Troll Hunter

Steven Vickers

The trollish poem, "*Nurosh Kha Dum,*" was taken in part from Maya Angelou's "Letter to My Daughter."

Contents

To my family, whom I love and adore forever. So many people had a share in crafting this story, but I am most grateful to the No Apologies and Peaklings writing groups, who were endlessly patient. This story was conceived nine years ago for the Graduate Program in Creative Writing at Western Colorado University. Thank you, Candace Nadon, Russell Davis, and all the rest, for your guidance. Jacob Hendrix, your maps are amazing.

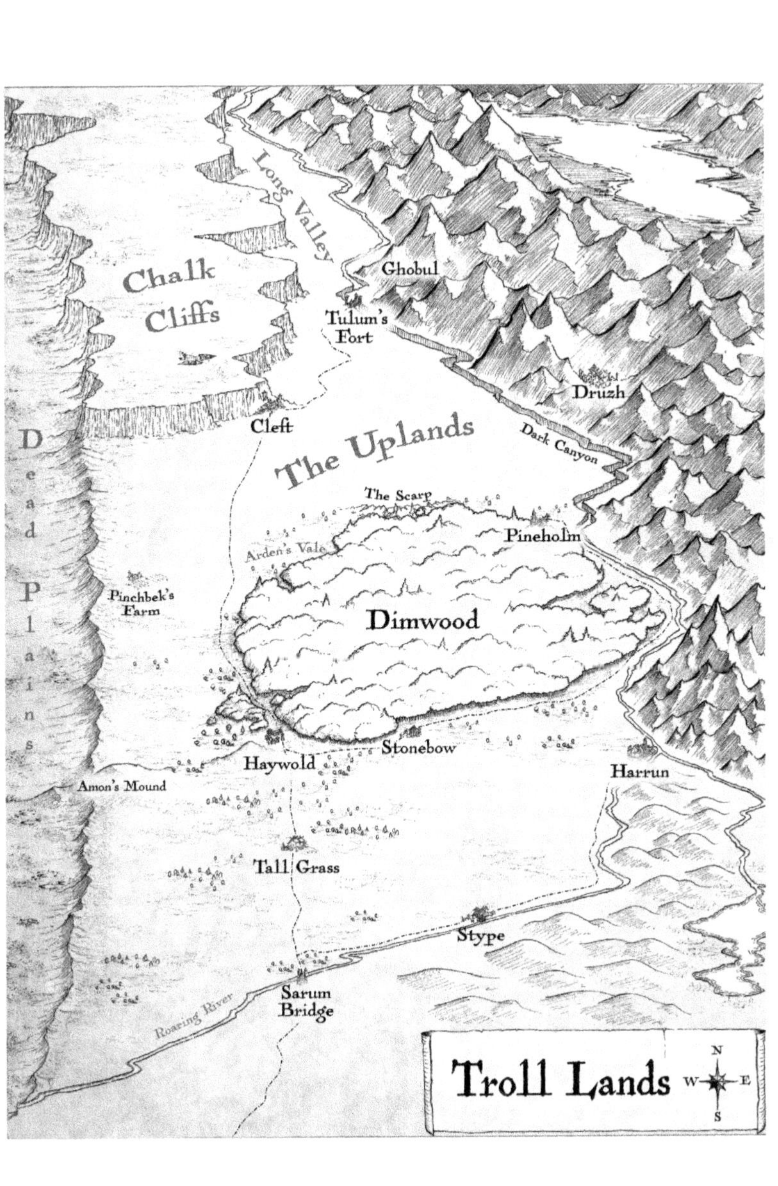

Chalk
Cliffs
Long Valley
Ghobul
Tulum's
Fort
Druzh
Cleft
Dark Canyon
The Uplands
The Scarp
Pineholm
Arden's Vale
Dead Plains
Pinchbek's
Farm
Dimwood
Stonebow
Haywold
Harrun
Amon's Mound
Tall Grass
Stype
Sarum
Bridge
Roaring River
Troll Lands
N
W
E
S

Chapter One

Pinchbek Homestead

Gabril Cullen sniffed at the chill breeze. The Uplands prairie spread out eastward toward the distant line of the Blue Mountains. The earthy scent of mulegrass mixed with the damp, ashy promise of rain from the Dead Plains to the west. But overlaying that was the distinctive rotten apple and old cheese stink. And there was something else: burnt sod.

"Ounwe's breath," he cursed. "Come on. I think they're heading to the Pinchbek's homestead. We're close."

His daughter Isabo pulled a vicious scowl and shook her head. "Stupid idiots," she muttered.

Cullen's hunting partner, Arden Luck, grunted. They all picked up their pace.

It didn't matter if she meant the trolls or the Pinchbeks, though if she meant the trolls, she would have used stronger language.

The trio crested a low rise at a jog, and Cullen saw exactly what he feared.

There was nothing left, of course. Trolls never left anyone alive; they murdered outright or took captives, but they never left survivors. Ever. He scanned the smoldering remains of the homestead. A faint wisp of smoke lingered on the breeze. Trolls had kicked in the sod home, burned and strewn its contents about the area. A single set of bones — human bones — lay beside the hut. He couldn't tell if they belonged to Vana or Emitt Pinchbek. They'd been stripped clean and stacked in the distinctive, orderly pile the trolls always used for human bones after they had taken the meat.

"We're too late." Isabo kicked at a broken bucket. "The fools lived too far out on the plains for anyone to respond in case of attack. If you're too stupid to live near help, you deserve what you get."

Cullen gave a grim acknowledgement. Troll raids were a common occurrence in the Uplands. The Pinchbeks had moved up from Tall Grass in the south early in the spring, lured by the fertile soil but heedless of warnings about trolls. Now they were dead, and everything they'd owned lay scattered about the ruins.

"Look at this!" Luck called from the other side of the ruined homestead.

Cullen glanced to see what he'd found. In a clear place in the dirt, someone had drawn a symbol in dark, sticky blood. Fat gray flies buzzed thickly. The image was two halves of a rough circle separated by a jagged mark.

"That's the sign of the Stone Breaker trolls." He stooped to pinch a bit of the bloody mark and roll it through his fingers. "The blood isn't completely dry, so it's only been a day or so," Cullen said, pointing to the bones. He added, "That's probably Emitt, which means they took Vana."

"How many were there?" Luck asked, fingering his sword.

Cullen stood and cast about for the lingering scent. Even with the smell of blood and smoke, he should still pick out day-old trollstink. In his brain, the distinctive, almost overwhelming smell slowly weaved into a clear pattern and then into the reek of individual creatures.

He started to answer but paused and turned to his daughter. "Isabo?"

She turned her head to catch the breeze. After a moment, she said, "Four of them."

Cullen chuckled and nodded. "Well done. I think one was from the party that attacked Tulum's Fort last fall. I remember his smell in particular. But why come all this way to take a single slave?"

Luck shuddered. "The attack on the fort was Stone Breakers as well. That clan is wicked cruel."

"More so than any of the others? They're all murderous beasts, Arden, lower than animals."

"Why do they always stack the bones like that?" Isabo asked. She waved at the mindless destruction of the homestead. "They're animals that murder and destroy everything they touch, yet they always put the bones in a careful pile."

Cullen raised an eyebrow. "It's some kind of unholy ritual for them. I guess they show enough intelligence to do that, but you're right, they're just animals. Nothing else they do makes me think they're very smart."

He sniffed, looked at the smoking remains of the homestead, and then east across the plains toward the Blue Mountains. Storm clouds hung low over the peaks. To the southeast lay the dark shape of the Dimwood and the village of Haywold Home. The village had a stout palisade and was well-defended, unlike Pinchbek's isolated farm.

"Are we going after them?" Isabo asked.

"Yeah," Cullen said. "For a few days until we can be sure they're heading back to their holes in the mountains. But we need more than us three if we're going to kill this band. We could never hope to take four of them."

"But they need killing," she said.

Cullen nodded and tightened his pack on his shoulders. "Aye, they need killing."

But this is the third time someone has spotted them this year, he thought. *The attacks are getting bolder and more frequent.*

Each time the troll bands had come raiding, the villages of the Uplands assembled hunting parties to track them in hopes of freeing any captives they took. If they were fortunate enough, they'd kill a few of the ugly brutes. But casualties were high on these hunts. Lately, many of the villagers had taken to hiding when the hunting parties came looking for help against the monsters. Some were moving away from the fertile lands to scrape out a living in the Dimwood or even fleeing to the Southlands, away from danger. At this rate, the Uplands would be abandoned to the trolls and the roving herds of grazing aurochs.

Was that the choice, to either suffer the raids and strike back feebly or slink away from the threat?

Luck turned to gaze southward toward the relative safety of the Broadwater and the distant south. Trolls rarely ventured that far from the mountains.

Cullen gave a weary shake of his head. "You thinking about leaving, too, Arden? We need every sword we can get."

The young hunter nodded. "Araya is pregnant, Gabril. I have to think of her. I'll go with you, but this is my last hunt."

Cullen clasped him on the shoulder. "Let's track these beasts, then head to Haywold. We'll gather a bigger party and go after them. Once that's done, you can think about going south."

"I'm not afraid, Gabril."

"I know that. You never have been. But we need to send someone for help. Arden, do you want to go to Haywold and gather fighters? It looks like the trolls headed straight east. Gather as many people as you can, then make your way north to cross our trail. You can do that easy enough."

Luck scowled. "No. Cullen, you and I can track them while she goes back to get help."

"Now, wait a minute," Isabo growled, "I'm nineteen. I can track and fight with the best of them. I'm not running away, not after what trolls have done to us."

Luck shook his head but gave a smile. "Isabo, you and your dad are special. You've both got the scent-gift. There isn't another scout between here and the mountains who can track the creatures by scent the way you can. We can't risk losing you both."

Cullen grinned and chucked his daughter on the arm. "You *can* track and fight with the best of them, but Luck is right. You can sniff out these bloody animals almost better than me. Almost. But that's why I trust you to make it home on your own and bring help." He nodded toward the heavy tracks in the dirt. "Arden and I can follow these beasts easily enough." He paused and looked around at the ruins of the Pinchbeks' home. "You get home and stir them up. You'll find our trail again. We've got to end these raids, Isabo. Folks know that."

"Fine," she said with a huff. "I'll bring an army."

Cullen leaned over, kissed her on the forehead, and brushed a wisp of tawny brown hair from her eyes. "Then bring an army." He nodded to a low, stone-faced well the settlers had dug beside the sod cabin. A ruined table covered the wellhead. "Better fill your water skins before you go."

Isabo grumbled but nodded. She untied the nearly empty skin from her pack and slid the rough-hewn planks from the well. "Ounwe's blessed teeth," she swore, slumping to her knees.

Cullen hurried to her side. "What's wrong, Iza? What —"

Floating in the narrow well was the tortured body of Vana Pinchbek.

***

A day later, the image of the battered, floating woman still hovered in Cullen's mind. The brutality of troll raids never ceased to affect him. He'd sent Isabo away with a warning to circle southward and east if she caught even the faintest scent of the creatures. For all their senseless brutality, the beasts rarely went south of Haywold. It was as if the Dimwood was some sort of boundary. And that's why Arden Luck wanted to take his young wife south, like so many others.

Since the well was tainted, he'd given his daughter half his remaining water. There was plenty enough for her to reach Haywold. They'd probably get rain before dark, and if not, there were plenty of stream beds and low places in the area that held water. Field lore that had long since become second nature sprang to mind.

Dig in the bend of a dried stream bed. Look for green grass in dry places. Follow animal trails to water holes. Look for —

"Why did they do it, Cullen?"

Geese fly to open water.

"Cullen?"

He stopped, suddenly realizing he had wandered off the trail left by the trolls. He shook his head to clear his thoughts, making his way back to the intermittent line of scuffed earth and trampled grass that showed the trolls' path across the grasslands.

Arden Luck watched him, his eyebrow raised.

"What did you say, Arden?" But his mind had already pieced together the man's words. "I don't know. Maybe they didn't do it, or at least didn't throw her in the well. They likely attacked in the darkness, and she somehow escaped and hid there."

"Was she pregnant, Gabril?"

Cullen halted and stared at his hunting partner. "I have no idea. How could I?"

Luck shrugged. "Araya's pregnant. That's all."

"You told me that. I'm happy for you. We have few enough babies around here anymore." He paused and placed a hand on Luck's shoulder. "Arden, these beasts are nothing but evil. I know that, and so do you. That's why we have to kill them or at least drive them back to their forsaken mountains. I need you for that. And I need you to be focused on what we're doing, okay? Afterward, you can go back and take care of your family, even if it means moving south."

The young hunter nodded. "I'm with you. And I'll do what I said I would." He squinted eastward into the distance. "Like you said, though, they came all this way. For what? To terrorize those few still living in the open? It's thirty leagues or more to the mountains. It doesn't make sense."

Cullen squared his pack on his shoulders. "You're right. That's been itching at me. If it were for slaves, they could come in force against Haywold or Pineholm. They'd lose some of theirs, but there would be a better payoff for them. This is different — as if they were hunting humans for sport." He looked back in the direction they'd come and then ahead, following the obvious path of the trolls with a practiced eye. The beasts' line of travel now edged southeast, past the road to Haywold and more in the direction of the Dimwood. It didn't make sense, but then, what did about this hunt?

Chapter Two

Raising an Army

I sabo topped a low rise and gave a grim smile. Her legs were sore from the long trek, but it was a good kind of sore. She was almost home. Watcher's Hill was in sight, and at its base lay the town of Haywold. From the east came the homelike baaing of sheep on a hillside.

She smiled as her ears caught a distinctive whistled command to a dog. A gray shape darted across a nearby hillside and circled a pair of sheep wandering aimlessly away from their herd. It was Jocko, her brother's dog, doing what herding dogs do best. She gave a sharp whistle of her own. The dog paused, looked up, wagged its tail twice, and then resumed its task of herding the aimless — and seemingly mindless — sheep.

"Iza, is that you?" A shaggy head popped up over a low cluster of scrub.

Isabo smiled at her brother and jogged on to meet him. She leaned down to give him a quick hug.

Amon peered around her into the distance. "Is everything okay? Where's Dad and Arden?"

Isabo slid her pack off her shoulder and shrugged her shoulders twice, trying to work out the knots. "We were at the Pinchbek's farm two days west. Trolls burned the couple out and killed them. It was pretty ugly."

"Morons," he said, shaking his head in disgust. "People warned them about living so far out. Are Dad and Arden tracking the trolls?"

"Yeah." Isabo nodded. "They sent me back to raise a hunting party. It looked like the beasts were heading straight back east toward the mountains. If we're quick, we can cut their trail and catch up."

"We? You're finally taking me on a hunt?"

Isabo snorted. "You're not ready yet — you're only fifteen."

Amon kicked at a tussock and stared down the hill at the flock of woolies grazing on the tough mulegrass. "But I'm ready. I can handle a sword as well as anybody. I knocked Zizzo Bracken's sword out of his hand twice this week."

"Zizzo isn't a troll; he's a knucklehead. This is serious business. Besides, we're scouts, not fighters. Have you found the troll's head that Dad hid yet?"

He sighed heavily and shook his head in resignation. "No. I thought I smelled it this week. Is it near the forest?"

Isabo gave a grim smile and picked up her pack. "I could smell trolls when I was half your age. When you can sniff it out without help, I'll take you on a hunt. Now, I have to get moving."

"Good luck. The Suleks said they're moving south, and probably the miller and his family, too. Folks are scared witless of more troll attacks."

"Well, I aim to stir up those that will fight. This is our home, and I'm not letting those beasts run us off. It's time to wipe them out completely."

Amon snorted. "I'll fight. I don't want to be stuck here watching stupid sheep."

"That's your job — for now. I'll see you at home later."

He glanced up at the sun lowering over the western plains. "Wait, Iza. The sun's going down. Help me drive the sheep back."

She laughed, shouldered her pack, and headed toward the village. "You've got Jocko for that. I'll see you at home," she called again over her shoulder.

***

The west gate of the village was closed as she approached. "Hey, it's Isabo," came a voice from atop the palisade. "Open it up, you morons."

She smiled. It was Will Perban, an old friend and companion.

He leaned over the palings and waved. "Welcome back! Where is your —?"

"Hey, Will. The trolls are raiding again. They burned a homestead and killed that couple that moved up from Tall Grass. Dad and Arden are tracking them."

"Are you going back out after them? I'll go with you!"

Another stocky figure appeared beside him on the wall. Isabo shook her head. It was Suza Bracken. Suza was Isabo's age, but her mother ran the Black Goat Inn and sat on the council. She chewed a fat quid of tobacco and spat a stream of brown juice into the breeze. "That's nonsense, Will Perban," the big woman said. "The full council will have to decide whether we risk any more lives hunting this band of trolls. We're far better safe behind stout walls than wasting lives in the wilderness."

Isabo shook her head. "Suza, you don't speak for the council. That's your mother's job. Besides, there's no time for that. Did you hear what I said? The Pinchbeks are dead, and my father is on the trail of the trolls that killed them. You can tell your mother and the council what you like. I'm gathering a war party." She turned to glance up at the peak of Watcher's Hill, then back at Suza. "I'll light the signal fire up there myself if I have to."

"There'll be hells to pay if you do that."

Isabo snarled. "Then there's hells to pay."

The woman scowled at Isabo and then turned to Perban. "Well, what are you waiting for? Sound the bell, and then send someone up to light the signal fire. Little good it will do, though. Them fools at Stone Bow and Tall Grass will take at least a day to get here, even if they do send anyone."

Isabo chuckled. For all her bluster and self-importance, Suza Bracken could usually be pushed to do the right thing. Usually.

She shook a finger at Isabo. "This is foolishness, but it's on your head, Isabo. You're throwing lives away to no purpose."

But Isabo wasn't listening. Perban rang a quick double stroke of the great brass bell, then repeated it twice. A moment later, a lad of ten or twelve ran out of the gate and up Watcher's Hill carrying a small bundle. She knew what it contained: kindling, flint, and steel. The bell would alert the townspeople that trolls were in the area, and they were to meet at the Black Goat. The signal fire on the hill would alert the neighboring villages to send fighters.

She had feared that Suza would convince her mother to convene the village council to consider the issue, but there was no time. Trolls near the village were an immediate danger. That might have been a stretch since the Pinchbeks lived so far west, but the old woman had acquiesced — to a point. "On your head" meant, "You help pay the bounty on dead trolls."

Well, her father had said to raise a war party. He knew what that meant — and the cost.

***

The common room of the Black Goat had once been a wide hall running the length of the inn. As the population of Haywold had dwindled through the years, the Brackens had partitioned half of the Great Hall into comfortable guest rooms, but even those were rarely used. The vast hearth had once burned great logs from the Dimwood; now, even the fireplace had been partially bricked up.

It took less than an hour for the room to fill up. Suza Bracken and her mother, Stura, busily filled mugs of the potent local beer.

Isabo began in a tone calculated to reach the room's far end. "Ten days ago, a traveler from up north found a leg — a human leg, with a troll's tooth marks. My father, Arden Luck, and I went out to hunt them down. We found them, sure enough. We think they were looking for easy prey, or they would have come here. Instead, they went after the Pinchbek's homestead two days west. They're the couple who came up in the spring from Tall Grass to start a farm."

15

There was grumbling in the room and shaking heads at the southlanders' ignorance. It was a hard world, and even harder when you didn't have the common sense that Blessed Ounwe gave a goat.

"Was they dead?" someone asked.

Isabo nodded.

"And eaten up?"

She nodded again. "Trolls killed one of them, ate him, and stacked his bones like they always do. We found the other, the woman, half butchered and dead in a well. She probably got away and crawled there herself to hide. The trolls lit off eastward."

"Eastward? That's toward us." It was Hupp, the butcher.

"The Pinchbek's farm was west and a bit north of us. The trolls went straight east, toward the mountains. If we haven't seen them here by now, I think they got what they wanted, which was plain murder. There were four of them, and my father and Arden are tracking them. I'll take a party of whoever is willing and able to carry a weapon."

The room erupted in a babble of talk. Maybe it was better to stay within the safety of the palisade. Maybe they should head south, where it was safe. Did she think they could really kill four trolls? It would take three or four stout fighters to kill even a single troll. Had the creatures really gone straight east? What about the council? Had the council voted?

Isabo ground her teeth, then nodded and waved to Stura Bracken for a beer. When she had the full mug in her hand, she raised it, then dashed it to the floor, spraying beer and broken crockery. The room went quiet in an instant.

"The alarm has been sounded, and the signal fires lit," she said, reciting the ancient call to arms. "I'll not take another drink until our dead are avenged."

"Till our dead are avenged," a smattering of voices in the crowd repeated.

***

Outside the door of the inn, Isabo was stopped by a strange pair of figures. The smaller of the two was a thin, pasty-looking man in rough, travel-stained monastic robes. His much taller companion was stout and looked like he could handle himself in a fight.

It had been months since the last wandering monks had visited Haywold. They came in ones and twos from their monastery in Harrun or Stype or somewhere in the south. Isabo shook her head. Her father didn't like the preachers much, always insisting that everyone lay their weapons aside and just love each other. She could abide the sentiment to love her fellow humans, but trolls? "We don't have time for peace so long as the trolls are about," her father had said. "A fellow can be as peaceful as he wants most days, but if trolls come raiding, he better carry a sword."

The wiry monk looked like he'd never seen a sword — or the outside of a monastery. It must have been a long trip from wherever that was because his once neatly tonsured scalp was stubbly and burnt from the sun.

"I am Brother Ambros Yoren of the Monastery and Temple of Ounwe in Harrun. Are you the daughter of Gabril Cullen? I bear a message from the abbot of my order to your father."

Isabo gave him a hard glare. "My father is tracking trolls in the Uplands, and I must get to him. If you'd like, I can carry a message to him."

"Yes, well," Yoren began. "That is most gracious of you, Lady Cullen, but it is only for your father's ears. I'm to give it to no one else, not even his daughter. We'll accompany you."

She laughed bitterly. "We're hunting trolls. Do you even know what that means? And don't call me 'lady.' I've no plans to be married."

"I —, I —, uh... My apologies," Yoren said. He straightened his robes and ran a hand through his stubbly hair. "I see that we have arrived too late to give him a warning in person. If you're going to him, then we must accompany you. It is of greatest importance that we take the message to him."

Isabo gazed at the monk, then at his companion. "Um, yeah. I'll pass on that you want to talk to him, but there's no way in blazes you're coming with us. You'd only slow us down when lives are on the line. If we're blessed by the heavens, we'll kill some trolls and be back here in about a week. If you won't give me the message, you can tell him yourself then. Now, I have to go."

Chapter Three

Ambush

Cullen peered down into the wooded valley and gave a grim smile. After a week of tracking, he and Luck finally had caught up to the stinking trolls. It had been a grueling chase that took them nearly to the Dead Plains and back, but the murderous creatures had finally gone to ground.

Looking back, he saw Luck standing in the open. Cullen grimaced and motioned his partner to stay, raising two fingers to indicate the two trolls below. Luck nodded in acknowledgment to the signal, retreated to the cover of a stand of pines, and loosed his sword in its scabbard.

Cullen studied the trolls' position. After a moment, he looked back at Luck and signaled again: *Two trolls, no lookout. I'll circle to the left. You stay here.*

Where were the others? The party they'd tracked had at least four of the beasts, but where were they all? Was this a different group?

The trolls were camped in a narrow valley beside a stony brook. Cullen crept around pines and lichen-covered clumps of granite, careful to avoid twigs and loose stones that might betray his presence. He glanced backward to see Luck camouflaging his position with branches and loose grass.

Quiet, Luck, he pleaded. The big swordsman fought well, but was getting sloppy. He was too worried about his young wife to focus on the job at hand.

He inched forward to get a better view of the valley below. A troll turned a pair of skinned rabbits on a spit over a large greenwood cookfire. Even from this distance, the troll's pale green skin, thick tusks, and turned-up snout were clear.

Smoke billowed in the hazy dusk. It was damned poor woodcraft to let the fire smoke so. Stupid trolls.

He moved slowly, putting the camp between himself and Luck.

The troll at the fire muttered something in its harsh guttural language, then laughed. Where had its companion got to — and the rest of the party? Cullen paused to sniff the failing breeze for the scent of other trolls. Nothing. The damned smoke obscured their smell. He craned his neck to see down into the valley. Only part of the encampment was visible from his vantage point, but across the small stream from the cook fire lay a jumble of boulders. The other troll must be there. The others might be out looking for game. Two rabbits that size might feed a single troll, but not several. He needed Isabo. The two of them worked well together, though she had a wicked temper. If she were here, one of them could get downwind to try for a better scent.

The lone troll uttered another harsh croaking laugh and continued his conversation, looking at someone or something amidst the boulders.

Cullen withdrew from the valley's edge to try to taste their scent on the breeze. Still nothing. He paused. *No, not nothing*. He focused, and there it was — the sharp tang of trollstink not quite masked by the resiny pine smoke. On a good day with clear air, his scout's nose could detect trolls from hundreds of yards away. He wished that others had the 'gift' of being able to smell the stinking creatures as easily. He sniffed again. The odor was similar, but not quite the same as he had smelled at the Pinchbeks'. Had others of their kind joined them? Were they gathering for a raid on Haywold?

The woods were silent and gloomy in the fading light. From below came the occasional crackle and sputter of pine boughs being fed into the fire. Cullen moved forward again to peer into the narrow valley. The single troll still sat piling branches onto a fire that now engulfed the rabbits on its spit. In the glare of firelight, the troll smirked and muttered.

He's burning that meat, and with all that smoke, it's going to taste like... Damn! Not even trolls are that foolish. It's a trap.

Cullen straightened and broke into a sprint, heedless of the noise. He drew his short sword and prayed that Luck's attempt at camouflage was successful. He cursed the trolls and himself. Lured into an ambush like the simplest child.

He rounded the stand of trees at a dead run to find the second troll standing over Luck's body. The hunter's severed head lay at the creature's feet. The troll licked Luck's blood from a jagged black knife. Cullen didn't break stride but charged, driving his sword straight at the creature's chest. As he feared, its leather armor turned the blade, but the force of the attack knocked the troll backward against the trunk of a twisted pine.

The green-skinned brute lashed out with the knife, slashing at his face. Cullen jerked back, but a searing pain shot from his jaw to his ear.

He swung again, hoping at least to knock the troll off balance. He was tall, but the ugly creature stood half a head taller and a full two stone heavier. His blade cut deep into the troll's upper arm. It howled. Cullen backhanded his sword hilt into the thing's jaw with a satisfying crack. From behind, he heard the troll's companion crash through the underbrush thirty yards away.

Cullen considered his position for the space of a heartbeat, slashed again at the troll, and ran. Luck was dead, his lifeblood now soaking into the forest floor.

Luck. There's a poor name if there ever was one.

He ran, knowing at least one troll was drawing close behind him. The woods were dark, but he had a reasonable idea of where he was. He darted from cover to cover, angling for the top of the ridge. Once on the other side, he'd make better time and lose his pursuers in the steep valleys leading east toward the river.

For all his skills, he'd somehow botched this hunt. The trolls' almost meandering track to the Dead Plains, the raid on the homestead, then back east across the grasslands, and now this. It didn't add up.

Cullen fumbled in his pockets and found his kerchief. He pressed it to his face to staunch the blood now streaming from the knife slash. His head swam, and he fought to clear his mind. An arrow whistled past his ear and thunked into a tree ahead of him. Fifty yards more, and he would be over the ridge crest.

From behind came the guttural, rumbling "Holooo!" of the troll's hunting call and then the answering call of a troll in front of him, from the top of the ridge.

This mess just gets deeper and deeper. Damn! The injured troll couldn't have gotten ahead of him. Another howl sounded from the trees far to his right. He scanned the hillside. A clump of boulders lay between him and the top of the hill, and to the left, a clutter of deadfall trunks and branches.

Cullen sprinted for the boulder pile. Trolls were big and fierce but couldn't match humans for agility or speed. He could lose them. He must lose them.

The low "Holoo!" came again from behind and was answered from the top of the ridge. They were herding him, and he was nearly surrounded. His heart sank within him.

To hell with that. His face burned, and blood soaked his chest. He shook his head to clear it, spraying dark droplets from the wound. His heart pounded. Sprinting up the ridge wasn't a wise thing to do, but he was alive for now. His knees grew shaky, and he fought to hang on. He leaped onto a waist-high chunk of granite and turned. That smell of rotten apples and old cheese returned — trollstink, but there were more than before.

"Come to me, trolls!" he shouted with more confidence than he felt. "I'll kill you here, or I can hunt you down!"

In front of him, the troll from the fire emerged from the woods. It laughed. "Throw your sword to the ground, human!"

Cullen wavered and shook his head to focus. The beast had spoken in the common tongue. Could they do that? "No, troll. Come closer."

The creature shook its head and drew a bow. "I can kill you now, ugly human. Throw your sword to the ground!"

From below came another sharp shout. "Kill him, Durok!"

The thing fired, and Cullen crouched a second too late, the heavy arrow tearing through his scalp. Pain lanced through his skull, and he staggered.

At once came the clash of swords and the twanging of heavy bowstrings.

Someone shouted in a deep, guttural voice, "Get down, foolish *pakh-hu!*"

That sounded like good advice. Someone had come to his rescue — or was trying to. He didn't recognize the speaker or know what a "pokku" was. Dizziness made it hard to hold onto a thought. He slumped to his knees and slid from the rock. He hoped the boulder would protect him from the accursed trolls. His head throbbed, and blood coursed down his face. With an agonizing effort, he raised himself high enough to see what was happening around him.

He shook his head and tried to make sense of what he saw. On all sides, the sounds of a battle rang. It was trolls, but they weren't fighting a rescuing body of humans.

They were fighting each other.

Another stab of pain shot through his head. Blood poured from his wounds. He reached up to touch his cheek and felt naked bone. The coppery taste of blood filled his mouth, and the afternoon light faded.

Chapter Four

Aftermath

Cullen awoke to a fuzzy light filtering through the trees. His face was numb. It should throb with pain from wounds like that. How odd. He tried to raise his hand to his face, but his hands were bound with a leather thong. He brought both hands up. A rough cloth bandage covered the side of his face and half his scalp.

"Don't touch it. Let it heal."

It was a human voice.

He opened an eye to see who spoke, but couldn't focus. What happened? Trolls. There was a battle. It came back: the troll at the fire, Luck's body, running up the hill, and then... one group of trolls fighting another.

"What happened to my face? Did you bandage me? Cut me loose; there are trolls about!"

"Quiet. Grimmun will want to leave soon, and you must eat."

"Grimmun?"

"Take this."

Something hot and greasy was pressed into his hands. He sniffed it. Rabbit. He bit into it and chewed. The well-seasoned meat settled his sour stomach. This wasn't the rabbit that the troll burned in the fire last night.

"Grimmun-ush is a warrior scout of the Three Valleys troll clan. I am Wogan. I am a healer, and I cook for the trolls. I belong to Grimmun, and now you do too."

"Belong to...?" Cullen said, almost choking on the rabbit. "I'm no slave."

Wogan shrugged but said, "Do not say that, or they'll hear. They won't hesitate to kill a human. Even you."

"Even me? What does that mean?"

Wogan didn't reply, but after a moment said, "Let me check your bandages."

His eyes cleared a bit. As the man knelt before him, Cullen squinted. He could just make out Wogan, a lean, gray-haired figure dressed in a sturdy doe-skin tunic and trousers. The man touched the bandage on his face with deft fingers.

"How does it feel?"

Cullen worked his jaw and tried to decide if it hurt. It didn't for some reason. As with his eyes, he found it hard to focus his mind.

"It's sore, but it should hurt like hell. That animal split my cheek wide open, and then someone shot an arrow that should have taken my head off."

Wogan pressed the back of his hand to the bandage. "It doesn't feel warm, so no infection yet. I stitched you up and got some mandragora and licorice root down your throat last night. When that wears off, your vision will clear, but the pain will return. Now, be quiet and eat. Grimmun returns soon."

The healer turned, picked up a skin, and tossed it at Cullen's feet. "Drink as much of this as you can stand. It's what passes for wine among the *trollim*. You won't like it much, but it will keep you on your feet."

Cullen picked it up, fumbled to open the skin, and took a taste. He shuddered and spat out the vile liquid. "Ounwe's teeth! What is that, fermented pine sap?"

To Cullen's surprise, Wogan grabbed a thick stick and swung it deftly, catching Cullen on the shoulder. "Don't despise the generosity of Grimmun, Gabril Cullen!"

Cullen struggled to stand but tumbled to the ground. He hadn't noticed the leather thong binding his feet. "Damn your skin, Wogan! Whose side are you on?" He struggled back to his feet. "And how do you know my name?"

Wogan shrugged again. "I told you I belong to Grimmun of the Three Valleys clan. I know your name because I sought you out. I led these trolls to you, though the other trolls — another clan — got to you first and nearly killed you."

"Why would you help these Three Valleys trolls find me? Why did the others — the Stone Breakers — want to kill me?"

"Because, Cullen, the Holy One of this clan needs you. He is the one who commanded Grimmun-ush to bring you to him. I was not told why. As to why the other *trollim* tried to kill you, I cannot say. Such things are not for me to know. Sit and rest until it is time to leave."

"You're not told why, and you blindly obey."

"I belong to Grimmun-*ush*."

"What's a Grimmun-*ush*?"

"I will tell you this, Gabriel Cullen, and I pray it will save your life. You speak to the troll who holds your life in his hands with the honorific -*ush*. This is how you are to address Grimmun."

"'Holds your life in his hands?' You mean he owns you?" Cullen snorted and turned away. Wogan was demented. A sane human would never assist trolls in kidnapping another human. His head swam from the exertion and loss of blood, and whatever Wogan had given him. A dull ache returned to his cheek and scalp, seeming to throb from one to the other.

"Ounwe's arse," he muttered. He closed his eyes and lowered himself to the ground. Maybe rest would help him think of a way out of this madness.

***

Cullen woke. He blinked and rubbed at his eyes, trying to clear his still-foggy vision. At his feet lay the remains of the rabbit and the skin of putrid wine. Wogan was nowhere in sight. He must have gone to tend to the trolls.

He examined the cord binding his hands and feet. It appeared to be supple leather, but the more he worked at it, the tighter it grew. He sat back down and tried to will his muscles to relax. The cords loosened somewhat, but not enough to remove his hands or feet. He looked around for his sword belt. It was gone, of course, along with the knife he'd worn on his right hip and his rucksack. Damn. *Focus, Cullen.*

He breathed deeply. A stream gurgled not far away. He looked around and saw they were back in the narrow valley. Wood smoke hung lightly in the morning air. With some satisfaction, Cullen realized that at least part of his hazy vision had come from the smoke. It was a small hardwood fire, not pine. He shook his head, which throbbed like he'd drained a keg on his own. Wogan and the trolls had indeed played him for a fool.

The great billows of smoke from the ambush were long since gone, and the thin wafts from the fire couldn't obscure the pervading trollstink. He turned his head and closed his eyes. In time, the bitter, musky cloud once again resolved into distinct scents. There were fewer trolls here than before. What had happened? He now smelled three trolls by the fire, two or more hidden among the boulders, and Wogan's fainter human scent.

He also detected a different, rancid odor that faintly pleased him. He had killed the beasts before and knew the bitter reek that lingered when they died. Anyone who killed trolls, even other trolls, must be okay. His confused memories of the battle and Wogan's later words rang true. One group of trolls had attacked another — maybe over him — leaving several of the creatures dead. Were the dead beasts the ones he had tracked from the Pinchbeks' homestead?

What did it all mean? A twisted flurry of thoughts ran through his aching head. Human settlements in the Uplands lived under the constant threat of attacks by trolls from the Stone Breakers or one of the other clans from the Blue Mountains. He'd never heard of the Three Valley Clan. Was this raid a precursor to a larger concerted attack or a battle between the clans for raiding lands? What did he have to do with it? Why was he singled out? He'd been a scout for years, hunting the nasty beasts when they came too near human settlements. Was he that much of a threat to them? One group at least thought so, and they tried to kill him, but another had intervened to save him. To what end? And poor Arden. Why had they killed the big fighter and left him alive?

He kicked at the skin of nasty wine and drew a deep breath. There was another troll nearby. Where? He turned again, trying to catch the breeze just so. The thing was close by, no more than ten yards away. Cullen stood, balancing against the bonds on his hands and feet. He leaned, hoping to catch a clearer scent. It was *there*, in that clump of scrub oak.

"I know you're there, troll."

"Hur!" A deep laugh came from the knot of vegetation. With a rustling of branches, a troll pushed through into the open.

"Very good, sniffer! You find me with nose. Hah! Wogan-thing was right."

Could this be the troll he'd fought yesterday over Luck's body? Its jaw was swollen, and its right arm hung in a loose sling. All these beasts looked alike to him, but it could be the same one. He'd taken a good cut at the thing's arm, but the sleeve he'd slashed now bore neat stitches, and the blood had been washed away.

The thing laughed again. It hooked a finger into its mouth and opened it to show a gap in its pointed yellow teeth. "See, you knock two teeth from me! Hur! You good fighter, but we told not to kill you, else Gheen would have lopped off your tiny head!" The troll made a throat-cutting gesture with a clawed finger.

Then the thing paused for an awkward moment. Its eyes glazed, and it wavered as if on the verge of fainting. Then it shook its head and peered at the human. "Cullen. You are Cullen-thing. A silly human name, like Wogan-thing." He pointed to himself. "I am Gheen, warrior of Three Valleys Clan."

"Gheen, *pakh-hu jha*!"

The troll hung his head and took a step backward as a hulking figure of a troll — presumably the one Wogan called Grimmun — stormed across the stream and up to Cullen. Wogan and another troll followed close behind.

The troll leader unleashed a furious stream of blows at Gheen and what Cullen guessed were curses in the harsh Trollish tongue. The fighter stood meekly, receiving the abuse, then withdrew to the edge of the tangle of scrub oak like a whipped dog. Grimmun snarled and turned to stare at Cullen.

Cullen blinked. His eyes cleared, yet the more he saw, the less he understood. Just two days ago, he and Arden had tracked a party of Stone Breaker clan trolls, creatures he considered fierce but not particularly intelligent. They were barbarians at best.

Now Luck was dead, and he was a captive because he'd underestimated the trolls. But had the trolls themselves crafted the clever trap, or had Wogan done it, as he said? And what was the business with the other clan? One group wanted to kill him, and the other to capture him. Either way, Wogan would pay. Humans don't help trolls in their butchery.

Yet Wogan had said the trolls needed him. Well, the hell with that. He turned toward the ugly troll. "You're Grimmun."

Wogan shot him an admonishing look and said, "Slaves do not speak to the *trollim* unless bidden to do so. And you must speak using the language of respect, as I told you."

Cullen barked a laugh and glared at the troll. "Perhaps slaves do, but prisoners — or free men — will do as they please. What do you want from me, troll? Say your business or turn me loose."

It stared back at him, not speaking. Was there anything behind those red-rimmed eyes and thick skull?

The troll leader remained motionless. Then his face broke into a hideous grin, and he laughed, his barrel chest rocking. "Hah! I like this one, this Cullen-thing. He has — What is the human word? Bravery? He has the bravery."

He wagged a finger at Cullen. "Be careful, Cullen-thing, you'll scare the other human. If he is frightened, he may not see to your wounds."

"If you need me, as the other human says, you'll see that he does."

Grimmun stopped laughing. "You would give me commands?"

He sneered at the troll. "No, but if you need me, you will keep me safe."

"Do not value yourself too highly, human. We captured you; we can kill you and find another who shares your particular skills."

Cullen ignored the threat. "You stopped another group of your kind from killing me, so I don't think you'll do that. You need a scout, don't you? Someone to hunt down others for you? Is that what this is about? That's why you killed my companion and left me alive. You can train a dog to follow a set of footprints in the mud. My companion Luck could do that much." He pointed to Gheen. "But few have the gift, as that one says, of being a sniffer. I can track your kind by smell from a distance. But you knew that. Or Wogan did, and I'm guessing the others, the Stone Breakers, knew it as well. That's why I'm here. But tell me why they wanted to kill me."

Grimmun chuckled, a deep, rumbling sound. He nodded to Wogan and walked away.

Wogan bowed and threw a bundle at Cullen. He recognized his rucksack. It was heavier than when he last carried it. What had they put in there?

"Prepare to travel. Grimmun graciously provisioned your pack with all that is needed for the journey to the mountains."

Cullen eyed Wogan, slave of the trolls. "What happened to you, Wogan? Are you no longer human? Why do you do their bidding?"

Wogan lowered his eyes. "Of course, I'm still human. I'm the property of —"

"The property of Grimmun of the Three Valleys clan. I know."

"Make light of me if you will, Cullen, but there is more at stake than you know."

"And what is that? Why do they need a scout? And why did the Stone Breakers want me?"

Wogan wrung his hands. "It is not for me to say."

Cullen sniffed and tugged at the cords on his wrists. "You're pathetic. I count six trolls here. If I could break these cords and head over that ridge and be gone, I would. Maybe I'd make it, and maybe I wouldn't, but I'll not help these things raid our lands and kill our people."

"Do you think I'm the only human living among the trolls? Hundreds of humans — our people, Cullen — dwell with the *trollim*. They're fighting for their lives, humans and trolls. We are all at risk from —"

"Trolls and their willing servants. Why should that concern me?"

Wogan met his eyes. "I am not privy to the councils of the *trollim*, but I know that what they fight is a greater evil than any troll raid."

"What could be worse than trolls?"

Wogan shook his head. "I do not know, and I have said too much. It is for Grimmun-*ush* to explain. Please, do not resist or try to flee. They — we — are desperate for your help."

"Maybe so," Cullen spat, "but you betrayed me into their hands. You helped trolls capture a human, one of your own kind. Be glad they took my blade because I won't hesitate to cut your throat."

***

They traveled throughout the day, always north and east. They walked in a file, first Grimmun, then another troll called Malbah, then Wogan and Cullen, followed by Gheen. At some distance behind came another troll, whose name Cullen hadn't heard.

Cullen wondered at the group's unaccountable speed and relative silence once they finally got moving.

He watched Grimmun and the other trolls pick their way through the forest. They were concerned with the signs they left behind, but not overly so. Grimmun approached, considered, and then circled a muddy patch, careful not to leave tracks, but then bulled his way through a thicket of young alders, snapping branches and trampling the soft grasses beneath. They also made more noise than any self-respecting scout. For all that, they were far quieter than any band of trolls he'd ever seen, certainly more than the Stone Breakers. And the troll leader sent scouts ahead; it wasn't clear whether they were watching for humans or others of their kind. He'd encountered trolls many times over the years, sometimes tracking them for a week or more. He tracked them by scent alone or by the signs of their careless passage: trampled turf, discarded skins, still-smoldering cookfires. But until Grimmun and these Three Valley trolls, he'd never known them to worry about leaving signs of their movement. This band understood at least the rudiments of moving stealthily. Someone had taught them. If trolls could learn this, they might become even bolder and their raids even deadlier.

"Wogan," he said, "where did these creatures learn woodcraft? Who taught them?"

The slave stumbled over a root and sprawled headlong in the dirt.

"Not from you, I warrant," he said, lifting Wogan to his feet.

The man pulled away from him. "It's not for me to say."

"You haven't given me a direct answer since I met you."

Wogan shook his head and lowered his eyes. "It's not my place."

Chapter Five

Setting Out

As day broke over the Dimwood, Isabo eyed her assembled party of volunteers. In addition to Will Perban, eight men and two women stood ready at the west gate. Each was grim-faced and knew the danger they were putting themselves in. Trolls were a present-enough threat that no one took the task lightly. In answer to the signal, two had arrived from Stone Bow and one from Tall Grass, both well-armed. A few of the locals carried swords while the rest carried bows or the thick, fire-hardened spears that were the village cooper's specialty.

Isabo started to speak when the gate creaked open, and two more figures joined them.

"Hey, Wulf. Hey, Hiram," Perban said to the latecomers.

Isabo glanced at the sun climbing over the trees. "It's about time. We have to go."

"Sorry, Iza," Hiram Tanner said with a smile. "Wulf here had to grab another bundle of arrows."

A small group of townspeople stood watching from atop the palisade. She saw that Amon had joined them, and she winked at him. He wiped something from his eye and waved back.

She looked back at her compatriots for the journey. Will Perban was, well, Will Perban. She gave a half smile. He was sweet on her, but she'd made it clear that he was her friend, and only her friend. He'd taken it well, and they'd stayed close. Will had taught her much about fighting with her mother's short sword.

Wulf Wheatley and Hiram Tanner were brothers, though not by blood. They were as unlikely a pair as she could imagine. Wulf was short, stocky, and reserved, while Hiram was tall and slim with a ready smile. Wulf had lost everything to trolls five summers ago. His family's small farm lay along the edge of the Dimwood, a mile from the safety of the palisade. When trolls came in the night, they burned his home, killed his parents, and took his brother. Twelve-year-old Wulf had been found wandering in the woods two days later.

Isabo remembered playing Trolls and Villagers with the boys. Wulf became a deadly shot at the stuffed figure tied to a tree and painted with the image of a snarling troll. He put arrow after arrow into it until the bag they used for a head was nothing more than tatters, and he handled a spear like he was born to it.

Hiram could hold his own with a bow but was better with a sword. While the others had worked on their archery skills, he sparred with Will Perban and Arden Luck.

As Wulf shouldered his pack and bow, Isabo saw him stuff something inside his shirt.

"What's that?" she asked.

He gave her a thin smile, then pulled out something on a leather cord. He held it up. Two items clicked against each other on the cord: a broken, yellowed tusk and what looked like a finger with a sharp claw.

She gave a knowing smile and nodded. Two summers before, Wulf and Hiram had hunted trolls. Arden Luck had killed the beast, and her friends had taken souvenirs.

Looking at the group, she did another quick count: fourteen total. She'd told her father she'd bring an army. *It's a damned small army.* But still, she'd never been in charge of such a large group. Her father was the natural leader, not her.

She stepped over to Perban and leaned close to her friend. "Will, I want you to lead them. I'll do the tracking, but I can't be in charge of all these people."

He raised an eyebrow. "What are you talking about? You came back here to raise a group of fighters, and you did. We haven't had this many to go after trolls in years." She shook her head fiercely, but he continued. "You're the best of us at this kind of thing, Iza. When you talked to Mother Bracken at the gate, she acted like she'd been caught stealing apples from Mulin's orchard. I thought for sure she'd make you petition the council before sounding the alarm, but you walked right over her — and she went along."

"I don't know, Will."

"I do. You'll be fine."

She considered. You could apprentice to become a cooper or brewer, but who was there to train someone to lead others? Certainly not the village council. They were either puffed-up busybodies like Stura Bracken or the butcher Hupp, or they were weaklings who always voted with whoever had the loudest voice at the table. No, when something important like this came up, it was easier to do what she thought was right and deal with the consequences when they arose. Was that leadership?

"Okay, Will, but on one condition. Hiram, come here."

She spoke quickly with her two friends, both of whom first expressed surprise, looked at each other, then gave nods.

"Listen to me, you lot," she said, turning to the gathered band of fighters. "If you can't hold your own in a fight, stay home. Half of you will be under Will Perban here. He's First Sword and my deputy. Those under him are part of the First Sword element. Got that? The rest of you are under Hiram Tanner. He's Second Sword, and those under him are the Second Sword element." The two leaders raised their hands. "You have questions, talk to them. They both report to me. Now, it will take us a few days to catch up. When we're not moving, Will and Hiram will drill with you to make sure you're all ready to fight. If you don't like that plan, I don't care. Stay home."

Perban and Tanner moved among the group, making a quick division. Perban took Wulf Wheatley, the two from Stone Bow, and half the locals from Haywold. Tanner took the rest of the locals and the lone fighter from Tall Grass, a tall, well-muscled man named Shamus Dorse who handled his heavy sword like it was a part of him.

"What do we call you, Missy?" Dorse asked with a chuckle. "Big Sword?"

"She's the Chief of this band," Perband growled. "Any problem with that?"

"Nope," the big man said. "I'm just checking, is all. It's good to know who's in charge."

"Isabo." It was Amon, her brother. He wore a bulky, awkward backpack. The dog Jocko sat at his side.

She straightened and gave him a smile with as much confidence as she could muster. She ignored the pack he wore. "Amon, we'll be back as soon as we can. You stay and tend to the flock. There's food in the larder and the garden. Gran Willis will look in to seeing that you don't starve."

"But I'm coming with you, Iza," he declared, his arms crossed and defiant. "I'm fifteen. That's old enough. I told you, I can almost track scent like you and Pop, and I can handle a sword."

"You have to stay to watch the farm," she said. "You're staying safe here!"

"Ounwe's bollocks I am!"

Isabo grabbed Amon's earlobe and squeezed hard as he tried to wriggle loose. "Now, don't swear and don't defy me," she said.

He winced and tried to pull her hand away. "Okay, okay. Let go!"

She chuckled and released his ear. "That's better. You have to stay and watch over things here. We'll be back soon, I promise."

"But —"

Isabo pressed her hand over his mouth. "You're as stubborn as I am, Amon Bray Cullen. Now, are you staying here to watch over things until we return?"

"Mmph. Mmmmph."

She smiled and said, "What? You'll be pleased to stay here and lovingly tend to things while your sister is away?"

He shook his head and nipped at her hand with his teeth. Jocko gave a confused growl beside him.

Isabo drew Amon into a hug and kissed him on the forehead. "Good. We'll be back quick as we can."

He suddenly squeezed her tightly and whispered. "Isabo, if anything happens to you and Pa, what'll I do? You're all I got."

She smiled and tousled his long, sandy hair. "Nothing will happen to us. I promise."

Amon walked away slowly. Isabo watched him, hoping he wouldn't do anything stupid, but fearing he would. That's what little brothers did. She wished she had time to talk to Gran Willis to ask her to keep a sharp eye on him.

She bent to tighten the straps on her pack, double-checking to ensure everything was securely in place.

"I would like to come, too."

It was the monk who had spoken to her outside the inn. Isabo hadn't noticed him in the group at the gate.

"If you're going after your father, then Brother Dunken and I must accompany you. There is a great danger, and I must see him."

Isabo glared at the little monk. "Look, my father's on the hunt for trolls. Do you know what that means? I don't suppose you do, hidden away in your safe monastery in the south. Trolls are murderous beasts. They don't leave survivors; they kill, or they take slaves. Unless we can catch up to my father and kill these things, they'll be across the river and into the mountains. That means we have to move fast. We can't afford to wait for you clerics to catch up."

Brother Yoren glanced up at his tall companion, who nodded for him to continue.

"We have little gear, and we carry our own food and water," the smaller monk said. "Brother Dunken here is a marvel at snares and traps. He can catch fresh game. Please. The abbot would not have sent us if it were not of the highest importance." He leaned close. "Miss Isabo, it involves your father and perhaps the very trolls he is pursuing."

She stabbed a finger into the man's chest, pushing him backward. "I told you before, you can wait here. Out of respect, I will tell my father you want to speak to him, and that you will be here when we return. I'll not say it again; you're not going with us."

"But I must. I —"

"Brother," she snarled, "this is not a mission of diplomacy. If all goes well, we will slaughter the trolls that are raiding our lands. If it doesn't go well, there may still be a slaughter, but not one we like. Anything you have to say can wait until we return."

She motioned to Perban, who had returned to stand at her side. He took Brother Yoren's shoulder and led him and his companion back to the gate.

Isabo brought two fingers to her mouth and whistled, calling the assembled group to attention. She scanned the dozen or so faces. "My father and Arden Luck are tracking at least four trolls. They killed the Pinchbeks and burned their home. We move twice as fast as any troll, so we can still catch them before they reach the mountains. We've all lost loved ones to these beasts. I won't have us lose more. We'll kill as many trolls as we can and get back to our families. They're big and strong and tough to kill, but that's what we aim to do. I'll find their trail. Don't any of you forget that *I* decide when and how we fight. But when it's time, don't leave any of the creatures standing."

All eyes were on her. She drew her sword and raised it. "Vengeance is ours!"

Everyone in the party and most of those gathered on the palisade responded with a hearty, "Vengeance is ours!"

***

Isabo led the party along the North Road for three days. She moved quickly, her eyes scanning the five leagues of rolling grasslands stretching from the Dimwood on the east to the gray Dead Plains in the west. Far northward, the Chalk Cliffs just scratched the morning sky. A low cloud of brown dust told of a herd of aurochs grazing in that direction. But she still hadn't seen or smelled any sign of her father's trail or the trolls.

Will Perban joined her at the crest of a rolling hill north of the road. "Anything?"

She shook her head and grunted. After a moment, she said, "From the direction they were going when they left the Pinchbek's, I'd have thought we'd have crossed their path already."

"Do you think they went farther north?" he asked. "Maybe toward Cleft or Tulum's Fort?"

She shook her head in frustration. "That's possible. Maybe they wanted to stay clear of the settlements near the forest. But why would they come all this way to burn a single homestead?"

Glancing back down the hill at the band of volunteers, she sighed. She had said she'd lead them to her father and the trolls. "How are they doing?"

Perban gave a worried smile and shrugged. "They're all eager to get at the trolls. The two from Stone Bow, Filip Humah and his brother Daron, look to be a couple of tough nuggets. They'll be good in a fight, I think. Hiram says the younger ones from Haywold — Kurtis Hupp and his buddy Zollar — are whining a little. They expected to be fighting trolls by now. We'll see if that holds up when we actually find some, but Hiram and I have some ideas on that. By the way, I sent Wulf and one of the two from Stone Bow back on our trail a bit to see if anyone else from town or from the other villages was trying to catch up."

"Well," Isabo said, "then we're it. I expected to be fighting by now, too. I just have to find the trail. Let's head toward that bluff out there. Maybe the creatures were using it for cover."

A sudden gust of wind blew grit in her eye — and something else. The wind had shifted to the east. She turned to sniff at the breeze. "There's something there," she said with a grim smile. It was the unmistakable smell of rotten apples and moldy cheese — trollstink, as well as the stronger scent of recent blood.

"Isabo, look! Someone's coming." Perban pointed eastward along the edge of the forest.

A lanky figure jogged toward them along the forest road. He was probably a quarter mile away, but she saw the easy loping stride of a plainsman. "I know him. He's a tracker from Cleft, up by the Chalk Cliffs. His name's Moze Tallard, and he's a friend of my father's. Maybe he's seen him."

"How can you recognize him this far away? What color are his eyes? Does he have a ring in his ear?"

She ignored the jibe. "Get everyone ready to move. I'm going to go see what he has to say."

As he drew nearer, Isabo waved and moved down the hill to the road to meet him.

"Welcome, Tallard," she said to the man. "Have you seen my father and Arden Luck? What news of the trolls?"

The scout met her eye. His face was lined and weathered, and he wore a travel-stained cloak. He nodded and gave her a half smile. "You're Cullen's daughter. I remember you from when I was last here in these parts. There's news, but you won't like it. You out here by yourself looking for your father?"

"No. I have a dozen fighters over the hill," she said, nodding westward. She whistled, and from the top of the hill, Perban gave an answering trill. She motioned for him to come down.

The weathered scout nodded, but gave a pained smile. "I crossed the trolls' trail north of here, on the other side of that bluff. Their track bent south to the forest up ahead. I don't have your father's scent-gift, but I'd guess there were two parties of maybe a dozen trolls total. I was heading to your village to give warning, but it seems you already got the word."

She told him about their foray westward, the Pinchbek's homestead, and her efforts to gather fighters to join her father and pursue the trolls.

He reached into a pouch at his belt to draw forth something wrapped in a worn kerchief. Opening the small bundle, he revealed a pale green sheet of woven mulegrass and pine needles a little smaller than his palm.

Isabo gasped. "It's a tale-teller. Is this from my father?"

Tallard nodded. "Aye, I believe so."

"Can I read it?"

Tallard handed it over. She examined the braided strands, trying to decipher the woven patterns in the grass, just as her father had taught her. "It says something about the new moon and a direction. East?"

She looked up and glared at him. "There's something you aren't telling me, isn't there? I just caught a whiff of trollstink and blood, but was faint — a couple of days old, at least."

"Aye. Take another look and read it close."

She glanced down. The grass plait was frayed at the edges and starting to dry out. Bits were missing. "It says three, no, four days after the new moon. That's when I arrived back in Haywold. That makes this... a week old. Ounwe's teeth." She examined it more closely. "'Traveling east with... trolls?' And 'Don't follow.' Why would he say that?"

Tallard shrugged.

A chill ran through her heart. "This makes no sense," she muttered. "He's been captured, and he's trying to keep me safe. Well, he's lost his mind if he wants me to turn back without trying a rescue."

Perban joined them, and Isabo gave a hurried introduction.

"Why don't you gather your group," Tallard said, "and then I'll take you to the place I found this in the forest. You weren't far wrong. Trolls camped there — and there's plenty of blood." He paused awkwardly. "Arden Luck was your father's hunting partner, wasn't he?"

Isabo nodded.

"He's dead. Near as I can tell, the trolls fought someone, possibly other trolls, but whoever won took your father."

Isabo looked eastward, where the tips of the Blue Mountains broke the line of the horizon, and shook her head. "I just came from my father and Arden, what, four days ago? Arden was going to go south with his wife. He wasn't the smartest man alive, but he was a good man. He didn't deserve to be slain by inhuman beasts." She glanced at Tallard. "We'll look at the camp, but we're not staying long. Luck is dead, but my father's still alive." She glanced at Perban. "If Kurtis Hupp wants to fight trolls, he'll get the chance. Let's go."

***

Crows had been at the bones, but the trolls hadn't left much meat for them to scavenge. Isabo shook her head.

Tallard poked at the remains of the fire. "From the condition of the camp, it's been at least five days since the trolls were here. Maybe six." He pointed at three small holes equidistant around the edge of the fire and a bundle of charred leaves a short distance away. "This greenery is called *kinnikkinnick*. It's used for smoking meat. The holes are where they made a tripod to hang the drying meat."

Six days. She'd moved as quickly as anyone could, but was too late. She cursed. "The meat? You mean Arden Luck?"

Tallard gave a grim nod. "I'd say they killed him, gutted him, and sat here to smoke the meat."

Isabo ground her teeth. What inhuman creature could do such a thing? Arden was — had been — a tough fighter, as quick with a sword as anyone she'd ever known, yet these beasts had butchered and eaten him. Just like Emitt Pinchbek — and so many others.

She knelt to examine footprints in the soft earth. "There are lots of their prints here, but look at this." She pointed to a jumble of footprints around the fire and along the narrow stream. "These big ones surely belong to trolls. You can see the impression of their hobnailed soles. But there are human prints, here and here."

Tallard moved toward the stump of a tree. "Isabo, would you recognize your father's footprints?"

"Yeah. Last fall, I had the bootmaker fashion him a nice pair of boots with a doeskin I tanned myself." She bent to inspect the marks by the stump. "These are his! I recognize the shape of the heel. He sat here? That means he's alive!"

Tallard shrugged. "We don't know that he's still living, but it looks like he was here. And there's something else. Follow me."

He led Isabo and Perban around the clump of boulders near the stream. Three troll bodies lay neatly arranged in a broad, grassy glade beneath the trees. Each bore the evidence of being in a battle: one's head was nearly severed, the leather armor protecting the second's chest was slashed through, and the third's skull had been caved in with something heavy. The ground beneath them was a large, drying patch of brownish-black.

"Look at their arms," Isabo said, leaning closer despite the intense troll-stink. The left sleeves of the trolls' rough tunics had been cut away, and a large gobbet of the flesh removed from each.

Tallard nodded. "I've never seen that before. My guess is that these three were killed by other trolls. Then they put them here and... did this."

Isabo glanced up at the nearest granite boulder, which towered over the scene. Scratched in the stone was a circular figure with a slash through the center. "These were Stone Breakers." She turned back to the trolls and sniffed their scent. "Yeah. These three were part of the group that killed the Pinchbeks. But one of them's missing. There were four that attacked the homestead."

"Then I have a good idea where he went," Tallard said. "Just east of here, I found troll tracks heading away. There was a big group, but one set of tracks broke off to the northeast, while the rest led straight east toward the Scarp. Maybe the one got away, and the rest didn't follow him."

"Wait a minute," Perban said. "Then part of the group — or another band — attacked these trolls." He glanced back in the direction of the campfire near the stream with its pile of human bones. "They took a chunk of meat from these three, but stripped all the flesh from whoever that was back there."

Isabo shook her head and spat on the nearest fly-ridden corpse. "My father thinks there's some ritual involved when they kill their enemies. Maybe it's a different ritual when they kill a human. But who knows why trolls do anything they do? They're just beasts."

She had turned to walk back to the campfire when Kurtis Hupp and his friend Zollar came in sight around the boulders. Hupp was the butcher's son, tall, stocky, and — Isabo had thought — not very bright. But she had seen him training Zollar and anyone who would listen in the use of a pair of long, machete-like knives. He handled them well and seemed to have a gift for teaching others.

"Is these the ones that killed them Pinchbek folks?" he asked, pointing at the dead trolls.

Isabo nodded.

Without a word, he swung one of the heavy blades at the nearest. The sound was like chopping through a large summer melon. The troll's head rolled away and came to rest against the boulder. He moved to the next, repeated the action, and then repeated it again.

"Can I take their ears?"

Isabo chuckled and nodded. "You better clean your blade after. Troll blood is nasty."

He wasn't listening. The lad stared down at his blade. The surface of the heavy knife bubbled and hissed.

"Kurtis, look!" Zollar said, pointing at the trolls. The pale green-gray flesh around the second troll's neck swelled and twisted, quickly erupting in ugly boils and mushroom-like growths. In moments, the eruption slowed, and the skin faded to a dirt gray. In the third troll, the reaction was more violent and accompanied by a bubbling hiss from the wound, causing everyone to leap back from the corpse. It took longer to subside, and the growths were larger and more grotesque.

Hupp stood shuddering. He looked down at his knife, its edge now covered with a brown, stinking crust. "My blade did that?" He started to wipe away the filth on his sleeve.

"Don't!" Tallard called sharply. "Wipe it on the grass, then clean it with a cloth in the stream."

"What in Ounwe's heaven was that?" Isabo wondered.

Tallard shook his head. "I've only seen that once before, three summers ago near Cleft. A band of us took on two trolls that were raiding the area. We killed the first one. One of our party, Mirra, drove a sword through its neck. Then we went after the second. We cornered it in a box canyon and hit it with more than a dozen arrows before it went down. Mirra went to take its head; as soon as she swung at it, the same thing happened, only worse. The beast wasn't quite dead. It howled like it was being dragged through the Seven Hells. Where the blade cut, it looked like a second head was trying to grow. We finally killed it with more arrows and bashed it with stones. Someone else finally cut its head off. Mirra's sword was eaten away." He shuddered and looked back at the troll corpses. "I can only guess that these three have been dead long enough for whatever causes it to weaken."

"What about that one?" Perban asked. He pointed at the first troll Hupp had hacked. The thing's neck showed no evidence of the reaction.

Tallard tugged at his beard and considered. "Isabo is right — troll blood is nasty stuff. Maybe it acts as a poison between them. Who knows?"

Isabo glared at Hupp. "You still want to take their ears?"

He shook his head weakly.

She turned to Perban. "You're First Sword. Take your team and gather some wood. I saw a stack by the fire." She pointed at the trolls. "Burn these."

Back at the campfire, Hiram Boyer examined the neatly arranged pile of bones near the fire. He glanced up at Isabo. "The good news is that those remains are Luck's size, not your father's."

"Good news? Arden Luck was my father's hunting partner."

"No disrespect intended," Tanner said. "I only meant that your father is probably still alive."

Tallard nodded toward Luck's remains. "You should bury him proper. Arden was one of yours, and he deserves more than having his bones scattered about." He took a small camp shovel from his pack and began to hack at the soft earth above the stream.

"We don't have time for that," Isabo said. "The creatures that did this still have my father. We have to catch them before they make it to the river. They have nearly a week on us by now."

Tallard threw her a cold glare. "Aye, Iza, a week ahead of us. If you have time enough for burning the trolls, you can bury your father's friend." The scout stopped and cocked an ear.

From the top of the ridge came a low, trilling whistle.

Isabo glanced up and saw one of Hiram's men pointing westward.

"What is it?" she called.

"Someone's coming!" he replied. "I can't tell who, but there are three of them."

"Human?"

The man nodded. "Looks like."

Tallard said, "I'll go see," and dashed off toward the edge of the forest.

"Three? Who could that be? Someone from Haywold, maybe?" Isabo breathed hopefully. "Maybe my father got away and sent someone to bring us back."

Will Perban gave a doubtful smile. "Maybe, but how could he have gotten away? Maybe it's trolls trying to catch anyone who followed them."

She frowned but nodded. Tanner and Perban reached for weapons and scrambled toward the cover of the boulder pile. Isabo loosed her own sword in its scabbard and made for a cluster of scrub oak.

Instead of trolls, Isabo heard the sound of swearing. Human swearing. It was Tallard.

"Come on," she said to Perban and sprinted in the direction of the sound. She climbed the steep side of the valley with sword in hand and then stopped, open-mouthed. Twenty yards away stood Tallard, holding her brother Amon by the neck. Beside Amon stood Wulf Wheatley, the fighter from Stone Bow, and two weary monks.

***

"I told you to stay home," Isabo said with a disgusted shake of her head.

The gangly teenager smiled weakly. "I asked Gran Willis to take care of the flock and the house while we were gone. He's my dad, too, Isabo. I can help you track — and I brought my sword," he said, brandishing his heavy sparring blade.

Isabo grabbed her brother by the arm and pulled him close. "You don't get it, do you? You're fifteen years old; you can't fight a bag of oats, let alone a pack of trolls! You are all that's left of our family. What would Pa do if he came home to find both of us missing and maybe dead?"

Amon shrugged off her grip. "I'm not going home, and that's final. We tracked you here, and if you leave me or try to send me home, I'll just follow." He glared at his sister. "What are you going to do? Slug me?" He nodded toward the monks. "Besides, I couldn't leave those two to follow you by themselves."

"Why in the Seven Hells would you bring them?" she growled. "This isn't a party or a temple feast. We're going to find Pa and kill the trolls that took him!"

"Took him? Trolls took..."

She nodded.

47

She glared at the two figures in gray, then to Perban. He motioned with his eyes. She nodded.

"Come with me," Perban said. He turned away. Amon hesitated for a moment and then followed. The monks glanced at each other and then joined Amon. Isabo shook her head disgustedly and followed behind.

He led the newcomers down into the valley toward the scattered ashes of the fire. "Do you know what that is?" he asked, pointing at the pile of burnt, gnawed bones.

Amon stared at the horrific sight and shook his head. "A deer?"

"That's Arden Luck," Perban reached down, pulled out the cracked, bloody skull, and shoved it in the boy's face.

Amon retched but managed to keep it down. He gathered his courage and glared at Perban. "Then let's go catch the trolls that did this and took my father."

"If the trolls don't kill you," Isabo said, "when we get home, I'll wring your stupid neck myself." She glared at Brother Yoren, who gave a watery belch and looked as if he were on the verge of fainting. "As for you, you don't belong here. Go back to your monastery. Follow the edge of the forest west until it turns south. You'll get to Haywold eventually, unless the trolls get you first. You're on your own because I can't afford to send anyone to keep you out of trouble."

"Please, Miss. We must go with you," he said, imploring. His eyes were drawn to the pile of bones, as Isabo knew they would be. He turned back to her. "The abbot of our order saw your father. He's in tremendous danger. He's going to —"

"What do you mean, he saw my father? He hasn't been in the South for years."

"I, uh, don't like to say."

She jabbed a finger in his chest, knocking him backward. "You'd better say, and right now."

The other, taller monk stepped forward. "You shouldn't ought to touch Brother Yoren that way."

"What are you going to do, monk? Preach at me?"

Yoren went on, raising a hand. "Peace, Brother Dunken, I am well. The abbot... had a vision. He saw trolls leading your father through a forest."

The taller monk stared at that and frowned at Yoren.

Isabo gaped, dumbfounded. "There's a damned forest right here. I don't need mystical hand-waving to tell me that trolls took him through a forest."

The monk looked away, then continued. "There were four trolls, maybe more, and another prisoner."

Isabo looked to Tallard. "Did you see other human-sized prints that weren't my father's?"

The scout gave a noncommittal shrug. "Maybe. The tracks are jumbled. Now that we've been trampling the area, it'll be almost impossible to tell."

She jerked a thumb at the monk. "So he could be making it up."

"Maybe," Tallard said. "As we track them, we'll keep an eye peeled for other human footprints." He looked eastward. "But we best be doing something besides arguing. Do you want to find your father or not?"

She brushed a wisp of dark hair from her eye, cursed, and looked around. Wult and Perban waited grimly for her to make a decision, while Tanner deepened the hole beside the stream with his shovel.

"Refill your waterskins. We're leaving after we've buried Arden Luck. You monks, make yourselves useful and help with the burying, but do it quick. Say some words over it. When we go, keep up or we'll leave you behind. Amon, you stay by my side, or I'll box your ears."

***

As they walked to the makeshift grave, the shorter monk's eyes kept returning to the stack of bones. The long leg bones bore the marks of a blade that had scraped away the flesh. Isabo saw what must be tooth marks. One — an arm bone? — had been cracked to get at the marrow. Her stomach lurched, and she willed himself not to vomit on the spot.

Isabo watched from a distance as the monks and Tanner hacked at the dark soil, tearing away clods of dirt. Yoren stole glances at the gruesome skull as he worked, and she saw Amon doing the same. After a few minutes, Tanner muttered that the hole was deep enough. The big monk, Dunken, gently took the bones and laid them neatly in the ground, weeping silently. Tanner scraped the dirt and turf over the remains and tamped it firm while Perban and Tallard gathered stones for a low cairn.

When it was finished, Yoren walked to the stream, knelt, washed his hands, and then dried them on his robe. His fingers were raw and scraped. He looked at Isabo, wiped his hands again, and nodded. The others stood aside as he made his way to the largest stone marking the head of Arden Luck. It was to the east, so Yoren stood with the glare of the late afternoon sun in his eyes. He wiped his hands on his robe once more and cleared his throat.

"Get on with it, monk," Isabo growled.

He nodded and cleared his throat again. "Blessed Ounwe," he croaked, "take the soul of this man murdered by trolls. Visit vengeance and everlasting pain on the creatures who did this and all their kind. So be it evermore." He looked up to Isabo. "Is that sufficient?"

She chuckled and smiled grimly. "That was good enough, monk. Short and to the point. Now let's get after them."

Chapter Six

Travelling East

Cullen sniffed, trying to scent where the trolls had gotten to. They'd been in a fair hurry to get away from the valley where they'd ambushed him, but now, after a week's steady march, they seemed to be taking their time. They'd made it as far as the Scarp, a low ridge on the edge of the Dimwood looking northward over the green, rolling plain. Across the plain, he could just make out the rise of the Chalk Cliffs. Somewhere at the base of those cliffs lay the human stronghold of Cleft. His friend Tallard lived there, a skilled tracker. With luck, the old scout had hunting parties out. Gheen sat near a tree twenty yards away, and several of the others had disappeared in the direction of a rushing stream that tumbled from the heights.

Turning away from the troll, he reached down and tore a few blades of mulegrass growing at his feet. He worked quickly, knotting the grass and weaving a few pine needles into another tale teller. He finished and laid the woven message beside the stump, placing a small twig atop it. If anyone could recognize the grass plaits for what they were, it was Moze Tallard.

Gheen grunted and stirred, and Cullen turned his attention to his rucksack. Everything seemed to be there, except his knife. Wogan had given him several large seed cakes wrapped in leaves and some dried fruit. Strapped to the pack was a skin of the nasty wine. He sniffed at it and recoiled.

"Gheen!" he shouted.

The troll stood and lumbered forward from the trees, looked cautiously to locate Grimmun, and then approached Cullen. He didn't speak.

Cullen threw the skin to Gheen, who caught it and frowned. "What does Cullen-thing want from Gheen? Why give this to me?"

Might as well have a friend, even an ignorant one. "It's what we humans do, Gheen of the Three Valleys Clan. We give things to each other. Besides, your drink is too strong for me. What do you call the stuff?"

The troll scratched himself and cast a quizzical eye at Cullen. "It is called wine."

The beast shrugged and sauntered away. Cullen sniffed, trying to identify and isolate Grimmun's scent. Despite the troll leader's earlier comment, he doubted they'd be in a hurry to kill him. Still, the beast wouldn't take it well if Cullen were caught leaving signs for someone to follow.

After their long trek through the eastern reaches of the forest, Cullen gave Grimmun and his apparent second-in-command, Malbah, grudging respect. They'd led the group quickly and quietly. Cullen approved of the silent travel, both for trolls' budding wood sense and because he had no desire to speak to them. They'd tell him in their own time why they captured him.

He closed his eyes, breathed once, then again, and tasted the air. He turned and sniffed. *There they were.* Grimmun and Malbah lay ahead, near the top of the ridge. Gheen was now thirty yards to the left, pissing behind a rock; Cullen wrinkled his nose at the acrid waft.

Grimmun and his companion gave off the repulsive rotten food odor that Cullen associated with their kind. To this, Gheen added the rancid scent of troll wine. He'd drunk his own skin of wine along the trek, slopping much of it down his front.

The fourth troll remained below, somewhere back along the trail. Cullen had named him Tail because he always traveled far to the rear of the group. He'd fallen into a swift-moving stream two days ago and just managed to pull himself out. Since the troll's dunking in the water, Cullen struggled to detect him, especially since he followed far behind.

Cullen shook his head. He knew his own gift for scent was rare, but Tail aside, these trolls just plain stank. It was well that trolls didn't think much of bathing; otherwise, they'd be more difficult to track.

"Wogan," he said.

The little man puttered about the small cookfire preparing the noon meal. "I'm busy, Cullen."

"Just give me a moment," Cullen said.

Wogan sighed wearily and placed the cookpot on the ground. "What is it?"

"Do any of the trolls have my scent-gift?"

The wiry old man shook his head. "No. I've never seen a troll with the gift. We — they — captured only a few human scouts in my time with them. Just one scout, a woman named Dannick, had it. It's rare in humans, and I've never heard of it in trolls."

Cullen scratched at his stubbly beard. "Tilda Dannick? I knew her. She was from Tall Grass, away in the southern plains. She tracked a runaway boy almost twenty leagues on foot through the grasslands." He eyed Wogan and spat on the ground. "She was smart. Too smart to fall into such a simple trap as I did. Did you betray her to the trolls, too?"

"No, not me," Wogan said, shaking his head. "It was another."

"What happened to her?"

"It is not for me to say."

Was he lying? If these beasts had killed her...

Wogan stirred the coals. "The trolls needed her, as they need you. She was helping the *trollim*."

This made no sense. Why were trolls capturing scouts? Tilda Dannick would never betray her people by aiding these foul creatures.

From below and westward along the edge of the forest came a low, just audible "Holoo!"

The troll Gheen appeared from behind the pines to Cullen's left. He faced down the hill and repeated the sound.

A moment later, an answering call came, repeated twice.

Gheen smiled, his tusks flashing against his pasty gray-green skin. He looked at Cullen with an ugly, lopsided smile. "Toleg and Burnah come. They stayed in the valley where we capture Cullen-thing in order to smoke the... meat."

"Was it venison?" Cullen asked with a dark glare.

Gheen dropped his eyes and didn't speak.

Cullen grabbed Wogan's shoulder and swung the small man around. "This *meat*, it's Arden Luck, isn't it?" he snapped. "My companion, whom the trolls slew?"

Wogan nodded but didn't look away. "It is."

"And if I refuse to help Grimmun, the same will happen to me."

Wogan shrugged, then nodded.

Cullen glared at the troll slave. He couldn't think of Wogan as human. "You eat man-flesh as well?"

Wogan looked at the ground. "It is only for trolls. It is special."

Cullen spat again. "What stops you, slave? Is there some small hint of humanity left within you, or are you afraid of displeasing your masters?"

"You don't know the life of *pakh-hu*, of humans, living with the *trollim*. Cullen, if you hate what I've become, then help me. Help them. They're desperate."

"How would helping the trolls possibly help humans? Some bad thing is threatening the trolls — fine. How does that threaten you?"

Wogan gave a pained expression. "There is much I would say, but it is not my place."

Cullen shook his head and turned away.

***

An hour later, the six trolls gathered at the crest of the ridge. They conversed in low, guttural tones in their own language.

Cullen and Wogan stood twenty yards down the Scarp, preparing their gear for the march north and east toward the mountains.

Wogan drew a knife from his pack and passed it to Cullen. "We're going out onto the open plains and need to move swiftly. Grimmun gave permission for me to return this to you. You may cut your bonds."

Cullen nodded. Traveling quickly with bound wrists and ankles, even loosely bound, was difficult. "Grimmun gave permission, eh? You'll have to thank your master for me." Cullen drew the knife through the cords around his hands and feet. He examined the supple material for a moment and stuffed it into his pack.

"How did you know me, Wogan? Where are you from?"

Wogan cinched his pack tight and hefted it onto his shoulders. "I grew up Stype, away in the south, but my parents were from Tall Grass. Arden Luck was a sort of cousin. I knew he tracked with you on occasion and that you lived in Haywold. I told Grimmun-*ush*, and a month ago, he sent troll scouts to find your village. When he had confirmation you were there, they — we — came after you."

"Ounwe's eyeballs, man. You knew Luck and let the trolls kill him in order to capture me? I should kill you now out of respect for the man."

"Do as you will, Cullen. Use the knife Grimmun returned to you. But know that you'll be dead — or worse — if you do. I regret Luck's death. He was a close friend of my family. But we're trying to stop something far worse than anything you could imagine. Trolls and the *pakh-hu* among them are in danger. Fighters like Luck are important, but you're more so. Please, don't resist them."

Cullen shook his head. "And the other trolls — the Stone Breakers — what was their role in this? Was killing the Pinchbeks part of your scheme?"

"As far as I know, it was a coincidence. There was a meeting between the clans before we set out, but I'm not privy to what it was about."

Cullen spat on the ground. "It's time to end this, Wogan." Without a pause, he seized the old man by the arm and held the knife to his throat. The fierce, sharp blade drew a thin line of crimson across his throat.

Wogan didn't flinch.

"Grimmun!" Cullen shouted. "Come rescue your slave."

A collective growl rose from the top of the ridge. Within seconds, each of the trolls had a scimitar or a long knife in his hand. Malbah and Gheen drew near.

Grimmun growled a command. The two halted, and the rest sheathed their weapons.

"Wogan-thing," Grimmun said with a touch of anger, "you have served me well. Die now."

At that, Wogan lunged against the blade at his throat.

Cullen jerked the knife away in horror.

Blood coursed down Wogan's chest, but the man still stood. "I am sorry, Grimmun-*ush*," he said, dropping to his knees. "I was unable."

"Enough!" Grimmun roared. His shout echoed from the trees. "We've no time for this. Cullen, bind his wound!"

"Bind it yourself, pig." Cullen wiped the knife clean on his sleeve and returned it to its sheath.

Grimmun growled. "Do you think I won't kill you, human?"

"No, troll, I don't think so. Tell me now why you need a scout to help you."

The troll's face twisted into what Cullen took for a scowl. He made a harsh, phlegmy sound deep in his throat, spoke a few words in Trollish, and then walked away, back toward the top of the Scarp.

Gheen, Malbah, and the others stared wide-eyed at their leader.

Wogan moved to stand beside Cullen, a cloth pressed to his throat. Blood soaked his shirt.

"What just happened?" Cullen asked.

"Go to him, Cullen. Now. He said nothing is more important than bringing you whole to the camps in the mountains. He'll tell you what you want to know."

***

Grimmun stood beside a lightning-blasted tree at the crest of the ridge. He gazed eastward along the edge of the forest to the peaks of the Blue Mountains in the far distance.

Cullen couldn't read the troll's expression. Maybe it was the upturned tusks or the sneer baked into the creatures' faces. He sensed that some of the anger was gone from Grimmun, but he couldn't tell what emotion took its place.

"Wogan said you wanted to speak to me, Grimmun."

The troll looked at him, then turned back to the mountains.

"What do you know, Cullen, of the dark things under the earth?"

Cullen chuckled. "Fairy stories?"

The troll snarled and shook his head. "No, human. I speak of the dark, evil things that live in the belly of the earth."

Evil? Cullen shook his head. "Besides the things that raid our lands and kill our people, you mean? I've no reason to think there are malevolent, evil creatures besides your kind, at least not under the ground. They're tales told to scare children."

Grimmun glared at him. His pig-like snout twitched. "You're a fool. Do you think there are no wind spirits or cave rats because you've never seen one?" He waved an arm to the mountains now gray and orange in the afternoon sun. "Do you see the double peaks to the right? Those are The Guardians. In their valleys live my people, my clan. Some of your people live there as well."

"Come to the point, Grimmun."

"Something is stealing my people."

Cullen leaned back and laughed long and hard. Great peals of laughter echoed from the ridge. Grimmun stood silent, waiting for him to finish.

At last, Grimmun cuffed Cullen, knocking him to the ground. "Enough!" he shouted, pointing a clawed finger at him.

Cullen stood and wiped the tears of laughter from his eyes, but when he finished, his face was set and grim. "Grimmun, your arrogance makes me want to vomit. Ounwe's arse! How could you think I'd help you after your kind has killed and kidnapped my people for generations?"

"Wogan-thing tells me you have younglings, a daughter and a son. Perhaps they also have the scent-gift."

"Troll, are you threatening my family? How long has it been since humans and trolls fought in open war? A generation? It can happen again."

Grimmun growled low in his throat and clenched the hilt of the sword at his hip. "Don't anger me further, human." The two glared at each other for tense moments. At last, Grimmun chuckled. "You are a fierce one. You would make a fine troll."

"Is that meant to be a compliment? I'll never understand your kind, troll."

Grimmun shrugged. "I don't ask you to do that but to aid my people. And yours."

"What do you mean, 'and yours?'"

"The *pakh-hu* among us are also at risk."

Cullen grunted. "Fine. When this is done, I will walk free, as will any other humans you've taken."

Grimmun laughed. "We'll discuss the specifics of this understanding when we arrive at our camp in the mountains. But yes, if you find our people, you'll be freed."

"Me and all the humans."

"That decision will be made by the Holy One of our people, but I suspect he would look favorably upon your... request."

"And how do you know it wasn't Stone Breakers or some other troll clan who took your... people?" It was hard to think of them as people. Humans were people. Trolls were creatures.

"All clans have lost trolls," Grimmun said. "Three Valleys Clan, the Deep River clan, and yes, the Stone Breakers as well. And the rest. It is not trolls doing this thing against us."

"What thing? Where have they gone? Tell me what in blazes you think I can do, Grimmun."

"They've gone into the mountain. We need you to find them, human. Or find what became of them."

Cullen looked from the troll to the distant peaks and back again. "I need a drink."

Grimmun raised a bushy, dark eyebrow but handed over his wineskin without a word. After a moment, he said, "Two seasons ago, our old ones began to have dark, terrible dreams, terrifying dreams. They left our camps and went into the caves. They would not be stopped. They said a gray thing called to them, bidding them to come. 'He is called Azuk, and he will slay us all if we do not come,' they told us."

"We followed them into the caves and down to the very limits of our tunnels. We found a new opening none had seen before, a new tunnel. It was as if some great beast had chewed its way up through the stone from the fires of Morag itself."

Cullen sniffed. Grimmun's scent had changed. It now carried the sour note of fear.

He uncorked the skin, held his breath, and swallowed a mouthful, then handed it back. The foul wine burned his throat, but he suppressed the urge to spew it out.

"You couldn't block the tunnel or keep them from going in?"

Grimmun swallowed deeply from the skin and shook his head. "We filled in the entrance to the tunnel, but our people pulled at the rocks until their claws bled. We restrained them with cords, but they cursed and spat and howled until we released them. When we let them go, they went straight to the tunnel and entered. Our hunters and scouts followed them, but it was as if some power drew the lost ones in hidden ways through the tunnels. We could not find them. We lost many hunters seeking after them."

"How many have gone?"

"Dozens from the Three Valleys Clan. As many from the other clans, or perhaps more."

The tall troll glanced down at Cullen. "The first was Urgan, once chief of our clan, then others. Our shaman, the Holy One of the Three Valleys Clan, said we needed a human scout with the scent-gift. You're not the first scout we captured."

Cullen nodded and whistled low. "Dannick, I know. She's smart. Was it she who taught you woodcraft?"

Grimmun would not meet his gaze. "We learned much from Dannick-thing. She could not find the old ones, though she tracked them far under the mountain. Only someone with the scent-gift like her — and you — could find their way through the maze of tunnels."

"What happened to her? And why would she help you in the first place?"

The troll secured the skin to his pack.

"Grimmun, damn your eyes, what happened to her?"

"She made several journeys deep in the tunnels. She found a cavern with a dark river far under the mountain. There she lost the scent. On the last journey, Dannick-thing did not return to the mouth of the tunnel. We entered in as far as we dared. That's where we found her. Her body was whole, but she raved and gibbered like a wild thing. She died in terror a few days after. Some *thing* had flayed her mind. Those who were with her — the trolls — were gone and not seen again. None have gone searching since then, though every few weeks Azuk calls more trolls into the caves."

Grimmun glowered at Cullen, but the human saw something — desperation? — in his features.

"Human, if you can find our people or find the thing that is doing this, the Holy One and the leaders of the other clans will reward you, and set free those of your kind who live among us."

"They have authority over all the troll clans?"

"Yes."

He sneered at the beast. "Then the freedom of my people is the least that I would demand from you."

"Demand? You would demand from —" The troll paused, turned away, and growled low in his throat.

Cullen raised an eyebrow. This creature was clearly forcing itself to be patient and not rip his arms off. It must be truly desperate. "I don't know what this beast is that is taking your kind," he said. "It must be a great evil if you look for help among those you would kill or enslave."

Grimmun nodded, and his face broke into what Cullen had to assume was a grim smile.

"At last, you understand, human. What else would you 'demand' for doing this?"

"I want your kind to die in the pits of hell, Grimmun. Azuk can have you all."

Now it was the creature's turn to laugh. "As I said, you would make a good troll."

"What if I don't do this thing?"

"In truth? We will kill you and find another with the scent-gift."

Isabo had the gift, and probably Amon, though the lad hadn't shown it. If he did nothing, he would be dead and probably his family, but eventually, this Azuk would kill all the trolls. If he helped them — and the trolls kept their word — the humans would be freed.

He stared westward along the edge of the Dimwood and the rolling grasslands. "My other demand is that trolls stop raiding our lands."

"I can't promise that," the troll rumbled.

"Then who can?"

"Only the Holy One and the chiefs of our clans."

"Then take me to them."

Chapter Seven

Gheen

Gheen watched the insect flit from leaf to leaf on the low shrub. It was *gzz,* what the humans called a horsefly. *Horsefly is a stupid name,* he thought. It didn't look like a horse or sound like one. It sounded like "gzzz" in your ear. Humans used poor words. How smart could they be if they always used the wrong names for things?

He inched an open palm toward the *gzz* from behind the bug, where it didn't see well. He paused as the thing settled on a leaf and shook its tiny wings once, twice. Before it could flutter a third time, his hand flashed forward, stunning the insect and trapping it in a closed fist.

The troll smiled. He shook his fist sharply to daze the creature within and then popped it into his mouth. He rolled it across his tongue, savoring the sharp, gritty taste, then glanced across at the human. The *pakh-hu* Cullen fidgeted with blades of grass and bracken stems.

"Why does Cullen-thing do this?" he asked the human.

"Do what?" Cullen said.

Gheen pointed at the grass, now plaited into a small rectangle with repeated patterns in the weave. The human started, like a troll youngling with his hand caught in the *ghor-nok.* He tossed the grass-thing to the ground.

"It's just a habit," Cullen said. "Just something to pass the time."

Gheen scratched himself and smiled. "Teach Gheen to make habb-et with weeds."

The human covered it with his foot. "No, it's not a habbet, it's called a—okay, fine. Yes, it's called a habbet."

Gheen pointed at the *pakh-hu*'s foot. "Show what you dropped."

Cullen shifted and made a strange expression. Gheen wished he could better read the *pakh-hu*'s face. Like their words, their faces carried confusing meanings.

"That one was bad," Cullen said. "I'll show you how to make a better one. Easy to do." He ground the thing underfoot.

Gheen raised an eyebrow. What was the *pakh-hu* — the human — doing?

"Is there meaning in the pattern of grass?" he asked.

Cullen shook his head. "No. I used to make these for my daughter at home."

"Then why you destroy with your foot?" Gheen shouldered Cullen aside and reached down to retrieve the object from the ground. The pattern of woven lines was just recognizable in the tattered remnant. He pointed to the skies. "Warriors of the Heavens give skills to all, even to the *pakh-hu*. It is wrong to destroy thing made by such skill."

Cullen snorted. "Warriors of the Heavens? Heavenly creatures may do such things for trolls, but they don't involve themselves in the lives of humans."

The troll shook his head and carefully pocketed the plaited grass. "Cullen not know."

"Gheen!"

Grimmun appeared through the trees, with Malbah and Wogan close behind.

Gheen shot to his feet and bowed his head to the troll leader.

"The *pakh-hu* Cullen is in your charge," Grimmun said. "If he attempts to escape, kill him. If he leaves your care, I will take your head."

Gheen touched his forehead in assent.

***

Grimmun led the party down onto the northern plains as the sun fell into the west. Gheen watched Cullen and Wogan-thing as they picked their way down the slope. Though their facial expressions remained a mystery, it was clear that Cullen didn't like the other *pakh-hu*. For what reason? Weren't they both of the same skin? Gheen wondered at the way these creatures treated one another. He'd been taught the Kinship of Trolls from an early age. Trolls, no matter caste or rank or clan, treated each other with honor. He shook his head. *Pakh-hu* — humans — had no such teaching and were only animals.

***

They set a brisk pace, marching past the edge of the forest and then, thankfully, eastward toward the distant peaks and home. *It will be good to cross the river and leave the human lands*, Gheen thought.

He settled in, loping along beside Cullen. Though the human was a full head shorter and scrawny, he kept up with the trolls' pace.

The moon rose in the early evening, and a chill breeze blew down from the northern wastes.

"Will you try to flee from us?" Gheen asked, panting.

Cullen shook his head from side to side.

Gheen nodded at that. He recognized the gesture shared by trolls and humans. "Can trolls trust the word of a *pakh-hu*?"

Cullen laughed. "Do trolls always talk so much?"

The moon rose clear of the mountains ahead of them, casting silvery light on the plains.

"Why run at night?" the human asked.

Gheen grunted. "Might be *pakh-hu* tracking parties on plains in day." He watched as the human gazed northward. "Do not forget the words of Grimmun. It will not go well for you — or me — if you try to escape."

Cullen spat. "Gheen, I don't care a lick about your tribe or clan or whatever you call it. They could all be swallowed up by this demon creature, and I wouldn't weep. But I gave Grimmun my word that I would do what I could to help. In return, all the humans, all the *pakh-hu*, will be freed. If they aren't, if Grimmun is false, my people will come to your precious mountains and kill every troll living, demon or no." The human looked up at the troll loping along beside him. "I like you, Gheen, if that isn't some kind of heresy. I'd hate to have to kill you if it comes to that."

Gheen gave a panting, rumbling chuckle. "I am glad *pakh-hu* Cullen can make joke." He looked down at the human, but Cullen wasn't laughing.

***

When the moon was high overhead, Grimmun called a halt beside a broad stream. Chest-high banks and low thickets of arrowbrush and chokeberry gave enough cover for the entire party to spread out without being seen.

Gheen pulled off his pack, sat against the bank, and took out a large seedcake. He broke off a chunk and began to gnaw at it.

Cullen stood a little apart, scenting the breeze and turning this way and that.

"What does Cullen-thing smell?" Gheen asked.

The human didn't speak for a moment but stood as if savoring the taste of the breeze. It pointed and said, "There's a herd of aurochs and antelope a league or so northward. They're moving eastward as well."

Gheen chuckled again. "You tell this from sniffing?"

Cullen nodded and pointed southward. "Grimmun and Malbah are a hundred yards south and east, probably looking at the way ahead. Wogan is in the same area, but I can't smell humans as well. They don't stink like trolls." He faced north again. "Toleg and Burnah are at the stream in that direction, fifty yards, in a patch of chokeberry. May they choke for what they did to Arden Luck."

Cullen turned to face west. He sniffed, shook his head, and sniffed again. "The other troll, Tail, is —"

"Gurmah," Gheen said. "He is Gurmah. He has no tail."

"Gurmah, then, is back behind us somewhere."

Gheen nodded and motioned for Cullen to sit. "Eat, Cullen-thing. Keep up strength. Fill skins with water if you won't drink wine." The troll chewed for a moment, then said, "You are good sniffer. Grimmun and Wogan-thing chose well when they pick you to find the stolen trolls."

"What do you know about these disappearances, Gheen? Did you know those who were taken?"

Gheen nodded. "Is always the oldest and wisest ones; never the young. Those who go, the gray demon calls them in their dreams. Demon is from Morag, the Dark Place. Who else has power to enter dreams?"

"There are no such things as demons, Gheen."

Gheen looked at the *pakh-hu* in the darkness. Of course, there were demons. How could anyone say such a nonsense thing? "Cullen not know," he said with a dark, petulant look. He chewed in silence for a while. "You must find them, hooman."

"I gave my word to Grimmun that I would try."

"Do not try. Do. You must."

Cullen shook his head in the pale moonlight. He said coldly, "It's urgent for you, is it? Imagine that, Gheen. I do this for my reasons — to help those humans you trolls hold captive, not from the goodness of my heart. There is no 'goodness of my heart' where trolls are concerned. Your people enslave and kill, and eat my people. You eat my people!" he repeated. "Don't you see that's wrong? My wife, Magda, died in a troll raid when she tried to run from our burning house. My daughter Selia — my Isabo's twin — tried to help her. I watched as a fat, hulking troll bashed that little girl against a tree, killing her on the spot. I killed him with my bare hands after I hunted him down."

He took a long drink from the skin, then went to the stream to refill it. When he returned, he sat against the bank and closed his eyes. "Gheen, I said before there's no such thing as demons, but I was wrong. It's you and your kind. I will rescue my people from the demons in any way that I can. If it takes going under a damned mountain to free a few trolls, I'll do that."

Troll and human sat silent for long moments. The wind whistled in the grass and the thickets, gusted a few times, and then dropped. From northward came the heavy lowing of the aurochs grazing in the darkness.

Gheen reached into his pack and pulled out a small bundle wrapped in leaves. It smelled faintly of wood smoke. "Cullen, can I tell you a thing?"

He waited, silent, until Cullen said yes.

"I am Gheen, the son of Guruk and Ama. I am only a mountain troll of low caste. Grimmun is high troll of different caste. He will be leader of my clan one day. We are different but of the same Three Valleys clan. Grimmun and Gheen could never be friends, but we honor each other because we wear same skin. *Trollim duruk* is most important thing among trolls."

He continued without looking at Cullen. "What is word for all humans who are of your family? Your Magda and children and brothers and cousins?"

"Kin," Cullen said. "They are — were — my kin."

Gheen grunted. "*Trollim duruk* is kinship of trolls. No troll would dishonor another, though we are of different caste. Does Cullen understand?"

The human shook his head. "No, I don't. Grimmun sometimes yells at you and treats you like an animal. That doesn't sound like 'kinship of trolls.'"

Gheen grunted. How could he make this creature understand? "Grimmun is troll of highest caste. On this journey, he is also my... how do you say? Commander? Leader? It is his right to treat me this way. Still, our skin is same. We are both trolls and honor each other."

He raised a thick eyebrow and watched to see if the human got it. When Cullen didn't speak, Gheen glanced nervously down at the small bundle in his hand. "Second most important thing for trolls is to show honor to bravest foes in battle. We do this with *amok jala*, Feast of Warriors. From your words, Gheen knows it is shameful for humans to eat others' flesh, but for us is the way to share in their bravery."

He held up the small leaf-wrapped parcel. "This is *amok ur jala* for the *pakh-hu* you call Arden Luck. I honor him."

Cullen glared at the troll. Realization slowly came to his face. "It was you who killed him, Gheen. What do you want me to say? You want my blessing to eat my friend?"

Gheen shook his head. "It is a thing of honor."

Cullen snorted.

Gheen stared at the human. How could he not understand the importance of these things? It would have been shameful, even sacrilegious, to leave the flesh of the human for beasts to scavenge.

At once, it dawned on Gheen what the human Cullen meant. "You think me a beast, *pakh-hu*." It wasn't a question.

Cullen gave an angry laugh. "You are worse than the beasts, troll. And you seek to instruct me in the *noble* ways of the trolls."

"The *trollim* are not evil, not beasts. Maybe we learn from you, and you from us."

"Don't hold your breath."

Gheen raised an eyebrow. "Why would Gheen hold breath?"

From their right came the sound of someone tramping along the stream bed. Grimmun and Wogan appeared.

"The time to rest is over," Grimmun said. "Fill your water and make ready to march. It is still two days to the river."

Chapter Eight

Into the Mountains

The massive pinnacles of the Blue Mountains grew taller as the party marched eastward. Through deep gaps, still more blue-gray peaks faded into the distance. On either side, the range extended far to the north and south.

At the foot of the mountains, hidden by a deep gorge, lay the Roaring River. Cullen heard it a few leagues away, the sound first registering as a low, continuous rumble in the chest. As they approached, it rose to a consuming roar.

Near the edge of the gorge, Cullen sat on a stone and drank deeply from his water skin. He considered the deep expanse of stony peaks rising steeply across the canyon, then turned to look back in the direction they'd come. Rolling, grassy hills dropped away into the far west. Somewhere leagues beyond the hazy horizon lay the emptiness of the Dead Plains. To the south hung the dark expanse of the Dimwood.

There's so much space here. Surely there's enough room for humans and trolls. Why did they have to come ravaging across the river into our lands?

He turned to the knot of trolls at the canyon's edge and shouted above the sound of the river below. "How will you cross, Grimmun?"

Grimmun didn't speak but sent trolls scouting both directions along the lip of the canyon, scanning the eastern side. After an hour, Malbah came trotting back southward and spoke to Grimmun.

Cullen watched the interaction between the two. He'd thought all trolls were the same: green or gray-green skin, protruding tusks, and upturned piggish snouts. A troll was a troll. But there were differences. About half of this group, including Grimmun and Malbah, carried themselves more confidently. They were taller and broader in the shoulder, and their speech was easier to follow. Gheen was in the other group — smaller, with an odd, halting speech.

Gheen had mentioned being a different caste than Grimmun. Were the differences in speech related to caste or family?

When all the trolls returned, the group headed south. They reached a point where the canyon narrowed to no more than thirty yards from edge to edge. About halfway down on the other side lay a cave half-hidden by trees.

"I'll have their hides for not posting a watch," Grimmun snarled. He nodded to Malbah and Gheen, who gathered large stones and began throwing them down at the cave.

No response came. Grimmun uttered a command to Malbah, who strung a bow and fired arrows down into the cave. After a few moments, excited shouts could be heard over the river's roaring. A troll appeared in the cave mouth; a shield raised against further arrows. Grimmun bellowed a command; the troll saluted and retreated back into the dark opening.

Grimmun glanced at the afternoon sun dropping westward. "Hurry now. There is work to be done to cross the river." He nodded to Malbah and stepped over the edge of the canyon onto a narrow trail.

Wogan pushed past Cullen, muttering quietly but loud enough to be heard over the river. He was agitated about something, but Cullen couldn't tell just what. The canyon was deep and the rocky sides steep, so it wasn't surprising that he was apprehensive, but there seemed to be something more.

The slave called to Grimmun in a shaking voice, and the troll halted. Wogan bowed low with his hands over his eyes, then spoke into the big creature's ear. The human was clearly shaking in terror.

Grimmun nodded and barked a few words to Malbah, who grasped Wogan's shoulder, guiding him down into the narrow defile. The troll leader turned and gave Cullen a curious eye. "You are not fearful in this place, pakh-hu Cullen-thing?"

His heart was beginning to pound slightly, but he wasn't about to let the hulking creature see it. He shrugged and itched at his beard. "Should I be? I've climbed rock cliffs before."

The troll considered him thoughtfully. "You are not like the other human. Not at all. This is interesting. Follow now."

Cullen did as he was bid, but not before looking behind him to see the other trolls. Gheen stood near him on the trail wearing an oafish smile, with the other two, Toleg and Burnah, watching eastward on the canyon's edge. The last of them, Gurmah, brushed the ground with a branch, obscuring the signs of their passing.

So much for leaving a message for anyone coming behind. Still, he fingered the weave of a tale-teller in his pocket. There might still be an opportunity.

As they picked their way downward through the rocks, he saw that the trolls on the other side were descending as well. They seemed to be making their way to a cluster of boulders about two-thirds of the way to the bottom.

Wind whistled through the narrow way, carrying a welcome dampness that cooled him after the dry air of the plains above. After more than an hour of stumbling downward, though, he was exhausted and fairly drenched from sweat and the damp air. But they continued on, trudging deeper into the canyon. He watched Wogan, who by this time was practically carried by the troll Malbah. The man had been quivering with fear, which only worsened as they descended.

The whole area was a jumble of jagged boulders, but they finally reached a flat space where they could rest. The trolls didn't seem fazed by the effort, but Cullen had rarely seen someone as shattered as Wogan. It surprised him because the slave appeared to be older, but fit. Had a few hours' tough exercise taken that much out of him? Malbah tended him almost gently, easing him to a seat on the ground and giving him water from a skin.

No, it wasn't exhaustion. Wogan had been in terror of something, and the strenuous hike had only worsened his condition.

Cullen eased himself to the ground next to Gheen and massaged his own aching calves. He nodded to the other human, trembling on the ground. "What's the matter with him, Gheen? He looks terrified."

Gheen glanced fearfully at Grimmun, who gave a slight shake of his head. "Is nothing," his guardian said. "Wogan-thing is afraid of the canyon. Is deep and rocky. He... fears he may fall on slippery rocks."

"Maybe. People can be afraid of different things, right? But that doesn't bother me."

Gheen busied himself with his pack and didn't speak again.

Cullen watched the trolls across the river. They had made their way to the odd cluster of boulders and began moving rocks. With some effort, they uncovered a dark shape and began assembling it. He was too far away to tell exactly what it was, but after some time, they added what looked to be handles and began to manipulate the thing. He couldn't see any effect, but then noticed a line running from the pile of rocks to the river. As they turned the handles, the line tautened and began to rise.

In a moment, he realized that his jaw was hanging open. It was a winch, and they were pulling something from the river. It looked to be a heavy rope. But what was at the end? After a few moments, it became clear, but he was no less amazed. The contraption was pulling not one but several lines from the bottom of the river. Gradually, the cables cleared the water, and he saw they were actually chains anchored on the near side of the river.

Grimmun barked an order, and Gheen, Malbah, and the rest of the trolls began uncovering sturdy planks a few feet long from a hidden stockpile. In short order, they began lashing the boards between two of the cables while those across the river worked in this direction — they were making a bridge.

Cullen shook his head. So, that was how the ugly beasts had been getting across the river to raid. None of the human scouts had ever discovered it. How long had it been hidden here?

In the end, they had a serviceable crossing, complete with a hand rope waist-high to a troll.

With the knowledge of this discovery came a sinking dread. Would the trolls let him survive now that he knew the secret of how they crossed the river? He casually reached into his pocket and slid the woven tale-teller onto the damp stone. There were no weeds or grasses at hand, so he couldn't add anything to the weave. It simply carried his mark and the number of days since the new moon. Maybe that would help Tallard or whoever came looking for him. He picked up a sharp rock and began scraping marks.

By the time the bridge was finished, the sun had long since fallen westward, and the canyon was in darkening shadow. Grimmun shouted another order. Gheen, Malbah, and Gurmah returned from their task and began gathering their gear. Wogan had rallied, or was at least conscious, though he still moaned and shivered piteously. Cullen watched curiously as Malbah took a vial from Wogan's pack and poured the contents into the prostrate human's mouth. Within a few minutes, Wogan was still, but his chest rose and fell evenly.

"What was that?" Cullen shouted over the noise of the water. "What did you give him?"

Malbah ignored him, but Grimmun gave a low chuckle. "It is for his fear. *Pakh-hu* are weak, though you, strangely, are not troubled. The potion will enable me to carry him across. He will wake again soon, but we must go. Come. Gheen will guide you." He gave the other troll a sharp look. "If the human falls into the river and drowns, you will follow him."

They shifted the unconscious Wogan onto Malbah's broad back and secured him with ropes. Without a word, Malbah turned and climbed onto the swaying bridge, and in a few minutes, was safely across.

Cullen attempted to swallow his mounting unease. The bridge swayed perilously over the water, and the planks dripped with the spray. Near the center, one of the planks had come loose and dangled just above the river, leaving a gap of four or five feet.

Grimmun chuckled and gave a command. Gheen nudged Cullen to step onto the planks. He had crossed bridges like this once or twice before, but they had been over dry gullies within the Dimwood. This was another matter. He steeled himself for the effort, grasped the hand rope, and began to cross.

Gusty winds caused the bridge to sway, but the chains were heavy, and the sheer weight of the thing kept it from moving too much. The wind and spray seemed more of a threat than the bridge's rhythmic movement. His foot slipped awkwardly on the wet planks until he found his balance. By the time he reached the gap in the center, his confidence had grown, and he crossed the broad opening without a downward glance.

At the end, he stepped onto solid ground with a broad sigh of relief. Gheen followed close behind. He turned to watch Grimmun cross easily. Only Gurmah remained, and that troll appeared to be inspecting the area around the bridge for signs of their passing. With a renewed sinking feeling in the pit of his stomach, he saw Gurmah pick something up from the ground and inspect it. He shoved whatever he'd found into a pocket and then turned to the bridge. It had been the tale-teller, surely.

Well, if he found it, he found it. There was nothing to do about it.

The troll stepped onto the first plank and then the second. At that, he turned around, drew a blade, cut the lashing of the first board, and heaved it into the river. He was making sure no one could follow, at least, not without clambering across the wet cables. He continued across quickly, slicing ropes and dropping planks. In a quarter of an hour, he was across. The trolls released the winch, and the cables dropped back into the water. There was now no sign the bridge had been there at all, except for a single, distant plank of wood bobbing in the current.

Gurmah approached Grimmun, bowed his head, and pulled something from his pocket. It was the vial Malbah had used to dose Wogan. Grimmun cursed and cuffed Malbah across the head.

Cullen sighed wearily and drank from his water skin. Maybe Ounwe was looking out for him after all.

They gathered their gear and began their ascent up the eastern side of the canyon. To his surprise, he saw that Wogan was conscious now and clambered quickly up the thin path. How had the old slave recovered so quickly? Had it been the potion? As he climbed, his legs ached, but with each step, he breathed more easily. He glanced back across the river at the tumble of boulders and the hidden bridge. Would he ever make it back to tell the trolls' secret? There had to be a way.

In another hour, the late afternoon sun was far down in the west, painting the canyon in deep oranges and reds. If he hadn't found himself a captive of trolls, he might have appreciated its beauty.

They neared the cave in which the trolls had been waiting, and Cullen leaned against a tall pole set in the ground to catch his breath. He glanced up and immediately stopped breathing. Mounted on the pole was a weathered human head. Empty eye sockets peered westward across the canyon. Crows and the elements had taken most of the flesh and remaining tissue.

Ounwe's bollocks! These trolls should be dead under his blade, but here he was in the midst of them.

"What is this, Grimmun?" he shouted over the roar of the river.

The troll glanced his way, then snorted and gave a grim laugh. "It's a warning of what happens should humans come across the river unbidden. Don't fear. Perform the tasks we ask of you, and you will be unharmed."

"You don't see irony in this, troll?"

"I don't know that word."

He pointed at the head. "It means I'm an idiot — or worse — for helping the beasts who would do this thing."

"It is a simple warning," the troll said. "It has nothing to do with why we need you."

Cullen shook his head. "A simple warning?"

Well, so be it. He would perform the task he was given, free the human slaves, and be gone. If the trolls reneged on the deal, Grimmun at least would die by his blade, and then it would be his ugly head on a stake. Gheen had said that Grimmun would one day be the leader of the clan, but that would never happen if he were dead.

He watched Grimmun harangue the three trolls from the cave for not keeping watch. Each received his share of blows and curses, but none seemed the worse for the abuse. Afterward, the three disappeared into the cave and retrieved provisions for the group.

"Eat and rest, human," Grimmun said. He pointed upward into the mountains. "Soon, you will meet the Holy One of my clan. He will tell you more of the demon Azuk."

Cullen shrugged and turned to the staked head. "After I kill your demon, I will tear that down, and I will kill any troll that tries to stop me."

The troll gave a low, growling laugh. "Your anger will defeat you one day, Cullen-thing. Perhaps it will aid you against the demon, but I doubt it. Eat. Rest."

***

From the river, the way led into thick forest. Grimmun and Malbah led the group upward on a well-worn path.

"How far is your camp from here, Gheen?"

"Tomorrow we there. We go up to tunnel, then through to Three Valleys," the troll said.

"A tunnel?"

Gheen nodded. "The Tunnel of Sukkuz goes through part of mountain. Trolls long ago dug it."

"How long ago?" he asked. "How long have your people lived here?"

The troll shrugged and mumbled, "Gheen doesn't know." He moved up the trail, and Cullen followed.

How long *had* it been? How long had the things been raiding across the river? The oldest stories from his remotest youth had always included the evil creatures. As long as there had been people, there had been murdering, raiding trolls. Sometimes it was years between their raids, but they always came. Humans and trolls were enemies, plain and simple. And yet somehow, he was supposed to forget all that and help his fiercest, most implacable enemies against a scary demon.

The more he walked and climbed, the more he willed himself to set aside such thoughts. Grimmun and Wogan both spoke of human slaves, humans captured in innumerable raids going back hundreds of years. There was a chance, just a chance, that he could do something to help them or even set them free. That wouldn't end generations of enmity between the two races, but there was a slim thread of hope for such an outcome. And if all else failed, he would find vengeance for Arden Luck, Magda, Selia, and all those the trolls had slain.

The path was well-maintained and smooth, but Cullen wasn't used to so much climbing. When they camped that evening, Wogan gave him a pouch of dried berries and another seed cake.

"What is it?" Cullen sniffed at the contents of the pouch.

"Hawthorn berries, elder fruit, and a few others. It helps with muscle soreness. Drink all your water."

Cullen nodded but otherwise didn't acknowledge the food. Wogan had apparently recovered from whatever odd fear had struck him at the canyon, but he was still "one of them," and Cullen couldn't warm up to the slave. The wiry old man had given himself over to his slave status.

He chewed on the berries and glared at Wogan. What had changed in the man that made him accept his condition? How long had he been among them? If Cullen stayed with the trolls, would he become subservient to these beasts like the old man?

He spat out a berry and glared at the blood-red pulp on the trail. He forced himself to remember the faces of all those the trolls had taken from him. There was no way in the seven hells he could ever forget. He tugged at a few blades of grass and plaited them quickly into a pattern, careful to hide his actions from Gheen — and from Wogan.

***

The next morning found them high up in a wide valley. Cullen turned and looked back westward. At the foot of the valley lay the forest and below that, the gorge of the Roaring River. The plains stretched away in the distance, green and lush. As he watched, the sun crested the mountains and bathed the far western grasslands in amber-green light.

Cullen sighed, turned back to the path, and breathed deep, inhaling the scents of the place. Pine wafted from below, along with scrub oak and other trees. He recognized the scent of laurel and half a dozen flowering shrubs. Twenty yards ahead came the sharp, bitter tang of a badger or other animal moving in the trees.

"It smells different up here," he said to Gheen.

"The mountains are our home," the troll said with a wide grin. He waved an arm westward to the plains across the river. "Humans have that land. We have the Three Valleys."

Cullen shook his head and sipped from his waterskin. "We each have our homes. Perhaps if trolls kept to theirs, both could live in peace."

Gheen clambered over a fallen tree, the heavy bough creaking under his weight. "Trolls and *pakh-hu* live in same world," he said. "Only deep canyon is between. Both us and you do what we have to to stay alive."

"Only a deep canyon," Cullen repeated. "Yeah, it's a mighty deep canyon."

They climbed through the morning. Grimmun and Malbah led, followed by Cullen, Gheen, Wogan, and the rest. When the sun was high above, they reached the valley's head. The trail led to a narrow cleft in a towering granite wall. Rather than make for the cleft, Grimmun turned to the right around gray slabs of stone. They entered a low cave that opened into a wide tunnel leading into the mountain.

As his eyes adjusted, Cullen saw that the floor and walls were pale, dressed stone. A line of runes and carved figures extended at eye level along the right wall. He recalled Gheen's words that trolls from long ago dug this way through the mountain.

Cullen couldn't make out the runes or pictograms, but they were clearly writing of some sort. One of the runes repeated: a horizontal slash with a triangle at the end. Among the symbols, he saw depictions of trolls in battle and a single troll on a high throne.

"Grimmun," he said, "what is this writing on the walls?"

The troll looked over his shoulder and shrugged. "It's old. Who knows what it says?"

"You don't know?" Cullen asked. "You're not curious about what this means?"

The troll gave a dismissive snort. "It does not concern us. The Holy One alone can read, and now he is blind. What is written here is not for other trolls to know. Humans are curious, trolls are not."

Cullen ran a finger along the characters and shook his head. He wasn't a learned man, but he knew these Trollish letters and symbols told a story. Why didn't Grimmun care? There might be something relevant here.

The pale walls somehow held the light, and even a hundred yards in, Cullen still made out the writing. The way curved to the left. Far ahead, a light appeared, and as they drew nearer, he saw that it was the other end of the tunnel.

They emerged blinking into the open air, the sun still high above. A cold wind whistled about them, bringing the smell of wood smoke. A thousand feet below, on the floor of the valley, sprawled a town of sorts. A twisting road led down from the tunnel into the valley. It had once been paved with the same pale stone as the tunnel, but it now stood weathered and cracked.

Their way switch-backed down the steep slope. Runoff from the mountains fed a stream alongside the road. Other streams joined it, and by the time it reached the valley floor, it grew into a small rushing river. The river followed the floor of the valley eastward and disappeared around a shoulder of rock. Midway down the south side of the valley, a canyon opened up. Another small river flowed from it to join the first.

"Behold, human," Grimmun said. "There lies the camp called Druzh. It is the home of the Three Valleys Clan."

The town boasted a stockade enclosing a cluster of small wooden cabins and houses, all arrayed around a central structure. Beyond the stockade lay a network of fields, but few appeared to be tended.

"Trolls live in houses?" Cullen asked, scratching himself. He ached for a bath.

Grimmun growled low in his throat. "You think we live in pits in the ground?"

Cullen shrugged. He'd never thought about it. "How many trolls live down there?"

"At one time, Druzh held over a thousand. Today, only a third part of that. Other camps of our clan are in two valleys to the south and east."

"And humans? How many humans live here?"

"A few hundred," the troll answered.

"And the other clans? The Stone Breakers and —"

Grimmun snorted. "They are nearby. You ask too many questions, *pakh-hu*. Let us go."

"You said the Three Valleys Clan lost dozens of trolls to the gray thing under the mountains, not hundreds."

"We'll speak of it in the camp," Grimmun said, stumping away.

As they descended the road toward Druzh, Cullen pondered the trolls' situation. Where had they all gone? Surely not that many could have been drawn away by the demon. Some may be raiding across the river or hunting in the mountains, but not enough to empty the town. The fact that Grimmun didn't know or care about the writing in the high tunnel was odd as well. Why would they choose to be ignorant of their own history? Across the river — in human lands — and far to the south of the Dimwood lay the Monastery of Ounwe in the old city of Harrun. It was said that the monks there had written histories that spanned many hundreds of years. And here the trolls had writings from their own past, and they couldn't be bothered to read them.

Stupid trolls.

He adjusted the pack on his shoulders and followed the troll leader down the path. These creatures were different beasts, that was for sure. He was picking up bits and pieces of the way trolls lived and got along, but nothing made sense, and he didn't plan on staying long enough to figure it out.

***

It took a lot less time to descend into the valley than it had to climb up from the canyon. Cullen's shins and calves complained at the strenuous elevation changes, but he resolved not to ask Wogan for help. *Let him come to me if he wants.*

They reached the floor of the valley and crossed cultivated plots of corn, beans, and potatoes. Some of the fields lay neglected and overgrown. In the active fields, dozens of humans worked with mules or by hand. He saw an iron slave collar on each of the humans. Many of them looked up as he passed, but without concern or interest. There were few trolls about, but as the party approached the camp itself, Cullen noted several watching from atop the walls.

Wogan appeared at his side. "Be cautious with your words in the camp, Cullen. These trolls have no love for humans and won't hesitate to strike you down."

Cullen looked back at the slaves in the fields. "Trolls don't love humans? Why would I think that?"

"I speak in earnest," Wogan said. "They won't hesitate to beat you or kill you."

Cullen yawned. "We've been through this already, Wogan. What's going to happen now?"

"We'll meet with the Holy One of the clan. He is a great shaman."

Cullen shook his head. "I've no use for mystics. Does he read the future in chicken bones? He can't be that powerful if he can't stop whatever takes the trolls."

"He foresaw your coming."

"A human prisoner arrives guarded by a band of trolls. He's powerful indeed to foresee that."

"Quiet now, Cullen. We're entering the camp. Inside the camp, a human may only speak if spoken to by the *trollim*."

"You're insane, Wogan. Act the slave if you want, but I won't. Be a human."

Before the gates stood a tall wooden platform. Its dark planks were stained with fresh and dried blood.

"What is this place, Wogan? Is this where human slaves are executed?"

The healer looked aghast. "No, this is where the *trollim* perform *mok jura*. It's a religious ritual. The blood is from animals, not humans. Now, *please*, be silent."

Cullen shook his head in disgust.

The gates opened at Grimmun's call, and Cullen trudged into the troll town. Within the walls, he found tents and lean-to structures alongside well-built wooden buildings. Trolls went about their business in the streets, whatever that business might be. Many of the buildings — homes? — stood empty. Had so many been taken by the demon? They passed a small marketplace. Humans in metal collars tended stalls offering foodstuffs, stoneware, and woolen garments. A few trolls perusing their wares stopped to look up as Grimmun's party walked by.

There seemed to be no organization to the camp, save that everything centered around a wood and stone structure.

"Is that where your shaman lives? Some kind of temple?" Cullen asked, pointing to the building.

Wogan gave him an angry, fearful look but nodded and said nothing.

"Take Cullen-thing and see that he is fed," Grimmun said to Wogan. "Bring him to the house of the Holy One when the sun falls behind the mountains."

Wogan bowed. "I will, Grimmun-*ush*."

Grimmun and the other trolls departed, leaving the two humans standing in the road. Wogan stood with his head bowed until the trolls disappeared into a building.

When they left, Wogan took Cullen's arm and led him through twisting streets. Given the way humans were treated, Cullen expected to be shown into one of the dirty huts, but Wogan led him to a square cabin made of neatly trimmed pine logs. Whitewashed stones bordered a path to the door.

Once they were inside, Wogan said, "This is my home, Cullen. Be welcome."

Cullen saw a simple, well-tended dwelling. There was a small hearth and kitchen, and a screened sleeping area. The kitchen table seemed too large and sturdy for such a small cabin.

"You have a large family?" Cullen asked.

"It's just me. Sometimes they bring the injured to me. I need a place to examine and treat them."

Cullen nodded and rubbed at a thick scar on his shoulder. He'd been sewn up on a table such as this the last time he'd had a run-in with the trolls.

Shelves filled with pottery and glass containers lined two walls. Each of the containers was labeled in neat, precise script.

"Herbs and medicines for the trolls?" he asked.

"And for humans," Wogan said. "Do you detest me so much for being a slave, Cullen?"

"Not for being a slave, but for being a willing, compliant one. You forget you were ever a free man."

"Oh, I've not forgotten that. But I have a new life here. I am needed and useful to the *trollim* — and to their servants. Sit while I prepare a meal. There's wine in that jug."

Cullen cringed at that, and Wogan laughed. "Don't worry, it's a good wine. There is a vineyard further down the valley. The trolls don't like our wine either, thankfully."

A knock came at the door. Wogan opened it to a young girl carrying a covered basket.

"Thank you, Alanna," he said, taking it from her.

"Dureg-*ush* commanded that I bring this. It's fish and new potatoes," she said.

The girl bobbed in the doorway and skipped away.

"Who is she? Will she go hungry so you can eat?" Cullen asked.

"So you can eat, in truth," Wogan said. "You're of greater importance than I. But no, there's plenty of food in the camp and good fish in the river. Alanna is the daughter of Solia and Thomas. They were taken from a village in the Chalk Cliffs some years ago."

"I had a daughter named Seala once," Cullen said. "She and my Isabo were twins. Until the trolls came and murdered her."

"I am sorry for your loss," Wogan said. "The *trollim* can be quite brutal."

He opened the basket, and Cullen saw two fine brook trout and a container of small red potatoes. In a few minutes, Wogan had a fire going in the hearth and set to cleaning the fish.

Cullen pulled out a chair and sat at the table. He poured a mug of wine for himself and, after a moment, one for Wogan.

"Is '*ush*' a slave word for master?" he asked.

Wogan nodded. "Of a sort. It is an honorific used to address one's owner."

"So she and her parents are slaves belonging to Dureg. *Ush* is a word you won't hear from my mouth." He paused for a moment. "You're too comfortable with all this, Wogan."

Wogan closed his eyes for a moment, then replied in a tone of resignation and weary irritation. "You have made your point, Gabril Cullen. This life is what we know. I remember well the life I once had across the canyon, and what I have lost. But now I live here. And the *trollim* treat us well enough."

Cullen gave a low growl of frustration and then caught himself. It was the same kind of noise Grimmun made when the troll was frustrated. He shook his head and took a swallow of the wine. "Wogan, is there more than one kind of troll? Gheen and a few of the others — Toleg and Burnah — look and sound as if they are almost a different race of troll. They're smaller and speak differently than Grimmun and Malbah."

Wogan smiled and nodded. "That's perceptive of you. Yes, Grimmun and his kind are High Trolls. They came, I think, from the east over the mountains in the far distant past. Gheen and the others are Mountain Trolls. I don't know where they come from. Here, I suppose. There is no animosity between the two groups. High Trolls tend to be more intelligent and take leadership roles. All have lived here together for generations. They even intermarry on occasion."

"Intermarry?" Cullen asked, raising an eyebrow. "I've not seen a female troll, nor any troll children."

"Oh?" Wogan asked. "But Malbah is female. She's Grimmun's wife. And Burnah is Toleg's. I thought you knew. Female trolls are a little stouter, and their ears are lower on the head. The *trollim* are not given to outward displays of affection. As for children, they don't have many. I've not seen a troll family with more than one child."

Cullen chuckled at that, finished his wine, and poured another. "The ones taken by the thing under the mountain, were they both High and Mountain trolls?"

Wogan seasoned the fish and potatoes, placed them on a gridiron over the fire, and paused. "I hadn't thought of that, but it's only been the High Trolls."

Cullen drained his glass and poured a third — the wine was really quite good. "Tell me about this shaman I'm going to see. Which caste is he?"

"He is the Holy One, and he is very ancient, well beyond the normal age of the *trollim*. He is certainly a High Troll. Guram Kan — you will meet him — may be the leader of the clan, but the shaman wields true power. Guram Kan defers to him by right."

Cullen watched the fire in the hearth. There was so much to take in. "I told Grimmun that I would help defeat this demon creature on the condition that the trolls would free their human slaves. Will the shaman accept that?"

Wogan shrugged, but it was clear that the notion disturbed him. "Trolls are honorable, but who can say? Guram Kan would resist — humans perform many vital tasks here. It is in the hands of the Holy One."

He poked at the fire and looked at Cullen strangely. "You are not just a human captured by trolls, Cullen. You are a scout with the scent-gift. Tell me, in all your years of hunting and tracking, have you ever heard of trolls killing one such as you?"

Cullen mused. "Trolls have captured and killed hundreds of our people over the years, including scouts. What are you getting at?"

Wogan smiled. "Yes, but have you ever known them to kill a scout with the scent-gift?"

He swirled the wine in the cup. No, he had to admit. He'd seen and heard of dozens of raids and battles with the twice-damned trolls, but now that he thought about it, he'd never heard of a sniffer intentionally killed by one of these creatures. The thought turned in his mind. He'd always considered himself lucky not to have been injured or killed in a troll attack.

"Why? What is it about the scent-gift? How would they know if a scout had the gift?"

Wogan shrugged and pulled the gridiron from the fire. "I honestly don't know, Cullen. People like you — humans with your gift — are a kind of Holy One to the trolls. You are somehow different from all the other *pakh-hu*."

Cullen slumped into a chair. *Ounwe's eyeballs. A Holy One. What did that mean?*

Grimmun had certainly treated him differently. The trolls could have killed and eaten him just as easily as they had Arden Luck. But that was the whole point: they needed his ability. He'd always thought the scent-gift was something hereditary, like being left-handed. He'd even tried to teach Arden to identify troll-scent, but the big fighter just couldn't get it. It was a thing that Cullen and most in his family could do, but few others could. But was there more to it than that? How did it make him a Holy One to the trolls? And how could he use that to his advantage?

Chapter Nine

Battle and Death

A day's journey north and east of the Scarp, Isabo signaled the troop to a halt. Her initial anxiety over leading the fighters was growing again. Perban and Tanner had taken to their roles as First and Second Sword, but they reported grumbling among their fighters. The townspeople had come to fight trolls, but so far, all they'd done was march across the prairie, practicing with their swords and heavy spears when the small army stopped to rest.

Food supplies grew thin, though the monk Dunken had proved adept at setting traps and snares. He had caught several of the large hares that skittered across the plains, a gamey but welcome change from trail rations.

Isabo slammed her fist into her palm. It had been a frustrating hunt: either the trolls who took her father had stayed within the edge of the forest, or they had gone much further onto the plains than she expected. She almost started to doubt her tracking skills. Almost. Neither she nor Tallard had seen signs of the trolls' passage since leaving the valley where they'd found Luck and the dead trolls, but the rising breeze finally brought what she'd been seeking: trollstink. She smiled, then swore as she realized that the scent was different from before. Trolls were near, but they weren't the ones who had taken her father.

"There," Tallard said, pointing to a low haze of dust in the distance.

Perban smiled. "Aurochs! That's a good-sized herd. It's about time we had fresh meat."

The old scout nodded. "It is, but look closer."

Isabo shaded her eyes and looked as well. "There's smoke," she said grimly. A thin plume rose from the edge of the dust cloud. "I can smell the trolls, but they aren't the ones we're looking for."

Tallard raised an eyebrow. "You can smell them this far away? That's at least a thousand yards."

"Yeah," she said, "but it's muddled. The aurochs' stink doesn't help. I can tell there are trolls. Maybe half a dozen or so of them. And that they're different."

The old man laid a weathered hand on her shoulder. "Isabo, I've come out of respect for your father, but I need to get back to my own people."

She glared at the distant line of smoke. "I know, and I'm grateful. But please help us do this. You've come this far." She turned to Perban and Tanner. "We need to scout out these trolls. With luck, they'll speak at least a little in Common Tongue. If we can take one of them, maybe we'll find out if they've seen the ones who took my father."

Both perked up at the suggestion, but Tallard shook his head. "You said half a dozen of the things. That's a lot to take on. Every time I've been up against them with your father or with others, it's taken three or four of us to bring down even one troll."

"I said we'll scout them," Isabo said with a look of frustration. "I'm not interested in throwing lives away. Too many people have died because of those creatures. If there's too many to kill, we'll circle wide. You can head home, and we'll find the ones that took my father." She nodded toward the fighters, who were lying on the ground, massaging their travel-weary muscles. "On the other hand, we didn't come all this way to walk away from a fight — and we have a new weapon."

Isabo peered in the direction of the aurochs herd and then at the sun lowering in the afternoon sky. "We need to get this done. Tallard, how well do you know the area?"

"Fairly well. I've been to Pineholm a few times. That's southeast a few leagues. The Roaring River gorge is due east of here, probably four leagues off. It's rolling hills most of the way there."

She nodded toward the trolls. "Will you help us? These things always set a lookout, right?"

Tallard hesitated, then nodded. "Aye, I'll help for now. And yes, they always post a lookout. They're stupid creatures, but they do that at least."

Perban and Tanner drew closer. Isabo noticed that their fighters had also moved in to hear the plan.

Isabo gave them a grim smile. She raised her voice so that all could hear. "Then we find that sentry and kill it, but quietly. I have an idea what we can do with its blood. But first, we should scout all the way around them to be sure there aren't a dozen more lurking about. First Sword will go left around the herd, and Second will go right. The hills should give you cover, but we need to be sure how many there are. Everyone catch that?"

There were nods all around.

"Once we know better what we're up against," she said, "we can decide what to do then."

"What about us?" It was Brother Yoren.

Isabo shrugged. "If you don't want to stay here, then you're coming along. Don't get in the way and don't make noise."

Yoren bowed his head in assent.

Tallard gave a thoughtful look and then pulled Isabo aside. He leaned close and whispered. "What about your brother? Does he have the scent-gift like you?"

She considered for a moment. "Don't get any ideas. He should stay safe with me. He and I will go with First Sword. You go with Second."

She looked over at Amon, who was chatting with Brother Yoren. "As for the scent-gift, it's starting to come in for him. When we were back at the ambush site, he told me he could smell the trolls. I'm not sure he was entirely telling the truth, but he seemed to be getting the hang of it."

Tallard nodded. "He's not a child anymore; he's fifteen. And you need all the help you can get to do this. Send him with Second Sword. Two of your kind sniffing will help your chances. Don't worry, I'll keep him safe. If nothing else, it's good training if he wants to be a scout like you and Cullen."

Isabo couldn't argue that. Amon was showing the monk something on the hilt of his sword. The boy — the young man now — *could* be a scout one day. And she had started training with her dad even younger than Amon was now.

"He's all that's left," she found herself whispering. "My mother, my sister Seala — they're dead. Killed by these evil monsters. Amon shouldn't be a scout. He should be something else, something —"

"Something safe?" Tallard asked with a smile. "Life isn't safe, especially with trolls around. Let him hone the skills he needs."

She cleared her throat and looked away, wiping a fleck of grit from her eye.

After a moment, she looked back to the scout and asked in a louder voice. "You've hunted these things more than any of us here. Where's the most likely spot for them to put a lookout?"

He glanced in the direction of the dust cloud, then back toward the point where the Dimwood approached the eastern mountains. "The nearest human settlement is Pineholm, to the southeast. If these beasts were smart, they'd set a watch in that direction. On the other hand, if these are the ones that captured your father, they'd watch for someone like us following them. Are you absolutely sure these don't smell the same?"

She nodded.

He pointed to a larger, wedge-shaped hill overlooking the herd. "My guess is they'd put someone there. If not, it's a better place for us to see what they're doing."

Isabo nodded. "First Sword, you know what to do. On your way, send someone to scout that hill. I'll go with you. Tanner, take Second Sword, circle the herd, and send a few scouts southeast. Tallard and Amon will go with you. Both parties have to be back here before sundown. That gives you about two hours."

Perban and Tanner nodded and moved to give orders.

The two groups rose and set off quickly. First Sword angled northward, making for the wedge-shaped hill. Second Sword moved away along an eastward-running stream bed. Within a few minutes, they were almost out of sight, with Tanner leading, the old scout and her brother close behind, and the rest of the group strung out behind.

Isabo tried to shove away her concerns about her brother. Tallard was probably right: it was a chance for Amon to learn. She considered asking the monks to say a prayer for him, but then noticed that the two robed travelers had gone with Tanner's group. Maybe they would bring divine protection to Second Sword.

She walked with Will Perban for some time, but then drew back to watch him. Her friend had a gift for encouraging and chiding the fighters under his charge. Usually, he walked at the front of the line, but sometimes he let others take the lead. A few times, he sent one of the men from Stone Bow off to climb a low hill to make sure they were heading in the proper direction. It was hard to believe that Will was the same gangly, awkward friend she used to play Troll and Villagers with.

Before the sun had moved too far down the sky, they approached the back side of the wedge-shaped hill. Isabo caught up to Perban.

"What do you think, Will?"

"You tell me, Iza," he said with a broad smile. "Can you make out the troll smell any better?"

She sniffed at the air. "There's one scent that's pretty strong toward the taller hill. Maybe that's their sentry. Why don't you take the rest of your group farther on? Maybe get north of the herd and see what you can find. Look for tracks coming or leaving the area. I'll take..." She looked at the fighters. "I'll take this one. Daron, right? And we'll go up the hill to find the sentry."

"It's Filip, ma'am, Filip Homah at your pleasure. That there is my brother Daron," the grizzled man said, pointing to his companion. The two looked like they'd been cut from the same piece of wizened oak.

"Filip, then," she said with a quick nod. To Perban, she said, "We'll meet you back here in about an hour."

Will nodded and moved off with his group.

"Yer a sniffer then, like your father?" the man asked with a ready smile.

She nodded.

"I met him a few years back. We don't get many trolls down our way in Stone Bow, but we always try to send help when they're in the area. Daron and I answered the signal for the ones that was raiding down by Tall Grass a few summers ago. A great man, your father."

Isabo nodded again and said, "We can talk later. Let's go find that troll."

"Oh, aye, ma'am. Right, indeed. Sometimes I get to talking and —" but Isabo was already moving quickly up the slope.

The pair crested the hill, careful to stay low and close to a boulder sitting at the pinnacle. The eastward face of the wedge dropped away steeply in a clutter of brambles and fallen stone. From below came the muted lowing of the grazing aurochs. Isabo sniffed the air carefully. She didn't count, but guessed there were nearly a hundred of the great beasts. Their scent was strong and earthy and not, she thought, completely unpleasant. It was a homey smell. On the other side of the herd was the trolls' fire. It sat at the entrance to a gully running between the two hills. To the southeast, she caught the line of the streambed Second Sword had traversed. A few isolated cottonwoods were spaced along it, and near one, she caught a brief glint of metal. She prayed it was Tanner's team. It wouldn't do to give their presence away to watchful trolls.

She glanced back down to the troll's encampment. Near the fire lay a slaughtered aurochs, and near that were six of the biggest trolls she'd ever seen. Even from this distance, she could tell the monsters were huge. She also saw another smaller figure in the shadow of the distant hillside. A human, maybe?

Filip nudged her, wrinkled his nose, and pointed downward to a stony out-cropping overlooking the herd. Isabo nodded. That would be a good spot for a sentry. Not as good as where she and Filip lay, but good enough for trolls, she supposed.

"Can you smell trolls down there?" she asked, raising an eyebrow.

"Nope, not like you can. But there's something that stinks down there."

She drew in the breeze, willing her brain to filter out the heavy, bovine smell. At last, there it was: the clear scent of trollstink — and something else. She focused and turned her head slightly to catch the distinctive odor. After a moment, the melange of foul troll smell resolved itself into individual signatures. From the traces of scent, there were seven of the things in the area, but one stood out more distinctly. It was closer. She moved her head again and was sure. It was indeed coming from the rocky outcropping below. They'd found the sentry.

The other scent came from there as well, rancid but with a strangely pungent fruity smell, like spoiled wine.

She scanned the area again, making mental notes of the hillside, its crevices, and possible lines of attack.

"I think our troll companion down there has been drinking," she said finally. "That may work to our advantage. Let's get back to the others."

***

Isabo gathered her army in a broad, shallow ravine out of sight of the trolls and their sentry. Perban's First Sword sat to her left, and Tanner's Second Sword to her right, checking their weapons. Amon and Tallard sat at her side. The two monks sat nearby, conversing in low tones. She did a quick count. They were four short.

"Do you have patrols out?"

Perban nodded. "Filip and Daron are keeping watch on the troll sentry and the pack of them near the fire. Their tracks come in from the north. It was hard to tell, but there were at least half a dozen. We didn't see signs of another sentry besides the one you found. And even that one doesn't seem to be too interested in anything but the aurochs. He hasn't budged from his spot."

She gave a grim smile. "I didn't detect any more than seven. That's good to know. How did Amon do?" she asked Tanner in a low voice. "Could he smell anything?"

Second Sword gave a noncommittal shrug. "He said maybe, but he wasn't sure how many."

She nodded. Her brother's scent-gift was developing, but she'd need to work with him. "Who else is missing?"

Tanner jerked a thumb behind him. "Two of mine, Hupp and Zollar, are keeping an eye north and south. No sense in letting anyone sneak up on us if we're going to sneak up on trolls."

"What else did you see when you were out?" she asked.

"I don't think there's any more of the beasts, either," he said. "We circled wide around them and then came in up the other side of the two hills. We could see down into the gulley between. We counted six of the things down there. There's something else," he said, his face going grim. "They have a human with them. A slave."

"I saw him, too," Isabo said with a nod, "but I was too far away to get a good look."

"Tallard and I — and Amon — got within fifty yards or so. I... I recognized him."

Everyone crowded near, and a babble of hushed voices whispered questions. "One of ours? Who was it? Was he from home? From Haywold?"

Isabo raised her hand for silence. To her surprise, the group quieted immediately.

"Who?" she asked.

Hiram looked up at Wheatley. "Wulf, it was your brother. It was Thomas."

Wulf's jaw fell open, and he staggered. He looked as if he'd be clubbed. Perban steadied him with a hand on his shoulder. "It was Tom? You saw him? You're sure."

Tanner nodded. "He's not looking good, Wulf. It looks like he's starved half to death."

"Trolls took him when they killed my parents and burned our farm. We have to get him back!"

Isabo straightened. "I guess there's no question, then. We're going to kill trolls and rescue Tom Wheatley." She looked at Tallard. "Do you still want to go home?"

The grizzled old scout chuckled and shook his head. "Are you kidding? I wouldn't miss it for the world. No one has ever taken back a human captive."

"Okay, get our lookouts in. We can use every blade we have."

Tanner and Perban nodded and sent runners to recall their people.

When everyone had returned, Isabo knelt and sketched a map of the area in the dirt. "Gather close and listen up. Here's us, and here's the main group of trolls. The aurochs are here, between the trolls and their sentry, who's probably been drinking, from the smell." She glanced west toward the lowering sun. "It will be getting dark soon. Anyone have an idea how to rile up the herd without causing them to stampede?"

No one spoke until Asha Maris from Second Sword raised her hand. "We have a few cows at home for dairy and meat. Aurochs are naught but big cattle, though they're a terror if they get angry. My dad tried to breed one of them to our cows. It nearly killed the cows — and my dad."

Isabo scowled. "Get to the point. They just need to make enough noise to cover the sound of us killing the sentry. Can you do that or not?"

"Aye, I can do that," Maris replied, looking abashed. "They're slow to get excited, but I can get them on edge."

"Slow is good," Isabo said. "If they suddenly start moving, that will alert the trolls." She pointed back to her sketch on the ground. "We'll put our three best bowmen here and here on both sides of the sentry. Will, those three will have to be your archers. Tallard will be here." She paused with a smile. "My father has told me what he can do with a bow."

Perban nodded agreement and pointed to Wulf and two others, who readied their weapons.

Isabo continued. "Once the aurochs are making a commotion, on Tallard's signal, all four of you will shoot at once. The trolls have tough leather armor but don't usually wear helms unless they're going into battle, so aim for the thing's head. Can you lot do that from thirty yards?"

The three bowmen and Tallard nodded.

She smiled at Wulf. "Sure you're up for it?"

"Just try and stop me," he said.

She glanced to Kurtis Hupp. "We'll need your heavy blades. When the troll sentry is dead, you take its head. I don't want it rolling around screaming at its friends across the way."

Standing, she looked at the faces of the rest of the troop. Each showed a grim, eager fierceness. "Everyone else will wait behind this shoulder of the sentry's hill in case it all goes to hell. I want that stinking troll dead before it can raise an alarm. If anyone has a bottle or cup or some cloth, gather as much of its blood as you can. We need plenty for what comes next." She pointed back to the diagram on the ground. "We're here. The rest of the trolls and Tom are by the fire between these hills, on the other side of the herd. Now's not the time to get skittish, but I don't think any of you are. Once we kill the sentry and collect its blood, Tallard, Amon, and I will go with Perban and First Sword. We'll go left around the herd to the back side of the troll's hill. Tanner and Second Sword will go to the right. Meet where this gully comes out between the hills. Any questions?"

Filip gave a broad grin. "Let's kill us some trolls. Me and Daron are ready."

Isabo smiled and nodded. They'd come all this way and were finally going to do something. She had promised her father to bring an army, and she had, more or less. Looking up, she caught sight of the two monks whispering together. She had half-hoped they'd have wandered away on their journey across the plains. "What about you two? Anything to say?"

The smaller one shook his head. "I pray this is the right thing to do. I see what you want to do with the creature's blood. It seems unholy before Ounwe."

"Unholy? You saw what those monsters did to Arden Luck back there — and to their own kind. Now the beasts have one of ours, and it's our turn to draw blood. If you two don't have a taste for battle, stay out of the way. Everyone else, get ready."

Amon glanced at her tentatively. His skin was flushed, and his hand quavered slightly. Isabo couldn't tell if it was nerves or something else. "Why not capture this one and see if it knows what happened to Pop? I mean, that's why we're here, right?"

She tried to give her brother a reassuring smile. "We can't risk attracting the other trolls. Besides, its blood will help us kill the others."

"You're sure about that, Isabo? I think we should —"

Isabo cut him off and motioned to Perban and Tanner. "This is the plan. We're going with it. We're losing the daylight, so let's go."

***

The huge aurochs grazed contentedly on the tough clumps of mulegrass and bluestem. Their immense yard-long horns swept almost rhythmically as they tugged and munched at the grass. Isabo watched as Maris crept closer to the herd in the fading light, careful to stay out of the troll sentry's line of sight. The smallest of the great animals was as tall as the farm girl. Isabo chuckled at that. There was no way the trolls on the other side of the herd would see her.

The girl picked up something — a clod of dirt or a rock — and lobbed it into the herd. A young bull snorted, tossed its head, and then returned to grazing. A few seconds later, Isabo saw another clod fly and then another. Within a few minutes, many of the beasts were raising their massive heads to look around, curious to identify the source of the disturbance. A few gave a deep, lowing call and shifted uneasily. They seemed faintly irritated at having their dinner disturbed.

Maris had done her job. With luck, only the aurochs would be spooked and not the trolls.

Isabo signaled to the scout, who gave a three-two-one-shoot signal to the archers. She heard the faintest twang of bowstrings against the rumbling of the aurochs and wished she were close enough to see the kill. She would be too far away to hear if the thing made a death cry.

Within seconds, Tallard gave her a thumbs-up. She saw Kurtis Hupp race forward, a heavy blade in each hand. She sprinted toward the sentry's position, arriving just as the butcher's son swung. With a thunk, the troll's head rolled away. Thick, deep purple blood pumped from the creature's neck, staining the ground.

Isabo pulled a cloth and a wooden cup from her pack. She held the cup into the pulsing stream. "Quick, soak up as much blood as you can and wipe it on your blades and arrows. This stuff is poisonous to the other trolls."

It took nearly a minute for the thing's heart to stop jetting blood.

"Damn," Hupp muttered. "These things are tough to kill, but we did it."

Isabo gave a tight smile. "Well done, all of you, but we aren't done yet."

***

Isabo and Tallard crawled the last ten yards to the crest of the hill. The late afternoon breeze carried the acrid scent of the bovines and the trollstink from the six monsters below. They inched forward until she could just see them grouped around the slaughtered aurochs. Tom Wheatley was nowhere in sight.

She gave a low curse. It didn't make sense. Just how many troll bands were there wandering the Uplands? One group had attacked the Pinchbeks and then

100

gone east toward the forest where they, maybe, had fought another group. The second group, presumably, had defeated them and taken her father, then fled toward the mountains. Yet this was definitely a third group. Who knew how many others were roaming the Uplands?

"They don't look too worried about anything," Tallard whispered. "Just out for meat. Let's hope they don't send anyone to check on their sentry."

Isabo nodded faintly. "If they're less careful," she mused, "then they'll be easier to kill. I just hope the troll blood on our blades will do the trick. We have to kill them — kill them all. Still, where's the group that took my father?" She seethed, then motioned back down the hill. The two withdrew from the crest of the low rise to join the others.

The rest of the party waited silently, the monks standing to one side.

Tallard spoke in low tones. "We counted six trolls around an aurochs carcass. No sign of the captive. They'll be busy for a while gutting it and gorging themselves. That's a lot of trolls to kill."

"It is," Isabo agreed, "but I think we have enough weapons — and the troll blood. But we need to grab Tom. If they see us coming after him, they'll kill him outright." She looked to Wulf. "What's it been? Four years since they took him?"

"Nearer five," he said.

She considered that for a moment, then said. "I'd guess they wouldn't keep him if they couldn't communicate with him. Either he's picked up Trollish or they know some Common Tongue. Either way, maybe we can use Tom to get information. I want to know if these things have seen the band that took my father."

Wulf shook his head. "No way. We have to get him free. From what Tanner says, he's in no shape to fight them. These things killed the rest of my family, Isabo."

"I know that," she hissed, "and my mother and my sister. I don't want him to fight them. That's on us. But I need to know about my father. We kill all but one of those things, then Tom can help us find out."

Wulf looked doubtful.

Tanner grinned and fingered his bow. "Now we're talking sense. Filthy beasts. Sooner this land is clear of 'em, the more I'll like it. Right, Amon?"

The boy nodded uneasily.

Perban cleared his throat. "I have an idea. Filip, Daron, and I can sneak up on them, none too careful. Pretending to sneak, if you understand. They'll likely send out one or two to try to catch us. Meantime, Wulf and a couple others can sneak down this gully and grab Tom while they're distracted. Then the rest of you come at them from behind over this hill. We catch them unawares. Hiram has his bow; he can take out one with a good shot, even without troll's blood. And, like Isabo said, then we kill all but one or two to find out what happened to Cullen."

Isabo stared at Perban. "That's a brilliant plan. Where in Ounwe's heavens did you come up with that?"

Her First Sword leader smiled. "From your father. He was always telling stories of his troll hunts. It seemed a logical thing to do."

Isabo turned to Wulf. "Well?"

Her friend ran a weary hand through his tangled hair. "I can bring my brother out? I'm ready."

Isabo gave a sharp nod. "Okay, but Will, I want you and your team with me. Tanner, it'll be Maris and two more of yours to draw out the trolls. They'll make noise like they're out to round up an aurochs. Maris seems to know cattle well enough. They come at the trolls through the herd, but not too close. How about Zollar and Hupp with her? Those two know how to handle blades if it comes to a fight. And with the troll blood on their weapons, the three of them should be able to take down at least one troll between them, if not more."

Tanner glanced at the three fighters Isabo suggested. Each nodded grimly. "Okay," he said.

Isabo considered each of her gathered fighters in the fading light and then turned back to her Second Sword. "Hiram, you're the best shot we have. You and the rest of Second Sword will cover them from the hillside. Don't let any of the trolls that come out get back to their friends. When the trolls are dead, fall back toward the fire. Tallard and I, with Amon and First Sword, will be there taking care of the rest of the stinking beasts. Any questions?"

Perban raised his hand. "The trolls are at the far end of the gully between the two hills, near the fire closest to the herd. I'll send Bromlin and Crumble with Wulf. They'll grab Tom and serve as a rear guard to stop any of them from getting away."

Isabo peered at Perban's group, trying to remember which Bromlin and Crumble were. She kicked herself. The two were from Haywold, but she kept getting them mixed up. Any leader worth their salt should know her people.

"Yeah, do that," she said, "but they need to be near enough that they can come running if we call." She looked at Wulf Wheatley. "That said, get your brother clear. He's spent long enough with those horrid things."

The stout townsman nodded.

She looked at the rest of the group. "Did everyone smear troll blood on their weapons? It caused a wicked reaction on trolls that had been dead for a few days. I'm guessing it will be even worse on a live one. It's nasty stuff, but clean it off later, *after* we've killed these things."

"There wasn't quite enough to go around," Perban said, "but everyone has at least one blade or spear with it."

She glanced up to see the monks watching her. She'd forgotten about them. "You two stay where you are if you're not going to help us kill these things. We'll find you later. Try not to get killed. Better yet, you wait at the far end of the gulley. When Wulf brings Thomas out, get him away. That will free Wulf to come back and help us."

They nodded but didn't speak.

Tallard spoke up, a look of concern in his eyes. "Isabo, you're counting on troll blood to do wonders. I hope for your sake, and Tom and your father's, that you're right."

She nodded. "I know, Tallard. But you saw what it did yourself. The monks can say a prayer that it works."

He chuckled. "That probably wouldn't go amiss. Still, no one has ever done what you're trying to do."

She glanced eastward toward the horizon. A waxing moon hung pale in the darkening sky. "The moon will give us a bit of light when it gets dark. Now let's get on with it and kill these things."

***

The sun faded behind a thick layer of clouds in the west, leaving a dusky, dusty light. Isabo, Tallard, Amon, and Perban crept up the back side of the hill overlooking the troll camp. The rest of the First Sword fighters came behind, fanning out to either side. They slowly made their way in the deepening gloom, their weapons and gear muffled against inadvertent sounds that might alert the trolls. Isabo tensed at every noise, and prayed that it would be covered by the crackle of the fire and the milling of the aurochs.

When they were within fifty yards, Isabo signaled for the group to wait. She and Tallard slowly raised themselves in the near-darkness to survey the troll's camp.

"They built up their fire," she breathed.

Tallard nodded and replied, his voice a barely audible whisper. "That's a good thing. With dark coming on, their eyes will be dazzled by the blaze. They won't see us coming until we're right on them."

Isabo sniffed and glanced at the nearby herd. "These damn things have killed any scent I had of the trolls. Tallard, are you sure you can hit one of those things in the dark?"

The scout nodded. "It will be easier if they're silhouetted against the fire."

"Once Hiram's people draw one or two of them out," she said, "we'll spread out and take them from above."

She stooped and made her way back to the group. She leaned close to her brother. "Amon, you stay right by me. If things go bad, you run like your tail was afire."

The boy scoffed. "I can handle myself."

"Isabo?" Perban's voice whispered in the gloom. "Daron is good with the bow. Want him to take a shot as well?"

She nodded and waved the man forward. "Troll blood on your tips?" she whispered.

"Yeah, on four of them," the man replied.

Tallard put a finger to his lips and disappeared to the left, circling lower toward the fire. In a few minutes, he returned and whispered, "There are still just the six. They haven't missed their sentry. The others are sitting around the fire. They carved up the aurochs and are roasting bits of it. Wulf's brother is about ten yards back down the gully in the shadows."

Isabo looked to the group and mouthed "Ready?"

There were nods all around.

"Give the signal."

Tallard nodded and melted away into the darkness, back toward the herd. After a few moments, they heard the churring call of a nightjar off to their left.

Isabo leaned close to Amon. "That's the signal. You sure you can do this?"

He drew the sparring blade from its sheath. "You know I can."

Even in the dim light, she could see the fierce edge he'd put on the sword. "Remember, if the fight goes bad —"

"Just see that it doesn't go bad."

A pale crescent moon had risen in the southeast, shedding just enough light for Isabo to pick out the scout making his way up the hill. The scout motioned to Daron, and the two edged closer to the crest of the low hill. She could just see Tallard as he nocked an arrow, nodded to Daron, and silently tested the pull of his bowstring. Out of the still night came three voices in a chorus of "The Barman's Dog."

Isabo smiled. Tanner's fighters had also heard the signal.

From below, she caught the trolls' guttural chatter suddenly cut off.

One of them uttered a low barking command, and two of them rose. They drew long, dark swords from sheaths and crept toward the herd.

Tallard raised his hand, waiting until the two large figures left the glare of the firelight and disappeared into the darkness. Then he tapped Daron on the shoulder.

The two stood, arrows drawn and ready, and inched forward until they could see the trolls in the firelight.

Isabo tensed and gripped her sword. There was no sense in hoping everyone was ready. They would have to be. By now, Wulf and the two others should be approaching his brother. With Ounwe's blessing, Tanner's Second Sword would take down two of the creatures, and she and the rest of her fledgling army could handle the remaining four.

She tapped Perban, and he motioned for the fighters to stand ready.

"To my count, Daron," Isabo heard Tallard whisper. "Three, two, one."

Two bowstrings twanged, and Tallard cursed. He rapidly drew another arrow, nocked, and fired again. This time, he was rewarded with a sharp howl that turned to a piercing, wailing scream.

"Attack!" Isabo shouted, and she leaped over the edge of the hill with her people behind her. One of the trolls clawed at an arrow that transfixed his neck. It yanked the shaft free, still howling in pain, staggered, and fell. Another clutched at the arrow in its arm and screamed.

The wounded troll and its two companions bellowed madly in the fire-light, struggling to find weapons. Isabo was on the nearest with her sword. She slashed madly, and the hulking figure staggered backward, tripping against the aurochs carcass. It fell, and one hand landed in the fire. It howled again and leaped to its feet, waving a black sword and shaking the other hand in pain. Isabo pressed in, beating at the huge creature with fierce blows. Out of the corner of her eye, she saw Tallard launch himself at another troll.

"Amon, here!"

The boy jumped forward and raised his sword for a blow.

By now, the shouts and screams had roused the lumbering aurochs. The herd lowed and bellowed, milling about and raising a low cloud of dust.

Isabo's troll gave a croaking laugh, but the laughter faded as more humans pressed inward, hacking and slashing. It managed a backhand strike against Amon and caught the boy a glancing blow across the forehead with the hilt of its blade.

She couldn't see if Amon was all right or what Perban and his people were doing. She lunged and buried her own blade in the troll's thigh with a cry of triumph. It jerked the blade out but wobbled and struggled with her for control of the weapon. It gripped the blade with its hand, and Isabo jerked the sword upward, slicing through its fingers. Its leg collapsed, and it went down on one knee. The hissing and bubbling of the poison in the wound could be heard over the tumult of battle. It lurched to its feet, but staggered again. In the flaring light of the fire, Isabo saw hideous growths sprouting on the troll's wounded leg.

Someone beside her — Filip? — swung, and the troll's arm spun through the air. In an instant, the man's sword flashed again, missing Isabo's head by inches, and buried itself in the monster's neck. Isabo drove her blade into the thing's face.

Amon screamed and leaped back into the fray. His forehead dripped streams of blood across his face. He stabbed awkwardly at the closest troll, but could not connect. The thing bellowed at him and swung a looping roundhouse blow that caught the boy across the cheek. He slumped heavily to the ground.

"Amon!" Isabo cried, but still another troll wheeled about to face her. She saw Tallard behind it with a heavy spear in his hand, preparing to drive it into the troll's back. She feinted left, turning the troll to give Tallard a clear shot. In an instant, he drove the fire-hardened weapon through the beast. It fell with a whump into the fire, spraying blood and scattering a flurry of sparks. It jerked once and was still.

Isabo ran to Amon, who lurched heavily to his feet. In the flaring firelight, she could see the side of his face was a giant bruise. "You okay?" she asked, squeezing his arm.

He gave a weak smile, nodded, and wiped blood from his eyes.

Further up the gully away from the fire, she heard the sound of fighting. Hopefully, Wulf was clear with his brother, and it was Crumble and Bromlin making short work of the remaining troll. Tallard and Perban dashed away to assist, but they soon returned with Wulf Wheatley and the rest of First Sword.

Wheatley's face was bloody, but he wore a look of weary satisfaction. "It's dead. Bromlin took its head."

"How's your brother?" Isabo asked, her hand on her friend's shoulder.

"Alive," Wulf said, "But he's —"

"We're not done yet," Tallard yelled. "There are two more in the herd with Tanner and Second Sword."

"Here they come!" Daron shouted. He knocked an arrow and shot, but it glanced off a troll's leather armor and hit an aurochs. The oversized cow bellowed in pain and bolted past the fire, nearly trampling Amon. Sparks flew as the spooked herd bellowed and called, turning the scene into a hellish vision of flames and confusion.

Isabo spotted the single troll charging out of the herd, fearsome black sword raised in clawed hands. Tanner, Hupp, and Maris followed close behind. The monster charged at Wulf Wheatley, who was struggling to draw his sword.

Tallard sprang at the beast as it swung its blade, jarring its elbow. The troll roared with anger, turned, and drove its mallet-sized fist into the scout's chest. The scout staggered, and his face registered surprise for a brief moment, then he dropped lifeless to the ground.

Isabo leapt at the troll, crying in anger. She slashed at its face with her blade, missing wide.

Blows rang and fell as the troll hammered at the humans with furious strokes. It pressed forward, backing Isabo and Amon toward the fire. The remainder of Isabo's army closed ranks behind it, raining sword blows and jabbing at the immense thing with spears.

"Ho, ho," it laughed. "Orma was right. We feast on *pakh-hu* flesh tonight!"

"Your friends are dead!" Isabo shouted at the creature. "All of them." She glanced left and saw Hiram Tanner nodding grimly.

The troll started to raise its sword again, but slowed, seeing its dead compatriots littering the floor of the broad gully. All around it stood puny humans — humans who had decimated its entire pack.

Behind the creature, Will Perban gave a fierce growl and drew a broad dagger. He motioned for Hiram Tanner to do the same. Perban pointed, and with a nod, both men slashed across the back of the monster's thighs. It howled, staggered, and crumpled to the ground.

"Hold!" Isabo shouted.

Perban looked up, startled. "What are you doing, Iza? Kill him, Amon!"

Isabo stepped between her brother and their foe. She wiped sweat and dust from her eyes, then pointed her blade at the troll's face. "Do you yield?"

With a savage, mocking grunt, it tossed its weapon aside.

"Lie flat on the ground," Isabo demanded.

The thing chuckled at her but did as directed. "Foolish *pakh-hu* things. I kill you all."

Perban raised a booted foot and stomped on the creature's head. It groaned and fell silent.

"Tallard had rope," Tanner said with a bitter curse. "Keep a sword on the troll, Isabo. I'll tie it up."

Isabo nodded and rested the tip of her sword on its neck.

Tanner worked quickly, and soon, the surviving troll was tightly bound hand and foot.

"Perban," Isabo said. "Check the other trolls. Make sure they're dead. Then set lookouts. Wulf, go find the monks and have them bring your brother here. Tanner, you killed the other one in the herd?"

Hiram nodded as Perban and Wulf moved off into the darkness. "Hupp brought it down, and an aurochs trampled it to death. But Zollar is dead, and Shamus Dorse took a wicked swipe with the hilt of that one's sword. He might have a broken arm."

She looked up to see Filip and Daron Homah standing beside her. The brothers had fought well, though Daron's eye looked to be swollen shut, and Filip had a great gash on his cheek. "Filip, do you have a clean blade?" she asked with a snarl at the bound troll.

"Clean enough. You want me to kill it?" the man asked. "I will."

With a grim smile, she shook her head. "Only if it tries to get up. Wipe your blade as clean as you can. We'll save the blooded blades to use against him later."

She turned away and breathed deeply. The heady scents of blood, trolls, and aurochs threatened to overwhelm her. She focused and found that, with a little effort, she could tune them all out. She'd never been able to do that completely before. Either the scent-gift was fickle, or she was learning to use it better.

The flaring firelight showed her the crumpled bodies of three dead trolls — and Willim Tallard. Amon knelt beside the old scout with Asha Maris, arranging the dead man's limbs so that he looked to be merely resting. Tears streamed down Amon's cheeks, mingling with crusted, drying blood.

She wiped and sheathed her sword, then called for young Hupp to stand guard over the troll with Filip, again emphasizing the need for a clean weapon. The butcher's son shook his head and muttered angrily something she didn't quite catch. Then she recalled that Finn Zollar, Hupp's friend, was one of the dead.

I got my wish, she thought, *but at what cost?*

"It's merely blood," a cold voice said within her. *"And what's a little blood for your valiant cause? Seek vengeance for those the trolls have killed."*

She started, looking around to see who had spoken. No one had, apparently. People were resting or tending to the wounded. That was odd.

I must be more tired than I thought.

This was met with an eerie, amused chuckling, and a memory — *the* memory — of the troll attack from her childhood, when the monstrous creatures attacked Pineholm and killed her mother and sister. The image in her mind was more vivid than she ever remembered, with viscous, leering trolls who tossed a flaming torch onto their cabin with her mother inside. Another beast grabbed Seala by the ankles and swung her like a club against that horrid tree.

She shuddered and shook her head to clear her images, but they wouldn't fade. She ran unfeeling fingers through her tangled hair. Her arms and back seemed a mass of cuts and bruises, and more than anything, she wanted to sit and rest, but she needed information. She turned back to the troll with a dagger in her hand.

Chapter Ten

In the House of the Holy One

As the sun sank to the valley's western rim, Cullen and Wogan arrived at the temple home of the shaman. The single-story building was constructed of mortared stone and trimmed pine logs. Cullen glanced up. A long, horizontal mark with a triangle at one end was painted over the door. It was the same symbol he'd seen in the cave.

Grimmun stood in the road near the door. Wogan bowed, and Grimmun muttered a few words in Trollish. The slave replied in the same language and backed away.

"Give me your hand, Cullen-thing," Grimmun said.

Cullen frowned but put out his hand. The troll took it, drew a small black knife, and nicked the pad of Cullen's little finger, just enough to draw blood. He forced himself not to jerk away. Grimmun did the same to himself. Cullen saw that Grimmun's finger bore many small scars. He'd done this before, many times.

"Do as I do," he commanded.

Grimmun turned and entered the building, pausing to let a few drops of his blood fall onto the threshold. "Now you."

"This is ludicrous," Cullen said, but he held out his hand to allow blood to fall. The threshold was already dark with both dried and fresh droplets of blood. Gray flies buzzed about the blood.

Cullen shook his head. *An offering to the shaman? Or to their gods?*

They moved into a small anteroom. A bearskin curtain hung across a doorway leading further into the building.

"We meet with the Holy One. If you have questions, ask them to him or me. The chief of our clan, Guram-Kan, is here also. He hates the *pakh-hu* — humans — and those of us who would make use of a human scout. He will not speak to you. Yet he must obey the Holy One in all things. He is the one who sent us to find another scout. That rankles Guram-Kan."

"How lucky for me."

"Don't be arrogant, Cullen-thing. Guram-Kan will kill you if you show disrespect."

Cullen shrugged.

Grimmun pushed aside the curtain and led him to an inner room. Torches burned on the walls, illuminating a dark chamber. Along one wall, an ancient troll reclined on a stone couch. All the trolls Cullen had seen were lean and muscular. This one was withered and grotesque. His left tusk was long and yellowed, but the right was shattered and broken, giving the creature a lopsided appearance. On his forehead was a round gray stone the size of a walnut. He couldn't see a thong or cord holding it in place; it appeared to be embedded in his skin.

The shaman's eyes held a vacant but aware look. Was he blind?

Over the couch was painted the same red horizontal slash-and-triangle symbol as on the front of the building, but something was different. He stared at it, wondering. There was something different, a vague shimmering in the air before it, and an eerie sense of hidden power. It was paint on a wall, but the odd force of it unsettled him like the thundering roar of the river.

Grimmun nudged him forward, and he shook himself. Heavy wooden chairs surrounded the shaman's couch, their varnished surfaces reflecting the wavering torchlight. In one of the chairs sat another troll. Other than graying tufts of wiry hair, he had the same features and bearing as Grimmun.

"Guram-Kan, my father," Grimmun said with a slight nod.

Father? More surprises.

The other troll returned the nod but did not move.

Grimmun nodded Cullen to a chair and sat next to his father. The two looked like an almost identical pair of hideous statues carved from gray-green stone.

The troll on the couch cleared his throat with a long, rumbling sound that reminded Cullen of boulders clashing together.

"The *pakh-hu* has come, as I have foreseen," the shaman said.

Grimmun stood and bowed low before the shaman. "He is called —"

"I am called Gabril Cullen," the human said, standing and interrupting. He pointed to Griummun. "This troll captured me across the river and brought me to this place because I am a scout with the scent-gift. What do you want of me?"

The shaman chuckled deep in his throat. Grimmun growled.

"You do not lack for pride, Gabril Cullen," the shaman rumbled, his eyes fixed on a point over Cullen's head. "You may suffice." He paused, as if listening, then said, "You have the scent-gift. It is most... potent. Tell me, do you know the significance of this thing to the *trollim* — and to me?"

"I know that it has helped me to track and hunt down those of your kind who raid our lands."

"That is true, Cullen-thing, but it is certainly more than simply the skill of a human scout."

He glared at the ancient troll with the unseeing eyes. "What does the shaman of the Three Valleys Clan want of me? Why have you taken me from my home?"

"You are direct. That is a trollish quality." The shaman waved a palsied arm at Grimmun, but he spoke to Cullen. "Be seated, my *pakh-hu* friend. I will be direct as well. Grimmun told you that trolls of our clan — and others — were called into the mountain by an evil, gray demon named Azuk. This creature comes to them in the night, in their dreams, and draws them to him. None can resist his call. To hinder them from going is to hasten their madness and death. You must track them to find where he has taken them. Return them to us. Or find Azuk the demon, so that he may be killed."

"That is all?" Cullen asked. "I don't believe in demons. But I'll find your trolls, for a price."

The ancient figure chuckled again. "We will speak of your belief once you have found our people."

Guram-kan angrily muttered something to Grimmun. The shaman silenced him with a blind glare.

"Grimmun said you captured another scout — Dannick," Cullen said. "She also had the scent-gift."

At this, the shaman nodded and clapped his hands. Through a side door, a tall human slave appeared, bowing low.

Cullen eyed the slave, who stood a full head taller than he, but the man would not meet his gaze. What village had he been taken from? Was he now a willing thrall like Wogan?

"Aydin-thing," the shaman said, "bring the other *pakh-hu* scout's gear."

The slave bowed and backed out of the room.

"Dannick-thing was useful," the shaman continued, nodding his huge head at Cullen. "She taught our scouts, and she sought after Azuk and the lost trolls. She was wise, for a human, and she was related to you."

Cullen raised an eyebrow. "She is — was — a distant cousin, but how in blazes could you know that?"

"Not all humans have the scent-gift," the shaman said, waving a hand. "It is carried in the bloodline."

The slave Aydin returned carrying a rucksack and a staff and laid them on the floor in front of the stone couch.

Damn. He recognized the items. He'd tracked and hunted with Dannick several times in the last ten years or so. He'd known skilled trackers, but none like her. She was as smart as they came. Yet the shaman said she'd taught troll scouts. He couldn't imagine her as a slave like Wogan. Had she helped them voluntarily? She wouldn't. That was ridiculous.

"Give him the paper," the shaman said.

The slave drew a folded paper from the rucksack and handed it to Cullen.

"What do the symbols on the paper mean?" the shaman asked. "Dannick-thing carried it when we took her from the tunnels of Azuk." He tapped his own forehead with a shaking finger. "She raved and could not speak clearly, though she had no wound on her. The gray demon had taken her mind. Yet she clutched the paper in her hand."

Cullen sat again and looked at the symbols: a flowing river and a tree. They were scout symbols. He knew what they said, but not what they meant. A tree of that shape meant tall or up. Tall at the water, or up at the water. Up at the water. Go up? Look up?

"I don't know," he said. "I will have to think on it."

"This *pakh-hu* is lying," snarled Guram-Kan. The troll looked at the shaman. "There are two symbols. How difficult can it be? He is hiding something from us."

Cullen looked at the chief, but the older troll wouldn't return his gaze. "It could mean anything, depending on where she was or what she was doing at the time."

Grimmun spoke. "At the last, Dannick-thing was found where the tunnel becomes a twisting maze of passages. She made several journeys in the tunnels. She said she found a dark river in a great cavern a half day's journey under the mountain."

"The river may be the water symbol," Cullen said. There was no sense in giving more information than the trolls needed. It was a message from one scout to another. A human scout. He glanced back at Grimmun. "No trolls ever went with her?"

The troll looked at the floor. "Two went on her first journey, but none returned. Dannick-thing said they went mad and slew each other."

"In the end, she went mad as well," the shaman grumbled. "Humans are less susceptible to the demon's power, though not immune, as she found out. You must go for us, Gabril Cullen. Only a scout with the scent-gift can track the trolls who have been taken."

"When were trolls last called into the mountain?" Cullen asked. His eyes caught the oddly compelling symbol over the shaman's bench. Had it moved? He shook his head to focus and glanced back at the shaman.

"Only three days past, two elders of our clan went into the mountain." Guram-Kan stared at the shaman's blind eyes. "And today, messengers arrived from the other clans. They also continue to lose trolls. Boru-Kan of the Deep River Clan said they will lose no more; the entire clan is leaving to go east of the mountains, away from this thing."

"Is that where the rest of your people have gone, Guram-Kan? East over the mountains? This camp lies more than half empty. They didn't all go into the tunnels, did they?"

Guram-Kan growled with the rumbling sound Cullen now knew meant rising anger. "The *pakh-hu* does not need to know this."

"Be still, Guram-Kan," the shaman said, raising a hand. "I will determine what he needs to know."

The shaman turned his blank eyes to Cullen. "It is as you have guessed, *pakh-hu* Gabril Cullen. A month ago, half of our clan left this valley. They went to find the ancient home said to lie east of the mountains. In truth, I am afraid that none knows where that home lies. We few hundreds are all that remain. Do this thing for us, and we will give to you all that you ask."

Cullen sat silent for a moment, his eyes fixed on the strange symbol. For a simple decoration, the pattern unnerved him. "What is the marking on the wall? I saw it in the high place that Gheen called the Tunnel of Sukkuz."

The shaman shook his head. "It is *vurad*, an ancient and powerful glyph that was said to protect our people. I fear it no longer holds that power."

Cullen shuddered. It still held some kind of power.

He glanced from Guran-Kan to Grimmun and back to the shaman, considering all that had been said. Suddenly, it was clear: they were scared. The mighty trolls were in terror. They were helpless against this Azuk creature, who might destroy them entirely in time. Humans hunted and killed them — rightfully — when they crossed the river. The creatures had only these few camps in the mountains or the faint prospect of an unknown place somewhere to the east. And perhaps a vain hope in a human scout. Still, it required belief in demon creatures, and that was a step he was unwilling to take, just yet. Demons were children's stories, no more real than water sprites or prairie dragons. He gave an inward smile. *This is leverage. They're desperate and they need my help.*

He stood and moved to pick up Dannick's things. "I'll do this for you, though I don't yet know how. My price is simple and is not subject to discussion: you will free all the humans your kind have taken." He thought of Wogan. "That is, every human who wants to be freed."

"I will do more, Gabril Cullen. If you succeed in finding and returning those we have lost, all troll clans will cease from raiding human lands."

"No!" Guram-Kan shouted and leaped to his feet. He whirled to face Cullen. "We cannot give up what is ours. We will not. The lands across the river are rightfully ours since the most ancient times. You dirty *pakh-hu* merely occupy them. In time, they will be ours again."

"Silence, Guram-Kan," the shaman said. "You are *kan* of the Three Valleys, but to protect our people, we must send a *pakh-hu* to do what is needed. And pay the cost."

"The other human scout could not save us," Guram-Kan spat, "yet you trust this one? You are old, shaman, and slow-witted. You would have trolls subservient to these creatures. Perhaps it is time for a new Holy One."

He drew his curved scimitar and lunged at the shaman. In the same moment, Grimmun sprang toward his father, dagger in hand. Cullen leaped from his chair, away from the trolls.

The shaman signed with a bony finger and uttered a low word. A blast of searing light and heat erupted from the finger, catching Guram-Kan full in the face. The scimitar fell from his hand. The troll staggered and dropped to his knees, clutching at his head. The troll chief's flesh bubbled and melted with a stinking, sizzling hiss. A weak croak escaped his throat as he slumped to the floor and was still.

"I am old, and I am blind," the shaman said with a grim smile, "but I am not powerless. Grimmun-Kan, you will now lead the Three Valleys Clan. Take the body of this *shakh-huz* to the refuse field."

Grimmun bowed without a glance at his father's still-smoking body. "I will do this, Holy One."

"*Pakh-hu* Cullen, do what is needed. If you succeed, we'll pay your price, though it cost us dearly."

Cullen sat stunned. Talk of demons could be dismissed as simple superstition, but this, this was different. He recalled Wogan's words that the Holy One held the true power within the clan. True power indeed.

The shaman stared at Cullen, his eyes white with cataracts. "Grimmun-Kan, draw near to me."

The younger troll moved to the shaman's side and sank to one knee. Cullen strained to hear what was said but caught only a few Trollish words. Had he heard Gheen's name?

Grimmun nodded, and the shaman chuckled deep in his chest. He coughed long, dismissing Grimmun and Cullen with a wave of a trembling, gnarled hand.

***

Grimmun walked Cullen along the wide streets of the camp in the direction of Wogan's cabin. Trolls and humans went about their business, oblivious to what had just happened.

"What just happened, Grimmun? Or should I say 'Grimmun-Kan?'"

"Yes, the Holy One spoke it. I am now Grimmun-Kan. The Holy One wields great powers, but rarely does he use them. My father would have gone east over the mountains with the others, but stayed to lead those who remained. He chose poorly. The trolls of our clan are divided, Cullen-thing, and we seek help from humans." His face grew grim. "But do not mistake need for weakness. If you try to take advantage of this and somehow seek to bring humans to fight us, we will kill you."

"Guram-Kan was your father. He was —"

"He challenged the authority of the Holy One in his vain anger. I accept the justice of the Holy One against my father."

Ounwe's blood, these are cold creatures. Aloud, he asked, "If your shaman has such powerful magic, why can't he use it to defeat this Azuk and get your people back?"

The troll shook his head and glanced quickly back to the shaman's temple. "He is a single troll, long in years, but the Holy One carries the knowledge of his predecessors going back a score of generations. He truly has great power, and yet the demon has more, Cullen-thing. Do the thing the Holy One asks of you. Only then may Azuk be defeated."

"But how? How can a mere human hope to —?"

"Enough!" Grimmun growled. "Your task is to find the lost trolls and bring them back, or find what happened to them. You are not called to defeat the demon."

Two trolls approached them along the road. When they recognized Grimmun, they nodded and touched their chests, ignoring Cullen.

"Did the Holy One mean what he said? Would you really stop raiding our lands?" he asked a moment later.

Griummun rumbled low in his chest and snarled. He began to speak, paused, then started again, saying only, "The Holy One has spoken it."

"Can he speak for the other clans?"

"He can, and does in this case."

Cullen shook his head distractedly. *Demons, magic, shamans.* This was a different world from the one he'd grown up in.

They walked in heavy silence, and then Grimmun asked, "Why did you ask about the symbol of the Holy One?"

"It was on the walls of the high tunnel," Cullen said. "Does no one truly know how to read that writing? It may be useful."

Grimmun-Kan made a gurgling sound in his throat. "No. It is old. If anyone could read it, it would have been the Holy One, but those who scrawled on the walls are long in their graves. Their letters are meaningless now."

"I might be able to learn something, even if I can't read the writing. That's the difference between humans and trolls, Grimmun-Kan — we honor those who came before us and seek to learn from them."

"Those who came before us are dead," the troll said.

They reached the whitewashed stones that marked the path to Wogan's.

"What will you do, Cullen-thing?" Grimmun-Kan asked.

"How far is the cave where the trolls go?"

"A few hours march down the valley," the troll said. "There are many old caves there."

"Will no trolls go in?"

"No."

"Then I'll go alone. Maybe Wogan will go with me. As for now, I'll plan the journey. Maybe Dannick left something I can use. Tomorrow I'll travel back to the Tunnel of Sukkuz to look at the writing. May I take Gheen?"

Grimmun-Kan's face twisted in an odd smirk. He nodded. "I will send him to you at first light. If you try to flee, he will kill you." Then the troll laughed. "He likes you, human, despite your pride and arrogance. He is a simple troll."

***

Wogan gave a low whistle when Cullen related the events at the shaman's home.

"Light came from his finger and burned Guram-Kan's head to a greasy ember," Cullen said with a shudder. "I've never seen such a thing. Either it was dark magic, or he had some kind of hidden weapon, though I've never seen a weapon that could do that."

"Nor I," Wogan said, grinding herbs in a pestle. "It was said that the shaman had such powers, but I've never seen such a thing either. You'd do well to heed him."

"I will heed him, but can I trust him? I've never trusted trolls, and I don't know if I do now. He said that in exchange for my finding the lost trolls or somehow killing a demon creature, he would free any human who wanted to go — and that the clans would stop raiding our lands. That's a big thing to promise."

Wogan inspected the contents of the container and gave a grim smile. "You may trust the Holy One, but you must do what he asks."

Cullen shook his head and poured himself a drink from the bottle on the neatly arranged table. "Ten days ago, I'd have laughed if someone told me I could trust one of these creatures. Now I'm making deals with them." He drained his cup and motioned with it to the village outside. "How many humans are here?"

"Two hundred and seventy-three in this camp and another hundred or so down the valley. There are about as many as there are trolls. But we are needed here, Cullen."

"I don't know what that means, that you're needed here. You're a human, not a troll. Everything I've seen tells me they are brutal, arrogant beasts. Why do you defend this life?"

Wogan looked around his home. "I have a place here, but it's more. For all their brutality, the *trollim* say there is a bond between humans and trolls."

"Gah! You mean 'trolls think humans should be in bondage.'"

But even as he said it, Cullen began to wonder. The shaman had hinted that the scent-gift had meaning beyond his ability to sniff out trolls. But what did that mean?

He looked around the small cabin. "Where do I sleep? Gheen is coming in the morning to take me back to the Sukkuz Tunnel."

Wogan laid his tools aside and led him to a smaller cabin that had been prepared next door. "This was Garon's home. He was my assistant at one time. He was very old and died a few months ago."

Cullen looked around the small room. It held a bedplace, a hearth, and a small sitting area. The cabin wasn't as neat and trim as Wogan's, but it would do.

Wogan handed him an oil lamp and turned away.

Cullen paused, then called out to him. "Thank you, Wogan. I don't understand what's happening, but I'll do what I can to help the people — our people."

"Help us all, Cullen."

***

When he'd lit the hearth fire, Cullen turned Dannick's rucksack out onto the small table. He perused the items she'd carried: a few clothing items, a knife, a flint and steel, a hunting sling. He'd liked the woman. They'd gotten along well the few times they'd tracked trolls together. Why had she turned to help the trolls? Had the Holy One made her the same offer he'd made Cullen? She must have thought that by helping them, humans would benefit.

He turned her blade over in his hand. It was a fine thing, perfectly balanced, its well-worn handle made from aurochs' horn.

There was nothing else of interest among her things except the paper with the scout symbols. *At the water, go up. What in seven hells did that mean?* He tucked it into his jacket pocket and placed the other items back in the rucksack.

He reached for his glass, marveling again at how the world had changed in his short time with the trolls. The murderous creatures were suddenly eager to employ sniffers, offering unbelievable concessions. They might still prove vicious — as the shaman showed with Guram-Kan — but there was more to them than he'd supposed. They were fighting for their lives. And some of them wielded powerful magic.

After another swallow of Wogan's good wine, Cullen turned out the lamp and lay down on his cot.

Chapter Eleven

Answers and Questions

Isabo glanced up from the captured troll. Wulf Wheatley had returned to the fireside with the two monks and his brother.

The sight of Tom Wheatley's emaciated frame made Isabo want to kill the captive monster outright. Wheatley wore a ragged, dirty woolen tunic that dwarfed his pale, bruised body. She had known Tom as a tall, strapping teen who came to town with his family on market day. The figure before her was hunched and twisted. His neck was a mass of sores where the iron collar had been removed. Some of the wounds, even in the firelight, looked to be infected. Two fingers on his right hand were missing. One had healed some time ago, but the little finger, which looked to have been taken at the first knuckle, still bore a tattered and bloody strip of cloth.

"We tried to give him some bits of dried meat," Brother Yoren said with a pained look, "but he's lost most of his teeth. It looks as if his jaw was broken some time ago and not set properly. Brother Dunken gave him some dried fruit to chew on."

She shuddered at the abuse the man had taken. Clearly, he was a slave, but why had the trolls brought him here? She spoke quietly to him. "Tom, do you remember me? I'm Isabo Cullen — from Haywold. I'm Wulf's friend. We'll see you home safely, but we're hunting for the trolls that took my father."

He nodded and coughed weakly. In addition to everything else, his lungs sounded deeply congested. How had he survived this long?

Tom pointed to a cooking pot at the edge of the fire and mouthed, "food."

Isabo had to lean in close to make sense of the man's words. He was weak and looked as if he'd barely be able to stand in a stiff breeze.

She couldn't guess how the pot survived the battle without being knocked over. "Wulf, is there anything in there?"

Wulf checked the pot, sniffed at the concoction, and gave a wry smile. "Looks like aurochs stew. Even trolls have to eat, I guess."

"Get a bowl for Tom. Let him eat as much as he can."

The beaten man quickly hobbled to a sack on the ground. He rummaged for a few moments, then triumphantly produced what looked to be a thick loaf of bread.

"I'm not sure I'd want to eat what trolls have been at," Will Perban muttered. "Who knows what else is in that pot?"

Isabo shook her head. "If it's kept Tom alive so far, it can't be that bad. Did you set a lookout?"

"Yeah."

The emaciated man ate his fill, soaking the crusty bread in the thick stew and savoring each bite. Wulf sat beside him, excitedly reassuring his brother that he was safe now and telling him all he could of what had happened since the trolls had attacked their home five years before.

At last, Isabo moved to the bound troll lying on the ground. Hupp and Filip still stood over it with swords poised over its throat. Hupp's heavy blade appeared to have already drawn blood. "That one's still alive," she said, calling to Tom. "Can you help us get information from it? We need to know about other packs of those things in the area."

Tom may have been weak, but food and anger had revived him. He nodded eagerly and glared at the troll. "That one's Appa," he rasped through broken teeth. "Do what you want to him. He was the worst of the lot. And then... and then, you'll kill him?"

Wulf steadied his brother with an arm around his shoulder. He squeezed tightly, drawing a painful wince from the frail man. "I'll do it myself, Tom, for everything those stinking beasts did to you."

"I want to kill it... for Finn Zollar," Hupp said.

Isabo cleared her throat. "Everybody has lost someone to trolls. We'll sort all that later, but right now, I want information."

The troll's misshapen head lolled slowly as it regained consciousness. One of its tusks was larger than the other, giving it a fierce, but crooked appearance. Isabo drew her dagger. She glanced to see that it was clean and pushed it across the thing's cheek. It drew a thin line of blood across its face. "You understand me, troll. I know it. I heard you before, but I didn't think your kind were smart enough to speak Common. What are you doing here? Did you come to kill humans?"

The troll coughed and gave a hoarse laugh. It spoke a few words in the guttural troll language and turned its head away from the blade.

Isabo leaned in and pressed harder, drawing a steady flow of dark blood.

"Speak to me, you piece of filth," she said with a snarl. "Tell me if you've seen other trolls with captive humans."

The thing shook its head. It glared up at its captors and muttered something else in Trollish.

"It's lying," Tom said excitedly. "Appa is lying!"

Isabo stared at the former captive. "What did it say?"

"He said he's seen no other *pakh-hu*... other humans, but he has!"

"Where?" Isabo asked.

"To the south! We... we came from the north, but yesterday at just about sunset... they saw another band. I heard them cursing about the other *trollim* they saw." Flecks of spittle flew from his lips as the words tumbled out. "They, they had two captives."

"Two?" Isabo asked.

Tom nodded eagerly.

"Which way were they going?"

"East toward the river, I think, but I didn't see them because I was preparing the meal. I only heard what Bruz and Appa were arguing about."

"Any idea how many trolls were in the party?"

He shook his head.

She glanced down at the leather armor on the creature's chest. She hadn't noticed earlier, but in the light of the fire, she saw what she half expected to see — the broken circle symbol of its clan, just like the ones that had attacked the Pinchbeks. The smell was different, though. They had the same symbol on their armor, but these weren't the same trolls.

"Tom," she asked gently, "do you know about their clans? Are these Stone Breakers?"

The man gave a sharp nod. "They are, and they can rot in the seven hells. I don't know much about the others, only that the clans don't all get along. Stone Breakers hate everyone else."

The troll cursed and barked what must have been a command. Tom instinctively cowered and looked away, muttering apologies. Then he turned back and glared defiantly, as if realizing that the troll no longer had power over him. With a curse, he spat a gobbet of phlegm in the thing's face. He tried to launch a feeble kick at it, but stumbled and had to be steadied on his feet.

With a deep rumbling laugh, the beast shook its head sharply, flicking a trail of dark blood. "Appa will kill all of you stupid *pakh-hu*. Is not for you *pu cha* to speak without permission in my presence. My kind will —"

Without a word, Isabo grabbed the troll's great triangular ear and jerked her blade across it, severing the ear. She examined the leathery piece of troll flesh as the beast howled in pain and wrenched sharply against its bonds. Filip and Hupp pressed their swords against its throat.

"Let me do it, Isabo," Hupp said. "I'll end this thing right here."

Isabo glowered at her captive. The blood streaming from the wound where she'd cut away its ear still flowed, reminding her that they needed to collect more if they were going to attack other trolls. "Tom, how much Common does it know? Will it understand if I ask it detailed questions?"

The man wavered on his feet, but nodded. "Most of them know some. They need it to talk to their slaves."

"In that case, troll," she said fiercely, leaning over the creature, "you have one chance to tell me what I want to know." She glanced up at Filip and Hupp. "Otherwise, these two will take turns slicing every bit of flesh from your body. And then we'll kill you. Or maybe we'll just cut you and send you crawling back to your kind in your slimy holes in the mountains. You'll serve as a warning to any other troll that tries to show its face on this side of the river."

"You are fierce for a *pakh-hu*," the creature said with a hoarse chuckle. "I would know your name, so I can add it to the song of those I have slain."

By now, its face and throat were criss-crossed with seeping knife wounds. Sticky, dark blood flowed freely, staining the ground around it. Isabo stabbed quickly, pinning the troll's remaining ear to the ground.

"Appa, isn't it? I don't think you're listening to me," she said, and she smashed the hilt of her dagger into its forehead. "Tell me about the other trolls you saw yesterday. Which clan were they? How many were there?"

It snarled, but its breath was coming in pants now. "We came from Ghobul in the north for meat. We would eat this beast," he motioned to the slaughtered aurochs, "and then we drive as many of the creatures as we can to Kishik."

Tom nodded. "Kishik is the troll name for the Tulum Bridge, fifteen leagues or so to the north. It's the only way across the Roaring River I know of."

Isabo shook her head and jerked the dagger from the beast's ear. "That's not what I asked you, troll."

The troll snarled fiercely and glared. "You are foolish, *pakh-hu*. There were a dozen or more *trollim* warriors. They were Deep River or Three Valleys clan. You could never attack them and hope to live."

She picked up the severed ear and waved it in the troll's face. "No one thought we could attack your party, but we've killed every one of your companions. And now I'm sitting here with your Ounwe-cursed ear in my hand. We will cut you apart if I find you are lying to us." She threw the ear aside and then moved the tip of her blade against the creature's jugular — or where a human jugular would be. "You know, I think I've heard as much from you as I care to." She turned to Tanner, who had drawn close. "Give me a blade with troll's blood on it."

Second Sword smiled and handed her a sword sticky with dark blood.

The troll cringed at that. "You must not use one troll's blood against another. That is forbidden. It is evil beyond telling."

Isabo gave a hoarse laugh. "Get used to it, beast, because that's how we're going to kill you stinking monsters. I'm surprised that throughout this battle, no one cut you with a dirty blade. That's a real shame. We're going to use your own blood to wipe your kind from the Uplands."

Amon laid a quavering hand on his sister's shoulder. "Iza, how is this helping find Pa?"

She shrugged away the touch. "This filth needs to know what's coming — before we kill it."

Brother Yoren also stepped near. "Isabo Cullen, your brother is right. Kill the creature quickly, if that's what you're going to do, and be done with it."

She spat and glared at him. "Stay out of this, monk. If you're not up for trolls' blood, then go back to your monastery."

"I'm with you, Iza," Perban said. "Do what you need to do."

"And me, too," Hupp growled. "They cut Finn to pieces — and killed Tallard. They deserve to die a long, painful death — every last one of these stinking things."

Isabo looked back at the troll. "It looks like it's, what, a dozen to two. I win, you lose." With a sharp jerk, she drove the blade up under the beast's jaw and wrenched it side to side.

The creature lurched, jetting blood across Isabo's face. It gave a gurgling groan and its muscles spasmed against the ropes for long seconds until it finally lay still.

"Who's the monster now?" Yoren asked.

She snorted, drew herself erect, and wiped the blade on her tunic. "Maybe it takes one to kill one, monk."

Glancing around to find Perban and Tanner, she said, "Make sure everyone cleans their weapons, but gather as much blood as you can; we have more trolls to kill. Set sentries through the rest of the night. Then let everyone get some rest, because we move at first light."

"What about Tallard and Zollar? We're going to bury them first, right?"

"Ounwe's teeth," Isabo muttered, shaking her head. "You've got two choices: build a pyre for them with what firewood the trolls have left, or somebody can spend the next few hours digging graves in the dark."

Perban gave Tanner a grim look, then turned back to Isabo. "I say we bury them. Only barbarians burn their dead."

Tanner nodded in agreement. "We'll get to it."

***

Isabo slept uneasily, haunted by mocking whispers just at the edge of consciousness and the unfading images of the family and friends that the trolls had taken from her. She'd tried to lie still, convinced that if she ignored the voices and her own racing thoughts, she'd eventually be able to drift off. That hadn't happened until someone built a fire nearby. The popping and cracking soothed her for a while, but within the homey sounds of the campfire, she could still hear the taunting voice. Had Will or the others heard it?

Her army had camped in the gully, away from the dead trolls. No one had wanted, or had the strength, to move the troll bodies, but no one wanted to sleep too close to them. The fighters — her fighters — had dragged away the trolls' firewood to make their own campfires. Those still sleeping were curled near a handful of smaller fires.

She tried to calculate how many days it had been since her father had been taken. There still had to be time to catch the trolls that had captured him before they reached the canyon and the safety of the mountains. The grass tale-teller said he had been at the valley four days past the new moon. She'd arrived at that grim place nearly a week later. Then she'd traveled with her army for four days to the battle with the trolls. Or had that taken longer? That meant... she had no idea what that meant.

The bright moon overhead waxed toward the full, mocking her, like the voices in her head.

In the end, she just lay there recalling the events of the day and yearning for sleep that didn't come.

Hiram Tanner nudged her with his foot before dawn. The sky was just tinged with gray light. "There's fresh-cooked meat, Chief. The monks and Kurtis Hupp have been at it most of the night."

"Doing what?" she mumbled as he handed her a plate of roasted meat strips. She sniffed at and realized she was ravenous.

"Them monks have been seeing to the wounded. Then they helped Hupp cut up and roast what was left of the aurochs. I don't think Hupp slept last night. He and Zollar were good friends."

She nodded and tried to force her thoughts to clear. "Is that going to be a problem?" she asked at last.

Tanner shrugged. "Who knows? Everybody's lost somebody to trolls, but it's different when you see it happen in front of your face. I talked to him last night when they went after Zollar's body. From what he said, Asha Maris stabbed the first troll that went into the herd with a blooded spear. She caught it under the arm and opened a great gash. It went wild and screamed like the seven hells were after it. Then Zollar went to attack it with his sword. That's when the second troll showed up. The fecking monster drew its great sword and split poor Zollar in half. It probably would have gone after Hupp and Maris, too, but they got away through the herd."

She mumbled thanks for the food, but realized she wasn't awake enough to deal with Hupp or much of anything else just yet.

"I want us moving in half an hour. See to it."

"Right, Chief."

"Thanks for the food."

***

It had taken longer to set out than Isabo wanted. Hupp, Maris, and a handful of the others had insisted that Tallard and Zollar be properly buried with words said over them by the monks. That had been done, with Brother Yoren solemnly intoning the Prayer for the Dead. Someone had collected the troll weapons and arrayed them over the bodies before the graves were covered. But at last, the small troupe was on the move. A thin layer of clouds hid the mountain peaks to the east, but that would burn away all too soon. They had wasted so much time.

Perhaps Amon had been right, she mused. She could have led them closer to the forest, where she would certainly have picked up the trail of the other troll party, the one that had taken her father.

She glanced back at the two hills, the site of the battle, with fierce elation and satisfaction. She had wiped out an entire pack of trolls. But there were more out there. All she had to do was find them.

Both Tom Wheatley and the dead troll Appa said the other troll band had been spotted to the south. They could be moving to attack Pineholm and the settlements along the Dimwood, or they could be heading directly eastward toward the mountains.

It would depend on whether it was just another raiding party like the Stone Breakers, or if it was indeed the other clan that had taken her father. If it were raiders, they would likely attack Pineholm, carry off what they could, and return north. But as far as anyone knew, there were no crossings along the Roaring River between Tulum in the north and Harrun in the far south. Why had her father left the message that said they were heading east and not north? Was there another crossing no one had found?

Tallard might have had a better idea, but he was dead.

As they crested a low rise, the dark green line of the Dimwood lay before them. She directed her lieutenants to make for Pineholm at the eastern edge of that line, with First Sword spread out to the right and Second to the left in hopes of finding signs of the trolls' passage.

Find them. Find the trolls and kill them all.

The thought came to mind unbidden, like the voice in her sleep. She tried to shake it off. Of course, she would find and kill the trolls. What else could she do? Her father could take care of himself while she cleared the land of murdering trolls. Then she would go after him. He would be so proud of what she had done. Surely, he would be fine.

She shook her head, trying to make sense of the jumble of conflicting thoughts racing through her head. Maybe defeating the evil creatures that held Tom Wheatley had shaken her more than she realized. Or it was just the lack of sleep.

"*...and kill them all,*" echoed in her thoughts along with the vivid memory of past troll atrocities.

She scanned the rolling prairie, looking for heavy boot tracks or other indications that a dozen trolls had tramped through the area. All she saw was the wind blowing swirling patterns in the bluestem and mulegrass.

The wind. That was it. She turned her head to catch whatever faint traces of trollstink lingered on the breeze. But there was nothing, not even the particularly rancid smell of dead trolls she had caught earlier when she woke. Whatever was out here, she must be upwind of it.

She glanced back at Second Sword trooping behind her. She'd decided to march with Tanner's fighters for a while. They'd done well in the battle with the trolls, but had taken a beating. Hupp and Maris moved stiffly, while Dorse, the lone fighter from Tall Grass, wore his arm in a sling and sported a dark bruise on his cheek. Tanner said the man had taken a stout blow from a troll. Then came Barty Naggs from Haywold and Eber Crumble.

"Hiram," she called, "did you move Crumble over from First Sword?"

"Yeah, Chief," Tanner said. "Will and I discussed how to balance things between the two teams since I lost Zollar. Crumble's a good 'un."

She nodded. "Just let me know when you move people around."

"Yes, Chief."

Fifty yards to her right, First Sword marched. They seemed to be in a little better shape. Will Perban was followed by Filip and Daron Homah, Bromlin, and Messick. Behind them tramped Wulf Wheatley, Amon, and the monks. Someone had fashioned a clever harness that Brother Dunken wore on his back to carry Tom Wheatley. That would have been a hard thing to do five years ago, but Tom looked to have lost about half his body weight.

Isabo shook her head. The shell of a man would be lucky to see his home again. The trolls must have beaten him frequently and nearly starved him to boot.

She caught the monk Yoren watching her, but at this distance, she couldn't tell his expression. Was it fear?

"Press on toward the end of the treeline, Hiram. That's where Pineholm is. I need to get things straight with that monk."

She wasn't sure why she'd taken such a dislike to the cleric, other than his refusal to listen to her when she'd repeatedly told him to stay at Haywold.

Angling across the intervening distance between the two groups, she let everyone pass until Wulf, Amon, and the monks caught up.

"What's going on, Isabo?" Amon asked with a smile as she fell into step with them.

She returned a half-smile and shook her head, taking in the contraption of leather straps on Dunken's back holding Tom. "Nothing. I just wanted to chat with the monks. That's quite the sling you've put together."

Brother Dunken nodded his head meekly. "I made one like it for my sister once. That was 'afore she passed and I went away to the monastery."

Isabo cleared her throat and looked away. She really didn't want to hear the fellow's story. "Tom, are you holding up all right?"

The man gave a gap-toothed, crooked smile and coughed painfully. "I'm right as rain, Isabo. I'm powerful grateful to you for killing them beasts and setting me free. You don't know what it was like."

He reached out and laid a twisted hand on her shoulder. The monks — or someone — had put a clean bandage on the missing finger, but it still stank of infection.

"We'll talk again when we get to Pineholm. Right now, I need to speak to Brother Yoren."

She pulled the shorter monk aside and let the others move on ahead.

"Yes, Miss?"

She waited to get some distance between them and the troop, then began walking slowly. "I'm obliged to you for saying the words over Zollar and Tallard, like you did for Arden Luck. And for your care of our wounded."

He gave her a polite bow as he walked. "Of course. The wounded deserve our mercy, and the honored dead gave their lives for —"

"That's fine," Isabo said, cutting him off.

"Uh, Miss, may I say something?"

"What?" she asked curtly.

"I apologize if I gave offense when you were interrogating the troll Appa, but the creature was suffering."

She gave a harsh laugh. "I know that. I wanted it to suffer."

He wrung his hands as if gathering his courage, and she continued. "I'm leading this troop, and what I say goes. I will do what it takes to wipe trolls from the Uplands."

"And find your father?"

"Of course."

He tripped over a clump of mulegrass and sprawled on the prairie.

She snorted and grabbed his arm, pulling him roughly to his feet.

"Thank you," he muttered, rubbing his arm.

They walked in silence for a few minutes. At last, Isabo shook her head and began to walk more quickly, leaving him behind.

"Wait, Miss Isabo, please," he called.

She rounded on him and jabbed a finger at his chest. "I've no use for you, monk. Like I said, I'm grateful for what you've done for my people, but you're slowing us down. You and your companion will leave us in Pineholm, along with Tom and Wulf. You can accompany them back to Haywold."

"Please," he said, "there is more I must tell you. I must continue on to find your father. If... if Dunken and I must travel alone in the mountains to find him, then we will."

Isabo was dumbfounded. "What is so blasted important, monk? Why come all this way when you could have just waited for him in Haywold?"

Yoren brushed the dust and grass from his robes and gave a pained sigh. "The abbot of our order, directed me to seek out your father. For over a year, I have been given visions of a great, looming darkness. Each time the visions came, a single figure — Gabril Cullen — was the central figure, sometimes in company with a priest of the trolls' dark magic. I must stop him before he unleashes a war in which thousands will die — perhaps all of humanity. I was too late to find him in Haywold. Now I must travel with you in the hope of still finding him. Or alone, if I must."

Isabo raised a skeptical eye and shook her head. "My father and a troll magician? He would never have anything to do with those evil creatures, particularly if sorcery were involved. They captured him, and we're going to get him back. That's all there is to it."

Yoren picked up his pace, making his way carefully across the uneven ground.

Isabo caught up to the little man. "Don't run away from me. You're spouting mystical nonsense and babbling about visions. I've got no time for any of that.

I'm here to kill trolls. I will not let you interfere with that. Go off on your own if you must."

The monk paused, took a deep breath, and then continued. There was a blend of fear and wariness in his demeanor that hadn't been there before — or at least that she'd never seen when he talked to anyone else. *Well, that's his problem and not mine.*

"There is more," he said. "Miss Isabo, do you know of Sayala?"

"No. Never heard of it."

He walked quickly, his eyes nervously scanning the ground for tripping hazards. "It's not an 'it.' Sayala was a person."

"Then I never heard of him either."

He spoke rapidly and insistently. "Within the archives in the Temple of Ounwe are accounts which date back hundreds of years — perhaps a thousand. One of the oldest describes the man, Sayala. He, too, carried the scent-gift, just like your father and you. He went among the trolls in his time and set in motion events leading to a great cataclysm. It was, perhaps, the event that created the Dead Plains and decimated our people." He paused, looking warily at her. "I heard your discussions with Tallard regarding the tale-teller. Did your father truly say he was traveling with the trolls and not that he had been captured by them?"

Isabo shrugged. "What does it matter? Now you're saying my father is conspiring with trolls to start a war?"

Yoren shook his head sharply. "I don't know what he is trying to do. The visions were unclear in that. The abbot of my order — Brother Merren — believes that all you who carry the scent-gift are descendants of Sayala. He fears that whatever your father is doing risks igniting another dark inferno that will destroy us all."

"All this because he was taken by trolls?"

He looked away toward the Dimwood. "There is more in my visions, but I cannot reveal it to you. I dare not. I must speak to your father before he does something that cannot be undone. And last night, I sensed a great evil. It was beyond even the malicious evil of raiding trolls. It was drawing near to you. You must be cautious and flee from darkness, for it seeks to engulf you."

She laughed derisively and shook her head. "Is it there now? Do you see demon creatures hanging over me? No?" She glared at the once-pale young cleric.

"Please consider what I've said, Miss," he said.

She stabbed a finger in his chest, knocking the little man backward. "Don't speak to me again, monk, unless you're spoken to. Do you understand?"

***

They marched on, and the sun drew near to noon. Isabo had moved forward to join Will Perban and to put some distance between her and the blasted monk. Now, she halted to scan the countryside. From her left came a sharp, piercing whistle. She turned to see Hiram Tanner waving from a few hundred yards away.

"Wait here," she said to Will. "Let them take a rest."

"Right, Chief," he said with a cautious smile. "Are you okay? You look tense."

"Didn't sleep well last night."

She adjusted the rucksack on her back, called for Amon to join her, then turned and jogged to Tanner.

As she drew near, she saw why he had called to her. Despite the stiff breeze swirling through the grass, crushed stems and broad scuffs in the turf were plainly visible. Trolls had been there, and they were heading in the direction of Pineholm.

"How many?" she asked, turning to Amon.

Her brother shifted awkwardly. "I can't smell anything here."

"Get closer," she said impatiently, waving him forward. "Get down over the tracks. It's been more than a day, so the trollstink is fading, but it's still there."

139

He knelt, and she watched him draw the scent into his lungs. His eyes grew big, and he leaned still closer. He staggered as the full impact of the smell hit his brain.

Isabo gave a genuine smile. She remembered the first time her father had led her to the trail of a group of trolls. The pungent smell of a pack of trolls had nearly overwhelmed her until —"

"There were nine of them," her brother said, wonderingly. He looked up at his sister with wide eyes. "Iza, there was just this mass of... stink, but suddenly I knew. It was like watching threads unraveling in my brain. There were nine trolls! Is that right?"

She nodded and clapped him on the shoulder. "Well done!"

He started to stand, but sniffed again. "Three of them are different. They're the same, but not. What does that mean?"

Isabo shook her head. "I'm not sure. Females, maybe, or they're from another clan of the beasts. I haven't seen that — or smelled it — before."

Her brother nodded excitedly. "We'll have to ask Pa. Do you think these are the ones that took him?"

She didn't reply to that. She knew the answer from the trollstink. Instead, she walked back along the trail the monsters had made through the grass. Examining a broad boot print in the dirt, she finally shook her head. "No. These tracks come from the north and are heading toward Pineholm. The ones that took Pa would be coming from the west and going toward the mountains. My guess is that these are the ones the band we killed saw."

The mocking voice spoke at the edge of her thoughts. *That means more trolls to defeat and more blood to spill. Well done, Isabo Troll-Slayer!*

Was this the creeping darkness the monk had warned her against? She gritted her teeth and squeezed her fist to chase away the thought.

Turning back westward, she signaled Perban to rejoin. When all of First Sword was present, she pointed to the crushed grasses and heavy prints in the turf. "These are troll tracks. There are more of them than last time." She glanced southward toward the Dimwood, where individual trees could just be made out, and then east, following the edge of the forest. "They're heading straight to Pineholm. We need to move quick."

Chapter Twelve

The Tunnel of Sukkuz

A chill, early morning wind whistled through the pines near the high tunnel.

Gheen grinned at the *pakh-hu* rubbing at its shins beside the road. "How will Cullen-thing find lost trolls and defeat the demon?" Gheen asked.

The human scrunched his face and bent down to refill his skin from the stream beside the road. "I don't know yet, Gheen. Everyone asks me that. You trolls wanted a scout so badly; I thought you'd know what I was to do. Besides, your Holy One never said I had to defeat the demon, just find the lost trolls. I didn't agree to anything else."

"Sniffer can find lost trolls," Gheen said. "Use nose."

"It's not that simple. Finding trolls is the easy part. Assuming they're still alive, we'll need to get them out."

Gheen watched Cullen massaging his legs for a few moments. They'd nearly come to the Tunnel of Sukkuz. The valley spread out behind them, bathed in morning sunlight. Surrounding the valley, jagged steel-blue peaks pointed to a bright sky.

"I thought Cullen not believe in demons," Gheen said idly.

"I don't. Or at least I didn't."

He looked back down the valley toward the village, then back at Cullen. "Can I tell you a thing, Gabril Cullen?"

The human shrugged. "Tell me what?"

"Across the river, when we first capture you, you sniffed and knew I was hidden in trees."

"I remember. So?"

"When Gheen came out of the trees and spoke to Cullen, he had — what is hooman word for things in your head? Pictures of things that happen before?"

Cullen gave a quizzical look. "Memories?"

The troll's eyes lit up. "Memories. Yes, memories."

"What's your point?"

"When Gheen came near to Cullen-thing, I had the memories of time before."

Cullen shook his head and drank. "I never saw you before you captured me. Not that I would remember," he said with a dry laugh. "You all look alike to me."

Gheen did not laugh. He turned and began walking toward the tunnel, then stopped. "Was not memories of you or me," he said awkwardly. "Was Holy One, when he first became shaman of Three Valleys Clan."

The human gave a quizzical look. "I don't know much about your kind, but the Holy One is very old. You don't look that old."

"Gheen was born long after Holy One became shaman of the clan."

"You're not making sense," Cullen said, catching up to the troll. "How could you have a memory of him from before you were born? You must have imagined it."

Gheen looked down at the road and resumed walking. "Was not imagining. Was memory — but shaman's memory, not mine. But was in Gheen's head." He looked down at the human walking beside him and shrugged. "Was not only time. When Gheen and Cullen walk together, Gheen has other memories, from before Holy One was alive, even. But does not happen when Cullen is not around."

Cullen shook his head. "You trolls are a weird lot. You'll have to ask the Holy One about that."

***

As they approached the mouth of the tunnel, Cullen leaned down to examine the stonework of the road and tunnel walls.

"Grimmun told me that trolls made this tunnel long ago. Do you know how long ago? Were they from the Three Valleys Clan?"

The troll shook his head. "Gheen not know. Tunnel of Sukkuz was old when the father of my father was young, and he is near two hundred years old."

"Your grandfather is two hundred years old?" Cullen asked, his eyes opening wide. "He still lives?"

Gheen nodded. "And his father is older still."

"How old is the Holy One?"

"Who can say?" Gheen shrugged. "Much older than the oldest in our clan."

Cullen gave a low whistle.

They walked into the wide tunnel and stopped to examine the writing extending along the wall at eye level. Gheen pointed at the figures engraved on the stone. "Here, mixed with writings, are little pictures. Some show trolls." The icon he pointed to showed a troll's face, complete with tusks and an upturned nose.

"And here's the shaman's symbol," Cullen said. He traced the sign with a finger.

"This mark is vurad — is sacred to trolls — but Gheen not know why it's here. Must ask Holy One. He is wisest of all trolls living."

"'Ask the Holy One.' I was afraid you'd say that."

Cullen eyed the characters engraved on the wall.

"What do you look for?" Gheen asked. He looked at the line of inscriptions, then at the human. Why did Cullen-thing want to look at the tunnel wall? He liked the *pakh-hu*, though he did strange things.

Cullen shook his head but kept tracing the figures with a finger. "I'm hoping to see a pattern or something recognizable besides mystical runes and troll faces. Something to help me find your trolls."

They followed the tunnel to the other side and back again. At last, Cullen tapped the wall. "There are several groups of letters and figures here that repeat, always followed by the vurad symbol."

Gheen stared at the letters. They seemed to dance and shift, moving into new patterns.

"Ho," he said, pointing at the wall. "Does Cullen see?"

"See what? The wall? Yeah, I see it."

"Letters moved."

The human had busied himself copying down the groupings with a charcoal pencil. "What? You're dreaming, troll."

"Not dreaming. Gheen is awake." He touched the inscriptions, but they were fixed and unmoving.

Cullen looked at the symbols on the wall and compared them to what he'd written. "With luck, I can make some kind of sense of this."

Gheen shuddered and looked up at the human. "Luck? Luck was the name of the other *pakh-hu* Cullen hunted with. He is dead."

"Luck is dead, you're right, Gheen. I meant —"

Now, the human stood for a few moments, shaking his head from side to side. "Gheen, I've seen enough. Let's head back — as soon as I rest my legs a bit. You know, I've journeyed for leagues and leagues across my land, but mountains are new to me." He shook his head. "All this hiking up and down makes me sore."

Gheen smiled, showing a wide, gap-toothed grin. "I will carry you. Cullen-thing is small compared to troll."

Cullen laughed out loud, the sound reverberating through the long tunnel. "I'll crawl on my hands and knees before I let you carry me, troll. But I thank you."

Gheen grunted and turned to lead Cullen back through the tunnel. "We must go to Holy One. He has much wisdom."

He paused at the tunnel's eastern end and looked back at the wall. The letters in one grouping shifted and danced, forming new combinations. He shook his head. Had he really seen that? Could such a thing be? He looked again, and now the characters were fixed and unmoving. He walked to the wall and touched them, but they were merely inscriptions etched into the solid wall. He looked to Cullen, but the *pakh-hu* was looking in another direction on the other side of the tunnel.

For a moment, he considered telling the human again what he had seen, but no, Cullen-thing would think him a fool. Besides, they were going to see the Holy One.

***

Gheen and Cullen made their way back to the shaman's temple home. At the doorway, Gheen drew his blade and nicked his palm, allowing a few drops of blood to fall in a sacred offering.

"What, this again?" Cullen asked. He reached for the knife, shook his head, and performed the same ritual.

In a few moments, they stood on a wide porch at the rear of the building, with a view of the stockade wall and the mountain peaks to the east. A pair of young trolls stood at either end of the room. Each carried a long, curved scimitar. They glared at the human who dared to come within the presence of their Holy One.

Cullen placed the sheet with traced characters on the table before the Holy One. "There's a pattern here that repeats."

"What characters?" the shaman said.

The human smoothed the paper. "Well, there's one that looks like a troll's head, then a circle that's open at the top, and a straight line that's bent at the end, and a —"

"Stop," the shaman ordered. "That means nothing to me."

"But at the end of the group — at the end of each group — is the character vurad," Cullen said.

The shaman waved a dismissive hand. "Gheen, explain the symbols to me."

Gheen bowed his head and shuffled from side to side. "Holy One, Gheen does not read letters."

The shaman smiled at that. "I must see the writing. It has been many years since I visited the tunnels. Describe them to me."

Gheen bowed and moved to the table. He pointed to the letters traced on the paper. "First is troll's head, but is angry troll. Next is shaped like water jug. After that, one is one like blade of *ukar* knife."

He continued, describing each character in each of the letter groupings Cullen had copied.

"Holy One," he said when he had finished. "There is other thing. When Gheen was in Tunnel of Sukkuz with Cullen-thing, the letters, they moved and danced on the stone wall."

The Holy One gave a dry chuckle and nodded faintly. His face carried the trace of a smile. "Gheen, put this aside. I will return to it in a moment," he said, looking toward the younger troll. "Your mother was Ama, wasn't she?"

"Yes, Holy One."

"I remember her well. You have her gift of patience. She served here in the temple in her youth."

The shaman fixed unseeing eyes on the human. "This one's mother was a beauty among trolls."

Cullen shook his head. "Shaman," he said, tapping the paper spread over a low table, "I'm sure she was wonderful for a troll. Do the symbols Gheen described sound familiar? Is there anything here that will protect me from the demon Azuk?"

The shaman growled. "Hear me, human. Gheen has his mother's patience. You would do well to learn it." He muttered, coughed for some minutes, and finally said, "I must see the letters. Gheen, come near to me."

Gheen moved his chair next to the shaman's.

The old troll reached out a hand and touched a misshapen hand to Gheen's forehead. He uttered a few sing-song words and said, "Look at the letters the *pakh-hu* copied down and point again to each with your finger."

Gheen looked down at the paper and pointed to the first.

"Gom," the shaman said. "Next?

"Kora. Next?

"That is mok."

Gheen pointed to each letter in succession, and the Holy One named them, ending with vurad.

"How did you do that?" Cullen asked.

The shaman said nothing but kept his hand on Gheen's forehead. Gheen's eyes were blank.

After a moment, the shaman withdrew his hand, and Gheen sat back, breathing deeply. The words and symbols from the tunnel still swirled and danced in his head, but they began to take on *meaning*. A memory not his own washed over him. It was the Holy One, only much younger, with bright eyes, carefully writing words on a scroll. The ink smelled faintly of blackberries. Then, just as suddenly, his mind was clear. He sat beside the ancient, sightless shaman.

"Remember the words you have read, Gheen."

"Yes, Holy One. But I saw —"

"I know what you saw, Gheen, son of Ama."

The shaman turned whitened eyes to Cullen. "The words are a prayer to the First Ones."

Gheen interrupted. "My pardon, Holy One. They... they give thanks for delivery from a hidden darkness."

The shaman and the *pakh-hu* both turned to look at him, Cullen-thing with cautious wonder, the Holy One with a faint smile.

"Are the First Ones your gods?" Cullen asked.

"They are *the* gods, human," the shaman said. He coughed again and summoned his human slave. "Aydin-thing, fetch the book."

The slave bowed and backed away. A few minutes later, he reappeared carrying a thin book bound in gray skin. He placed it on the table and withdrew.

"This is all that remains of our people's history, *pakh-hu* Gabril Cullen. Now that I am blind, none can read it." He turned blank eyes to Gheen. "Unless I teach it to someone. What you saw in the tunnel, the moving letters, was *kur anesh*. That you see meaning in them is the opening of wisdom, a sign of your lineage. There is power within you to learn sacred reading — and the way of the Holy One. When Azuk is defeated, come to me, and I will teach you."

"Gheen is a Holy One?" Cullen asked.

The shaman ignored the human's words.

Gheen stood open-mouthed, staring at the Holy One.

Cullen reached for the book and opened it. He flipped the thick parchment pages, eyeing the figures written there. After a few minutes, he closed the book and pushed it to Gheen.

The young troll leaned over the book. Some of the letters were the same as the ones he'd read to the Holy One. He recognized the vurad rune among them. But what did they mean? He willed the words to move and explain their meaning, but they remained fixed on the page. Why could he find meaning in the others but not these?

Cullen spoke at last. "Shaman, I can make nothing of your book. What does it say?"

The old troll settled back on the couch, grumbling. He spoke a few words, and an attendant brought a tumbler of wine.

Gheen turned from the Cullen to the Holy One and back again. The *pakh-hu* sniffed and wrinkled his face at the strong scent of the wine.

The shaman drank deeply and wiped his mouth with the back of a clawed hand.

"It is ancient, older still than I, and I have lived many, many lifetimes," the Holy One said. "It's a part of a longer book that has been lost to us, called First Things. It tells of the trolls coming from — or was it over — the mountains? I carry the memories of many shamans before me, and I dimly remember bits of these things. When I was younger, the memories were clear. I fear I am forgetting much that I once knew. We were a great people, and none could stand before our might. We built great cities, the strongest of which was Dhugash. All brought tribute to the city, even the *pakh-hu*, Gabril Cullen. Does that surprise you?" He waved a clawed finger. "And then, at the height of its power, mighty Dhugash was no more. Its streets lay empty, and the trolls scattered."

"What happened, Holy One?" Gheen asked.

The shaman smiled at Gheen. He tapped his forehead. "Who can say? I think that I once knew. What is clear to me is that only through the power of vurad were trolls saved from destruction."

"Was it Azuk that brought the destruction?" Gheen asked.

The shaman finished his wine and fixed his eyes somewhere over the younger troll's head. "Perhaps."

"Shaman," Cullen said, "yesterday you used magic to —"

"To kill Guram?" the old troll asked. He settled back on his couch and waved his cup. The attendant brought a pitcher and refilled it. He motioned at Gheen and Cullen, and the attendant poured cups for each of them.

The shaman turned unseeing eyes to Cullen. "You want to know if my strong magic could kill Azuk. Again, who can say? The trolls of old had such power. If Azuk had destroyed the great city of Dhugash, the trolls would have fought against him using strong magic. And no doubt they had more than a single feeble shaman to wield it. It was only through the power of —"

"Vurad. I get it," Cullen said. He stood and took the cup. Without a word, he drained it and replaced the cup on the table. "Tomorrow, I will go into the deep tunnels where the trolls have gone. I've not seen such magic before yesterday, but if there is any help you can give, magic or otherwise, this would be a good time."

The shaman shifted on his couch and gave a low rumble. "To you, I will say that Dannick-thing was close to something she thought would help, either to find the lost trolls or to somehow fight the demon. I don't know which — or how she would use it. Return tomorrow before going to the caves. I will teach special words to Gheen, if he can learn them. They may be a help to you in the deep tunnels."

"So Gheen is going into the tunnels with me?"

The Holy One shrugged, rattling his necklace of bones and twigs. "I did not say that. Gheen alone must decide that."

Gheen closed his eyes. There was so much to take in — learning letters and words of power, the reminder of his mother's service in the temple, and what that could mean. And the looming fear that he might have to enter the tunnels with Cullen-thing to find the lost trolls.

He breathed deeply, bowed over the table, and touched his forehead. "Gheen is honored for Holy One to teach him words."

"I will come too," the *pakh-hu* said. "I would learn also."

The ancient troll laughed, but the laugh devolved into a fit of coughing. After a time, he spoke again. "No, human. These are words fitting only for a Holy One. Gheen-*buruk* carries the blood of a shaman within him. I will teach him alone. You, Gabril Cullen, are *pakh-hu buruk-ush*. You have a separate fate. To my people — and yours — you have the ability to sniff out trolls, but your gift is much more. You seek knowledge but are not ready for what you must learn. Together, perhaps, you will find that knowledge."

The *pakh-hu* slapped the table. "Don't you think it's a good time to tell me what that is? What in Ounwe's green heavens does that mean? You're sending me off to —"

The Holy One raised a crooked finger and gestured.

Gheen shivered sharply, and Cullen fell silent as a sudden icy chill encompassed the room. A line of frost lanced across a wall. He placed a warning hand on the human's shoulder and bowed to the Holy One. "We go now. Gheen will return tomorrow as the Holy One says."

Chapter Thirteen

Battle and a Rest

"Wulf, we have to move quickly to catch these trolls," Isabo said. "Tom can't keep up, even with you or Brother Dunken carrying him, so you'll just have to follow after us." She pointed southeast along the trampled path. "Pineholm isn't more than a few hours' march that way. Do you have troll blood in case one of them comes back?"

"I do, but we'll meet you there," the fighter said with a nod and a grim smile. "You just make sure none of the buggers get away."

"If there are that many of the beasts out there, you'll be sitting ducks. Tallard said the town has a stout wall around it, like Haywold, but there are unprotected homesteads and small settlements running westward along the forest's edge. If anything happens, keep your head down and get everyone home that way."

Wulf shook his head. "No. Like I said, we'll meet you at Pineholm. We'll be fine. You go kill them things."

Isabo ground her teeth at his stubbornness but clapped her friend on the shoulder. She gave a sharp command, and the two columns took off at a quick jog. Their pace wasn't as brisk as it had been. Perban and Tanner confirmed what she already knew: her people were drained. The exhaustion and injuries of the past week, not to mention the battle with the trolls, had taken their toll.

But, oh, what a battle it had been.

"We'll rest in Pineholm," she'd told the fighters, "after we deal with the beasts."

In her heart, though, she knew she was lying to them. Maybe they'd have a short rest for the time it took to recruit more fighters. But there were still more trolls loose in the Uplands. There would be little respite until every one of them was dead.

***

"The smell's getting stronger!" Amon said with a grin. "We're going the right way."

Isabo grunted. "Of course we are. But look at the tracks; don't just smell them. You can see the boot prints leading this way. It's good you're using the scent-gift, but don't ignore what's in front of your eyes."

Her brother looked abashed for a moment and glanced guiltily at the marks in the dirt. Then his smile broadened, and he returned to the scent of trollstink.

She started to berate him again, but Filip Homah shouted, "A runner! There!" She looked up to see the swordsman pointing toward the forest.

"Human?" she asked, joining him on a low hilltop and squinting at the distant figure.

"Aye, it is. I don't see any trolls."

She judged how far away he was and quickly glanced at her remaining fighters. "Amon, Maris, you're both fast. Drop your gear, hightail it out there, and bring him back. Make sure there are no trolls chasing him first!"

Both nodded, stripped off their packs, and raced over the waving grass toward the lone figure.

"Let's go," Isabo called to her lieutenants, and the entire party moved off.

Daron and Hupp picked up the dropped gear and rushed to catch up.

The group didn't take long to meet up with their compatriots who were returning along the path, supporting an exhausted figure.

Blood seeped from a loose bandage on his arm, and a livid bruise covered the side of his face.

"You've come," he panted. "Ounwe be blessed. We saw you from the forest. Trolls are attacking Pineholm. You must hurry before they break through the gates!"

"How many are there?" Isabo asked urgently.

The man shook his head. "I couldn't see them all. A dozen, maybe. Once Faulken closed the gates, we lit out for the forest, but one of the things nearly took my arm off with its sword."

She nodded to Perban, who pulled a rolled bandage from his pack. He winced as he removed the blood-soaked cloth from the man's arm and wrapped a fresh one. "He'll need stitches."

"There's no time," Isabo said. She glanced at the man. "What's your name?"

"Mika Span."

"Well, Mika, I'm Isabo Cullen, and these are my fighters. There are two monks following close behind us." She pointed north, where Yoren, Dunken, and the Wheatley brothers could be seen moving steadily toward them. "Wait for them, and they'll see to your arm properly."

The man shook his head. "Like you said, there's no time. I'm to bring you back." He looked at Isabo's fighters and clucked. "So few. Come with me and we can protect you."

That drew a growl and a few wry chuckles.

"We just killed half a dozen of the creatures," Filip said with a grin. "I don't reckon a full dozen would be that much harder."

The man stared. "You'd go to your deaths with so light a heart?"

Isabo gave him a tight smile. "We know how to kill trolls. How far is it?"

"No more than half a mile over that hill."

"Troll's blood on all weapons," she said to the group. "Arrows, blades, spears — everything we have. This time we won't spare a single one of them. Lead on, Span."

***

Pineholm sat in a high corner of the Uplands where the rolling prairie met the forest. To the east, across the dark canyon of the Roaring River, lay the stark cliffs of the Blue Mountains. Isabo had never seen the peaks or the river, except from a great distance. Part of her marveled at the immensity of the granite formations, but another part dismissed them as nothing more than the hideout of filthy trolls.

Supported by Perban, Span led the group toward the trees, then eastward along a shaded trail just inside the forest. A gray haze of smoke hung thick in the pines. "They burned the Raffas' farm. I don't know if the family made it to Pineholm in time. We only had a few hours' warning."

Isabo sniffed at the breeze, then prodded her brother. "Smoke masks the trollstink. You have to concentrate to catch it, but it's still there."

He nodded but didn't speak.

Span halted and waited for everyone to catch up. To Isabo, he said, "Just up ahead, we'll break out of the trees. The village is in the middle of a clearing. It has a tall palisade, and the trolls were trying to break down the gate."

"How far is the wall from the edge of the trees?" she asked.

"Sixty or seventy yards. Less on the east side. This isn't the first time trolls have attacked. We cleared the ground so they couldn't sneak up on us."

"Like we're trying to do to them," Will Perban said with a grim smile.

Isabo nodded. "Let's get closer."

They crept closer, and through the trees she made out the harsh bellowing of trolls, an occasional frenzied human curse, and the twanging of bows.

"Here," Span said after a few moments. He motioned Isabo off the trail and into a tangle of scrub oaks.

The sheltered thicket gave a clear view of the walled village. The ground had indeed been cleared all the way to the trees as far around as Isabo could see. A stone-cobbled road led northward from the city gate toward the plains. Beside the road lay an overturned wagon. Another way led eastward toward what Isabo could only guess was the canyon.

She could make out at least six trolls near the gate. They had piled logs and brush against the gate and were attempting to set it alight. Townspeople on the wall pelted them with rocks and arrows.

Isabo tasted the acrid pine smoke that hung in the air. It would be nearly impossible to sniff out the other three trolls.

"Don't you want to go inside?" Span asked.

Isabo raised an eyebrow. "You want us to just go up and ask the trolls to step aside?"

The townsman shook his head and gave a sly grin. "Like I said, this isn't the first time trolls have attacked. A few years ago, we dug a tunnel that leads to a thick clump of trees on the south side."

"That makes sense. We should do that back home." She nodded toward the wall, where two men hefted a heavy stone over the edge. It crashed down, knocking one of the trolls to the ground. "So they're not in any danger?"

"They are. We never underestimate those beasts," he said. "They could catch the wall on fire or just batter it down. But most of the families are ready to flee through the tunnel and then southward toward Harrun. We'd better get your fighters inside."

Isabo ignored the remark. The smoke in the clearing was growing thicker. "Where's that coming from?"

"Raffa's farm is just west of here. They burned it and probably a few of the smaller holdings nearby."

She stared at the overturned wagon. With all the smoke, it might provide enough cover for a few fighters to creep close, especially if the trolls' attention was elsewhere.

"Can you get word to them inside?"

"Of course. There is a guard and a runner at each end of the tunnel."

"I have an idea." She motioned him back to the trail. "But first, we need to know where the rest of them are. Who is your leader? Will he give us fighters?"

"To defeat trolls? I should think so. Alastor Faulken is the mayor here. He'll do anything to fight these things if it'll keep his people from fleeing south. We've lost too many families. This is the second attack this season. They rarely come at us directly or so frequently. Something is stirring up the creatures."

Isabo considered for a moment. "You'd best go then. Get yourself stitched up and send someone back who can tell us where the other three are."

Before Span could move, the question was answered. Two trolls slowly emerged from the edge of the forest a hundred yards to their left, dragging a heavy log between them. Another larger beast bellowed what must have been curses, haranguing the other two and cracking a short, thick whip over their heads.

"Go now," Isabo urged. "Tell them inside to put everyone they can on the wall. Keep the trolls at the gate occupied and make a lot of noise. We'll kill these three and then come after the rest!"

The townsman disappeared through the trees.

"Perban, Tanner," she snapped. "We have to get closer. Put every archer we have on those three. Check to see that there's troll blood on each arrow. No slip-ups. No one shoots unless they have a sure shot, and not until the trolls at the gate are distracted!"

In a quarter of an hour, activity on the wall suddenly increased. The people of Pineholm clustered over the gate, hurling curses and stones. Two trolls stepped back from the wall and took aim with heavy bows of dark wood. Near-simultaneous twangs sounded. One arrow buried itself in the top of the wall, but the other caught a defender full in the face.

The troll with the whip redoubled his efforts to encourage his companions.

"Now," Isabo called in a harsh whisper.

Hiram Tanner drew his bow, standing beside Katya Bromlin and two others. Tanner muttered something, and they fired. Immediately, all three trolls screamed. Two clutched at their faces or necks, and the third grabbed at a shaft buried deep under its arm. Even through the haze of smoke, Isabo could see that the troll blood had been effective. The creatures bellowed and dropped to the ground, writhing in agony. Blood jetted from one's throat as hideous growths erupted from the tainted flesh.

Isabo drew her sword and tightened the straps of her helmet. "Perban, take a squad and finish them off. When they're dead, make for the gate. The rest of you, follow me!"

She stepped from the trees and sprinted toward the overturned wagon, only twenty yards from the gate, angling to keep it between her and the enemy. She slid to the ground and heard the others coming in behind her.

One of the beasts under the wall glanced back to see what had happened to its companions and gave a sudden warning howl. It was cut short by a heavy, jagged stone dropped from above. It staggered, cursed, and shook off the injury. The huge creature's face registered surprise and fear as it pointed to the three trolls sprawled on the ground, each with a human fighter hacking at it.

Daron Homah drew a leather sling thong and grabbed for a smooth stone. Isabo had hunted squirrels and small game with such a weapon when she was a child, but what damage could a small stone do against such beasts? She reached up to drag the fool to the ground, but he stepped away and swung the weapon twice over his head. With a sharp *whirr*, the stone flew straight at the injured troll that had called a warning. The smooth rock clipped the troll's ear and caromed off into the dirt.

The troll swatted at the injury as if at a fly, but suddenly it, too, grabbed at the seemingly minor, bleeding wound and gave an awful, howling scream as if it were being skinned alive.

Daron dropped to the ground and gave a wide smile. "I wiped the stone in troll's blood, Miss Isabo. Figured it couldn't hurt — or at least it couldn't hurt us — but that bugger won't be bothering us none."

But Isabo was already on her feet, calling for fighters to attack. The weariness of a week-long march followed by a battle and another day's march fell away in an instant. She glanced quickly to find Amon and realized to her horror that he was not with her, but there was no time to worry. She was around the wagon and sprinting for the gate.

"Now!" shouted a voice from the wall. Buckets crashed down on the trolls, splashing the ground and two of the trolls with slick liquid. Torches followed. Flames engulfed the beasts and crept toward the gate.

Hupp and Crumble shot past Isabo toward the trolls. Hupp swung his heavy blade at the nearest of the brutes, but the blow was deflected. Before the lumbering creature could respond, Crumble dodged in and drove a heavy spear into its gut. Something struck Isabo's helmet, knocking her sideways, but she regained her feet and joined the fight. Arrows whizzed by overhead, and the scene devolved into a cacophony of shouts, heavy blows, and the crackle of flames.

The trolls' heavy leather armor and helms made it difficult to land a solid hit, but even a glancing strike with a blooded weapon had its immediate effect.

Filip nearly fell, struck by a heavy club. His brother leaped into the fray, swinging a sword that took the creature's arm off at the elbow. Katya Bromlin finished it off by driving a blade hilt-deep into the monster's face.

By now, six of the creatures lay dead. Another moaned piteously on the ground amid crackling flames. That left two standing, as one had succeeded in smothering the oily fire with dirt. But the thing looked like a grisly, burned porcupine as arrow after arrow poured into it from above. It staggered madly, swinging a heavy sword at anyone who approached. Hiram Tanner took steady aim and calmly shot it in the throat. It gave a gurgling shriek and spun around, only to trip over its still-burning companion and collapse on the ground.

The last troll, seeing it was surrounded by determined fighters with still more approaching, gave an angry snarl and dropped its sword. In barely distinguishable Common Tongue, it rasped, "You *pakh-hu* are vermin. You have no honor. We will —" But Filip Homah picked up a fallen spear, jabbed it into a dead troll to coat it with blood, and with a mighty grunt, drove it into the thing's neck. It gave a strangled scream and died as its flesh bubbled and twisted.

Isabo looked around. It was over. She staggered and slumped to her knees. They had done it again. They had slain an entire party of trolls. "Tanner, make sure all of these are dead. Messick and Crumble, douse that fire before it goes up the wall."

Unbidden, a harsh voice cackled in her thoughts. *You're not finished, young one. There are more to kill northwards and in the mountains. You must fight them!*

She shook her head sharply to clear the thought. With a glance up at the figures on the battlement overhead, she saw Mika Span and a score of others. To a man, they stood gaping at the scene below them.

***

The scarred and still-smoking gates opened smoothly with barely a creak. A small crowd of townspeople crept out warily, peering nervously at the slain trolls. At their head strode a sharp-faced man of forty or so, with thick, graying hair and a cautious smile.

Not unlike her father, Isabo mused, if her father had been a merchant.

She untied the strap of her helmet, tucked it under her arm, and ran fingers through her sweat-soaked hair. "I'm Isabo Cullen," she said, waving to indicate her troops. "I lead this band. They are the Uplands Fighters."

"And my name is Alastor Faulken. I'm the mayor of Pineholm. Welcome and..." He glanced at the motionless troll beside him and the men moving from beast to beast, ensuring they were dead with quick, sure strokes. "...and thank you."

Isabo nodded and shook the man's hand. "We've traveled far, from Haywold and beyond, chasing trolls. These aren't the first we've killed and won't be the last."

"How have you done this?" a man asked wonderingly. It was Mika Span. "To kill so many of the evil things with so few is... unheard of."

Isabo gave a weary chuckle and pointed to the nearest body. Tanner stood nearby with a bloody sword. "Hiram, did you cut this one?" she asked.

He shook his head.

Isabo took his sword and jabbed it into the dead troll's arm. Immediately, the blood on the sword hissed, reacting against the creature's flesh. At the same time, cancer-like growths bubbled and twisted from the wound in grotesque spirals.

"Merciful Ounwe..." someone whispered.

"It's their own blood," Isabo said, as if she were teaching a group of youngsters. "Blood from one troll is poison to another. These nine, plus another seven two days ago, makes, uh, sixteen of the things we've killed this way. For the first, we took blood from three more that someone else, maybe other trolls, had killed west of here."

Low mutters and gasps came from the crowd.

"How have we not known this?" the mayor asked. "I've seen a dead troll before, but it took three strong men to bring it down after a fight that lasted for hours. And two of the men died from horrendous wounds."

She shrugged. "There's some weird power in their blood. Magic, maybe, or just how the things are built."

From beside the wall came a great gasp of pain. It was Shamus Dorse, the taciturn fighter from Tall Grass. He lay slumped against the wooden palings. Blood seeped from a wound across his chest. Asha Maris knelt beside him, pressing a cloth against the blood.

Isabo bit her lip. Dorse had taken a blow from the trolls in their last encounter. How had she let him stay with them? She should have forced him to travel with the monks.

"Mika, run for Healer Shuta," Faulken said. To Isabo, he said, "Your people will have everything they need. Everything! Come inside the gate. The inn is nearby."

Faulken saw to it that each of Isabo's fighters was treated to the finest Pineholm had to offer. Dorse had taken the only significant injury, a slash across his chest that required a great many stitches. The man wouldn't be able to swing a sword to any effect for some time, but he might be able to manage a spear. No one else had taken more than minor cuts and bruises.

The feast to celebrate their victory was epic. The public room at the Rook's Roost, the town's inn, rang with laughter, stories, and song. Tom Wheatley finally arrived, escorted by his brother and the monks. When the story of his rescue was told, the hall erupted in raucous cheers once again. He had insisted on walking through the gates under his own power. As rare as it might be to see trolls slain, the presence of a captive rescued from the beasts was unheard of. He wasn't up to much celebration, and the innkeeper found a quiet room at the far end of the house for him and Wulf.

Isabo smiled to herself at the sight of Tom being led away to cheers. Such a thing would make it difficult for the mayor to rebuff her request for more fighters.

"I'll see that the healer attends to him as well," Faulken told her, pouring her another tumbler of honey wine. "Anything he needs, absolutely anything, will be done. Your army's actions are nothing short of miraculous! Miraculous, I say!"

The wine was as good as any she had ever tasted, and the opportunity to sleep in a soft bed was more tempting than she realized.

"Begging your pardon, Alastor, but may I join you and the commander of these fine fighters?"

Isabo looked up to see a tall, thick-set, balding figure with beefy arms and shoulders.

The mayor gave a grunt of irritation, but waved to an open spot on the bench beside him. "This is Tomas Figg, the butcher."

Isabo gave him a noncommittal smile.

Before she could speak, the man gave her a respectful bow of the head and said quickly, "It's just that I was on the wall when you was explaining to the mayor here about how you did what you did with the blood. We could do the same thing — I mean, take the blood and have it ready in case those terrible monsters attack again."

Isabo nodded, and he continued, explaining that the best way to collect the trolls' blood was to shackle the creatures by the leg, hoist them into the air like slaughtered beef, and drain their blood into tubs.

The mayor's eyes widened, and he quickly agreed to the idea. To Isabo, he said, "We'll see to it that you have as much as you need." He poured her another drink and one for the butcher. "Though we'll keep what your people don't take to make sure everyone in the area has some — and knows how to use it."

Isabo drew her dagger from its sheath and held it to the torchlight. "Be careful with it. I've already cleaned this blade, but you can see how the blood has stained the metal. It doesn't damage it as far as I can tell, but it darkens the blade."

Figg drained his cup and stood. "I'm obliged to you, Miss. We all are. Me and my mates will get right to collecting the blood. Thanks for the drink, Alastor."

"We've been fighting trolls as far back as anyone can remember," Faulken said as the butcher moved away through the crowd. "It's a wonder that no one discovered it. It would have saved many lives over the years."

"Someone must have," she said, "but they probably didn't live to tell the tale." The strong wine was going to her head. She replaced the glass on the table and pushed it away. "Mayor, we're looking for more trolls — the ones that took my father. They may have passed east through the area in the last week or so."

She glanced up to see Brother Yoren and Brother Dunken — and Amon — standing near the door, speaking to another figure in monastic robes.

The mayor followed her gaze and smiled. "I see your monks have found Brother Ignatus." Looking back to her, he continued. "I'm sorry the beasts took your father. And, yes, there was another troll band. It was five or six days ago. Where are they coming from — and going to? Usually, there are a few raiding bands every season, but this is three or more groups of the horrible things inside of a week."

Isabo shook her head. Who knew what had changed to rile up the trolls?

"Yes, well, we sent a scout — my daughter Mayra, actually — up north along the canyon. The things didn't see her, for which I'm grateful, but she lost them a league or so away. Their trail was still there, but it led right to the edge of the canyon and disappeared. As if they took a running leap and flew across."

"Were there humans with them? Captives?" Isabo asked eagerly.

"Aye, two of them that she saw." He reached into his pocket and pulled forth something wrapped in fine cloth. He pushed it across the table. "She also found this."

With trembling fingers, she opened the thin bundle. Her heart raced when she saw the fragile, woven-grass tale-teller.

"Papa," she whispered, caressing the rough weave of bluestem and mulegrass.

"You know what this is?" Faulken asked gently.

She nodded. "It's a message from my father."

"What does it say?"

She examined the weave. "'Into the mountains. Do not follow. Danger and… hope.' It must be him."

"I've only seen these once before," the mayor said. "Another scout stayed for a while last year: Tilda Dannick. She showed me how this was used. Did you know her?"

Isabo shook her head. "Is Mayra here? I'd like to see the trail she found — and where she found this."

"She's at home. She lives just south of here along the canyon. I can send a runner, and you can meet with her tomorrow."

Isabo nodded, carefully rewrapping the tale-teller and placing it in her pocket. "I'd like that. We're going after him, you know, me and my group. We recaptured Tom Wheatley, and we'll recapture my father." She picked up the bottle and split the remaining golden liquid between her glass and the mayor's. "You said you'd help us, and I appreciate that. I aim to track down the creatures that took him, even if that means crossing the canyon and taking the fight to the trolls. To do that, I need more fighters."

Faulken's expression registered panic. "Into the mountains? No one has ever —"

"No one has ever done a lot of the things we've done. The longer we wait, the greater the risk to the Uplands, to Pineholm, and to my father. You were lucky that we arrived when we did, even with your wonderful tunnel. Would you have lived in the woods or slunk away south if trolls had broken down the gate or burned the village? They'd have hunted you down piecemeal, then killed or enslaved you."

The man's voice was calm, but his eyes grew hard. "Don't think me ungrateful, but do you honestly think you could track the beasts on their own ground, in territory you've never seen? You're from Haywold. How many mountains are there at your home? I would be sending my people to their deaths."

Isabo shook her head and smiled. The tale-teller had given her hope. He was alive, and she knew where they had taken him — at least the general direction. "Do you smell that, Mayor?" she asked, sniffing lightly. "That faint trace of moldy apples and spoiled cheese? It's here, even now, within the walls of the inn. It carries on the air."

He gave a thin smile and shook his head. "I smell nothing, except ale and the sweat of unwashed bodies."

She nodded. "You don't have the gift. I do, and my brother. My father has it as well. The smell is trollstink. But it's different from their usual stink because it comes from the dead trolls outside the walls. The smell changes when they die — or when we kill them. Have no fear that I won't be able to track these creatures into the mountains. Give me stout fighters. I'll take them into the trolls' stinking dens, bring my father back, and then we will rid the Uplands of any that remain."

Faulken sighed. "As I said, don't think me ungrateful. And I did promise you anything you need. How many fighters will it take?"

Isabo considered. "A dozen. More if you can spare them. And two leaders who will report to me. I'll also ask that you replenish our food and help us repair or replace damaged gear." She sipped thoughtfully at the wine. She could practically hear the man calculating the cost of her request. "Mayor, it's customary to pay a bounty on each dead troll. The bounty on nine trolls —"

"— would empty our coffers," he protested.

"Just so," she said. "Deduct the cost of our supplies — and your men's wages for two weeks — from the bounty. We can settle up the rest when we return."

The mayor glowered at her, but finally softened. "Very well. It would be... churlish for me to do otherwise."

When the mayor took his leave, Isabo scanned the room for her brother. The monks had disappeared, and she finally saw Amon sitting at a table near the fire with Asha Maris and Kurtis Hupp.

She made her way past crowded tables, refusing drinks from her own fighters and locals alike.

"It's the troll slayer!" someone called. "Drink!"

"They're all troll slayers," another slurred voice shouted. "Isabo is the Queen of Troll Slayers! To the troll slayers and their queen!"

Isabo shook her head and laughed.

"Amon," she said, reaching her brother's table, "let's go for a walk. I need to show you something."

As he stood, she saw Asha's hand linger on her brother's arm. Isabo grumbled at that but wasn't sure why. Maris was smart, from a good family, and a skilled fighter. At the moment, only the last was important.

She led her brother out the door and under the light of a torch on the wall.

"What is it?" he asked.

She removed the tale-teller from her pocket and carefully uncovered it. "It's from Pa. They found it last week."

His eyes grew large with wonder as he took it from her and held it to the light. "What does it say?"

"You can't read it?"

He shrugged. "You're better at this than I am. Just tell me."

When she told him, he stared. "Are we going after him?"

She nodded.

"And I can go?"

She rolled her eyes. "Against my better judgement, yes."

He smiled, but suddenly dropped his gaze. "Isabo, the monks need to go as well."

She shook her head firmly. "That can't happen. It was dangerous enough, them traipsing across the Uplands with us. We're going into the mountains — once we figure out how to cross the canyon — into the middle of troll territory. We just can't take them."

"They are going whether you let them or not."

"What do you mean?"

"I thought... I thought that you weren't going to go after Pa, that you were going to stay here and chase down more trolls. Everybody did. But Brother Yoren said he has to go after him. Brother Ignatus got swords and supplies for Yoren and Dunken." He looked away. "And I told him that if you stayed here with your army, I would go with him."

Her jaw tightened, and she glared at her brother. "Amon Bray Cullen, if you tried any such thing, I would tie you up and send you home in a wagon." Then she scoffed. "And I don't trust that monk. Dunken's harmless enough, but your precious friend Yoren is hiding something. He doesn't travel all this way and risk being killed by trolls just to wag his finger at Pa."

Amon leaned against the wall. "Iza, do you know who Sayala was? Brother Yoren said he was —"

Isabo rolled her eyes. "Yes, Yoren said he had a vision of this Sayala. He was some ancient guy. The monk is making out that Pa is the modern version of him or something. Said he was going to start a war or some nonsense."

"But the monks got a message from Harrun, from the monastery there. Yoren says it's more important than ever that he —"

"Amon, the monks' problem is not my problem."

"Please, Isabo. It's important to them."

She shook her head and glared at her brother. "You've been spending too much time with those fools. Fine, they can go with us, but only because I'd rather have that Yoren where I can see him. Don't say *anything* to anyone, especially the monks. I still have to work some things out." Then she softened. "Why don't you go back and sit with Asha? I think she likes you."

Even in the ruddy torchlight, she could see him flush.

"But this isn't the time for dallying," she warned. "Our job is to get Pa back and kill trolls. Keep your head about you — both of you."

Chapter Fourteen

Into the Caves

The entrance to the caves lay at the base of the mountains Grim-mun-Kan had called The Guardians. A near-vertical cliff loomed high over the tunnel opening, a blank granite wall whose upper reaches were lost in cloud. Beside the cave mouth, a spring bubbled from the rock. A village had grown up near the spring, thrived, and died. Just stone building foundations and cracked, empty cisterns remained.

"What is this place? It looks like there's good water here. How come nobody lives here?"

"None come here now," Gheen said. "In my father's father's day, some did. But bad spirits lived here long before the gray demon called our people to the caves."

"Hmph," Cullen said. "There are no spirits, no demons. Azuk is a creature, like a fox or a bird, and can be killed."

"Fox or bird doesn't call trolls into cave to die," Gheen said, lowering his burden to the ground. He carried torches and provisions for Cullen's journey under the mountain.

"Well, Gheen, you have my thanks for coming this far. I won't ask you to go into the tunnels. I never thought I'd say this to a troll, but I appreciate you being here."

"Cullen-thing is smart. Will find trolls and defeat demon."

Cullen laughed. "I don't have to kill it. I just have to find the trolls. Still, you have more confidence in my abilities than I. Do a favor for me, though."

"Gheen will do what he can."

"Call me Cullen."

"But you are *pakh-hu*. It is how —"

"It's how trolls refer to their human slaves," Cullen said. "I'm not a slave. I'm helping your clan for a price."

Gheen made a rumbling, considering sound, and then nodded. "Very well... Cullen."

"What words did the shaman teach you?"

Gheen fidgeted with the hilt of his sword. After a moment, he looked back at Cullen. "Holy One says Gheen's mother came from line of shamans. Her mother's mother was shaman long ago."

"But what did he teach you?"

"Words of protection and joining. Holy One said I would know to use them at proper time. Do not ask further."

Cullen watched the troll's face, but Gheen would not meet his eyes. After a moment, he walked away, leaving the troll to whatever was troubling him.

He looked back down the trail leading to the troll camp. Wogan promised to join him and to bring other humans. In the distance, he recognized the slave walking beside a tall figure, who might have been Aydin, the shaman's slave.

That's not a lot of help to get past a demon creature.

Cullen nodded toward the approaching humans. "They are allowed to walk free?"

Gheen gave a quizzical look. "Of course. The Three Valleys are their home."

Cullen was about to reply that their homes were far away across the river, but it dawned on him that perhaps Gheen was right. Wogan and at least a handful of others must live in relative comfort. Yet they had forsaken their real homes among their own kind. He wondered if those who tilled the fields were as satisfied with their lot.

When the pair arrived, Cullen saw they had no gear but a small bundle each.

"We cannot go beyond the upper reaches of the tunnel," Wogan said, his eyes toward the ground.

Cullen spat. "Is that because your masters said so or because you're afraid?"

Neither of the slaves replied at first, but then Wogan spoke. He handed his bundle to Cullen. "I put up some dried fruit and meat for you and some medicinal herbs and ointments."

He took the other package from Aydin and unwrapped it. "The Holy One sends this to aid your journey."

From the package, he took a gray stone carved with runes. The central character was vurad.

Cullen shook his head. "This is it? The Three Valleys Clan kidnaps me and asks me to find its lost trolls and kill a monster. To do this, I'm given berries and a rock? Go back to your master. I'll do this by myself."

"We'll go back if you wish it. But the stone is for Gheen, not for you."

Gheen raised an eyebrow. "Holy One sends to me?" He took the stone from Wogan.

Aydin bowed his head to the troll and spoke in a voice that seemed unused to human speech. "It is *kor-oba,* an affinity charm. It will aid in drawing the force of vurad to you. Holy One bound other charms to it as well. It will not relieve the terror of Azuk in itself, but it may offer protections at need."

"Then Gheen must go into tunnels," the troll said. He picked up the bundle of torches and moved to stand beside the scout. Peering into the darkness of the cave mouth, he said, "Trolls who go into tunnels will die, but Gheen must go with Cullen."

"You don't have to do this," Cullen said.

"Gheen will do this. Holy One has given protection, and human should not go alone."

The scout reached up and patted the big troll's shoulder. "You'd have made a good human, Gheen. I hoped you'd go with me."

They lit a torch, drew their weapons, and left the others at the tunnel mouth without another word. The passage led straight into the heart of the mountain, descending gently. After a few minutes, Gheen turned and looked back toward the entrance. Beyond the circle of torchlight lay darkness.

"Come on," Cullen said. "We're wasting time."

Gheen paused and sheathed his blade. As Cullen watched, the troll tapped his forehead, then stooped and tapped the floor.

"What are you doing, troll? We don't have time for this."

Gheen drew his blade again and moved to follow. "It is… custom of my family," he said, his voice a low rumble in the darkness. "In dark place or before battle, we ask protection of the First Ones."

"It's superstition, Gheen," Cullen said, moving down the tunnel. "It won't help you here."

"Cullen doesn't know." The troll considered for a moment, then looked at the human. "Why does Cullen swear by Ounwe's arse or Ounwe's Third Hell if he doesn't believe in gods or demons?"

"That's a good question. It's just something we say. Some humans believe in such things," Cullen said, "but I never saw the use. Life's hard enough without worrying about invisible gods."

The troll grunted and said again, "Cullen doesn't know."

***

"Gheen, when we were across the river, Grimmun told me a little about how the demon calls to trolls. What do you know about it?"

The troll visibly shuddered at the question. "Is in dreams that he comes. Gheen not know what he says to those he calls, but always they go mad. Then, they cannot be stopped. Nothing in their minds but to go into the tunnels." He looked in fear at the smooth walls. "These tunnels."

"But Dannick came here with two trolls," Cullen said. "Grimmun told me they weren't affected for some time."

Gheen nodded. "Burush and Ghan. Ghan was my, what is word? Cousin? He was son of my father's brother. Both were younger than Gheen."

Cullen paused at a narrow cross passage. He looked down the side tunnel, sniffed at the air, and moved on. "So Azuk exerts some kind of power over the older trolls he calls, but younger trolls are resistant to it." He looked up at his companion, who still trembled. "At least for a while. Don't worry about these tunnels, Gheen. We'll probably be fine until we get lower down."

At that, Gheen gave a weak smile. "Problem is not tunnel but demon that lies below. Are many caves and tunnels in these mountains. I explored them when I was youngling."

Cullen chuckled. "You can have them. Humans live on the plains and near the forest, where we're meant to live. I'm not used to hiking under — or over — mountains."

***

They moved rapidly down a smooth, broad tunnel made of the same finished stone as in the Tunnel of Sukkuz. Occasional side passages intersected the main downward tunnel. At each, Cullen handed Gheen his torch and listened. He heard silence, the occasional drip of water into some hidden pool, and the skittering of bats. Then he cast for troll scent; each time, the scent led him forward and downward. Most of the cross passages in the upper reaches of the tunnel offered moving air; yet, as they descended, he found only still, dead air and silence.

And were the walls narrowing? *Gah, get me out of here,* he thought. Outside, the skies had been blue and bright. The tunnels were things of darkness. How could anyone come here of their own will?

Images of Haywold and his children came to mind as he moved. He hoped Isabo and Amon were still at home, tending to their small flock of sheep and meager fields.

"Gheen, who made these tunnels, if not trolls? No human did this."

The hulking figure shrugged. "Was very long ago. Much longer ago than the time of my grandmother's grandmother. None living, except Holy One, maybe, knows of this time."

Cullen shook his head. "I'm no scholar, but there are monks — our Holy Ones — who keep records of ancient times. In my village, there are a few books and scrolls, but the monks in the far south are said to keep hundreds of them, maybe thousands."

"Gheen does not know the word 'thousands.'"

Cullen stopped to examine a pit in the floor of the tunnel. No sound or air came from below. "Thousand means a great many. Look, this is not a place for trolls or humans anymore, if it ever was. Let's do what we need to do and get out."

The troll grunted assent.

Cullen held the torch low. A clutter of trollish footprints skirted the opening and continued along the tunnel. "You don't need a scout to follow these marks," he said. "Where is the maze of passages Grimmun-Kan spoke of?"

"Further," Gheen said. "First come to wide chamber. Is where Dannick-thing was found."

After several hours, the tunnel walls fell away, and Cullen found himself in a large chamber. His torchlight flickered on damp walls.

"This is where they found her?" Cullen asked.

The troll nodded. He pointed to the far side of the cavernous area, where two tunnels continued downward. "Just there," Gheen said.

They walked across the chamber. The floor was finished stone worn by years of use, but the exiting tunnels were roughly made and more recent. Cullen again lowered his torch to examine the troll tracks leading into both tunnels.

Cullen stood in each doorway and cast for a scent. Each way held moving air, and the scent of trolls.

"If these are the tracks of the lost trolls, both ways likely lead to the same place. Flip a coin?"

"What is coin?" Gheen asked.

"Never mind, follow me."

Cullen checked to see which way held the most tracks and entered that tunnel.

Once they left the chamber, the passages began to twist and wind. The smooth, dressed-stone walls were gone in favor of roughly hewn passages. More frequent side tunnels and gaping holes in the floor appeared. Cullen's sense of unease grew. The dark tunnels and holes were big enough for a troll, but were no place for a sensible human.

They weaved their way forward, scenting at each tunnel and hole. Twice, they followed the scent down into the holes in the floor. For hours, they journeyed downward, lighting new torches as old ones flickered and died.

After a time, a new sound crept into Cullen's hearing. He struggled to identify it but found that Gheen's scent also changed, growing more bitter and musky. The sound was the troll's ragged breathing. Gheen was terrified.

"How are you coming along, Gheen? Do you need to rest?"

"No, no. Gheen is... fine."

"Let's sit and rest," Cullen said. "I could use some of Wogan's magic berries."

He sat and propped the torch against the wall. The troll slumped down beside him. In the flickering light, Gheen's eyes were wide and staring. Cullen recalled Grimmun-Kan's words at the shaman's temple house: the trolls with Dannick, Burush and Ghan, went mad and slew each other.

This place is nothing but death.

No trolls had come into these tunnels since, except those called by Azuk. Cullen took a drink from his water skin and held it out to Gheen.

"Drink. You'll feel better. Sorry, I don't have any of your nasty wine."

The troll didn't speak and didn't take the skin.

"Gheen."

Gheen's breath grew quick and shallow. His eyes darted left and right. With a heavy grunt, he staggered to his feet and turned back in the direction they'd come.

"Must go. Gheen cannot stay here."

Cullen leaped to his feet. "Gheen, blast you! What are you doing? Stop!"

The troll didn't answer but lurched back up the tunnel.

Cullen saw that the troll had drawn a long knife and was waving it before him. "Ounwe's teeth!" he swore and ran after Gheen, leaving his pack on the ground.

"There's no demon here," he shouted. "Gheen, stop, damn you!"

But the troll ran blindly forward, brandishing the blade. Cullen hurried after him, back up the tunnel.

It couldn't end like this, chased out like scared children.

After a few hundred yards, Gheen slowed, then stopped. He leaned heavily against the wall.

Cullen approached warily — the troll still carried the vicious blade in his clawed hand.

"Speak to me, Gheen. Are you okay?"

The troll panted, but his eyes no longer darted from side to side in the guttering torchlight.

"Is it the demon?" Cullen asked.

After a moment, Gheen nodded. "Yes. But is not summoning. Maybe Gheen is not old or wise enough troll for him to call. We draw near to where demon is. Gheen feels tongues of fear — like flame, only not — reaching out from below."

Cullen handed him the waterskin. "Drink. You'll feel better."

Gheen took it and drank, sloshing a good bit of it on himself.

"We'll have to get more water once we find the river," Cullen said. He looked into the troll's face, trying to gauge whether the hulking creature was up for it. "The further we go, the closer we get to the demon."

Gheen grunted and nodded, handing back the now-diminished water skin. After a moment of silence, he said, "Gheen go in other caves plenty of times and not feel fear."

"We left the rest of our stuff below when you bolted," Cullen said. "If we go on, that fear will return. Can you handle it?"

Gheen shrugged, then looked at the blade in his hand. "Gheen once fought trolls from Stone Breakers clan. He even fought wolves in high mountains. Also fought *pakh-hu* at Kishik two winters past." He looked sheepishly at Cullen at the mention of a battle with humans. "Always, I had sword or knife or bare hands. Not know how to fight against fear."

Cullen gave a dry chuckle. "In that, Gheen, you're no different than a human. Fear is the worst enemy. The two trolls with Dannick —"

"Ghan and Burush."

"How many times did they come here with her?"

"Two times, or three."

"And they didn't go mad with fear until the last time."

Gheen nodded.

"Then you can do this too."

The troll returned his blade to its sheath. "And I promised Cullen before that I would go with him, so I will. Tongues of fear come and go like ripples in pond. Is less now."

"Good, let's go back to where we were, eat something, and then go on," Cullen said.

Gheen gave an awkward nod.

***

After a short rest and a meal, Cullen and Gheen gathered their gear.

"Torches won't last," Gheen said, watching the human reach for another from their dwindling supply. "Gheen can lead in the darkness."

Cullen turned to gape at the troll in amazement. "You see in the dark?"

"Not see," the troll said in his deep rumble. He tapped an ear. "Gheen hears echoes. Can tell where walls of tunnels are and holes."

"While I stumble behind in the dark," Cullen muttered.

"Not have to. Tie cord to Gheen's belt. I stay in middle of tunnel. Tell human where side tunnels are, and holes. Then Cullen can sniff right path."

Cullen looked at the remaining stock of torches. There were enough for two or three more hours. They'd already traveled for six hours, and Grimmun said it was a half-day march to the cavern of the dark river.

"Why in —? Why in Ounwe's Third Hell didn't you tell me you didn't need torches?"

Gheen shrugged. His tusks and turned-up snout danced in the guttering torchlight. "Cullen not ask," he said.

***

Cullen guessed they'd been in the tunnels for most of the day. Either Dannick was a better scout than he or she'd taken the other, shorter passage. Still, the tunnels must converge at some point, else why two sets of tracks?

They continued in silence, with Gheen moving forward and Cullen tagging behind like a dog on a leash. They stopped whenever the tunnel forked or other openings appeared in the floor or ceiling. They couldn't travel as fast, but by all reckoning, they should be nearing their destination. The acrid scent Cullen associated with the troll's fear rose and fell. When it peaked, he questioned the troll about life in the mountains, his family, Grimmun, and, in particular, the shaman. Soon, his companion's fear subsided.

He told rambling stories of life in the troll camp, hunts he'd been on —
sometimes for food, sometimes for human slaves — and stories he heard as a
young troll. Sometimes, they made no sense, and Cullen wondered if he was
making them up as he went along. But if it kept the big creature from panicking,
so much the better.

"You said Azuk comes to the old trolls in their dreams. I don't understand
that. I've had powerful dreams in my time," Cullen said, "but I don't put much
stock in them."

"Gheen dreams, too. All things do, maybe. But what Azuk sends, how he
summons trolls, is not same as regular dreams."

"And why only older, wiser trolls, I wonder?" Cullen said. It dawned on him
that the demon — blast, now he believed in demons? — exuded some power
that caused the toughest trolls to cower in fear. It also communicated with some
in their sleep. Just what was this creature?

"Gheen, why didn't you join the others who went east across the mountains?"

Gheen considered. "This our home. Why not humans move when trolls
raid?"

"Fair enough."

Cullen bumped along behind the troll, knocking into him when Gheen
stopped short. He didn't necessarily fear dark places, but it grated on him to
be led about by a troll, especially one who might go mad when the terror of the
demon struck him.

In time, the sound of moving water joined the noise of their scrabbling and
Gheen's labored breathing. "I think we're close to Dannick's dark river, Gheen."

As they marched, Cullen noticed faint points of yellowish luminescence. He
stopped to examine them and found it was mold growing in the increasingly
damp air. The mold gave off a sweet scent that seemed out of place this far
underground.

"Side tunnel is ahead on right," Gheen said.

Cullen felt his way forward, tethered to the troll and one hand on the right wall. The faint troll scent grew stronger at the junction of the two tunnels.

"I wonder if I dare light another torch," he said. "This mold on the walls isn't enough for me to see the tracks on the tunnel floor. This is probably where the two tunnels from above converge."

"Is not far to cavern from here, I think," Gheen said. "Echoes change ahead."

They walked forward, and sure enough, swirling air patterns brought scents different from those in the tunnel. Even in the dark, Cullen knew they were nearing a large open space. The faint sound of water grew louder still. He felt his heart pounding more strongly. He'd been in a shallow cave in the Chalk Cliffs many years before, but this was something on another scale entirely.

"We're here, I think," he said when the wall on his right hand ended. "Wherever here is. I'm going to light a torch, Gheen. I need to see which direction the tracks go."

He slipped his rucksack from his back and pulled an unlit torch from the bundle. As he fumbled for flint and steel to light it, he looked around in the darkness. To his surprise, he saw that the darkness wasn't complete. Large patches of the yellow mold clung to the floor and walls, casting a faint, steady light.

Cullen sensed the cavern's vast size. A hundred yards or more to the left, he just made out a river pouring in a noisy cataract from somewhere above. It flowed in a broad channel and crossed the far side of the cavern, disappearing into misty gloom. To the right lay a faint jumble of boulders extending into darkness.

At last, he found the flint and steel and struck a light on the oil-soaked rag of the torch. As it flared to life, both human and troll shielded their eyes from the sudden brightness.

When his eyes adjusted, Cullen held the torch near the ground of the tunnel entrance.

"Look," he said, pointing. Troll tracks led to the left, toward the dark river. "But see? Another set goes the other direction, toward that pile of rubble. Those are smaller. I'd wager those are Dannick's tracks."

Cullen felt in his pocket for the paper with the other scout's symbols. He didn't need to see it, but took comfort knowing that she'd been here before and had found something.

"Gheen, I didn't tell the shaman and Grimmun-Kan everything I learned. Dannick found something here. She left me a message."

"What message say?" Gheen asked.

"Up at the river. If this is the river she meant, we need to look or go upward from here."

But what had she found? The lost trolls? Azuk the demon? He held the torch aloft. The cavern receded upward into darkness. Twisted shapes of stone glittered in the torchlight, descending from the unseen ceiling.

"Gheen, can you see anything up there with your dark vision, or however it is you see in the dark?"

The troll was silent.

"Gheen! What's up that way?"

The troll turned, his eyes blank. After a moment, he shook his head and gave a low, quavering "Holoo." The sound echoed and reverberated in the empty space until the noise of the water swallowed it.

Gheen hesitated for a moment, and then pointed, "Floor of cavern rises that way toward ceiling. Maybe a path leads up for a ways, but is buried by rubble."

Cullen turned back to the tracks on the floor. They led in the opposite direction. "We need to find the trolls first," he said. "Let's follow the tracks. We'll come back later and explore that upper path." He looked at the troll. "How do you feel, Gheen?"

The tall creature waved a shaking arm toward the river, toward the path of the trolls. His breath was becoming quick and ragged again. "Is safe here, but great, evil blackness is that way. Demon thing is near. But I will go that way if Cullen wills it."

Cullen cursed and spat. Toward great, evil blackness or Dannick's vague clue? "Listen, Gheen. The troll trail is down toward the river. I don't know if any are alive or not. I'd wager not. Dannick left me a clue for a reason, so if you're afraid of the demon in that direction, we can follow the upward path for now. Then, if there's nothing there, we come back and find Azuk." He ran a weary hand through clammy hair. "If you're not up to facing him, wait by the tunnel we came in, and I'll figure something out."

Gheen put a large, clawed hand on Cullen's shoulder. "Gheen will go where Cullen goes." He reached into his pocket and drew out the shaman's stone. "Besides, Aydin-thing said Holy One put charm on stone to help find vurad. Only with vurad sign can Cullen defeat demon. Holy One said so."

"Gheen, I wondered when you would get to whatever hocus-pocus the shaman gave you. No one knows what this symbol is or what it does."

"Is enough that Holy One says so. Use faith, Cullen."

Cullen shook his head. "Faith. We're doomed."

"Not doomed. Cullen here for reason; Gheen here for reason."

"I hope your faith doesn't get us and your whole clan killed, Gheen."

Gheen opened his palm and placed the stone in the center. Nothing happened.

"Do you feel anything?"

"Nothing," Gheen said in a deep rumble.

Cullen snorted. "So much for magic trinkets. Let's find the path up. You can throw the rock if anything comes at us."

"Is sacred stone, Cullen. If Holy One said it will help, it will help."

"Fine."

Cullen checked his gear, took a drink of water, and followed as Gheen plodded toward the dark rubble pile. "Ounwe's arse," he muttered.

Gheen's dark vision didn't fail them. The floor of the cavern rose to their right. For a time, a path wound among the boulders, and by the wavering torch, Cullen occasionally found Dannick's tracks. Her footprints were the only human-sized prints he'd seen in the tunnels. It had to be her.

Soon, the path faded as they climbed toward a larger cluster of boulders and fallen rock. At some point in the far past, the ceiling and cavern wall had collapsed, burying any pathway under tons of rock. Cullen held the torch high, looking for signs of Dannick's passage or a way through the boulders.

Gheen uttered low, holooing noises, sounding for a passage. At last, he called to Cullen from atop a large, flat rock. "Climb to here. Is easier way after the boulders."

Cullen made his way upward to where the troll stood. Carrying the torch made clambering over the shifting rocks difficult, but at last, he stood next to Gheen, surveying the cavern. The torch brought light to the area where they stood, but couldn't hope to illuminate the echoing depths of the larger cavern. Nearby, the light showed the strange, eerie shapes of stalactites and vast curtains of stone.

Gheen pointed downward to where the path wove around rock formations. The way led toward twin pillars at the very edge of the torchlight. Even at this distance, it was clear that the pillars were too symmetrical and evenly surfaced to be natural formations.

Cullen reached up to thump the troll's shoulder. "That's where Dannick went, I'll bet. Let's go see what she found."

They climbed down through teetering boulders and regained the path. The torch again showed Dannick's clear prints. Cullen led the way to the pillars, then stood open-mouthed at what he found.

The pillars guarded an arched doorway. Through it, illuminated by great patches of the luminescent yellow mold on every surface, lay an underground city stretching far into the distance.

Cullen looked up at the great pillars. Circling each at eye level was a carved scroll. The scrolls showed a single repeated figure: the ancient glyph called *vurad*, slightly altered from the symbol used by the shaman but recognizable.

Chapter Fifteen

Pineholm

The next morning, Isabo met Perban and Tanner in the common room. The two were midway through a heaping platter of bacon, eggs, potatoes, and brown bread. After more than a week on the march, fresh food was a blessing.

Perban applied himself to slathering butter on a thick slice of bread. Even after a night's good sleep, he looked as weary as Isabo felt. Tanner wasn't much better.

Isabo glanced around. Many of her fighters sat clustered nearby, engaged in the same task. She reached for the bread, pulled off a chunk, sniffed at it, and smiled. "I see you two wasted no time in gorging yourselves."

"Do you blame us, Chief?" Will asked. "I may never leave."

"We need to talk about that," she replied, and reached for a pitcher of brown ale.

A serving girl hurried over with more plates and a sizzling pan of chops.

When she was done and moved away, Perban gave her a worried look. "Yeah, we should talk."

"You go first," she said, filling her plate. "What's up?"

Perban cast an eye on Kurtis Hupp and a handful of others at a nearby table. "I'll be plain, Iza. There are some of our folks who want to go home and be paid for what they've done. They've killed more than a dozen trolls. The bounty on that would set anyone up for a year."

"That's true enough," she said. "I told Stura Bracken before we left that my father will pay his part of the troll bounty. The council will have to come up with the rest because we've killed a lot more trolls than anyone expected. And the mayor here will pay his share. He promised me that. Don't worry, everyone will get paid." She slid fried eggs and bacon onto her plate. "But the job isn't over, Will."

"There's more," Tanner said, leaning back on his chair. "Your father's still out there. You and Tallard — Ounwe rest him — were supposed to be the best trackers around. Some say we should have been looking for him the whole time and not haring off after random bands of trolls."

Isabo snarled, suddenly furious. "Random bands of — I'm the chief of this army. You both agreed to that. I will decide what we're doing, not anyone else. You tell those sons of filth that —"

Perban raised placating hands. "Peace, Isabo. We're on your side. Look, you're in charge. We get that. And I'm not saying they won't follow you. You've led us this far, and we've done well, but you need to talk to them. Some may need convincing."

Tanner nodded in agreement. "I've heard the same from Second Sword. Like Will says, there's grumbling. Most of it's nothing to worry about, but people want to know what's going on. They're over the moon about killing so many trolls, but they're tired. And, by the way, Kurtis Hupp is still mad because you killed the troll you interrogated the other night. He said you promised to let him do it."

"That's his problem. Will he still fight when it comes to it?" she asked.

"Yeah, he'll fight, all right. More than ever. But he still wants vengeance for Zollar. And he's kept trophies: he has a collection of trolls' ears on a string."

"And there's something else," Perban said. "You probably figured it out, but Wulf wants to take Tom home. You saw the man. Those trolls starved and beat him half to death. He's not up to a campaign against these things. Dorse is in bad shape, too. He needs to heal up before going out again."

"That's my fault," Tanner said. "I should have made him stay out of the fight."

Isabo sighed heavily and brushed wisps of hair out of her eyes. "Fine. Tom, Wulf, and Dorse can stay here for now to heal up. Dorse is a good swordsman, and I don't want to lose him, but he's no good to us in a fight. As for the rest of them, I'll talk to them. Look, we're learning as we go. There hasn't been a real army for who knows how long. And by the way, we're not on our own anymore. The mayor agreed to give us more fighters."

Will raised an eyebrow. "We're getting a Third Sword?"

"And maybe a fourth," she said with just a trace of a smile. "We'll know today."

Perban paused, reaching for the eggs, and gave her a worried look. "What does that mean? Are we going back out looking for more trolls? When does it end, Isabo?"

She crumbled a bit of bread in her fingers and said casually, "We're going after my father. We're going to follow the blasted trolls into the mountains and bring him out."

Perban and Tanner stared, their mouths hanging open.

"When were you going to tell us?" Will asked.

Isabo popped the bread in her mouth and reached for the bacon. "Now, I guess. Can you pass me the salt? You guys have done great. More than great. But, like I said, the fight isn't over. Finish eating, but I want everybody in the courtyard out front of the inn in an hour. They don't need to pack their gear yet. It might take another day to gather the extra fighters and supplies. Now close your mouths before your breakfast falls out."

***

What remained of First and Second Sword gathered in the inn's spacious rear courtyard. Tanner and Perban stood with their people. Following a night of revelry and drinking, their disheveled state was pretty well what Isabo expected — shabby. Kurtis Hupp, Eber Crumble, and Barty Naggs all sported bruises or black eyes that hadn't come from the battle with trolls. Isabo supposed that a few of the townspeople might look the same, or worse. To one side, Amon stood beside Asha Maris.

A small knot of locals stood near the door, including the mayor and a woman of about Isabo's own age — presumably his daughter.

Isabo caught Perban's eye and nodded slightly toward the newcomers. Will winked understanding and moved over to ask them to step inside.

"Hear me now," she said when they were alone. "You all did a fine job with the trolls yesterday. Everybody did their part. Together, we killed nine more stinking trolls in one fight. Be proud of that."

There were a few claps and shouts of agreement. From the back row, Filip Homah called out, "And they was big fecking trolls at that. We showed them what's what — again."

"Aye, they were big and we killed them all," she continued. "They've taken our blood and killed our kind for years. Now, we're paying them back. I aim to keep on killing trolls as long as I can hold a sword in my hand. Now, some of you are content with what we've done, maybe thinking it's time to go back to your homes and families. You're worrying about how you're going to spend the bounty on these trolls. Be sure that the bounties will be paid. You have my word on that. But I won't be satisfied until we've wiped out every one of those beasts. There's more of them out here, and your homes aren't safe until they're dead."

Crumble raised his hand. "I'm one of them that wants to get back to my family. No one here can call me shy, but I did what I came to do. You asked us to kill them things and we did. And how's your pa going to pay the bounty if you haven't even found him yet? These trolls that attacked Pineholm aren't the ones that took him."

Isabo nodded. "Most of you know my father, Gabril Cullen." There were nods and a few grumbles. "I talked to the mayor last night. Last week, his people saw another band of trolls heading toward the canyon. There were two human captives with them. One of them was my father. We're going after him."

"What do you mean?" Hupp said with a snarl. "Where did they take him? North?"

She glanced at the mountains looming over the trees to eastward. "No. We're going into the mountains. I aim to take the fight to them, but I don't want anyone who's had enough or doesn't want to fight. If you want to go home, go home. You'll be paid when you return. But every one of us has proved themselves in battle with these monsters. We know how to kill them. That's why I need you all to stay." Looking sharply at Crumble, she said, "Not a one of you is shy. We've come this far; I'm asking you to take the next step and finish this fight — or at least this part of the fight."

"What about getting more fighters?" Messick asked. "We already lost Zollar and Tallard. And Shamus Dorse can't fight much. Is he going with us?"

"Dorse will stay here and rest up till we return. Tom Wheatley will, too. But when Tom regains his strength, Wulf will take him home." She gave what she hoped was a confident smile. "As for more fighters, the mayor here has promised to give us as many as he can. I asked him for a dozen. When we have those and have replenished our supplies, we'll cross the river. I want to do that as soon as tomorrow, so spend today going over your gear. If you need blades sharpened or are missing anything, let Will or Hiram know. They'll get what we need from the locals. Otherwise, stay close to the inn."

"Hiram," Isabo said when they had finished, "keep an eye on things. I want to take Will to meet the mayor."

"Sure," he said.

She nodded to Perban, and they went back into the common room.

***

190

"Isabo, my dear," the mayor said, standing to greet her. "This is my daughter, Mayra. She was the one who picked up the trolls' trail north of here. She also saw your father."

The girl was lean and willowy, with sun-tinged auburn hair tied in a neat bun. Her tanned features showed that she spent a lot of time outdoors. At her side, she wore a long dagger in a plain leather sheath.

"I can't say that it was him," Mayra said, cutting in on her father. "I only saw them from a distance."

Isabo nodded and introduced Perban as her second. "We have two elements, First and Second Sword. Will leads First Sword. Ideally, we'd have six or seven fighters in each, with a good mix of archers and swordsmen. We've lost a few men, which is why we're eager to see your people."

Mayra gave him an appraising glance and a quick smile.

Faulken motioned for them to sit. "I've put out the word for volunteers to gather here at noon."

Isabo looked back at Mayra. "How many trolls were in the group?"

"I counted eight, but there may have been more. There were two human captives with them, but I only saw them at a distance. One looked to be older. Maybe sixty? He wore an iron collar. I guess that would make him a slave. The other was a plainsman, dressed like you are."

Isabo's heart raced. It had to be him.

"When they passed, I followed as closely as I dared. The trolls were big, ugly beasts, like the ones you killed here yesterday. But I lost them near the canyon. I started to feel uneasy, like something dark and evil was watching me. It got worse as I got closer. That part of the canyon has always been spooky."

"Can you take me there?" Isabo asked.

Mayra nodded. "It's only an hour or so north of here."

"Good. Will, you see to the new troops when they get here. You and Hiram check their skills as best you can. Run them through some drills." She gave the mayor a polite smile. "Don't take anyone who can't handle a weapon. And I told the mayor here that at least one of them needs to have some leadership skills. You know what we need. And they have to carry at least a week's provisions. We don't know how much game is in the mountains."

"Right, Chief," he said with a nod.

"I've already seen to your stores," the elder Faulken said. "And I know who the leaders will be."

Mayra groaned at that.

"Hush, girl," her father said.

She rolled her eyes. "I'm twenty-two, Father. Don't call me 'girl.'"

***

From Pineholm, Mayra led Isabo and Amon back onto the plains along the smoothly cobbled road. The way curved sharply westward, following the edge of the forest, but the girl led them east to the canyon. A few small cabins surrounded by low stone walls huddled near the edge. It wasn't even a day after the troll raid, but thin columns of smoke rose from their chimneys. All looked peaceful, though one looked to have been burnt and rebuilt at some point.

"My father always tries to have scouts out to give warning. I take my rotation doing that. When the monsters are spotted, everyone outside the walls comes inside."

"Can we look down into the canyon?" Amon asked, giggly at the prospect.

Mayra smiled and led the flatlanders north, past the last of the cabins, and then to a point where they could peer cautiously over the edge.

From below came a deep roaring that Isabo felt in her chest.

"Whoa..." Amon said with a look of wonder. He pointed to the boulder-strewn river below. "That's incredible. How far down to the water?"

"A hundred or more feet in this area," Mayra said with a smile. "Are you scared?"

He shook his head, picked up a rock, and threw it into the gorge. It spun end over end before disappearing in the churning foam, just missing a large tree branch dragged along in the fierce current.

"The canyon gets deeper the farther north you go," the girl continued. "They say at Tulum it's nearly half a mile down. To the south, toward Harrun, it drops away to almost nothing. This part here they call the Dark Canyon."

Isabo could see why. If the sun weren't directly overhead, the narrow walls would be cast in shadow. "We aren't here to see the sights," she groused, and she pointed across the canyon. The other side was covered with a dense pine forest. Occasional openings in the trees revealed steep clefts leading up toward the granite heights. "So if the trolls crossed the river, they went up there."

Mayra nodded.

"So how do they get from here to there?" Amon asked.

"No one knows. A traveler said they hold the bridge at Tulum," Mayra said, looking northward. "But that's thirty leagues away."

Amon craned his head over the edge. "Are there ways to get down to the river?"

She looked doubtful. "I suppose you could lower yourself, but you'd need an awful long rope. There are a handful of spots where it isn't so steep, but people have died trying it."

"Take us where you saw the trolls," Isabo said. "They obviously know a way."

"It's a couple hours' hike to the north."

"Then let's go," she said with a touch of impatience.

The dirt path they followed sometimes revealed dressed stones, as if there had once been a road. Mayra maintained a steady flow of conversation, which varied from the wonders of the local area to the depredations of the trolls, to the day-to-day goings-on of the people of Pineholm.

Amon, for his part, kept up the conversation, but sometimes stumbled because he was gazing at Mayra or at the strange beauty of the canyon and the looming mountains. More often, it was the girl.

Isabo kept her thoughts to herself. She thought over yesterday's battle and how well her army had done against the trolls, and of Alastor Faulken's willingness to give support. That would help a lot. Even the ominous voice in her thoughts was silent for the moment. She wondered at that. It seemed to ebb and flow, increasing with proximity to the trolls or to battle. In the fight before the gates, it had been insistent, goading her to drive her people forward to contact with the trolls, reveling in the bloody carnage.

There's nothing creepy about that, she muttered to herself. *If it drives me to kill trolls, what's wrong with that?*

And at least the monks had given her some peace.

Mayra prattled away, telling of her father's argument with a family that recently decided to flee south.

Isabo perked up as a thought occurred to her. "You didn't seem thrilled when your father told me he'd make sure your fighters have good leaders."

The girl shook her head, her expression one of distaste. "No. That would be Lim Voss or Marko Gaskun, or both of them. They're arrogant bullies. They're fairly good hunters, but they think a lot more of themselves than they should. I saw Marko Gaskun put an arrow through a squirrel in a tree from forty yards at twilight. Voss is almost as good, but he's better with a sword. Just ask him; he'll tell you."

Isabo gave a half smile. "I don't care if they have an attitude as long as they can fight. Have either of them gone up against trolls?"

"Gaskun did two years ago. Well… maybe. The things came in the night and torched one of the homes along the canyon. The owner was taken, a farmer named Oaken. The next day, Gaskun and a group of men went after them. They never caught the trolls, and there were questions about how it was handled. My father didn't want me to talk about it, but I think they gave up the chase too soon."

They continued, and the land gradually rose. After some time, the girl seemed to grow more cautious and peered over her shoulder occasionally.

Isabo sniffed the air for trolls but only caught the faintest hint. "What is it? You look nervous."

Mayra angled westward onto the plains. "We're getting close to where I saw them, but this is where the canyon gets creepy. I can't get close to the edge right there. It gives me the horrors."

Isabo frowned and scanned the area. "But we walked along it the whole way here, and it didn't bother you."

She shrugged. "I can't explain it. I live beside the canyon south of Pineholm, and it's never been a problem. There's just something about this spot. People don't come this way very often. That's probably why."

"I don't feel anything. Where are the tracks?" Isabo asked.

The girl pointed a little further ahead. "It's just up here. I was near that stand of pines in the distance when I saw them. I let them pass and tried to follow, but they went around this rise and disappeared. I couldn't see where they went."

Mayra found and pointed out a patch of exposed soil. "Here," she said. It looked as if someone had brushed it smooth, or at least tried to hide the tracks.

"Hmm. Trolls don't do that," Isabo said.

Amon smiled. "These did."

Isabo shook her head. It didn't make sense. She'd been on several hunts with her father, and the creatures had never shown an inclination to disguise their passage. They typically bulled straight through, leaving boot prints, crushed grass, and the litter of their camps. If these had somehow learned to employ stealth, that might explain why she and Tallard had missed their passage for so long.

Then she pointed west. "Back that way, it's more obvious. I found places where the grass was disturbed, and one place with footprints. That's where I found that grass weave thing I gave to my father. Most of the time, though, where there were troll tracks, they'd mostly been rubbed out."

"Can you show me the place you found it?"

She led them a few hundred yards back along the trail. "It was here, by this rock."

Isabo studied the area and what was left of the footprints, which wasn't much. There were a few heavy impressions where she guessed a troll had passed, but at least the marks hadn't been purposely obscured. She pulled back the grass that overhung the trail — and saw a single, clear print the size of her father's boot.

She turned to her brother. "What do you smell?"

Amon knelt and leaned close to the dirt. "The scent is really faint. There was more than one, but that's about all I can tell."

Isabo nodded. "That's what I thought as well. It's been at least a week." She looked to Mayra. "Did it rain here over the last week?"

She shook her head, wide-eyed. "A little. There were a few small showers, but they didn't last. You guys have the scent-gift? That's so cool. There was another scout through here about six months ago — Tilda Dannick. She had it, too, I think. Do you know her?"

"No," Isabo said. "Being able to smell the stupid creatures is no help if the trail is cold. It looks like this group may have been trying to cover their tracks. I've never seen them do that before."

She followed the trail in the direction of the canyon with Amon close behind. Mayra stayed, apparently not wanting to get any closer to the spot.

At the edge, just as the girl had said, the tracks vanished. The ground was harder, showing exposed brick or stone in places. Isabo sniffed at what soil there was and muttered a low curse. "There's nothing here. And this close to the edge, the damp wind off the canyon hides any scent." She peered southward along the edge. "Amon, walk that way a hundred yards or so and see if you can detect anything or see any tracks. I'll do the same to the south. And look to see if there's a way down."

A short time later, they came together again. "Anything?" she asked.

Amon smiled. "I couldn't smell any, but there were tracks — heavy boot tracks like they wear. They went seventy or eighty yards, then turned around. They weren't as careful to brush away their trail." He looked over the edge for a moment. "And this place doesn't look like a completely horrible spot for them to climb down. It would be dangerous as anything without a rope, though."

Isabo smiled. At last, they were getting somewhere. "It was the same to the south, with two sets of tracks going down and back. It's like they were hunting for a spot, but they came back here."

Her brother suddenly stared across to the far side, where the rocky canyon gave way to dense trees. "Is that a cave over there?" he asked, pointing.

"Yeah, maybe," Isabo said. "Yeah, it is. And look, there's something on a pole beside it. Maybe it's some kind of marker."

"Or a head on a pike," her brother said grimly.

Isabo shaded her eyes to get a better look. "I can't tell, but you may be right."

"It looks like a human head," he said. "Murdering monsters. It's a warning to stay away."

She waved for Mayra to join them, but Amon shook his head.

"Wait a second," he said in a low tone. "What do you make of her being so afraid of this place? I don't feel anything weird."

Isabo considered, then motioned for the girl to wait. "Other than the head on a stick? Who knows? Local superstition, maybe? I don't sense anything either. If she's too scared to come close, she probably hasn't seen the head."

Amon shrugged. "Could it be troll magic, maybe? Brother Yoren said the troll clans have shamans who can do weird things, magic things. Maybe they bewitched the spot to make people afraid."

She gave a snort. "You need to stop spending so much time with the monks. How would he know? And why doesn't it bother you or me?"

He considered that. "Because of the scent-gift? He says you and I and Pa are different from other people."

"I don't feel very magical," she said, not wanting to mention the dark voice that sometimes came to her.

She called to Mayra that they should head back to Pineholm. The girl nodded and began angling south toward the edge of the canyon, keeping her distance from whatever it was that bothered her so.

Before they joined up again, Isabo leaned close to her brother and whispered, "I saw you making puppy eyes at her earlier. She's at least five years older than you, and besides, I thought you were getting friendly with Asha Maris."

Amon flushed, but shook his head. "Mayra's just pretty, is all. And why do you care if I like Asha?"

"I don't, much. Just keep your head clear. Don't do anything stupid. This may be where the trolls crossed, or not, but that's obviously troll territory over there, and we need to get there. Try to think of a way over without us having to march way to the north. If they can do it, we can, too."

A few hundred yards south of the trolls' trail, they met up with Mayra. "Are you sure there's nowhere else to cross?" Isabo asked. "I'm fairly sure those things dropped down into the canyon and somehow came up the other side — with my father."

The young woman shook her head. "Not below —"

"Tulum's Fort," Isabo said with growing exasperation. "I heard that before. Are you absolutely sure?"

Mayra nodded. "The canyon just gets deeper that way. Though one of the other scouts said that north of here, part of the canyon wall had collapsed this spring. Nobody usually goes past this spot because it gives people the terrors."

"How far?"

"I don't know. Another hour, maybe."

Isabo looked up to the sun, which hadn't reached noon yet. "Let's go find it."

They walked back in the direction Mayra had come, away from the edge, until she no longer felt the uneasy chill, and then returned to the side of the canyon. Isabo picked up the pace, following the edge northward. In places, the plains grass grew right up to the edge of the cliff. In others, the turf was worn away, exposing more of the worn paving stones. But who would build a road here? Trolls? Ancient humans? There had once been a paved road leading south from Haywold toward Tall Grass, and some said another led far westward toward the Dead Plains, but there wasn't enough travel to warrant maintaining such curiosities. Better to let such things return to the prairies.

After another hour, they saw that Mayra had been right. The canyon wall fell precipitously away as the river hooked eastward. Thousands of tons of granite had slid downward, leaving a steep, but just navigable path down to a gray dome of rock above the river. Below that point, the riverbank lay thick with a tangle of dead trees swept downstream. Two of the trunks hung over the churning water more than halfway across. The opposite bank presented a sandy shelf well above the level of the river. A few twisted pines stood on the shelf, precursors of the forest above.

Isabo smiled. "How far is it from the dead trees over the river to those pines?" she asked.

"Iza, you're mad if you think we can dangle on a rope over that river," Amon said, looking dumbfounded at his sister

She nodded southward. "The trolls somehow did it back there, and I'd wager this isn't half as far across."

He gave a doubtful chuckle. "Aye, you're mad. Still, if we're going to cross, this is as good a place as any. We'll be as dead here as there. It's no more than twenty-five yards — easy bowshot. But look, if someone was to climb up on that hump of rock, they could shoot down into the trees on the other side rather than shooting up whilst hanging onto a dead trunk."

Amon scowled. "I don't like it, Iza. Even if we can shoot a rope across, it still has to catch snug enough to hold someone's weight."

"Aye," she said, "but what choice do we have?"

Mayra gaped at her. "You flatlanders are out of your minds. You'd be washed away in a second if you fell in the water.

Isabo smiled. "Then we don't fall in." She clapped her brother on the shoulder. "We just found our way across."

Chapter Sixteen

Dhugash

Cullen gaped at the city extending deep into a large cavern and gave a low whistle. He'd never seen a village of more than a few hundred people. A city of this size was beyond belief. Thousands could live here.

"What is this place?" Gheen asked.

Cullen pointed to the rune on the pillars. "A troll city. Or at least whoever lived here shared the same runes. It must be the city the Holy One mentioned. Dhurash?"

"Dhugash," the troll said, marveling.

He looked at Gheen. "Do you sense the demon here like you did in the cavern?"

The troll paused and touched the carved letters. "Is very faint. Holy One said vurad protected the trolls. Maybe demon can't come here."

Cullen pointed to the pathway leading into the city. Three sets of footprints approached the pillars, a smaller set that was probably Dannick's and two larger sets from troll-sized boots. "The purpose of Dannick's message was to bring me here," he said. "But look at the tracks,"

"They come near the pillar but don't enter the city," Gheen said. "Why?"

Cullen held his torch low over the tracks. The light revealed a dark stain in the gritty sand and dirt that littered the cavern floor. The footprints were disturbed and muddled as if there had been a struggle. Dannick's prints were to one side.

Had she leaped out of the way of her battling troll companions? The flame also caught the bright reflection of a broken knife — a troll knife.

He picked up the blade and examined it. The edge was stained with dark blood. He handed it to Gheen.

"I guess this is where the two trolls slew each other." He pointed again. "None of the tracks enter the city."

Gheen nodded grimly. "But where are bodies? When Dannick was found in upper tunnel, she was alone."

Cullen waved the torch around, scanning the area. Nothing was clear beyond the fact that there had been a struggle.

"Maybe they didn't die here but wandered off. Maybe the demon called them."

"This is evil place," Gheen said, shuddering.

Cullen fingered the paper in his pocket, his only link to the other scout. Had Dannick made her way through the twisting maze of tunnels to the upper chamber by herself after the struggle, only to die? But still, she'd had the presence of mind to leave a written clue for a scout to read. Why had she done that? Was it for any scout or for him in particular? Why had she helped the trolls in the first place? They'd captured her, but then she helped explore this blasted place. And even before this debacle in the cave, she'd helped train the trolls in scout craft. Why? Had she betrayed the humans? Or had she believed the shaman's warnings about the threat to trolls and humans? Like him, she was more likely trying to help the human captives.

Cullen shook his head. None of it made sense. "Let's go, Gheen."

They moved into the city following a broad avenue. The streets and buildings were made of fine-grained, smooth stone — the same stone he'd seen in the Tunnel of Sukkuz and the tunnels leading down from above. Yellow mold lit the vast area, revealing squat houses and buildings of one and two stories. The ceiling was lower than in the cavern they came from, making the light brighter.

Stone columns stretched between the floor and the ceiling high above. Around these streets, they wound deeper into the city.

Cullen noticed a steady current of fresh, dry air. Just how deep under the mountain were they? Somewhere nearby, shafts must connect to the outside.

"Let's look in these buildings," he said, pointing to a row of two-story structures.

"Maybe someone live there now," Gheen said with a faint shake of his head.

"Listen," Cullen said.

A profound silence hung over the city. "There's no one here," Cullen said. He sniffed deeply. "I smell nothing like live trolls here."

Cullen pushed and pulled at a door, but it refused to budge. Gheen nudged him aside, pushed hard with his shoulder, and the door opened inward with a loud scrape. Opening the door disturbed the thick dust covering the furniture and other dark shapes within. Cullen and Gheen both coughed as Cullen raised the torch to survey the room.

In the center of the low room stood a long stone table. On the table sat large bundles. Cullen drew his knife and cut the cord tying one of the bundles. Now thin and brittle with age, the outer cloth of the bundle fell to pieces, spilling the contents across the table. Cullen saw what looked to be clothing, a black stone knife, and everyday household items.

Gheen pulled something from the pile — a spoon. Ornate, carved filigree decorated its length. "My father's father and his father have spoons like this. *Trollim* lived here, Cullen."

Gheen stepped back and nearly tripped over another bundle on the floor. He looked down and gave a low cry. At his feet lay the remains of a troll.

Cullen held the torch aloft, revealing still more long-desiccated remains scattered around the room. The trolls' tusks and facial features were clear; their skin dried to a faded gray-green.

"Let's leave this place," Gheen said.

The scout nodded and turned for the door. Just visible on the back of the door was a large vurad rune.

Gheen pushed past out into the street. He leaned back and gave a low, wavering howl that rose in pitch and volume. Cullen made out words in the trollish tongue repeated over and over again.

The cry echoed from the ceiling of the city cave. Cullen cringed at that. He hoped he'd been right in assuming the city was empty. Were he and Gheen — and Dannick — the first to come to this city after hundreds of years? He hoped so. Anything alive down here must have heard Gheen's wail.

Gheen repeated the lament and then performed the ritual from the tunnel, tapping his forehead and then the ground.

Cullen laid a hand on the troll's shoulder. "I don't know what happened, but these were trolls. There's no telling how long it's been. Many lives of your people, I'd guess. It looks like they were preparing to flee."

Gheen nodded his large head. His eyes were damp. "Azuk. He somehow killed them."

Cullen stared back at the open door. "If it was him, maybe he caused them to go mad and kill each other, like the trolls with Dannick."

"Vurad did not protect them."

Cullen paused and then smiled. An idea had come to him. "Wait here," he said

He returned to the house and entered, holding the torch near the rune on the back of the door. He leaned close to examine the character and then returned to the street.

"Why does Cullen smile?" Gheen asked.

"I might have found something. Come with me."

He turned and ran back to the twin pillars at the city's entrance. Gheen came shuffling up behind him.

Cullen pointed the torch at the carved scroll on the pillar. "Look. What do you see?" he asked.

"Vurad, all the way around, on both pillars."

"But it's not," Cullen said. "Not quite."

They peered closely.

"What does the symbol look like?" Cullen repeated.

"Vur —" Gheen looked closely, tracing it with his finger. "Is vurad, but different, a little."

Cullen smiled. "The rune in the Tunnel of Sukkuz and at the shaman's house was a long stroke with a triangle on the left end. This stroke is curved and extends out from the triangle shape a bit. It looks like —"

"Like troll scimitar," Gheen said. "But what is triangle? Troll swords not have that."

Cullen *knew* the answer was right before him if only he could see it. Why were the symbols different?

He sniffed at the gently moving air and caught the faintest tendrils of scent from the lost trolls somewhere below in the caverns. He also took in the more pungent smell of Gheen. The acrid tang of the troll's fear seemed to rise and fall. He hoped his companion could overcome his terror of the demon if it came to a fight. He looked to the troll, whose massive hand sat lightly on the hilt of his sword.

Suddenly, a smile crossed his face. "You know, Gheen, maybe vurad isn't a magic rune. The shaman implied it had some magic or holy property to it. What if it's a weapon? Maybe that's how we are supposed to go after Azuk."

Gheen scratched an ear. "But where is weapon? And what happened to trolls in city?"

Cullen considered. "Do you remember what the shaman said? If they fought against Azuk, they'd have more than one shaman to wield the magic. And they'd have had temples to the First Ones, right? If the weapon still exists, the temple's a good place to look. I don't know how long ago they fought, but it was long enough for some trolls to flee and then forget this place. Gheen, the shaman was right. This city *must* be Dhugash. Your people must have lived here once."

Cullen turned back toward the troll city. "Grimmun-Kan said Azuk first came about two seasons ago. If this is the same creature that wiped out the city, the shamans here must have defeated him or at least bound him using the weapon. I think he is free again and is terrorizing your people, or at least building his strength until he can get free. You said that he calls the oldest and wisest trolls to him. Maybe he is somehow absorbing their life and their strength. Your Holy One said that he has lived many lifetimes of trolls and carries the memories of ancient shamans. I've never heard of such a thing. Maybe he was lying, maybe he wasn't. If he was telling the truth, how could he do that without somehow absorbing the life and strength of past shamans? That is some strange magic. Until I met you trolls, I would have thought it was the simplest nonsense, fit only for children's tales. But I'm starting to see that the world is larger and weirder than I imagined."

Gheen recoiled a little at the discussion. "It is not for me to know the deep magic of the Holy One, but..."

"But what? Tell me, Gheen."

The troll shuffled awkwardly. "Do you remember Gheen told you he had memories that weren't his? Memories of the shaman, but before Gheen was born?"

Cullen gave a low whistle that echoed strangely in the high cavern as the realization came to him. "Maybe I was wrong. Maybe it is for you to know. With his great age, the Holy One must somehow share memories, and you have the same bloodline. How many other trolls are in your family? Who has the same shaman's bloodline?"

Gheen shook his head. "I am the last."

"Isn't that a coincidence? You of the shaman's blood are here with me hunting demons."

"But Gheen chose to come with Cullen," the troll protested. "Is not... coincidence."

"I guess the shaman knew you would volunteer, or maybe he even arranged for you to volunteer. Why else would Grimmun assign you to guard me unless they already knew you would be involved?"

"Who can say? And Cullen-thing must not associate the shaman with the demon Azuk."

"Gheen, you said yourself how horrible it would be if the Holy One were taken by the demon. Why hasn't he been if he is the oldest and wisest of the trolls? Relax, Gheen. I'm not saying that the shaman is in league with Azuk, but he knows much more than he told us. He is somehow protected from the demon. Maybe you, too, since you have his blood."

Gheen's face twisted into an angry knot of frustration and confusion. "Cullen should not say such things."

Cullen raised placating hands. "I'm making guesses, Gheen, but it's the best I've come up with. What else do we have to go on? Let's find the temple and hope the vurad weapon is there."

***

Deeper within the cavern, they solved the mystery of the dry air currents. A broad road zigzagged up the side of the cave to disappear through a dark hole in the roof. Tattered banners hanging from the opening high above fluttered in the breeze.

Cullen examined the rutted, well-worn road. On either side, where it met the cave floor, stood two pillars identical to the ones at the other city entrance. They also bore the engraved representation of vurad. "This is it, Gheen," Cullen said with a chuckle. "I'd guess your ancestors or predecessors or whatever came and went from here to the outside world. The only question is where it comes out above."

The troll gave a quizzical look. "Are many caves in the mountains, but Gheen not know any with a road coming out. Near the abandoned village where we

207

entered, maybe. Trolls could have blocked it long ago to keep our people from coming back here.”

The city — Cullen already thought of it as Dhugash — filled not one but two adjoining caverns. After hours of wandering the city streets and entering buildings, Cullen and Gheen found homes, taverns, eating places, fountains, markets, and even a small amphitheater. Each was clad in the yellow glowmold. It wasn’t the same as the natural sunlight on the surface, but it provided more than enough illumination to see. Most buildings stood empty or held the ancient carcasses of the dead, many of those little more than dust.

Cullen was grateful for the glowmold that illuminated the lost city. He carried just a few remaining torches. Returning to the surface would be difficult — unless the road they’d just found proved a more direct route than the way they had come. He didn’t relish another trip through the dark, hanging on Gheen’s coattails.

Gheen marveled at the structures of the underground city. Each intricately engraved structure must have been the product of years of troll labor. “No troll makes houses or buildings like this.”

“Yes, Gheen, they do — or did. Trolls have forgotten how. Azuk took the smartest of your kind, remember? Who knows what else was lost?”

In the center of the city cave, they found what had to be the temple on a broad columned avenue. From several buildings away, Cullen saw the sign of vurad on the tall, domed structure.

As they drew nearer, Gheen’s breathing grew more and more erratic.

“Is Azuk here?”

“No, but is close,” Gheen said. He looked down at the paved street. “Maybe below.”

“Fight it, Gheen. I need you not to panic here.”

The troll nodded. “Is not bad fear, like in the tunnel, but Gheen can tell demon is nearby.”

They entered the building up a broad staircase from the street. At the top of the stairway stood a tall statue. On a plinth stood three tall, noble, and fierce trolls.

Gheen looked at the inscription at its base and read, "The First Ones. Charged by Umosh — the One Who Creates — to build and rule Dhugash, the City of Trolls. They brought might, justice, and the Light of Umosh to the city and the outer world above."

Cullen stared up at his companion. "How did you do that? You just read, Gheen."

The troll looked at Cullen in wonder. "The letters — words — were same as in Holy One's book, but in different order."

Cullen looked at the inscription. As far as he could tell, some of the figures were similar, but not all. "No, Gheen. There is more here than we saw in the book. How can you know all these words?"

The troll shifted uneasily, not meeting Cullen's gaze.

"Blast it, Gheen, don't keep secrets from me. We're in this together. Even your beloved Holy One said so."

But Cullen stopped as a growing realization came to him. The shaman had told Gheen to return to see him before they departed for the tunnels.

"The Holy One said he would teach you special words. Did he give you some kind of magic to help you read?"

Gheen looked away.

"Ounwe's third nipple! The shaman sends me — and you — down here to fight a demon practically unarmed, and you hold back secrets! Secrets that could help us."

"It is not permitted for me to speak of what you call magic. It is... holy thing."

Cullen gaped at the troll, dumbfounded. "What else don't I know? Can you fly?"

The troll raised a crooked eyebrow. "Trolls cannot fly."

"Gheen, blast it. I —"

"It is enough for you to know I can read some things."

"Some things?"

"Let us go into the temple, Cullen."

"If I live through this and the shaman keeps his word that there will be no more troll raids on our lands, I will go home to my village with my family and pray that I never see another troll as long as I live."

Once they entered the temple itself, Gheen led the way. They stood in a wide room. Carved into the walls were scenes of trolls digging and building an underground city. Each scene bore an inscription. Gheen studied them in turn. He nodded with a half-smile. "This *is* Dhugash."

"But what of vurad, the sword?" Cullen asked.

Gheen shrugged but moved toward a broad doorway in the far wall. They entered a chamber similar to the one in the shaman's house. Instead of the rune painted on the wall, Cullen beheld a mosaic image of exquisite jewels and colored stones. It depicted a troll brandishing a curved scimitar. Sparkling crystals showed a shaft of light emanating from the sword. Standing beside the troll was a smaller figure clad in red but without a troll's tusks or green skin.

Gheen went to the image and ran his heavy fingers over the words engraved below it. "This was Boruk-Kan, one of the First Ones. See his sword? He carries vurad."

Cullen saw from the image that his surmise about vurad was correct. The rune represented the shape of the curved sword, even the odd triangular cross guard above the handle. "Who is that?" he asked, pointing to the smaller figure in the mosaic. "A human?"

Gheen nodded. "Holy One said that in ancient days, even *pakh-hu* brought tribute to Dhugash. Why he is shown with Boruk-Kan Gheen doesn't know."

Cullen scratched at his stubbly chin. It made no sense. Trolls hunt humans today, but according to the shaman, humans in the past brought them tribute. That implies that trolls then and now saw humans as a lesser race of creatures. So why show trolls and humans together in such a powerful image? Why use valuable jewels and skills to depict a lesser race? There was a lot the old troll had not told him.

He stared up at the jeweled representation of the human. "When we were with the shaman, he said you were Gheen-*buruk*, which must mean something about being a shaman. Do you and he share the same bloodline? But he said that I was '*pakh-hu buruk-ush.*' What does that mean?"

Gheen looked away, then back at Cullen, but wouldn't meet his eye. "*Pakh-hu* means human."

"I guessed that. And the rest?"

The troll started to walk away, but Cullen grabbed his arm. "Tell me, blast it!" He pointed up at the image. "Does it have to do with that human? What is so special about sniffers and trolls?"

Gheen hesitated and stood, rumbling deep in his chest. "Is not sniffers and trolls," he said at last. "Is sniffers and... Holy Ones. Gheen does not understand fully. Holy One has deep magic. With sniffer — *buruk-ush* — Holy One Are can do more."

Cullen shook his head. "What exactly? What is it that I can do? Or what can you do with me here that you can't without me? That's why your Holy One had Grimmun drag me halfway across the Uplands into the mountains."

Gheen nodded. "But Gheen not know 'what exactly.' Has something to do with old memories."

Cullen slumped against the wall. "You mean we're both sent down here to do *something* and somehow rescue trolls and deal with Azuk without understanding what's going on?"

"Gheen has thoughts but doesn't fully understand either."

"Well, use whatever magic words or memories you have and figure it out," Cullen demanded.

The troll stood silent. Cullen spat and wandered around the room. His eyes kept coming back to the jeweled image. He considered the sword in Boruk-Kan's hand. "A pretty picture isn't a real sword, Gheen." He glanced around the room. "Vurad is a strong weapon. It has to be, but it's not here. Though I don't suppose they left it lying around. Let's check that room," he said, pointing to another doorway. "I have no idea what my role is supposed to be, but I won't abandon the other humans you've captured. Let's go."

Trollish writing and a carved image of scrolls were over the door. Cullen pushed through a tattered curtain of dangling threads into a small antechamber leading into yet another room. Tall letters incised on a wall within announced something: a pithy quote? Pride in a long-dead empire? The secret of vurad?

"Do the letters look familiar, Gheen?" Cullen asked, pointing upward.

Gheen craned his head back to look up at the inscription. He grunted and shook his head. "What is... archive?" he asked.

Cullen shrugged. "There were scrolls on the wall outside. Maybe it has to do with that," he said. "I don't come here often. I don't know."

Gheen didn't laugh at the weak joke, but to Cullen's mind, the troll seemed less tense than he had been. Perhaps being in the lost city of his ancestors eased his anxiety. Maybe the temple itself offered some meager protection from the demon. Or maybe there was more blasted troll magic at work.

He felt in his pocket for the scrap of paper from Dannick. She had wanted him to find the city. That could only mean that something here must be useful in fighting Azuk, or would it help the humans to escape the trolls' domination? He shook his head again. There were simply too many questions and too few answers. But they had to be getting closer to an answer.

A doorway to the right led still deeper into the building. Cullen led the way, following the glowmold that covered the walls and ceiling. It was everywhere here. Had it been painted on these surfaces, or did it grow here naturally? He stepped through the door, glanced around the room, and gazed in amazement. The yellow glow spread in vast swaths up the walls and across an arched ceiling five feet above. Shelves lined the walls, running back as far as he could see. One of the shelves had collapsed along the left wall, spilling its contents to the floor.

"Is books," Gheen marveled.

In his life, Cullen had seen only a bare handful of books. There was no telling how one made a book, but it must be ridiculously time-consuming; to inscribe that many letters on a page and then somehow bind them together must have been the work of weeks or months. And here were hundreds — thousands — of bound books and scrolls, like the wandering monks said they had in Harrun.

"Gheen," he said, "this is the knowledge of your people, their history." He looked at the shelves reaching far back into the room, and smiled. "You can read now. I'd say you have some work ahead of you."

Gheen shook his head. "How can I read all this or even know if things in books can help defeat Azuk?"

"The Holy One wouldn't have given you that ability if you weren't meant to use it. But I have no idea where to start."

Cullen reached down to pick up one of the volumes. The leather cover, now brittle with age, broke in his hand. The pages dissolved into a shower of gray flakes that settled to the floor. He moved to one of the shelves and examined a scroll. Its cover was also dried and brittle, but it held together. He unrolled a small portion of the parchment within to see rows of angular script.

"What does this say?"

Gheen peered over Cullen's shoulder and then took the scroll from him. His brow furrowed, and his lips moved as he mouthed the words. "Is listing of tribute paid in twenty-third year of reign of the First Ones."

"That does us no good," Cullen said, "but I'll keep looking."

Further examination found shelf after shelf of what must have been ancient documents. Some had already turned to dust, while others were suspiciously pristine and intact. Not even those gave them a clue how to proceed.

After nearly an hour, Cullen's stomach began to rumble. He looked around the long room. "We're wasting time, and I'm getting hungry. We need to find this vurad thing, then find the trolls and deal with that blasted creature. I think Dannick meant for me to find this place, and your Holy One certainly meant for you to be with me. What in Ounwe's third hell are we missing?"

Gheen shrugged and shook his head.

Cullen turned and walked deeper into the room as Gheen returned another scroll to the shelf. As interesting as all these books may be, they were meaningless to their task.

"Gheen," he called as he pushed past row after row of scrolls and books to the very back of the long room. Against the furthest wall, he found a high table holding a simple stone box. On the box was carved the single rune: vurad.

Chapter Seventeen

Aid and Assistance

The sun moved westward over the plains as Isabo, Amon, and Mayra drew near to Pineholm. Before reaching the cabins, they met a work party with a horse-drawn wagon at the canyon's edge. The villagers were dumping the slain trolls into the river.

Isabo recognized the butcher from their brief conversation at the inn. "Mister Figg, I see you've finished your business with the trolls."

"Just finishing it now," he replied with a satisfied grin. "It wouldn't do to have their carcasses stinking up the place, now would it? We'll let the crows and the fish handle the rest. By the way, we've collected their nasty blood — dark stuff, now, isn't it? It'll save a lot of lives, it will. I'll see that you have all you need. If only I had more time, perhaps it could be dried or made into something more easily carried. I gave the mayor and your Mr. Perban their swords, knives, and whatnot. We're surely indebted to you for killing these great beasts, Miss Isabo."

She smiled acknowledgment and moved on toward the village. Not every bit of the trolls had gone over the edge. Stepping back onto the road leading to the gate, she saw what looked like a gray-green bundle hanging from the branch of a tall pine. Getting closer, she noticed flies buzzing around a net full of trolls' heads.

They put a human head on a pike. We can do the same.

They approached the palisade to the clatter of swords and distinctive *thunk* of arrows striking targets. Instead of the screams of agony she might expect from a battle, Isabo caught the sound of laughter and good-natured ribbing. She growled at that. They were supposed to be building an army, not planning a festive outing.

Coming around the wall with Amon and Mayra close behind, she found Perban, Tanner, and two other men overseeing drills.

Perban gave her a broad smile. "You're back. What did you find?"

Isabo took in the scene. A line of men and a handful of women with practice swords were taking turns hacking at a mock-up of a troll under the eye of Kurtis Hupp. Several of the locals had good skills, and everyone showed at least basic proficiency.

Further along the wall, Crumble and Asha Maris watched as others shot arrows at colored cloth scraps hanging on hay bales.

She looked up to see Perban watching her expectantly. "We found where the trolls crossed, and we found a way for us to get across, but we need rope and some grapnels. But why aren't you two handling this?" she asked with a hint of frustration.

"Uh, sorry, Isabo, but our folks have it in hand. Hupp and Maris have weeded out a good handful, and we'll still have about a dozen recruits."

"That's not the point. You two are my leaders, and whichever two clowns the mayor gives us. This is your job, so do it," she said through gritted teeth.

Perban gave an awkward smile. "Isabo, this is Lim Voss and Marko Gaskun."

Gaskun looked to be about thirty, and Voss a little younger. She glared at the two, anger welling in her. "What are you doing? If you think you're coming with me and are going to laze around, I don't need you. We're out to kill trolls and get my father back. That means going into their —"

Gaskun wagged a beefy finger in her face. "You just calm yourself, Missy, and have some respect. Maybe it's better if Lim or I lead this expedition."

She grabbed his wrist and twisted hard, throwing him off balance. He crashed into the wall and howled with pain. He shot back to his feet and lunged at Isabo, but Perban caught him around the neck.

Tanner raised his hand and stepped in front of the two locals. Activities around them ground to a halt, and heads turned. "Isabo, we got off to a bad start. You're right. Will and I, along with Lim and Marko, should have been managing this directly. We were just discussing how to organize things. There are enough solid fighters here for four units. We think our new friends here would do well as leaders. What do you say? Third and Fourth Swords? Now, we can either keep First and Second as they are, or mix our people with theirs, or even —"

Isabo fumed. The voice in her thoughts intruded with an eerie, chuckling laugh. To Gaskun, she said, "I've heard of you two. Your mayor is helping us, so I won't turn you away... yet. I'm in command and I will make that decision." She nodded to Will and Hiram. "Perban is my second. If he and Tanner and the mayor think you're good enough to lead fighters, I'll give you the benefit of the doubt, but I won't hesitate to turn you loose if you're not up to the job."

"What about the troll bounty?" Voss asked. "Who's paying that?"

"Take it up with the mayor. I'll see to it that my people get what they're due. He's paying your share."

Gaskun considered and nodded at Perban and Tanner. "What do you call them? Do they have titles, like captain or commander?"

Isabo shook her head. "They're First Sword and Second Sword. You'd be Third and Fourth."

"But that's the whole element, right? A leader needs a title. It's only fair."

"You can call yourself whatever you like," Isabo sneered, "but you answer to me. You're Fourth Sword for now. Voss is Third."

The two newcomers looked at each other. After a long moment, Gaskun nodded. "That's fair enough," Voss said.

Isabo looked to Perban. "Don't make me regret this."

"All you lot get back to it!" Gaskun shouted angrily at the fighters standing around.

***

217

Isabo watched in silence as her 'captains' made the final selections.

Tanner disqualified one of the men despite being an excellent hand with the bow because he had a twisted leg. He took it with good humor, saying, "I heard you all were going into the mountains. I'm content to stay on the wall as a defender. I was the one who filled that ugly bugger full of arrows yesterday."

Others were too young or too old. In the end, they settled on ten.

"How are we doing for weapons, Will?" Isabo asked.

Perban glanced at Voss, who gave a thumbs-up. "All good, Chief. The blacksmith here has an assistant who serves as armorer. He's looked over our blades and given them all a good edge. He polished out the worst of the troll blood, but it stains metal deeply."

"As long as it still holds an edge. Anything else?"

"He's got helms for those that don't have them and as many bundles of arrows as we can carry, but he wants silver, twice as much as anyone would charge back home."

Isabo shrugged. "We'll take them. He can charge the mayor. What about spears? Messick and Naggs carried spears."

Perban smiled at that. "They have four apiece, all fire-hardened oak. That's one more each than they started with. The armorer fitted them all with steel tips. We couldn't be better off, weapons-wise."

"Good. Get all our people out here so I can talk to everyone together. Then see that they all get a good dinner. After that, none of our people leave the inn. I don't want anyone getting drunk or fighting. The locals can say goodbye to their families tonight. At dinner, you, Hiram, and your two new buddies will settle who belongs where. Let's balance ours and theirs, and swordsmen and archers across the four teams. I want to be off at first light. Understood?"

"Yes, Chief. What about a team of archers we can use as a unit?"

"Figure it out and tell me what you've done." She turned to Voss. "Mayra Faulken said you have a rope-maker. We'll need enough light stuff to get us all down into the canyon and something stouter in case we have to make a rope bridge."

"Okay, uh, Chief," he said awkwardly with a glance at Gaskun. "We should have that at the storehouse. I'll see to it."

A good-sized crowd had gathered on the wall to watch the proceedings. Isabo saw Mayra looking down with her father. She waved for Mayra to come down.

The girl and her father came down. Isabo made pleasant conversation with him for a few minutes and then called Tanner over to explain to the mayor how they selected each of the recruits.

"Mayra," she said in a low voice when they had moved off, "how long have you been a scout?"

"I started going on patrol at sixteen, so five years now. Why do you ask?"

"Amon and I are the only scouts we have. We lost our other scout, Tallard, to trolls. This is Amon's first troll hunt. He's only fifteen. I could use someone else with experience. Can you fight?"

She smirked. "I have three brothers. Of course, I can fight. To be honest, though, I'm just okay with the sword and bow. I do well enough with the sling that I can feed myself when we go out."

Isabo chuckled at that. "You'll have to meet Daron Homah. He took down a troll with a sling yesterday. It was a blooded stone, but still. Are you interested?"

Mayra looked dubious. "I don't have your scent-gift."

"Neither did Willim Tallard."

"My father will throw a fit. I'm his only daughter. Can I let you know in the morning?"

"We leave at dawn, so decide tonight."

***

She didn't waste words speaking to her now-larger army assembled in front of the gate. The plan was simple enough: cross the canyon, go into the mountains,

219

find her father, and return, killing any trolls who stood in their way. She let Perban explain how trolls' blood was to be used on all weapons when they were near enough to need it.

True to his word, the butcher Figg had provided an ample supply of blood in bladders and stoppered clay vials.

Looking around, she confirmed that all her people were present, Crumble included, despite his talk of going home. He'd helped Maris weed out the new recruits. To her relief, the tall, skinny archer was still there, but would he come along tomorrow? She'd have to have a word with him.

To their credit, the locals looked competent and eager to be at the trolls. Seeing her band take down nine of the creatures must have put heart into them. It remained to be seen how they responded when it came to fighting the monsters themselves.

***

Isabo was awake an hour before sunrise. Gathering her gear, she made her way to the common room, where the innkeeper Ellis had laid out a generous spread of bread, cheese, and cold meats. She knew she should eat, but her stomach was closed. On opening her pack, she was surprised to find that it already contained a bundle of dried sausages and fruit.

"Begging your pardon, Miss," Ellis said, laying another tray on the table, "but I took the liberty of giving you rations for the trail. We're grateful to you for killing those things."

Marko Gaskun pushed past her without a word, shoving Ellis out of the way.

"Don't mind him, Miss," said Ellis.

***

The gray light of dawn seeped over the peaks, barely illuminating the crowd of scratching, yawning fighters standing in a loose gaggle at the village gate.

Perban caught Isabo's attention. "We're missing a few stragglers, but Hiram and Lim Voss have gone to round them up."

"Get the rest into some kind of order. I want to get on the trail." She leaned close. "Keep an eye on Gaskun. If he puts a foot wrong, I'll send him packing."

Perban nodded and drew a parchment sheet from his bag. He began calling names and directing people into four separate groups.

Isabo looked up to see Amon standing nearby with the monks. All three had coils of rope over their shoulders. Brother Yoren, easily the smallest man in the assembly, was dwarfed by Brother Dunken. To her surprise, Yoren also carried a long, ornate dagger on his hip. At least he was doing something useful, though what he hoped to do with the dagger wasn't clear.

By the time Perban was finished calling names, Voss and Tanner returned with nearly all the missing people.

"Crumble's not going, Isabo," Tanner said in a low voice. "He's heading home with Tom and Wulf Wheatley."

She shook her head and glanced up to see if Crumble was with the cluster of people on the wall. "Ounwe's teeth. I didn't want to lose him. We already lost Dorse and Wulf, not to mention Tallard and Zollar."

Mayra Faulken arrived with her father. She wore a broad leather hat and had a short sword slung across her pack.

Her father's face was stern, but his voice pleaded. "May, you can't go with them into the mountains. It's too dangerous. Just lead them up the canyon and come back." He looked up to Isabo. "Tell her how dangerous it is."

Isabo shook her head. "I won't say it's not. You all know what trolls can do, but I need another scout, Alastor. If she wants to go, I won't turn her away. Now, we need to be moving. I hope to be back in a week or a little more." She pointed to Perban's element. "Mayra, you'll take Crumble's spot in First Sword.

For now, though, you're our advance scout, so stay ahead of us and watch for trolls."

The mayor gave Isabo a look as if she had betrayed him. "I'll hold you personally responsible if any harm comes to my daughter."

"Fine," Isabo said as the young woman eagerly sprinted ahead.

Marko Gaskun spoke up. "Wait, now. Lim Voss' brother, Arno, has good eyes. I think he'd make a better lookout, and since Fourth Sword are the bowmen and natural protectors of this little army, I'll send Dobsen along with him."

She ignored him. At a nod from Perban, she called, "Let's move," and led her fighters away from the gate. Despite the early hour, family members and friends lined the battlement, calling out farewells and prayers for a safe return. Isabo heaved a grateful sigh.

They met no resistance as they marched northward, though knowing that they would soon cross into hostile lands, nearly every eye searched the trees across the canyon for trolls. Perban and Tanner had established a marching order with First Sword in front and Gaskun's Fourth, thankfully, at the end of the line.

The dim pre-dawn gave way to pale morning light, and the first rays of the sun over the mountains cast the Uplands in a golden glow. It was nearly seventy leagues to Haywold, and back home, people were waking to go about their business. Isabo hoped they were doing so without fear of troll raids, but there was no telling. Haywold was on its own for now. Besides, her only family was here or in troll-infested mountains.

Isabo tried to put the thought out of her head. She had no business worrying about such things now. Ahead in the distance, Mayra disappeared over a low rise, and Isabo sniffed the breeze. There was no sign of trollstink in the air. In the open, with a faint breeze and ideal conditions, she knew she could detect the creatures from hundreds of yards away. She glanced at the treeline across the canyon and wondered what it would be like tracking in the heavy scent of the pines. Would it be easier or harder? Again, there was no telling. She would find out once they'd crossed the river.

Nearly two hours north of Pineholm, she saw her advance scout pause and then turn away from the canyon. Mayra must have found the crossing point.

"She must have seen something," Perban said.

"We'll stay along the edge of the canyon," Isabo said with a thin smile. What would Will — and the rest of her army — feel when they drew near to the spot where the trolls had crossed? Would they experience the same sensation Mayra had?

Within a few minutes, she saw her second-in-command twitch nervously. She stopped along the trail. "Keep going straight on, Will. I want to check something." Sure enough, Daron and Filip, and then the two recruits from Pineholm, Lupin and Kellick, put their hands to their swords and looked around anxiously, their eyes wide.

"What is it, Chief?" Hiram Tanner asked as Second Sword drew near. He scanned the far side of the canyon as if fearing an imminent attack.

"We're okay," she said in what she hoped was a reassuring tone and clapped him on the shoulder. She pointed to Mayra, now standing a hundred yards to the west. "Head that way." She whistled to Perban and pointed in the same direction.

Soon, all four elements had gathered around the scout. "What's happening?" Gaskun called. "Are there trolls about? We need to get away from here."

Isabo didn't tell the rest that they had passed near a troll-cursed place — or whatever it was that hung over the spot that instilled so much fear. She glanced at Amon and shook her head. "No, but I think that's where trolls got across the river. Mayra found their tracks. But we can't cross there." More than one fighter breathed a visible sigh of relief. "We've got another hour's march to the place where we can get across."

***

When they arrived at the place where the canyon wall had collapsed, most of the army nodded appreciatively. The gravel and rock-strewn incline was steep, but manageable. Gaskun, not surprisingly, voiced an objection to the spot. "There's got to be a better spot further along. Even if we could get down to that big rock, there's slim chance you'll be able to get a rope across, let alone fashion a bridge. It's madness to cross here. Why don't I take a hand-picked team further north and find us a better spot?"

Isabo was tempted to let the man do it, and good riddance. "No. We're crossing here." Her mind toyed with the image of Gaskun running away screaming, or better yet, throwing himself into the canyon in a panic. "We can make our way down to that big rock easily enough. From there, we throw or shoot a grapnel to that tree across the river. Once it's secure, someone goes across trailing the heavy line and ties it off. Everyone else follows."

A short, wiry middle-aged man from Second Sword raised his hand. "Begging your pardon, ma'am, but I'll go first to check the route down to that rock. I live on the canyon south of town. Me and my boys go birdnesting on the wall over the river in the spring. Many's the time we've climbed or let ourselves down on ropes."

"What's your name?" Isabo asked.

"Garnay, ma'am. Isaac Garnay."

"Okay, Garnay. What do you need?"

The man was already tightening his pack and checking to make sure nothing would fall out. "Just a bit of that thin rope under my arms so you can pull me back if I get stuck. It's stronger than it looks. Bayre, the ropemaker, does good work."

In short order, he had taken a coil of line from the monks and looped a bit of it around him. He gave the rest back to Brother Dunken, showing the brawny cleric how to brace himself and pay out rope as needed.

Everyone watched with interest as the little man picked his way over boulders and down the incline. He pointed out the best routes, loose rock, and spots too steep to traverse. In no time, he stood on the broad shoulder of rock, gazing back up at his companions. Before anyone could express more than muttered appreciation for the man's accomplishment, he began the climb back up, leaving his pack and the end of the rope behind.

"It's not so hard as it might seem," he said when he'd regained the top, panting a little from the exertion. "It would be better if we tie off the line on this outcropping. That way no one has to stay behind — and we have a way back up. We can let down the packs and such down separately, and then I can guide people down."

It took nearly an hour to get everyone and their gear down. Surprisingly, those from Haywold and the south had a tougher time with the descent than those from Pineholm. Katya Bromlin clung fearfully to a sharp chunk of granite halfway down, and Garnay had to come alongside, reassuring her and placing her feet. It didn't help that once over the edge, the wind whistled fiercely down the canyon. The tumult of the Roaring River became a real presence, making it difficult to hear instructions.

Tanner and Voss saw to collecting gear and getting the packs back to the right person. After a brief rest and a meal, spirits revived.

Isabo pulled Perban aside. She leaned close to be heard over the tumult below. "We're in it, now, Will. There's no going back unless we climb up." She pointed to a tree on the far side, overhanging the river. "What do you think? Twenty yards? That's an easy shot." She spoke firmly, but was fighting to keep the quavering note out of her voice.

He looked down from the rock they stood on to the tall pine across the river. "It'll do," he said. "We'll make a rope bridge between that pine and the tree trunks." He nodded to the twisted pile of trees washed against the base of the rock. "It's damned close to the river, but it's the best we're likely to find."

He gave her a concerned look. "Is everything okay, Iza? You aren't having second thoughts, are you?"

She shook her head but didn't speak.

"Iza, you've done everything right so far. Well, mostly," he said with a sly grin. "Seriously, with you leading, we've done better than anyone could have hoped." He pointed to the army of fighters, smiling and digging through packs for victuals. "They're in good spirits, and they trust you. Our folks will follow you anywhere, Iza, and most of the ones from Pineholm are in awe. You should have heard their comments yesterday. 'It's Isabo Troll Slayer!'"

His expression grew slightly more serious. "Do me a favor, though. I know Marko Gaskun is a pompous git, but throw him a bone. He's a solid archer, probably the best of this new lot. Most of the Pineholm folks like him, and even the mayor recommended him. Give him a chance to show what he can do."

She stiffened, but nodded agreement. "He needs to guard his tongue, but okay, since you asked."

Perban gave a nod and made his way down to the tangle of tree trunks on the shore.

Isabo walked to the fighters, most of whom were sitting in groups or lying with their eyes closed. "Don't get too comfortable. We need to get across the river and then find the trolls' trail."

Gaskun sat with Voss and Tanner. "All right, Marko," she said. "Let's see what you can do with your bow."

Leading him across the rock to a point over the water, she pointed to the tree. "We need a line to that pine. Can you make that shot with a grapnel?"

The man peered out over the river, giving her a confident look. "Of course, I could hit that tree. Anyone could do that. Well, almost anyone. I saw the line you brought from Pineholm — and the hooks. That's heavy stuff. It's not something an arrow would carry. Such things are only done in stories."

Isabo cursed.

"Now, young miss, don't get yourself worried. Old Gaskun has the answer, though we really would have been better off finding another place to cross."

"We're not finding another place," she snarled.

He wagged a finger in her face, and she considered shoving him into the river. "What would you suggest?" she asked, forcing a smile.

"It's simple," he said with an equally false smile. "I'll throw it."

Isabo muttered under her breath, cursing the fellow's arrogance, but forced a smile. "That sounds fine."

Gaskun called for the thin rope and grapnel. Fixing the hook to the end of the line, he moved to the edge of the rock overhanging the river and swung the hook over his head. "It's the simplest thing," he said, and threw the grapnel squarely into the river, missing the tree by ten yards. It took three attempts, to the hoots and laughter of those watching, but at last he draped the line across the tree and drew it taut.

"Come down and secure the line to that trunk," Perban called to the man.

Isaac Garnay made the rope fast with a solid, complicated-looking knot, wiped his hands on his tunic, and took hold of the line.

"Let me. I'll go across first," Amon said.

"Amon, what are you doing?" Isabo growled. She squeezed his shoulder hard, but he smiled. "You can't," she said. "This man knows ropes — and you're all I have left besides Pa. I won't allow it."

"Iza, I've done this a thousand times before with Zizzo Bracken, in the Dimwood. I know what I'm doing," he said. "And I'm grown enough to make my own choices. I have to do this for Pa."

Isabo turned to look at the assembled party. Amon was taller than Garnay, but lighter, and she knew that her brother and Zizzo frequently went into the woods to climb trees. "Remember when I said I'd box your ears when we get home? I meant it."

Perban pointed to the tree line higher up the canyon on the other side. "We'll keep an eye on the woods, Amon. If trolls come, drop everything and fly back to the rope. We'll cover you the best we can from here."

The boy nodded as Brother Dunken handed him the thicker rope.

"I will say a prayer for your safety," the monk said.

Isabo winced and hugged her brother tight. "I will absolutely kill you if anything happens," she said, thumping him on the back of the head.

Without a word, Amon smiled and hooked an arm and a leg over the rope. He pulled himself along quickly, paying out the coil of heavy line as he went.

Isabo shuddered as the rope swayed to his movements over the rushing torrent. She found she was holding her breath.

In a few agonizing minutes, Amon was across the river. Isabo scanned the trees above the river for signs of trolls. She watched as her brother tied the thicker rope agonizingly slowly to a bough at knee level.

She looked up to see the rest of the party clustered nearby.

"That'll do nicely," Garnay said. "Shall I skip across and make sure the knots are all secure?"

Isabo gave a quick nod. Why had she let Amon go across first?

"Give me a moment to get across and that all is well," Garnay said. "I'll give the thumbs-up when it's safe. When you cross, put your feet on the bottom rope like this and grab the top one. It's as easy as kiss-my-hand. The good thing is to not look down." The man gave a wink and began sidling across.

A short time later, he was across. He inspected the knots, nodded, and raised a thumb.

Isabo shook her head. If Garnay trusted Amon's knots, her brother must have some skills at this.

Isabo motioned for Perban to lead his team across. "Have them spread out watching the trees in case there's a welcoming party." He nodded and took his place. Cautiously, First Sword made their way over the rope bridge without incident, dangling above the roaring spray.

When they were safely on dry ground and arrayed facing the trees, she tapped Tanner and Second Sword. "Take Brother Yoren beside you. I doubt he's done anything like this before." She waved the monk forward.

She'd used such bridges before, but never this close to an angry river. She cut a measured length from the end of the remaining rope, looped it under his arms and over the top rope, and knotted it securely. "If your feet slip off the lower rope, you're still attached."

He smiled weakly. "Thank you, Miss Isabo."

"Go quick, and don't think about it."

Yoren mounted the rope beside Tanner, muttered a prayer, and began inching sideways across the bridge.

Isabo shook her head. It was good that the cleric was so skinny, or his weight would have dragged him perilously near the water. Perban and the Homah brothers' feet had almost touched the water when they crossed.

The monk almost made it without incident, but his foot slipped from the rope when he was almost to the far side. The loop under his arms caught him with a jerk, and he screamed, dangling over the water. Without hesitation, Tanner somehow managed to calm the monk and get his feet back onto the lower line. In a few minutes, they were safe on the far side.

"Ounwe protects fools," she muttered.

"And he takes care of his own."

Isabo glanced up. She hadn't realized Dunken was still there. "Can you make it across?"

The monk nodded with a smile. "I grew up in the trees. Well, not really in the trees. I come from Forest Glen on the south side of —"

"Just go, Brother," she said, shaking her head.

"Yes, Miss."

When everyone was across safely, Isabo spoke. "We've got to move quickly."

Perban gave a quick assent. "The trolls have a week on us, probably more. We'll need to find our way back downriver to where they crossed." He looked to Isabo. "You'll have to pick up their scent from there. We've no way of knowing how deep into the mountains they've taken your father. With luck, it won't be far."

Isabo looked back at the rope bridge, then up to the dark trees, and gave a faint shudder. Other than captives, when was the last time humans had been in the troll lands? Or were they the first?

Chapter Eighteen

Secrets

Cullen lifted the box to examine it. It was heavy, a foot square, and perhaps half that tall. Besides the rune incised deep in the lid, it held no markings. A thin crack around the box showed the edge of the lid. He reached out to remove it.

"No!" Gheen shouted. The troll took the box from Cullen and placed it back on the table. "This is for troll to do first, not *pakh-hu*," he said.

Cullen stared at his companion. This was the first time Gheen had spoken harshly or raised his voice to the human.

"What is it?" he asked Gheen. "Is this what we're looking for?"

Gheen didn't answer but took a deep, cleansing breath. Then, he tapped his forehead, stooped, and tapped the floor — the same religious ritual he had performed when they first entered the caves.

As Cullen watched, Gheen placed his right-hand palm downward on the vurad rune. The troll's eyes grew wide with wonder. He looked at Cullen and shrugged, but his face was hopeful.

"Place right hand here, like mine."

Cullen did as Gheen asked. "Now what?"

"You do not feel the power within?"

"Uh, no," Cullen said. But as he spoke, a tingle spread from his palm to his fingertips. He jerked his hand away. "What is that?"

"When Holy One read with my eyes," he said, "Gheen could feel power inside Holy One. This is same." He gave Cullen an odd, piercing look. "Holy One said only those with shaman's blood can feel."

"That's ridiculous. I'm not a shaman; I'm just a scout."

"Not only scout, but —"

"I know, Gheen. I have the scent-gift. But so what? Others do as well. Dannick did. Your clan needed someone to sniff out the lost trolls, and I'm living up to my side of the bargain to free my people. I brought us this far using my nose, but that's it. You're the one with shaman's blood, Gheen. The rest is up to you. I can't shoot lightning out of my fingertips like the Holy One did. If you put Wogan's hand on the box, he'd probably feel the same thing."

Gheen shook his head. "Wogan-thing not have same blood as Cullen."

Cullen slumped back against the wall, looking from the troll to the box and back again. This was beyond ridiculous. The scent-gift was rare, but not holy.

He remembered Wogan's words in his cabin. Wogan had said the same thing — that trolls practically revered humans with the gift. *No*, he thought, *I won't be drawn into this mystical gibberish. Ounwe's arse.*

He sighed and dragged weary hands through his straggly beard. How long since he'd slept?

"Gheen, let's open the box, take the vurad thing or whatever is there, and go back out to the tunnel. I need some rest."

But the troll shook his head. "Must do other things first, before rest." He fumbled in his pack and drew out the stone given to him by the shaman.

"What are you —?" Cullen said.

Gheen moved apart a few paces. He held the stone to his forehead, uttered a low phrase, and repeated it again louder. To Cullen's surprise, the stone gave a faint green glow, growing brighter as Gheen repeated the words.

Gheen withdrew the stone. The glow faded, and the stone lay pale gray in the luminescent glowmold. Cullen recalled the same type of stone on the shaman's forehead.

"How did you know to do that? What is the stone?" Cullen asked.

Gheen stood silent, but his lips still moved, and he repeated the same phrase.

"What is it? What are you doing?" Cullen repeated.

"Holy One gave me words of protection and joining. Since he read through my eyes, I have seen flashes of... other. At first, was just dreams or memories. I thought was my own. Now I see it was his thoughts and old, old memories. The *kor-oba* stone brings joining — and hopefully protection. What I now see, the Holy One also sees. What he knows, I know. I share his thoughts. Before we left, at the temple, he saw the letters I saw. When he saw them, I knew what the words were." He passed the stone to Cullen. "Thoughts came, and I knew it was time."

"He read those words through you." Cullen gave a slow shake of his head. For some reason, he didn't doubt Gheen's words, despite his earlier thoughts about mystical gibberish. A few weeks ago, he'd have laughed at the notion. Now, it was just troll magic. Something about Gheen had changed; that was certain. His words were different, less halting and awkward, as if he shared the shaman's speech patterns.

He glanced at the stone and moved to hand it back.

Gheen shook his head. "For now, it is for you to hold. The time will come when you return it to me."

"I don't know what that means, but fine."

Cullen put the stone into a pocket and glanced at the troll. He was different somehow. He sniffed. The scent of fear was still present in Gheen, but he was a strange mixture of confidence and terror.

"Can you shoot fire out of your finger like the shaman?"

Gheen inspected his finger and shrugged. "Gheen understands a little where the Holy One's powers come from. It is a very old place within."

"Old? What does that mean? Gheen, do you know what the Holy One is thinking?"

The troll shrugged with a very Gheen-like gesture. Whatever had happened, the troll he knew was still very much present.

"Holy One knows what I see and think."

"As if you're talking to him?"

"Yes. But that is not important right now. We must open the box."

He drew his long, dark knife, nicked his palm, and dribbled the blood on the box.

"I won't ask how you knew to do that," Cullen said.

The drops of blood ran together on the lid's flat surface as if into a curved bowl. As Cullen watched, the blood seeped into the rune and disappeared.

As the blood vanished, a piercing shriek erupted, reverberating through the temple. Cullen clapped his hands over his ears. The sound seemed to come from everywhere.

Gheen looked to Cullen and mouthed the word "Azuk." Then, unmoved by the hideous screech, he uttered a few words. The lid tilted open without a touch.

Cullen leaned forward to see what was within.

Gheen reached into the box. With an expression of awe and triumph, he drew out a short-bladed dagger in a shining black leather sheath. He pulled the blade from the sheath. Intricate, twisting letters covered the dark metal blade. In the troll's huge hand, the thing looked tiny.

"That's vurad?" Cullen shouted.

"Perhaps," Gheen said. He placed the dagger into his pack. "Azuk is below us. He knows we are here. Now, we should return to the tunnel."

Cullen wondered how Gheen knew where the demon was. But with a groan, he recognized the same tingling in his feet he had felt touching the box, only darker and somehow fiercer. How was this possible? He was no shaman able to work magic.

"I'm with you, Gheen. Let's leave this place."

As abruptly as it started, the noise ceased.

In an instant, Gheen staggered and fell to his knees. "Azuk," he gasped. "The demon is here. He calls." The troll writhed and clutched at his head. "I must go to him."

Cullen felt a palpable, dark shudder pass through him. If this was the demon summoning a troll, he wanted no part of it. "So much for protection from the Holy One," he muttered. He grabbed Gheen's shoulder and tried to drag him to the doorway.

"We can't stay here! Fight it, troll. Use the shaman's power. Fight it!"

Gheen groaned and staggered to his feet. He turned for the door and lurched forward. Cullen half supported, half dragged him from the room and the temple.

He led the troll down the steps to the street. "Move, move, move," he urged. "Run, Gheen, we have to get out of the city."

They moved at a shambling trot in the direction of the pillars. For a moment, Cullen considered taking the winding road they'd discovered that led up from the cavern, but there was no telling what lay above.

Gheen alternately gibbered like a lunatic and howled in angry fury. Cullen prayed the troll was receiving strength from the shaman.

Between gasps, he grunted to Cullen, "Flee. I must go to Azuk."

"We're in this together, troll. We'll go back to the tunnel. You said it was safe there, that the demon wasn't there."

Within his own mind, tendrils of fear shot through him. The horror ebbed and flowed but was clearly nothing to compare to what Gheen was experiencing. Even so, he felt his tenuous grip on reality weaken. With growing clarity, he understood what caused the other trolls to slay each other and drove Dannick mad.

Gheen lurched from side to side, barely able to stay on his feet. "I must go to him. Take the blade. Kill me before he takes me, Cullen-thing."

"Don't talk. You're joined to the shaman. Use that. Get strength from him; get knowledge of how to fight this thing. We've got to get out of the city.

Whatever this demon is, we'll face it together with vurad." He had no idea how they would do that, but he had to keep the troll moving.

Human and troll staggered through the streets of Dhugash toward the twin pillars. The dark fear slowly receded from Cullen's mind as they went, but still lurked at its edges. He found himself panting in fear, like Gheen. They made their way out of the city past the pillars. The haunting blackness finally diminished when they began climbing up the boulders in the outer cavern.

He led Gheen staggering through the tunnel opening, and both slumped heavily against the wall.

"How do you feel?" he asked.

The troll grunted but didn't speak. He wasn't raving and howling — or waving a sword around — so he must be better.

Cullen reached down for his water skin, but it was nearly empty.

"Gheen, are you with me? We need water. Maybe this isn't the best time, but I'm going down to the river."

The troll nodded and pulled two water skins from his pack. "Gheen is thirsty but better. Must rest."

Cullen rose in the twilit darkness and gathered his and Gheen's skins. He dug into his pack and found the dried fruits and berries Wogan had given him. Thankfully, Wogan included some dried meat as well. He grimaced and sniffed at it. It had the gamey scent of venison but was — something else.

They had enough food for another day and a half at most. He ate a handful of berries and a strip of meat. The dwindling bundle of torches was on Gheen's pack. He considered. The faint yellow mold in the cavern provided a steady light, but it wasn't bright enough to explore by himself. He'd use another torch. After all, he reasoned, he'd need to see the tracks of the summoned trolls.

He stood and found their tracks. They'd left the tunnel entrance and gone down the trail toward the river. Somewhere ahead in the shadows, the river and trail disappeared into another cavern or a still lower channel. Back in the city, Gheen said that Azuk was below them. That meant the trail must lead downward.

He stopped along the edge of the water. He washed his face and filled the skins, considering what they'd learned so far. *A lot, but not enough.* They'd found the ancient city of Gheen's ancestors, the temple, and maybe even vurad, for all the good a small blade like that could do. Gheen had some sort of link to the shaman through a holy rock. And he was even beginning to at least sense the presence of magic.

But all of that didn't tell him how to kill the demon. *Great. Heck of a day.*

Their supplies were dwindling, but they could stretch what they had for another day or maybe a little more. After that, they'd be dead or back on the surface. He hoped it was on the surface.

He tied the skins to his pack and trudged back up the trail to find Gheen.

He found the troll sitting up, rooting in his pack. Gheen pulled out a bundle and the vurad knife.

"Doesn't look much to take on a demon with," Cullen said, handing the troll his water skins.

Gheen nodded and turned the blade over in his palm. "It must be enough, or we are lost, and my people as well."

"Are you still linked to the Holy One?"

"I still feel his presence, but is not strong. With the words, I can join with him again."

"Gheen," he said after a moment, "you could sense the demon all through these tunnels, but it only struck you hard, it only summoned you, when you joined with the shaman and found the knife."

"Yes," Gheen said.

"Azuk calls the oldest and wisest trolls, right? When you gained knowledge from the shaman, you became more vulnerable to the demon. Something about the wisdom must make you more... appetizing to him. Yet somehow, having shaman's blood gives at least a measure of protection."

Gheen nodded and fingered the stone in his hand. "But Gheen needs the wisdom that comes from long learning. Apart from that learning, I am not smart troll."

Cullen chuckled. "Smart is overrated."

The troll opened his bundle and pulled out a strip of his own dried meat. "This is called *kherus*. Is big deer from high in the mountains. To eat it is to take on the strength of the animal."

Cullen nodded at that. It made sense that trolls might think that way. Eat *kherus* to gain the deer's strength; eat, what, owls maybe, for wisdom? Eat humans for — no, better not go there. He shuddered. "I'd eat a hundred shamans, though, if it gave me the wisdom to —"

Gheen cocked an eyebrow. "Wisdom to do what?"

The realization came to Cullen slowly. He watched Gheen chewing the strip of meat. "I was right, I think. It's what he's doing. I don't know if Azuk is a demon or just some evil creature. Maybe he was a troll himself at one time. But I think he's consuming the old trolls for their wisdom." He peered at Gheen in the yellowish light of the glowmold. "He took the oldest and wisest from Dhugash, and the rest fled to settle in the mountains above. He's doing the same with your clan and the other troll clans. That's why they haven't built great cities since Dhugash fell. Sorry for saying so, but trolls have gotten stupid over the years because of Azuk."

The troll made a low, grumbling sound. "It must be," he said, looking down at the dried meat. "I must kill him, or trolls will become like *kherus*, strong but just animals."

Cullen took a long swallow from his skin. The water was clear, cold, and refreshing after such a long day. "You're smarter already, Gheen. Trolls and humans aren't animals. I'll be honest: I don't think the other trolls are still alive. Maybe, but I don't think so. But between us, we can figure out how to kill this thing once and for all. That's saying a lot because we haven't even seen him yet, but we've felt what he can do."

Gheen gave a crooked troll smile. "I'm glad Holy One sent us for you, Cullen." He lay down and arranged his pack to serve as a pillow. "Was long day. I must rest. Yes, tomorrow we will find the demon Azuk and kill him."

Cullen thought about what he'd just said, that trolls and humans weren't animals. He'd spent his life hunting trolls to kill them and raised Isabo and Amon to do the same. He had considered trolls little more than beasts.

He glanced at Gheen. "We'll do this thing, troll, and then I'll take my people home. But what happens then? Do we go back to killing each other?"

The troll opened an eye. "Gheen not know," he rumbled. "Want to say no, but I am not the leader of my clan."

"We need to think on that. I'd hate to kill you one day. For now, sleep. Maybe the shaman or the First Ones will give you a dream of how to defeat Azuk."

***

Gheen tossed on the stony ground, unable to find a comfortable sleeping position. The horror of the demon still teased at the edge of his consciousness. He found a flat rock and shoved it under his pack for a headrest.

Uneasy sleep came at last, bringing horrific images of dread mingled with snatches of memory not his own. The Holy One stood with other trolls dressed in shamanic robes. On one, he recognized the sign of the Stone Breakers clan; another wore the markings of the Deep River clan. Others bore symbols from clans he didn't recognize. A gathering of shamans? The trolls towered over a smaller figure in red — a *pakh-hu*. No, this was *pakh-hu buruk-ush*, the human counterpart to the shaman. It must be. The human stood at ease, blood from his hand dripping into a bowl on a stone table. In the bowl was a round stone, like the *kor-oba*. Holy One spoke, and the bowl glowed with a pulsing, unearthly blue light.

The images were foreign and yet familiar. The purpose of the rite hung just outside his grasp. He reached out to touch the trembling, palsied shoulder of the Holy One. As he did, the shaman slumped wordlessly to the floor. Gheen reached out again to help him, but the others in the room motioned him away from the figure. The Holy One, ancient beyond days, shuddered and climbed slowly to his feet. His face was hidden in a deep cowl. He stood erect, facing Gheen, and pushed back the deep hood. Gheen stared into his own face.

***

He awoke in the black silence. From out in the cavern, no sound came, not even the tumbling of water from the waterfall. The yellow light of the glowmold faded, winked, and went out. He listened for Cullen's restless breathing but heard nothing. Where had the *pakh-hu* gone?

"Cullen," he said. Nothing. Even the echoes died when he spoke.

He stood and felt along the wall for the opening of the cavern. He gave a low "holoo," but only mocking laughter echoed from the walls, and then that too faded.

The echoes should have shown him the cavern walls and tunnel, but there was nothing. His dark vision showed only the black emptiness of a vast pit, and he stood teetering at its edge.

His heart raced, and he forced himself to breathe deeply.

"First Ones, protect me," he muttered. "Holy One, give me peace."

Mocking laughter returned, and from somewhere behind him came strange, unaccountable echoes that revealed nothing.

"I am Gheen, warrior of the Three Valleys Clan," he shouted. "I am afraid of no beast!"

The shout faded even as it left his lips. He reached for the scimitar at his side. It was gone.

A dark, harsh voice spoke in the blackness. "You challenge me, Gheen of the Three Valleys Clan."

"Who, who are you?" he said.

240

"I, Azuk, am the uttermost darkness," the voice said. "The *pakh-hu* was right, Gheen of the Three Valleys clan. I was once like you. We share holy blood. But you cannot defeat me, son of Ama, the whore. Instead, you will release me from the bonds that have held me for a thousand years."

This wasn't the same. In the city, the summons was frantic and demanding. Here, the demon — for he had no doubt that it was indeed Azuk — mocked and cajoled.

His pulse pounded, and Gheen fought to keep from throwing himself into the abyss. The voice of Azuk was a spear at his heart, almost gentle but blade sharp. It commanded him to obey.

Yet words — holy words, but not the ones the Holy One had given him — leaped into his throat.

"*Gor pakh ji hanam; Gor pakh na am.*"

Where had the words come from?

At once, the place he stood was bathed in a light of searing intensity. The light erupted from within him, illuminating the tunnel and the cavern with diamond brightness.

The pit and the darkness were gone. Azuk was — no, not gone. None of the images were gone, only dispelled for the moment. Nearby, in some stinking pit, the demon still lurked. He would face it again.

Within himself, he felt the ancient, feeble Holy One nodding approval. And there were others within as well, other Holy Ones that somehow he knew lived many ages of trolls ago.

Well done, Gheen, son of Ama, the voices within him said, *but it is not sufficient.*

His heart sank within him. "What must I do?" The Holy One spoke, now in Gheen's own voice. "My death comes soon. If you would defeat Azuk, you must take my mantle as Holy One."

"How can Gheen do this thing?" he asked.

"Take the blood of the Seeker, the faithless one."

Gheen looked around him. The voices and images faded. He felt the rough stone walls of the tunnel. A faint shine of glowmold from the cavern illuminated Cullen, who snored gently at his feet.

Gheen sat, leaned against the tunnel wall, and closed his eyes.

Chapter Nineteen

Over the River

It took the rest of the day to make their way southward through the thick woods on the eastern side of the river. They were aiming for a point closest to where the trolls had likely crossed. In the fading evening light, Isabo felt the weight of the mountains looming over her. Westward beyond the canyon lay the plains and forests where her people — real people, not monsters — lived. Trolls had killed humans for generations, and she had finally returned the favor. They had raided the Uplands, and now she was raiding them in return.

The grim woods were thick with the resiny scent of pine and the acrid stink of trolls. "We're close," she said to Perban, who turned and signaled to the rest of the party following fifty yards behind.

She pointed down the darkening slope to the lone tree in front of the cave opening. "Trolls hiding in that cave must have helped them cross the river."

"How do you know they aren't still there?" he asked.

"The scent is old. Maybe a week or more," Isabo said. She motioned toward the trail leading from the cave up into the trees. "They went that way. A whole herd of them."

Perban looked down at the cave, and the head on a stake. "You're sure it's a dead scent? I want to check the cave."

She nodded and pointed to what was clearly a human head on a stake near the cave. "Fine, and cut that thing down," she said.

"Gaskun," she said in a low voice. The townsman drew near, and Isabo pointed into the darkening woods. "Take your archers just up there and set a guard just off the trail. We don't want any trolls surprising us."

"Why me?" he asked.

"Because you're Fourth Sword, and we need bowmen for protection. And because I bloody well told you to," she said, struggling to keep her voice calm. "Keep troll blood close by in case you see any, but I don't think you will. None have been through here for a week."

With a curt nod, he ordered his fighters into the woods.

Perban scrambled down the slope to the cave, listened, and peered inside. Satisfied that no trolls were lurking there, he turned and pushed the stake until it tilted far enough for him to knock the head off the end.

Picking it up, he examined its features and then raised it over his head to display it to the fighters.

Isabo pointed at the grisly skull. "This was a warning to us and every other human not to enter troll lands. To hell with that," she spat. That elicited a low chorus of approving murmurs and curses at the monsters who would do such a thing.

"Should we bury it?" Perban asked.

She thought for a moment, then shook her head. "No. Put it by that tree and cover it with rocks. We'll give it a proper burial later. Voss, Gaskun, why don't you two do that?"

Gaskun raised a finger to protest, but Voss grabbed him by the arm and said, "We'd be honored."

Perban returned to the cave. A few moments later, he reappeared and climbed back up to the trees. In his hand, he carried a metal rod.

"What's that?" Isabo asked.

Perban held up the thick bar. "I'm not sure. There are two more in the cave. They're nicked and a little bent at the end, like they had been shoved into something to wedge or turn it."

She glanced down at the river far below and shook her head. "We don't have time to figure it out."

"There's something else." He pointed across the canyon. "That's where Mayra found their tracks, right? I can't explain it, but being there put the fear of the seven hells into me. The others felt it, too."

She looked up the trail to see Gaskun's people disappearing into the trees, but Perban continued. "I don't feel it over here. It's as if something was driving us away from the place."

Filip Homah spoke up. "Me and Daron felt it, too, over there. It scared the life out of me, but I didn't want to say anything. I don't feel it on this side."

"Mayra felt it, too," Isabo said, "when we were here looking for the way across. Amon and I can't feel it, but everyone else seems to."

Perban raised an eyebrow. "And you let us walk right into it?"

She looked away. "I wanted to find out where it started. Mayra never saw the cave and the head on a pike because she couldn't get close enough."

"There are, um, some who say that the trolls wield magic. Maybe they cast a spell to instill fear."

It was Brother Yoren, suddenly standing in their midst.

"I don't want anyone telling tales like that," Isabo growled. She glared at Amon. "Or believing them. Let's go. We're wasting daylight."

***

After an hour's march in fading light, the group camped off the trail and without a fire. Even in the gloomy darkness under the trees, it was clear that others had used the spot before them. Perban set guards above and below the site. None of the party was used to hiking in the mountains, so there were more than a few stifled groans or curses as they settled in for the night.

As everyone settled in for the night, Isabo took Perban a short distance up the trail. She checked to see that no one standing guard could hear. "There's something you have to know, Will. I've been hearing voices."

That stopped him in his tracks. "Uh, what do you mean?"

She clenched her fists tightly. "Since we first killed the trolls, near the aurochs herd. It's been driving me, pushing me to press on and kill more trolls. I hear it in my thoughts, especially when we're near them. And there are images that won't leave my head... of trolls slaughtering my family."

"If it's pushing you to kill those monsters, that can't be bad, can it?" he asked with a grim smile. "After all, that's what we came to do."

In the dim light, she saw his eyes grow wide. "Does it happen to Amon, too? Is this a scent-gift thing? Maybe it's the opposite of what happened at the canyon, when everybody but you two were afraid."

She shook her head. "Amon hasn't said anything, and I'm pretty sure he would. Brother Yoren thinks I'm going mad or something. That stupid monk 'senses a dark presence in me,' or some such nonsense." She put a hand on his shoulder. "If it does get worse the closer I am to trolls, I'm afraid what might happen as we go deeper into their territory. Don't let me do anything foolish."

He gave a hearty laugh. "You? Never! You're the Troll Slayer. But don't worry, I have your back. Hiram, too. Never forget that." His smile faded, and he tugged at his straggly beard. "Seriously, Iza, we're here to do a job, but you're my friend first. Me and Hi will take care of you, okay? Let us know if this thing gets in the way."

This wasn't the response she expected, or even hoped for. She stared for a moment, unsure how to respond. "Thanks, Will."

In the morning, Isabo, Amon, and Mayra searched the area around the campsite while the others prepared to move out. Isabo cast about for her father's scent, but the week-old troll stench obliterated any faint human trace.

"Look at this," Mayra called. Thin light streamed through the trees, revealing the remains of a small fire pit.

Isabo moved to her, careful not to obscure any tracks on the soft ground.

The scout smiled and pointed to two distinct human-sized bootprints. "There were two humans here. And this," he said, holding a small clump of plaited grasses.

"Yes!" Isabo exclaimed quickly, reaching for the tale-teller.

As with the others that had been found, it contained a pattern of knots and weaves. "'Two humans and twelve trolls. Safe.'" she read.

"It's Pa's weave!" Amon shouted.

"Blast it, keep your voice down!" Isabo hissed, then she waved her four element leaders over to show what they had found.

Tanner gave a low whistle. "A dozen trolls is a huge party just to capture two humans."

"There were nine of them on the other side of the river," Amon said with a half-smile. "I could smell them."

Perban nodded. "And three in the cave to help them across? We didn't explore the area around the cave too much." He stared blankly for a second, then turned to Lim Voss. "How do they open the gate at Pineholm?"

The man looked confused, but said, "Uh, the gate's attached to a pulley system by big ropes."

"Do they pull it up by hand?" Perban asked with a grin.

"Of course not. It's attached to a big winch."

"The trolls have a bridge," First Sword announced triumphantly. "They raise it and lower it with a winch using the bars I found to lever it around. That's how they get across." He looked cautiously at Isabo. "Add whatever magic hoodoo they used, and humans would never figure out how they crossed — until now."

Isabo tapped the tale-teller gently. "That's one mystery solved. Good thinking, Will. Don't spread it among the others that they're using magic. I don't want anyone running away scared." She glanced back at the footprints. "Who's the other person?"

Perban shrugged. "No telling. A slave they brought along, like Tom Wheatley, maybe."

Isabo scanned the rest of the ground around the fire pit. "There are plenty of troll marks here, and no human prints besides these. This has to be them."

Perban looked at the trail leading upward into the mountains. "The further we go, the closer we get to troll settlements. I'm surprised we haven't seen any of them on this side of the river."

Amon cleared his throat. "Um, these trolls don't smell like either of the groups we killed. And we didn't leave any trolls alive, so this band couldn't know humans are fighting back. Maybe they haven't set guards because they don't know we're here. They think their bridge is hidden, so why would they think we are?"

Isabo gave her brother a smile and nodded. "That gives us the advantage. They think they're safe. Even so, I want scouts ahead and someone watching behind."

***

Isabo knelt, rolling her bedroll into a tight bundle.

"Miss Isabo, can we speak privately for a moment?"

She glanced up to see Brother Yoren. "What do you want, monk? I don't have time for your visions."

The wiry young man shifted nervously, tugging at a small tassel on his robe. "Yes, well... It's just that..."

"Spit it out, man!"

"I've told you, Miss, that I had seen your father, and that he is embarking on a course that threatens the ruin of us all."

She scoffed. "You also said there was a great evil over me. All it's done so far is tell me to kill trolls. So what?"

The monk staggered, and his hand went to the odd dagger at his side. "It has spoken to you?"

"What? Not really. I just get a sense of it sometimes. It isn't like there's an evil demon possessing me or anything."

He flinched away. "You must go! Return to your home. You must not approach the trolls. You are in mortal danger!"

Kill this one. Strike him down! He seeks to keep you from your destiny.

Isabo jerked and felt her hand reaching for her sword, as if some other being controlled her muscles. She forced her eyes closed and gripped her wrist with her other hand, holding it tight across her chest.

The monk's words were quick and insistent. "If this thing speaks to you, it will only grow stronger and more difficult to resist as we get close to their camps. You must turn away now. Leave this task to others!"

"Get away from me!" she shouted in blind fury, grabbing at the man's robes. "I warned you before to leave me alone." With a fierce bellow, she hurled the monk to the ground.

All eyes were on the two of them. Tanner and Lim Voss rushed to her side. "What's going on?" Tanner said urgently. "Isabo, what happened?"

She drew herself erect, towering over the cringing monk with her sword drawn. "If this thing comes near me again, I will cut its throat," she snarled.

"Isabo," Tanner said in a placating tone, "what did he do?"

She shook her head sharply and barked, "What's everybody standing around for? Move out!"

Those on the ground leaped to their feet, and she heard Gaskun mutter to a compatriot, "I should have been in charge. She's not stable. You watch, it'll be a disaster, and we'll be lucky to get out with our skins."

***

249

They marched for hours through a broad wooded valley that narrowed as it rose. No one spoke as they climbed higher, moving farther away from the canyon and the Roaring River. The high forest thinned to a scattering of gnarled bristlecones. Isabo, Perban and Amon conferred in sharp whispers about the trail, which had faded into a rocky path.

"The scent is still there," Isabo said, "though just barely. We're still on the right track, but it doesn't make sense. We've followed the track for hours without seeing any other evidence of trolls. They must stay deep in the mountains and only cross the river to raid our lands."

Amon leaned low over the trail, drawing in the scent. "This is like we smelled across the river. It's the same bunch. I just wish I could catch Pa's scent this way."

Isabo chucked him on the arm as he stood up. "That's not how it works. It would be nice to track people or game with it, but for some reason, it's just stinking trolls."

"I expected some resistance, but there's nothing," Perban said with a worried expression. "I wouldn't count on our luck holding." He looked over his shoulder at the other elements hiking behind them. As the pathway rose, everyone labored to keep up with Isabo's pace.

"Iza, what did the monk say? What was that all about?"

She shook her head. "Just keep him away from me."

"Did it have anything to do with the voices you heard?"

She didn't respond.

They moved on, following the trail toward a cleft in a tall granite cliff ahead.

"They could be up there watching us," Mayra said, panting.

"Aye. The rest of you stay here," Isabo said. "Will, come with me. I want to look at those slabs of rock there to the right. That's a likely spot for an ambush."

He nodded, and the pair jogged away toward the rocks.

Isabo looked upward at the jagged cliffs looming overhead. Waiting trolls could dislodge boulders and send them crashing down upon them. She glanced back to see the rest of their party waiting, their weapons drawn. Crouching low, she scanned the gravelly soil for signs of the trolls' passage. She circled the stone slabs and quickly called to Will. Before her stood a low cave — a hidden entrance into the mountain.

"What do you make of that? Could they have gone in?" she asked.

"You tell me," he said in a whisper. "Any scent?"

She wrinkled her nose and nodded, then crept forward to approach the cave entrance. Instead of the rocky trail continuing into the opening, she saw smoothly joined stones lining the floor and walls. Writing of some sort extended along the wall.

She sniffed again at the air of the cave. "That's odd, in here I can sense that at least one troll has been through here within the last few days. Maybe humans, too. The scent outside was old. Could this be the start of the troll lands? I don't fancy walking in their front door."

Perban considered. "Our other option is to go up the cliff and through that cleft. I say we explore this tunnel. If trolls come, we have to fight — or run like fury. We've got no torches, so let's only go as far as we can see. I'll tell the others."

When he retreated from the cave's mouth, Isabo crept deeper into the tunnel. Though the paved path continued deep into the mountain, the smooth stones somehow managed to hold the light.

Maybe we won't need torches.

She walked further in, tracing the strange letters inscribed on the wall with her fingers. Before she knew it, she was twenty yards in. She continued and soon saw a bright square of open air at the other end of the tunnel.

"Isabo!" someone hissed. The sound echoed in the narrow passage.

She turned and hurried back toward the entrance.

"What were you thinking?" Perban asked.

She ignored the question. "There's enough light to see. It's not a cave. Someone — or something — made this. It looks to be a hundred yards long. I could see the light at the other end."

"And it likely opens on a troll village," he replied with a grimace. "We didn't come this far to be captured."

Isabo waved aside his objection. "Nobody has come this way for days."

"Even so, you're being reckless. We'll get your father, but it's too dangerous for all of us to go traipsing through there. Let's both of us go through to the other side and scout it out. Stay out of there, and I'll tell the others what we're doing."

***

They returned to find the others spread out in defensive positions behind boulders or low wind-blasted trees.

"What did you find?" Tanner asked. "Are there trolls?"

Isabo nodded. "Yeah, we're not too far now. A road on the east end of the tunnel leads down into a wide valley. We didn't see any guard posts along the road. There's a village with fields around it, half a league down the valley. Someone was working in the fields, but we couldn't tell if they were trolls or humans."

Gaskun chuckled. "Trolls working in fields? Those were humans, I'd wager — human slaves. How big was the village?"

"Big enough for a few hundred trolls," Perban said, "and plenty of slaves."

"Our people are down there," Voss said suddenly. "Trolls raided farms west of Pineholm last season. They burned and killed and plundered. Those they didn't kill outright, they took. We have to bring them back."

"We came for my father," Isabo said. "If we can free a few others, we will."

"But our people are here too. We have to get them out," Voss insisted.

Perban shook his head. "We'll take out who we can, but we're not an army."

Voss interjected, "If we don't take everyone now, the trolls will be on their guard. We'll never get back in here."

252

Marko Gaskun glared at Isabo. "Well, 'Chief,' you keep saying you're the leader. What's your plan?"

She chewed her lip and debated whether to drive a sword through the idiot's face. "I'd like to have more people to attack a village this size. I want to think this through and make sure we have a good plan. They want my father for something. I doubt they'd go to the risk, or send such a large party for just one or two slaves."

She looked around her small army. "Hiram," she said at last, "go through with Second Sword and watch the road down into the valley. Don't go more than a hundred yards from the tunnel entrance and stay in cover."

***

Amon gnawed a chunk of dried meat as he polished his already-gleaming heavy sword. In the bright sunlight, the troll-blood stain along the edge shone as a dark purplish pattern on light. "So, how are we going to get Pa back?"

Isabo sat with her back to the tunnel wall, just inside the west entrance. Even this high in the mountains, the walls were oddly warm. She smiled at her brother, trying to keep her expression positive. "I've got some ideas. Will said there were human slaves in the fields. We'll find out from them where the trolls are holding him. We should be able to get some of them to fight with us."

"Against the whole camp of trolls?"

"You aren't worried, are you?"

He gave a faint nod.

"Hey," she said. "We did fine against them across the river, even if it cost us a few good fighters. Trolls may be big, but they're stupid. We can outthink them. Plus, we have troll blood now. Besides, Pa will help us fight our way out."

"You're the boss, Iza." After a moment, he said. "Tallard was Pa's friend. Think he'll be mad that he's dead?"

She frowned at that. She'd forced herself not to think of the gruff, old scout since that first battle. "At the trolls, sure. But everybody's lost somebody to these things."

"He said he needed to get back to his family in Cleft."

"I know. When this is all over, I'll make a trip up there to let them know what he did."

Amon slid his sword into its sheath. "I hope we're doing the right thing, Isabo."

She laughed. "Of course, we are. We're killing trolls, and we're going to get Pa back."

***

When the sun was directly overhead, Isabo gathered the group at the stone slabs by the west end of the tunnel. "Our only hope is a fast raid," she said. "There's no telling how many trolls are down there, but from the size of the camp, maybe hundreds. We can't afford a direct attack that turns out a storm of angry trolls. Tanner found a second trail down to the camp. It leads along the south wall of the valley. That will get us closer to the fields outside the camp. Perban and I will scout the route and the camp if we can get close enough. We have to know what we're facing and, above all, where my father is. Everyone stays in cover until we return. We'll be back here before dusk and make final plans for the raid. When we have a plan, we'll likely go in at night. The moon is two days from full, so there will be plenty of light to get into the camp and find our way around."

***

The path was little more than a game trail, but it was well-used. Isabo couldn't imagine what kind of game animals were willing to live near trolls. She pressed forward, keeping the granite walls of the valley close on her right hand. The way meandered through the woods, dropping in a shallow line to a stream bed and rising steeply away from it.

"Why does the trail rise and fall like that?" she wondered aloud.

"Big animals," he said. "Deer, elk, or whatever big critters live in the mountains. Their heads are heavy, so they have a harder time coming down the hill. They'll make a careful, gentle path. Moving uphill's easier for them, so those trails are steeper."

That was the kind of thing her father would know, but she'd grown up mainly on the rolling plains west and south of Haywold. She pressed onward, more determined than ever to find her father.

"What about trolls?" Perban asked. "Any scent?"

She paused and cast about for any traces lingering on the light breeze. "Nothing on this trail. Just animal scent, like you said. It was a deer, I think. Back up on the road there was a more recent scent of a single troll."

They traveled eastward along the trail at a good pace for an hour, hopeful that trolls wouldn't indulge in a sudden desire for game. As the sun dipped westward, they turned off the trail at a rocky outcropping and moved downhill toward the farmlands through glades of aspen and scrub oak.

From the forest's edge, they looked out over an array of fields surrounding a stockaded village. Only half the fields were tended. An open gate was just visible in the western wall of the stockade. In front of the gate stood a broad platform as tall as a man.

"The sun is dropping, so they'll be leaving soon." She pointed to the trio of human slaves hoeing weeds in a field. She didn't recognize them, but it didn't matter. They were humans, and they didn't belong here. She looked around the farmland and then back to the village. "No trolls in the fields, but I can see and smell a few on the wall." She shook her head. "I thought their camp by the river stunk. This place reeks."

She glanced back at the slaves in the field. "What keeps them from running away?"

Perban scanned the area. "There." He pointed to a large stake fifty yards away, like the one they'd seen by the river. Atop the ten-foot pole was another human skull. "That's probably what happens to humans who try to flee."

Isabo hawked and spat. "Filthy beasts. Will, I want to creep out there and talk to the slaves before they're done for the day."

"Yeah, we could make it down to that stand of trees at the edge of the field. I have an idea."

They crept from the cover of the trees to a small cluster of alders. Perban moved forward on his belly to within a few yards of the field. He cupped his hands over his mouth and made a low churring call.

Isabo recognized the sound of an injured nightjar and smiled. The birds were common in the Dimwood, but she doubted they came to the mountains. With luck, humans would recognize the sound but not the trolls.

He made the call once, waited a few minutes, and called again. Isabo watched the humans for a reaction. Nothing happened at first, but finally, one of the three, a short, wiry man clad in a gray smock, looked up.

"Do it again," she whispered.

He repeated the call. The man leaned to one of his coworkers to say something, then turned and walked slowly toward the trees, chopping at an occasional weed with his hoe.

When he was within ten yards, he called, "Who's there?"

"Friends," Perban said in a low voice. "Who are you, and where are you from?"

Isabo watched the man's face take on a puzzled look. "I am Hursh, and this is my home. I belong to Nurag-ush."

"We've come for Gabril Cullen," Isabo said. "He's my father. Do you know him, or know where the trolls took him? They have brought him here in the last week."

Hursh grew agitated and turned away.

"Stop," Isabo called. "I have to find my father."

"It is not permitted for you to be here," Hursh said. "You must go."

"Not without my father."

The man quavered. "I saw when they brought him in. He was taken to the Holy One. The shaman. He lives in the temple building in the center of the village. I must go."

"Hursh," Perban said in a low voice. "We're coming for him and any other humans we can take. Do the trolls ever close the gate in the wall?"

Hursh shook his head.

"Do you know the people from Pineholm?"

A nod.

"Will you help us if we fight the trolls?"

"I must go." The man turned and hurried back to his coworkers.

"Why did he react like that?" Isabo asked. "He should have been eager to help us."

"The trolls have them cowed," Perban said. "We better not count on any help."

Isabo looked up at the head on the stake. "Then we need to do this before any more heads are taken. Let's go."

Chapter Twenty

The Demon Azuk

Cullen woke to find Gheen sitting quietly beside him in the tunnel. He held the knife from the box in his hand.

"I guess today is the day, Gheen."

The troll nodded.

"Any idea how we're supposed to use that blade to defeat the demon?"

Gheen eyed him with a strange, downcast expression.

Cullen shook his head. "Well, cheer up. You're tied in with the Holy One somehow. I'm sure that, however it works, he'll give you an idea. He wouldn't have sent us both down here helpless, right? We have the stone and the knife."

Gheen nodded, and Cullen busied himself, gathering his gear.

"Did you eat anything?"

"Gheen is not hungry," the troll said.

"We're going to find and fight a demon creature. Better get something in your stomach."

Cullen found the bundle of food from Wogan. He took a strip of dried meat and chewed at it, watching Gheen from the corner of his eye. "You're not saying much this morning, Gheen," he said, tying the waterskin to his pack. He looked around in the dim light of the tunnel. "If it is morning."

"No," the troll rumbled. "Let us go."

They gathered their gear and hiked across the cavern toward the dark river. Cullen sniffed the air — Gheen wasn't anxious. The troll's bitter, sour-apple stink hadn't taken on the sharper tang of fear that had been so redolent yesterday. And yet they were heading toward Azuk, the source of Gheen's earlier panic. The troll had found courage somewhere, but there was something else in the troll's demeanor. Resignation, maybe?

They reached the far wall of the cavern, and, as Cullen suspected, the river dropped over a fall into a lower chamber. The trolls' trail followed along a well-worn, downward-sloping ledge beside the river. The tunnel descended at a steep angle for fifty yards, then grew more shallow. Rushing water made speech difficult, and moisture masked any scents. Gheen could be wetting himself in fear, but somehow Cullen knew otherwise. Whether it was a shaman's charm or something else, the troll seemed calmer than Cullen expected. That would likely change the closer they drew to Azuk.

The river and trail curved to the right. Cullen guessed that if they weren't under the city, they were very close. The tunnel leveled out and entered an open cavern. To his dismay, the glowmold was thin here, casting only a faint light. They stood in a dim, twilit space. He drew close to Gheen. "You'll have to lead from here. I can barely see."

Gheen nodded and offered Cullen the end of a cord. "There is wide cavern here with many pits and holes. Hold rope and stay close."

The path turned away from the river.

Cullen wondered at Gheen's demeanor. He was no longer the almost timid creature he had been before. "I felt the demon in the temple," Cullen said. "It was terrifying, and I expect it will only get worse as we draw nearer to him. Can you handle that?"

Gheen grunted and nodded. "I can."

Cullen believed him.

***

Once they were away from the river, the scent of the lost trolls returned. The caverns and tunnels each carried their own unique smell, some salty with minerals, some faintly acrid, some musty and dank, but the bitter trollstink was a path as clear as anything above the ground.

The path veered sharply to the left and entered a low, twisting tunnel. The glowmold came and went, offering glimpses of the underground passage, but there was little to see. His faint interest in exploring this other world below the mountains had vanished. They crossed narrow chasms whose bottoms could have been a few feet below them or hundreds.

The tunnel widened into another broad chamber, and Cullen noticed a sickly-sweet, almost fetid smell. Something had died here.

"Gheen," he said.

The troll didn't respond but moved forward quickly, weaving around barely glimpsed openings in the cavern floor.

Cullen caught snatches of repeated words. Was Gheen using the shaman's words to ward off the fear?

The stench of death rose, mingled with that of troll.

"More pits here," Gheen said.

"Stop," Cullen said. "Do you smell that?"

"Yes," Gheen grunted, coming to a halt.

The roof of the cavern drew lower. A small patch of glowmold revealed an opening in the floor.

"Wait," Cullen said. He gripped the cord linking him to Gheen and edged closer to the hole, trying to catch the smell from below. After a moment, he leaned back and said, "There are dead trolls somewhere below. It's as I feared."

Gheen nodded. "And Azuk is there." He pressed forward along the trail, away from the edge. "This way. The demon beckons."

The hairs on Cullen's neck rose with a growing sense of dread.

Gheen led Cullen onward. Patchy clusters of glowmold grew larger, bringing a pallid light. Instead of the vibrant yellow of the city caverns, this stuff shed a thin, greenish-gray light. Cullen remembered the long-dead trolls up in the city. Their parchment-dry skin was the same color.

The path led to a blank cavern wall beside an open pit ten yards across. When they drew near, Gheen stopped.

The troll turned to Cullen and pointed at the pit. Surrounding it lay items of troll clothing, walking staffs, and more than a few skins reeking of the nasty trollish wine. "This is where they come. The demon calls them, and they cast themselves into the pit.

"Azuk is here. You have done your part, human, by bringing us here. I must go into the pit to kill him. Stay here. This is for a troll — one with the blood of a Holy One — to do."

Cullen drew his sword and put a hand on the troll's shoulder. "Holy One? Look, I know you are joined to the shaman, but how will you do this? Where is vurad, the knife?"

Gheen drew the blade from a pocket. It looked tiny in the troll's hand. He handed it to Cullen and looked away. "Take this from me and go from here."

"Go? No. This is the vurad blade. We need this. We came to find the trolls, and we've done that. If the demon is to be killed, we'll do it together."

"No!" Gheen roared. "Blade is not vurad. Blade is *ukar*, a knife of sacrifice... of human sacrifice. Take it, Cullen, and go from me."

Cullen stared at the troll and at the blade in his own hand.

"Human sacrifice? You're supposed to kill me to defeat Azuk?"

Gheen stood silent.

The realization grew like lighting a lantern in a dark room. "The Holy One manipulated us. To get us to come down here to find your city and this damn knife. Did you know? Were you in on his scheme? Or was it just me, the foolish, ignorant *pakh-hu*?" He looked at the troll clothing. "They were already dead, and he knew it. I'm supposed to be a damned sacrifice to your demon god to stop him from taking any more of your kind."

"No," the troll shouted again. "Gheen didn't know. Azuk is not demon god."

"But the shaman knew, and Grimmun too, I'd wager." Cullen looked into the troll's face. "And then you must have known also when you joined with the blind, forgetful fool."

Gheen nodded slowly. "When I was joined to the Holy One, I saw and felt the memories of shamans from very long ago."

"Then his promises were meaningless to me, weren't they? He had no intention of letting my people go. This is all some mystic, prophetic game to take my blood." Cullen laughed. "And now you can't do it. You can't do what you were sent to do."

He turned to look back in the direction they'd come. "Ounwe's teeth," he swore. "And I can't get out of here without you. So, Gheen, you and I are going to kill whatever is down here, and then you're going to lead me out. And then I'll take my people back where they belong."

"Cullen, do you remember the picture of Boruk-Kan in the temple?"

"What of it?"

"There was human figure in the picture."

"So?"

"Gheen doesn't know trolls' old history."

"So?"

"I think Holy Ones and Seekers — sniffer humans — worked together to defeat demon. Gheen and Cullen saw this in the temple in Dhugash. Was not only shamans like Holy One said."

"Maybe. If so, he lied again."

"Not lie, but didn't tell all of truth," Gheen said.

"It's the same thing. Look, I'm guessing that picture in the temple was made before the demon came. That means humans were already part of troll society. Or sniffers were, anyway. Why are sniffers so special to your kind?"

Gheen gazed down into the pit. "Last night, Gheen had dream — vision — from Holy One. He told Gheen to take Cullen's blood so that Gheen may become Holy One."

Cullen stared at the troll, but Gheen wouldn't return his gaze. "Is that how we defeat the demon? You have to kill a sniffer to become a shaman so you can use the magic of the old shamans to kill Azuk? Forget it, Gheen. I won't let you kill me."

"Gheen does not want to kill Cullen. Gheen won't kill Cullen."

Cullen inhaled deeply, breathing in the fetid stink of dead troll flesh rising from the pit. "Let's find this thing and get out of here. If I die fighting the demon, then so be it."

"Is not all," Gheen said, still not taking his eyes from the pit.

"Now what?"

"Vurad blade is not for trolls, but humans. For sniffer." He finally looked up at Cullen. "All Gheen knows is that your blood is holy to trolls."

Cullen snorted. "That again?" He slid the knife into his pocket, unshouldered his pack, and took out a torch, flint, and steel. "Well, this holy sniffer is going down into that pit. I'm not killing anybody but the demon. Are you coming with me, troll? Ow!"

He looked down at his hands, which throbbed with tingling energy — the exact sensation he'd felt in the temple. But added to that was a different note, a darker shudder of fear that shot through his mind in an enveloping blanket of terror.

From below came a squelching, bubbling noise. Gheen moved to the edge of the pit. "We won't have to go down. The demon Azuk comes to us." He drew his scimitar and held it over the pit. Even in the dim light, Cullen saw that the troll's eyes were wild, not with fear, but with some other ecstatic emotion.

Gheen chanted in a powerful, echoing voice, "*Gor pakh ji vurad hanam; Gor pakh na vurad Azuk.*"

The words echoed from the walls of the cavern.

From the pit, the bubbling sound grew louder, like a vast boiling cauldron of putrescent oil heated in the fires of hell.

Gheen's chant grew louder, echoing and filling the chamber with pulsing noise. Another voice answered, echoing the words. Cullen recognized the voice of the shaman, the ancient Holy One. He shot a glance around the cavern. The shaman wasn't there. He turned back to see Gheen standing over the pit. The voices, calling and answering, came from him.

"Gor pakh ji vurad hanam; Gor pakh na vurad Azuk!"

Cullen realized he had his sword in one hand and the vurad blade in the other. But what good was mere steel against a demon? He glanced over the edge of the pit, and his heart froze. The pit was filled with an oily, seething mass of gray horror. Troll faces and limbs writhed on its surface, appearing and then melting into the slimy whole. Great eyes a yard across formed and unformed. As it neared the pit's surface, the echoing chorus of Gheen and the Holy One sounded like a thousand voices.

Gheen stood exultant over the seething thing, his scimitar glowing with unnatural light. As he watched, it grew and transformed into the sword Cullen had seen on the temple's wall. Blazing light shot from its edge, filling the cavern with dazzling, coruscating silver fire.

The chant thundered and reverberated from the walls. Gheen himself began to change. His face shifted into the aged likeness of the shaman, broken tusk and all, then into another troll and another. A light grew within the troll, growing brighter and brighter until Cullen had to turn away.

"Almak gur an, Cullen!"

The voice spoke in Trollish, but Cullen understood as if his own father had spoken: "The blood of the faithless one, Cullen!" But he stood rooted to the ground, the light burning and dazzling his eyes.

From the pit, the demon's roiling shape rose and shifted, coalescing into a hideously twisted form twice the size of a normal troll. It also held a scimitar in a gnarled claw, the dark twin of the blade in Gheen's hand.

Gheen swung his blade in a two-handed blow that should have been powerful enough to shatter a tree. The blade crashed against the demon's scimitar with a shower of sparks that lit up the cavern.

Azuk gave a hideous, mocking roar of a laugh. "Gheen, son of Ama, it long, long years since I've tasted the blood of a Holy One."

Gheen panted and swung again, but Azuk's blade easily deflected the attack. Again and again, he beat against the dark form, hammering it repeatedly as the demon simply laughed. With a flick of its wrist, the creature's sword sent Gheen's flying. It was toying with him.

Gheen bellowed in anger and dove for his blade, rolled, and sprang to his feet. Suddenly, he stopped, and his eyes grew wide. "Cullen!" he shouted. "The ritual is not complete! The blood of the faithless. *Almak gur an!* It does not mean death!"

"Blast it! We don't have time for rituals."

Cullen lunged and swung his own blade at the creature, but the demon seemed impervious to their weapons.

"A Holy One and a Seeker?" the demon said. "Oho! At last, I will be free of this pit of death."

The demon swung its black sword at Gheen, swatting the troll with the flat of its blade. Cullen heard a loud *thud* as Gheen landed in a heap across the cavern.

He jabbed the demon with the vurad blade. The demon lifted its arms and laughed. "You don't know how to use the power! You're both mine to consume."

Cullen bolted to Gheen's side.

"*Almak gur an,* friend Cullen!" Clutched in Gheen's hand was the *kor-oba* stone, just like the one on the Holy One's forehead.

Cullen snatched up the stone. It glowed with a faint blue light. The runes inscribed on it burned his hand. He held it to Gheen's forehead in the faint hope that it would complete whatever joining had occurred with the Holy One. Nothing.

The demon thing howled with laughter and walked toward them, sword raised over its head. It chanted in foul mockery of the words Gheen had spoken.

The blood of the faithless, Cullen thought.

Cullen looked at the vurad blade in his left hand. It pulsed with the same blue light as the stone. As Azuk neared, the demon's dark magic lanced through Cullen like a thousand needles. Instinctively, he touched the vurad to the kor-oba stone. And suddenly, he knew what had to be done. He dropped to his knees, laid the stone and his sword next to Gheen, and plunged the vurad blade into the palm of his left hand.

Blood coursed from the wound and down the blade. He grasped the *kor-oba* stone in his bleeding hand and smashed it hard against Gheen's forehead.

Gheen convulsed, and the stone flashed with the radiant light of a hundred suns.

The demon howled.

Gheen shook himself as if awaking from a sleep and leaped to his feet. He dashed at the demon, catching up his sword from the ground.

"Gor pakh ji vurad hanam; Gor pakh na vurad Azuk," he shouted in the same thundering, echoing voice as before, but this time Cullen heard only a single thunderous voice.

Gheen swung his flashing scimitar at the creature. The demon snatched up its blade, raising it in defense, but Gheen's sword clove through the demon in a shower of radiant sparks.

The hideous body writhed and crumpled to the ground. In the same instant, a piercing scream emanated from the pit below.

Gheen threw his sword to the ground and picked up the demon's body. Though it was twice his size, he raised it high over his head and, with a mighty howl, hurled it into the pit. He raised both arms and chanted again.

Cullen felt the ground shake beneath him. From overhead, stones fell from the cavern's ceiling into the pit in a continuous, thunderous rain until the pit itself — and whatever remained of the demon — was buried beneath tons of rock.

He gazed in awe at Gheen. The troll lowered his arms and turned. The stone, red with the blood of the faithless, sat affixed on his forehead as if nailed in place.

"Well done, Cullen. It is over. The demon is trapped in this place. He is bound with stones and with enough dark magic to last a thousand, thousand years."

"Not dead?"

"No," Gheen said. "But sealed."

"For how long?"

Gheen shrugged. "Until it is not."

Cullen slumped to the ground. His hand ached. He held it up to examine the wound, but the flesh was whole. Sticky blood covered his hand, his clothing, and the ground around him, but there was no sign of the wound.

He reached for his water skin, but it was empty, torn open in — whatever happened.

Gheen handed him his own. It reeked of troll wine, but Cullen drank anyway.

"It is powerful thing," Gheen said, tapping the stone on his forehead. "What you call troll magic. Gheen was joined with Holy One and the Holy Ones of old. The magic was enough."

"The Holy One will be glad to hear that," Cullen said, rubbing his forehead.

"The Holy One is dead but is alive within me. I am now the Holy One of the Three Valleys clan."

He looked at the troll, shook his head, and chuckled. "Then you're in a position to honor the Holy One's promises."

Gheen nodded. "I am."

The troll put out his hand. "I have seen *pakh-hu* do this. I think is greeting between humans who are friends."

Cullen took the troll's hand. The clawed fingers felt wrong in his hand, but he shook it. "It is that. It is a greeting between friends, Gheen."

Chapter Twenty-One

Endings

The sun touched the cliffs above the tunnel behind them, casting the steep wooded sides of the canyon into shadow. "We're making good time," Perban said. "There's a high spot ahead near the road in a grove of aspens. When the sun goes behind the mountains, we'll be in deep shade. We can look down on the troll camp, but they won't be able to see us."

The rest of the raiding party needed to see the layout of the village, but Isabo begrudged every second. She glanced back at the four elements creeping forward cautiously.

They stopped at the rocky outcropping that Isabo and Perban had spotted the day before. The trail broadened, and the aspens thinned enough for most of the group to see their objective from above. Isabo pointed out the wood and stone building where the slave told them Cullen was being held and outlined the plan. "After dark, I'll go with First and Second Sword. We enter and make our way along the inside of the walls to a pathway marked with white stones leading to the building at the center of the camp. Even with a bright moon, we should be in shadow under the wall."

Looking at Voss, she said, "Third Sword will be right behind First and Second. You'll stand guard outside as we enter the building to find my father. We find him, and then you lead the way back to the gate."

"And what about Fourth Sword?" Gaskun asked. "And since we're all archers, it's only right that we be called 'First Arrow.' You know, even with the moon, it will be harder to find targets. Maybe we should —"

"You and the Fourth will do the job I give you. And that job is to bring out any humans who want to come." She pointed to the camp. "It looks like the houses right inside the gate are larger, so those are probably the trolls'. The smaller ones at the other end of the camp are most likely where the humans are kept. You're to rouse them quietly. If they'll come on their own, fine, but don't waste time convincing anyone. They may even know another way out. Otherwise, make your way to the gate and then back here."

"I thought you weren't interested in rescuing others," he said with a hint of accusation in his tone.

"Don't push me. If you can't handle the task, then stay here," Isabo said fiercely.

Gaskun raised his hands. "Now, now. We're all in this together. I was just making a suggestion, is all. We'll do our part, me and the Fourth. You can count on us."

Perban nodded thoughtfully. "It's as good a plan as we could come up with. The priority is to bring out Gabril Cullen and whoever else we can. That's it. If we can do it without alerting the trolls, so much the better. If it goes to hell and they're on to us, we'll fight our way out with Third Sword covering us. I just wish we knew the layout of the shaman's house. We'll have to go in and ransack the place until we find Cullen."

"A shaman?" Mayra asked with a cautious look. "You didn't say anything about a shaman."

Isabo scoffed at the girl. "You're worried about an old troll mystic scattering chicken bones to tell fortunes? We're here to kill trolls and get my father. Shamans be damned. If the thought of taking on a troll mystic is too daunting, leave him to me. I won't hesitate to stick a blade into him."

Mayra bristled at that. "I'll do my part, too, but I've heard stories. They say their shamans know dark magic and can turn folks to stone with just a word."

Isabo waved her sword. "Then I'll take his head off so he can't say a word."

Mayra lowered her head and fell silent.

A few moments later, Isabo pulled Perban aside. "Will, get them ready. Tell them what they have to do."

He gave her a questioning eye. "Is everything okay?"

She rubbed at her temples. "Just a little headache. I'm sure it'll go away once we start tonight."

He leaned close and whispered. "Is it the voices?"

She gave a faint shake of her head, but he didn't look convinced.

"Look, Iza," he said, "I'm getting a little worried."

"About attacking the trolls?"

"No, about you. You change sometimes. You're fine, and then sometimes you explode at people for no reason, like at Mayra just now. It's like there's two different people living in your skin."

He touched her hand, and she realized that she'd balled her fists so tightly that it hurt. She jerked away. "I'm fine, Will. Just get them ready, okay?"

"I will, Chief."

"One more thing," she said, willing herself to relax and silence the taunting voice in her head. "I don't trust Gaskun. He talks too much. Put Hupp with him. If Gaskun freezes up, we'll have one of our own ready to take over."

"Katya Bromlin is already in Fourth Sword, and besides, Hupp isn't a bow-man."

Isabo flexed her fingers, as if trying to work out a cramp. "It will be too dark for much shooting, though I'm glad we didn't put all the archers in the Fourth. Just tell Hupp and Bromlin they need to be ready if it goes badly."

"Right, Chief."

***

She stood apart as Will addressed the group. "Every blade, arrow, spear, or stone we have gets coated in troll blood before we go in. That stuff makes them shriek like demons before it kills them, so go for quick kills. The longer it takes us, the more likely it is that one of them will hear and sound the alarm."

Those from Haywold and the south nodded thoughtfully. They'd done this before.

"For those of you who haven't killed a troll yet," he said, "don't hesitate. It doesn't take much if you have their blood on your weapons. A blade to the face or exposed bit of arm or leg. Cut them where you can and get out of the way. The blood will do the rest. Ounwe's teeth, Daron Homah here killed one with a rock."

There was laughter at that, and Daron nodded eagerly. "I surely did, and from twenty yards away!"

"Where's Hupp?" Perban asked.

"Here," the butcher's son replied.

"What's on your belt?"

The man chuckled, untied a leather thong at his side, and raised it for all to see. From it hung a number of dried, leathery shapes. "I been taking a collection of trolls' ears," he said.

Perban continued. "You all know how big these things are, but all this shows they can be killed. We proved that, and we'll do it again. But have a care, because if you miss or hesitate, they'll cut you in half."

He pointed out the field from which they would approach, the location of the gate, and the rectangular platform in front of it.

Isabo turned and went to Amon's side. "Promise me something," she said, lowering her voice.

Her brother gave her a suspicious look. "As long as it doesn't involve turning around and going home."

"Just stay near me, or Will or Tanner. And don't do anything stupid, no matter what happens to me."

He ran a hand through his tangled mop of dark hair. "Iza, I won't do anything stupid. Well, not too stupid," he said with a grin. "You know I can handle myself against these things. And why are you making a big deal of this now, after all we've done?"

She shook her head. "There will be a lot more of them this time. I'm serious, Amon. You saw what they did to Zoller — cut him in half with one blow." She paused. "You know, you were just a babe when those things raided and killed Ma and Seala. It was the worst thing that ever happened. I couldn't stand it if anything were to happen to you."

"I wish I knew them," he said with a soft smile. "I barely remember Ma at all, and I can't even picture Seala in my mind. It must have been nice to have a twin."

Her face grew hard. "That's what they took from us, Amon." She glanced up to see Brother Yoren nearby. He faced Perban and the group, but he cupped his hand to his ear as if he was straining to hear what they were saying.

She cursed. "I thought I told you to stay away from me, monk."

He hurriedly retreated to the back of the group. She watched him for a moment, but he wouldn't meet her gaze. Something other than her presence had spooked him. Had he been listening to their conversation?

Perban raised his voice to get Isabo's attention. "The thing that worries me is where all the trolls are. A camp this size should hold hundreds of the creatures. Besides the few on the walls, we haven't seen one since we crossed the river. Where did they all go?"

"I don't know and don't care," she said, rejoining the conversation. "That just makes our job easier."

***

Cullen and Gheen stood at the foot of the road that spiraled up the cavern wall from the underground troll city.

"We must return quickly," Gheen said. "All is not well above in the village."

"How do you know? Never mind. If you say so. I want out of here anyway." He followed the curving road with his eye until it disappeared in a dark opening above. "How do you know this way leads where we need to go?"

The troll chuckled and smiled at the human with a gap-toothed leer. The troll's expression would have seemed almost comic before, but Cullen sensed a gentle humor and depth that hadn't been there before. Or maybe it had. He eyed the troll. Gheen was different. Whatever had happened to him in the battle with the demon had changed him.

He chuckled. *Maybe I've changed as well.*

He no longer saw a beast to be slain but a warrior fighting to save his people. And yet, trolls were murderous, savage creatures who raided and stole his people. He couldn't reconcile the concepts, but he knew he must.

The stone in the troll's forehead pulsed with a faint gray glow. "I know many things, friend Cullen. Not all things, but many. This road is called *Nuzh-an Burukh*, the Path to the Sky. It ends near the deserted village where we started."

"How could you know that?"

"I am now a Holy One. I see with the eyes of those who have gone before me. There is little time, *pakh-hu an*," Gheen said, motioning toward the road. He shouldered his pack and began walking. "Your people are going to attack my village, and I sense a great evil among them, not unlike the one we just defeated. They have blood weapons."

"Seven hells. What does that mean, and what are we waiting for? We have to stop it. Let's run."

Whatever reconciliation he'd come to with Gheen was on a personal level. Perhaps in the future, they could use it to broker some kind of understanding between the two races. For now, they had to stop a battle.

***

The group arrived at the edge of the field as the last orange glow of daylight faded from the mountain peaks to the east.

Isabo watched as Perban handed Tanner, Voss, and Gaskun lengths of knotted rope. "It's an hour until full dark," he whispered, "and not too long after that until moonrise. At full dark, we'll move quietly behind the platform in front of the gate. It should give us plenty of cover. Everyone takes hold of this rope when we move out, so no one gets lost or stumbles. Make sure your people don't draw their weapons until we're in place behind the platforms. Is that clear?"

All three nodded.

He pulled Tanner aside. "Tell the monks to stay under the cover of the trees. We'll likely have trolls after us when we come out of the gate. They'll need to help the injured, but they'll have to move quickly."

The minutes passed quickly. Isabo sat in the thicket and saw to her gear, making sure sword, daggers, and anything else metal were sufficiently padded against making noise. Looking up in the dim light, she saw Amon and the others doing the same. Her brother glanced at her and gave a grim nod, a thumbs-up, and a confident smile.

At last, she leaned back and breathed deeply a few times, forcing herself to relax. Not surprisingly, relaxation wouldn't come. She watched the stars brighten in the sky and picked out the constellations: the Bow, the Fish, and even the dim form of the Three Swords. Surely, seeing the Three Swords high in the eastern sky was a harbinger of luck. It had to be.

***

Isabo almost didn't hear him coming. The faint metallic snick of a dagger being drawn gave her an instant's warning, but it was all she needed. She spun to her feet, sword in hand, and knocked the blade from Brother Yoren's hand. With her sword at his throat, she watched the dagger spin harmlessly into the trees. The monk's overhand blow had been laughably clumsy. "It's you," he rasped,

274

clutching at his hand. "It wasn't the descendant of Sayala who would plunge us into destruction, but the twin — the twin of Seala. Ignatus warned me, but I wouldn't listen."

A hulking shadow rose behind Yoren, and a crashing fist drove the monk to the ground. "My apologies, Miss. Brother Yoren... He was not well," Brother Dunken stated meekly. I will stay with him."

Perban and Lim Voss pushed through the dark thicket to reach them. "What in blazes happened? What's all the noise?"

Isabo shrugged. "Brother Yoren is staying here. Dunken will watch him."

***

Isabo was grateful the moon still lay hidden behind the eastern mountains. The dark was a blessing, but two hundred yards of open ground still lay between the edge of the field and the odd platform at the gate. As she moved, Isabo felt the peering, searching eyes of the trolls in the heavy gloom.

A steady breeze from down the valley brought the scent of the woods, tilled earth, and trolls. The closer she drew to the village, the stronger the stench grew. In the field, tracking a small group of the creatures from a distance was simple; up close, the reek became overwhelming. She concentrated, trying to determine whether there were any of the beasts outside the walls. "I think we're safe for now," she whispered. "I can't smell any of them nearby."

She called Amon alongside and asked what he made of it.

He covered his nose and stifled a cough. "Smells like an orchard dungheap."

"Can you smell any outside the walls?"

He shook his head.

The open gate loomed up to her right. She held tight to the rope and followed Perban around the shadowy wooden platform. In a moment, the dark mass of the structure blocked whatever could be seen of the gate. She sniffed and leaned closer to the edge of the structure, then sniffed at it again. Blood. It wasn't troll's blood; that had its own weird tang. This was different. Human?

She reached out to Perban and drew him near. She placed her lips near his ear and whispered, "Stinks of blood. Human executions, maybe?"

Perban pointed at what might be feathers or bits of fur and shook his head. "Animal sacrifices? Or maybe butchering dinner for the slaves?"

She listened to the night sounds. Somewhere to her left, a wolf howled high up in the mountains. Its eerie call echoed strangely in the deep valley, unlike anything she had heard in the Uplands. Behind her, behind the blood-soaked platform, and behind the palisade walls came a deep, guttural voice, repeating a phrase over and over again. The voice was a troll's, and the words were gibberish, but she recognized it as a plaintive song. It almost sounded like a lullaby. This quiet, almost tranquil scene was not what she expected. What had she expected? Bonfires and raucous feasting? Never mind, she told herself. Quiet, peaceful trolls will be easier to kill.

The crests of the peaks westward above the tunnel glimmered with the silver light of the rising moon. Their timing was perfect.

Satisfied that everyone was in place, Isabo drew her sword and a vial of troll blood. Perban nodded and whispered to those behind him, "Draw your weapons and wipe them with blood. Once we're inside the gate, don't say a word, but if we meet trolls, kill them before they can kill you."

Isabo gave a tight smile. At last. All doubt and anxiety were gone. Even the phantom voice was silent for now. It had all come to this moment. The plan was simple, and that suited her: kill trolls and rescue her father.

She and Perban peered over the top of the platform at the gate and the stockade wall surrounding the camp. The rising moon cast a dim light on the hulking figures of two trolls slowly pacing the walkway atop the wooden wall. They were in no hurry, pausing occasionally and then moving on again, returning to the gate every quarter hour or so.

Once the trolls left the gate a third time, Perban waved them forward.

Slowly, they crept around the platform to the black shadows under the gate. Isabo took a deep breath and stepped through into the troll village. She remembered the rough layout of the troll camp from looking down on it: a few larger buildings inside the gate, a road leading left and right, and a hundred scattered buildings within the camp in no discernible pattern. They padded down the road to the left that led to the shaman's dwelling and her father.

The village lay before them in the still, clear night. They moved quickly and silently, passing neatly trimmed cottages, some with troll-sized doors and some human-sized. It didn't make sense that trolls lived in such nice houses. Trolls were mere beasts, after all. And they surely wouldn't build such homes for their human slaves. She hoped she had sent Fourth Sword to the right place to rescue the captives. It was too late to change.

She glanced up at the wall. Hopefully, any trolls up there were now looking outward.

The way broadened from a narrow road between buildings to a broad street. Perban stayed to the left, under the wall. Lights burned within some, but most were dark.

How many held trolls? Isabo wondered. Even if the village was partially deserted, enough remained to slaughter this small band without difficulty. She gripped her sword. They would pay dearly if it came to that.

From somewhere ahead on the road came the sound of an argument. Trollish voices rumbled and wrangled. One was distraught as if some great woe had overtaken him; the other grumbled and cursed.

Perban led the group into the shadow between two buildings as the trolls approached. They waited long minutes until the creatures passed and then cautiously resumed their journey. If all went well, Gaskun and Fourth Sword were under the wall on the other side of the camp, making their way to the slave quarters.

Several buildings later, Perban halted and pointed at a structure larger than any they'd passed — the shaman's house. It wasn't what she'd expected, but she wasn't exactly sure what she expected.

"Be ready," Perban whispered. "Voss, circle the building and see if there are guards. Don't get too close."

"That wouldn't be a wise idea." A figure appeared from the shadow of the shaman's home, then another one, much taller — a human and a troll.

"I am Wogan," the human said. "This is Grimmun-Kan, chief of the Three Valleys clan." He bowed his head to the troll and turned to the humans. "Place your weapons on the ground."

The troll drew a large curved blade whose edge shone in the moonlight. Two more trolls appeared at his side. In addition to their leather armor, they each wore a tight-fitting helm and a shaped steel plate with a high collar to protect their shoulders and neck. It would be difficult to find openings to insert a poisoned blade.

Isabo spat at his feet. "I am Isabo Cullen, Chief of the Army of the Uplands. We've come for my father, Gabril Cullen. Release him to us, and we will leave."

The troll leaned back and laughed, a deep, rumbling sound that chilled Isabo.

"You journeyed here to rescue the *pakh-hu* Cullen?" the troll asked. "Your effort was wasted. He is performing a service for the Holy One of this clan."

It was Isabo's turn to laugh. "My father would never betray his people to help monsters."

Wogan stepped forward. He wore the iron collar of a slave. "You must go, or the *trollim* will kill you. Your father is not here. He's —"

"Lies," Isabo said. "Attack!"

The few bows they had twanged, sending a spate of arrows at the troll Grimmun-Kan. Isabo leaped forward and swung her blade to strike down the hulking beast. Amon flashed past her, bringing his heavy sword up in a scything blow that bit deep into another troll's armor. Amon wrenched it away, but the troll drove the hilt of its sword into Amon's gut.

"Amon!" she screamed, but she couldn't see if he still stood. From the corner of her eye, she saw the climber Garnay tackle Wogan and drag him out of the fray. She lunged again at the still-standing troll chief, who parried her blow, but did not strike back. Mayra called a warning to someone. From somewhere to her left came the stench and heavy footfalls of more trolls joining the battle. A man crumpled under the sweeping stroke of a heavy sword. From her left came the heavy footfalls of more trolls joining the battle. Isabo hacked and thrusted again and again as the confrontation devolved into a mad melee.

"This one is mine," Grimmun-Kan called. He continued to parry and block her blows, but did not counter-attack.

"You must not do this!" Wogan shouted, but his words were drowned out by guttural curses, the clanging of swords, and the all-too-infrequent screams that Isabo now understood to be caused by a poisoned blade.

Hiram Tanner shoved Amon aside, but the boy swore at him and drove forward, hacking at the nearest troll. The creature growled and swung, missing Amon's head by inches.

A fierce spark of relief shot through Isabo that her brother still lived. She lunged at the troll chief with a sharp overhand blow.

Perban yelled in pain as another troll stumbled into him and fell, Mayra's sword protruding from its chest.

The young woman wrenched at the hilt and heaved, but not before a troll blade arced through the air, cleaving her head from her body.

"No!" someone yelled, leaping forward and throwing his bow aside. It was Arno Voss, Lim's brother. He tore his sword from its sheath and joined the fray, cursing and swinging wildly at the nearest troll.

Grimmun-Kan laughed as he swatted away the man's blows. He turned and swung a blow that sent the younger Voss's arm spinning into the darkness. Arno howled in pain, and the troll slashed at the man's head. Isabo watched in horror as the dark blade sliced through his helm and the man crumpled to the cobbles.

The troll chief lurched forward, drawing near to Isabo. "You are Cullen's daughter? You have the scent-gift as well. I would rather not kill one such as you, but I will if I must. Surrender now!"

Isabo ignored his words. She closed with him, sword in her left hand and dagger in her right. She swung a fierce blow at his neck. As he raised his curved blade to parry, she drove the dagger into his ribs. The blade caught on his armor and snapped.

Grimmun-Kan bellowed and brought his blade down on her head.

Her steel helm rang, and she staggered, blinded by the force of the blow. From somewhere behind came the sound of still more trolls — and humans — shouting and racing to the battle.

The sudden twang of bows was faint in the melee, but two trolls dropped, screaming. Someone lurched out of the darkness, taking Grimmun's knees out from under him. He bellowed what must have been a curse and fought to regain his feet.

Isabo cursed. She had thought the battle at the aurochs herd had taken a long time, but this fight seemed an eternity.

***

"Cullen must run more quickly," Gheen called over his shoulder. "The attack has begun. Your daughter is among them."

Isabo? Isabo is here?

They had covered half a league from the abandoned village at the cave mouth. Cullen had never seen a troll run like Gheen. The troll moved with an easy grace instead of his old lumbering shuffle. Was this the movement of some long-dead shaman? Whatever it was, the troll easily outpaced the experienced scout.

Cullen found his pace. He couldn't keep up with Gheen, but he stayed close. The walled village drew near, illuminated by the bright moon rising over the eastern peaks. He wondered who could be attacking the village. Had old Willim

Tallard brought an army from Cleft, and somehow Isabo too? Already, he heard swords clashing near the center of the village.

Ahead of him, Gheen paused at the broad eastern gate to wait for Cullen.

"Go," Cullen shouted, his breath coming quickly. "You know the way. I'll follow."

Gheen made his way through a warren of dark houses. Cullen found himself wishing he had some of Wogan's berries and herbs to vanquish the screaming of his aching muscles.

Gheen rounded a corner, and Cullen nearly ran into him. A furious battle occupied the wide dirt street in front of the shaman's temple home.

A familiar, tall figure battled a troll. In the light of the moon, he recognized Hiram Tanner, one of Isabo's friends, fighting Malbah, the troll Wogan had said was Grimmun's mate. Cullen started to shout, but his heart sank when he saw the troll chief fighting Will Perban — and Isabo.

"Gheen," he cried. "Stop them! Use your magic, damn you!"

***

Isabo lashed out with her blade as she tripped backward over a body. Her eyes cleared, and she saw with horror that the body was Amon's, illuminated by the nearly full moon. She leaped to her feet in a fury and spun, swinging and slashing at anything that moved. She hacked her way toward Grimmun-Kan, who stood locked in a furious battle with a stout man he didn't recognize. Neither held a sword. The troll's arms encircled the man in a back-breaking embrace while the human drove his thumbs into the troll's eyes. Grimmun-Kan staggered and threw the human to the ground, where he lay unmoving.

Isabo glanced around the area, her cheek torn by an unseen weapon. Trolls and humans lay motionless in the bloody street or groaned piteously.

Grimmun-Kan panted and growled low in his throat, panting but somehow unscathed. "Throw your blade down, *gruzhak pakh-hu!*"

She spat blood. "I want my father, you murdering pig beast!"

The troll laughed again. "You truly are a brave, but pathetic creature, human. Why will you not —"

She staggered but hefted her sword and lunged toward the troll. Grim-mun-Kan swung a clawed fist at her jaw.

"Isabo!"

At that moment, a coruscating blast of silvery light struck the human and troll like a torrent of icy nails. Isabo screamed and fell to the ground, clutching at her skin.

"Isabo, Isabo. What have you done?"

She looked up through the searing pain to see her father kneeling over her.

"I came to rescue you," she said weakly. She tried to blink away the blood to see him more clearly, but her eyes wouldn't focus.

"I'm here, sweet. We'll get you help. It's over now."

Another huge figure loomed over here beside her father — a hulking troll. "Get away from him, you filthy monster," she rasped, her breath coming in gasps. Her sword lay in her hand, but she didn't have the strength to lift it, to slash the creature's dirty throat, to watch it die screaming in agony.

"He's with me, Isabo. This is Gheen. We're working together to —"

No. It was wrong. The words made it sound like her father was in league with the monsters. The same monsters that killed her mother and Seala, and all the others. No one could do that. It was the betrayal of all humanity, and of all they had fought for.

Her eyes swam with tears and blood, and the voice came again.

You must kill them all. Kill every one of the trolls — and any traitor who stands in your way.

Chapter Twenty-Two

Conclusion

Cullen stood on the wide eastern veranda of the shaman's temple home — now Gheen's home. The morning dawned cold, and a chill wind blew from the peaks, foretelling early autumn and a bitter winter. A pale sun inched above the mountains, drawing a tear from his eyes. Cullen refused to look away from the piercing light to the row of human and troll bodies arrayed at his feet. If he looked down, he would have to gaze on the form of his son and all the others who died to rescue him. He could not face that.

Amon, what have I done to you?

A clawed hand took his shoulder and turned him from the harsh early sun.

Now arrayed in shaman's robes, Gheen handed him a stone cup. "Drink this, friend Cullen."

The human glanced at the cup and sniffed half-heartedly at it.

"Do not fear," Gheen said. "It is Wogan-thing's human wine, not trollish."

Cullen drank deeply, not tasting the sweet red liquid.

"These are honored dead," Gheen said, pointing at the row of bodies.

"Honored dead?" He nodded toward the bodies of Malbah and five other trolls he didn't know, their wounds sprouting hideous, twisted growths. "Yours, perhaps. They died defending their shaman's home. These humans, my people, my son, came on a fool's errand to find me. Their deaths are on my conscience."

The troll furrowed his brow. "I do not know that word."

Cullen snorted and shook his head. "I suppose not. You should learn what it means." He stared at his son's lifeless body. "You could have sent a delegation to come and ask for my help. All this could have been avoided."

"Would you have come quietly if such a delegation arrived at your door?"

"No, probably not."

"You are unlike most of your kind. You are *pakh-hu an*. We needed your gift. Without you, the demon Azuk would not have been defeated."

"I don't care," Cullen said tersely. He knelt beside Amon, caressed the cold cheek, and wept.

"My sight did not give me knowledge that he was here," Gheen said softly. "I mourn for you and for them. Come, let us leave the dead for now. Your daughter and the others still live."

Cullen looked into the troll's face and saw the grief there. In the confusion of his thoughts, it didn't make sense. Grief was a human emotion.

"Holy One, may I speak?"

They turned, and Cullen saw Grimmun standing at the doorway. Dark blood still seeped from a bandage on the chieftain's side. He wore a patch over one eye, and one of his tusks was broken. With him was Toleg, one of the party who had captured him.

"You must see to your wounds, Grimmun-Kan," Gheen said.

"In time, Holy One. Toleg has found two more of the *pakh-hu*. They were in the trees below the road to the Tunnel of Sukkuz. One was injured and has been taken to Wogan-thing. The other is with the other captives."

"Who is this, Cullen?" Gheen asked.

The scout shook his head. "I have no idea. I'd have thought everyone who could carry a sword would have joined in this foolish attack."

***

In a troll-guarded hallway, Cullen and Gheen watched Wogan tend to Isabo and Will Perban. The wounded were mercifully unconscious, thanks to the healer's potions.

Bandages swathed the left side of Isabo's face, hiding a wide slash from ear to chin. Cullen had seen the wound before Gheen did whatever it was that he did to stop the battle. Though Wogan had stitched it as neatly as he could, she would bear the scar for the rest of her life.

Cullen reached up to finger the scar on the side of his own face — the wound he had gotten in the ambush that killed Arden Luck.

Perban's injuries were less obvious but more immediately life-threatening. A thin coverlet hid the bandages over the man's chest and abdomen.

Gheen nodded toward the fighter. "Wogan-thing says this one may not live, despite his best efforts. Malbah slashed his belly and broke many ribs."

Cullen suddenly turned on the troll with more anger than he thought he had within him. "Say his name, Gheen. It's Wogan, not Wogan-thing. I don't care if he's here voluntarily or if he's a slave. Can't you and your people do that? Can't you just say his name?"

The troll stood a full head taller than Cullen, but he looked abashed. "Gheen will do what Cullen asks. My people will... take time. It is what we have always done."

"Aren't you the Holy One? You can make that happen, right? Things can be different between our people."

The troll nodded slowly.

Cullen sighed as every bit of energy seemed to be draining from him. The journey of the last few weeks leading to this moment had taken so much from him and those he loved. "I'm sorry, Gheen. You really are the Holy One now. I shouldn't talk to you this way. We can change things. We must."

"Can you speak for all your people?" the troll asked.

"That's a fair point," he said with a weary smile. "I suppose we both have work to do. We're not that different in that respect." He pointed to Perban, who lay on a pallet, breathing unevenly. "Can your powers do nothing for him?"

"Is not that kind of power. I can prolong his life for a short time, but his body must heal on its own. If the damage is too great, as I fear, he will die. But Gheen — and Wogan," he said awkwardly, "will do what we can."

Cullen nodded. The troll spoke in an odd mixture of the old creature he had been and the new. For some reason, that was comforting.

Hiram Tanner sat on the floor beside Isabo's bed, his broken arm splinted and immobilized in a sling. He glared at Cullen and Gheen and then looked down.

A third figure clad in a gray robe lay face down on a table. Wogan stood by, gently probing at a knot on the back of the man's head.

"That's a monk," Cullen exclaimed. "Tanner, what's he doing here?"

The townsman said nothing but spat on the floor.

Gheen leaned close to inspect the monk's robes. "The *pakh-hu* is one of your Holy Ones?"

"You could say that, but it's nothing like those of your kind. He can't do magic. I have no idea what he's doing here." He looked around dazedly. He was bone tired, and things weren't making sense.

Tanner struggled to his feet and lurched toward Gheen. "Don't you touch him, you filthy pig!"

Gheen motioned to one of the troll guards. "Take this one from here, but do not harm him."

With Tanner gone, Gheen again leaned close to the monk. His expression, as far as Cullen could tell, was a mix of sadness, wonder, and admiration.

"He came to kill you," a dry, faint voice said. "I should have let him."

Cullen's eyes leapt to his daughter, who turned her head away with a painful grimace. "Isabo!" he breathed, dropping to her side. He took her hand, but she pulled it away.

"I came to save you," she croaked. "I brought an army, just like you asked. You repaid us all by betraying us to these... monsters. You're helping them. Amon's dead — your own son — and Arden Luck and Finn Zollar and your friend Tallard."

Cullen had to strain to hear her words. "Isabo, sweet, I did this to help our people."

She gave a soft, choking laugh. "There's nothing you can say, Father, that will change my mind about these evil beasts. All these people came to help you, to rescue you, by Ounwe, and you've been in league with the filth the whole time. I told them in Haywold and in Pineholm that you were in danger, and they all believed it, so they left their homes and came with me. Even those hopeless monks came because of you." She paused and turned her head enough to see the still-unconscious gray-clad figure. "Yoren was right, wasn't he? He said you were going to start a war that would destroy us all." Her voice was thin and dry, but it strengthened as she spoke. "Well, let the war come, because we can kill trolls now. We know how. I've killed dozens of the merciless, murdering things, and I'll kill even more. I raised an army to rescue you, and I'll raise another, greater one that will scour the mountains and plains until every last one of them is food for the crows."

Cullen flinched and slumped wearily against the door jamb.

"You should go, perhaps," Wogan said softly, taking his shoulder. "She must rest. What she said... perhaps it is because of the potion I gave to her. It has disturbed her."

Isabo gave another sharp laugh and turned her head.

***

Outside, Cullen turned to the healer, who had followed them from the room.

"Will the monk live, Wogan?"

287

The healer gave a noncommittal half-nod. "Someone hit him very hard. His skull is not broken, but he is still unconscious. If he wakes, he should recover."

As tired as Cullen was, Wogan looked even more so. The frail old man's smock and hands were covered in blood, presumably both human and troll. He must have been up all night ministering to the wounded and dying.

He looked to Gheen, who wore a troubled expression. "Last night, when we were returning, you told me Isabo's attacking party had a weapon, blood poison, I think you said. What is that?"

The troll gave a low rumble and frowned. "It is the worst poison. It is unthinkable that a troll would use it against another, and its use is forbidden at pain of death. Your Isabo must have discovered its secret."

"But what is it?"

"It pains me to say, it is so foul." The troll looked at Wogan, who cleared his throat.

Even the captive human looked disturbed at the thought. He said, "It is simply the blood of the *trollim*. It is a deadly, corrosive poison when used against another troll outside its immediate family. You saw the cancerous growths on the wounds of the slain *trollim*?"

Cullen nodded.

"That is the result. It causes searing pain and not quite instantaneous death." He gave a thin, weary smile. "That is why I or other humans tend to the wounds of the *trollim* and not they themselves."

Cullen's mind reeled at the implication. "And that is what Isabo used on the trolls she encountered."

"Yes," Wogan said, "They likely smeared it on their weapons. Grim-mun-Kan was fortunate that he was not pierced by such a weapon."

"But he wore a bandage on his head. I saw the blood."

"The Holy One gave him warning of the attack," Gheen said. "Grim-mun-Kan wore battle armor. His injury was not from a tainted weapon."

Cullen nodded and looked back at Wogan. "I treated you badly. For that, I'm sorry. I see why the trolls value you. Do what you can for them all, our kind and the trolls."

"Of course," he said, stifling a yawn. "That is most civil of you, Cullen."

***

The sun rose higher over the peaks that hid the entrance to the tunnels, the ancient city, and whatever remained of Azuk the demon. Cullen turned away from that and stared up at the opposite end of the valley. On the other side of that wall of rock lay the Roaring River and the Uplands, and far away to the west, his home.

Gheen gave a low, rumbling chuckle and began a slow chant with an odd, guttural rhyme. "That was *Nurosh Kha Dum*. It is a poem that is in my memory, though I never learned it. It tells of a troll forced to escape from his home before it was buried under a slide of rock. He says, 'We are changed by our journeys and what befalls us, but our homes remain. A troll carries the shadows, the dreams, the fears, and dragons of home under one's skin, at the extreme corners of one's eyes and in the gristle of one's earlobe.'"

Cullen turned and cocked an eye to study the troll. "Poetry? You are not the troll you once were, Gheen. You are changed, and not just because of the rock on your forehead."

Gheen smiled and touched the *kor-oba* stone with a thick finger. "Changed? Yes, I am changed. Among the *trollim*, I am no longer Gheen. A Holy One does not need a common name. I carry the knowledge and memories of all the Holy Ones of our clan since Azuk first perverted the holy rituals, maybe further."

"Azuk was a shaman? Not a demon?"

Gheen looked thoughtful. "Maybe demon is good name for what he became. He sought to use the *mok vurad* ritual to acquire limitless power and knowledge."

"And yet you now have the knowledge and magic of all the shamans who came before. What's the difference?"

"I will endeavor to learn that."

Cullen gave a low whistle, but then smiled. "Be careful with that. Can a *pakh-hu* still call his friend by a common name?" Cullen asked.

Aydin, the old shaman's servant, padded up silently. "Holy One," he said, "Grimmun-Kan craves the honor of speaking with you again."

"Come, my friend Cullen," the troll said. "There is much to be done. You have helped to save my people and have freed your own."

***

Grimmun-Kan stood when the new shaman entered the room. He growled at the sight of Cullen but bowed to Gheen.

Cullen watched the interplay between the two trolls, still amazed at the transition in his friend and the readiness with which Grimmun acknowledged the shaman's authority. It was as if a simple farmer had become the king of an empire overnight, and no one had batted an eye.

"How many of the *pakh-hu* will go?" Gheen asked.

Grimmun-Kan shrugged. "More than half. It will cripple us. You cannot allow this, Holy One. Who will tend our fields and gather the harvest? We have relied on human slaves for years. Perhaps my father was right. Defeating the demon came at too high a price."

Gheen barked a few words in the troll tongue, and Grimmun-Kan bowed. Cullen had never seen Gheen speak to another troll in such an authoritative tone.

The shaman turned to Cullen. "Your sacrifice against the demon Azuk has made you *troll-hu zur anush*, the Strong Hand of the Trolls. You are bound to us, and as *pakh-hu an*, to me. But I and my people are no less bound to you. Help us to learn your ways. In turn, we will teach you ours."

Grimmun looked as if he'd eaten something nasty.

Cullen glanced down at the mark seared into his palm. When he smashed the stone against Gheen's forehead in the cave, the vision of the ancients, both troll and human, flooded him, if only for an instant. Humans and trolls in the distant past had indeed coexisted. Could they do so again? Yet years of distrust and outright butchery lay between them. Many on both sides would resist the thought of mutual trust between the races.

Isabo, for one. She still had not spoken to him. If anything, her anger had deepened.

Cullen looked up at the shaman and the troll chief and spoke. "I can promise nothing, but I will speak to the humans. Both our peoples must change, but if it is in my power, I will work for that."

***

In two weeks, a hundred and fifty humans and two trolls stood near the path at the edge of the Roaring River canyon. A stout, planked bridge now spanned the river. Cullen glanced down at the tree by the cave. The staked head was conspicuous in its absence.

"We'll bury our dead across the canyon. Humans will set up guards on the other end of the bridge," he said to Gheen. "I will speak again to Isabo and will do what I can to avert further hostilities."

The shaman spoke sharply to Grimmun-Kan, who glared at the departing humans. "As I live," the troll chief said, "no trolls from the Three Valleys Clan will raid human lands. We will meet with the other clans to discuss our arrangement and share news of our victory over Azuk and our discovery of the marvels of Dhugash."

"Will they go along with this new arrangement?"

The troll shrugged. "Some will, but many will resist. My people can be slow to change their ways. Other clans are far away in the north and east. It will take some time."

Cullen nodded. "And mine as well. I will return with as many as possible to help in your harvest and teach what we can."

"Return soon. I would be honored to speak again with Cullen, Strong Hand of the Trolls."

He winced at the title but nodded in response. Whatever the mystical event was that took place in the tunnels under the city, he was now linked to the trolls and to his friend, the Holy One.

"Ounwe's arse," he muttered.

He waved to Tanner to take the humans across the river and back to their homes. Isabo stood beside her friend. She glared at her father and the trolls. Without a word, she turned and walked toward the bridge.

"I am truly sorry about your daughter," Grimmun-Kan said. "She is a fierce fighter and a worthy adversary. It is not well that there would be strife within families."

Cullen nodded and shook hands with the troll chief. He turned to Gheen for a last time and took both of the troll's clawed hands in his own. "I will return, Gheen, Holy One of the Three Valleys clan."

Gheen bowed his head to the human. "I know that you will."

***

Once they crossed the swaying bridge, Isabo pulled Tanner to the side. She cast a dark look at the bridge and her father midway across. An odd tingling ran through the soles of her feet and her hands. She looked at her palms. "We will return," she said slowly, "and burn it to the ground."

The saga of the Troll Lands continues...

About the Author

Steven Vickers writes SF, fantasy, and historical fiction, but has a thing for werewolves and trolls. He lives in Colorado Springs and has an MFA in Creative Writing/Genre Fiction from Western Colorado University. Troll Hunt, a novella in the Troll Lands universe, was his first published work. It was selected for the Cannon Publishing 2024 High Caliber Awards Anthology. He is completing a novel set in the same universe. Steven is also the Senior Editor at SC Visel Edits, LLC, (scviseledits.com) providing copyediting and proofreading services to other fiction and non-fiction authors. He served in space operations fields for 24 years in the US Air Force, and continued supporting the Air Force and Space Force after his retirement from active duty. He is married, with two sons and two dogs of questionable intellect.

More from Cannon Publishing

Join the Crew!

Sign up for our newsletter for the latest news on new releases and more.

Follow our authors at their Amazon Pages!

Shane Gries (Dragon Finalist)

Lucas Marcum

Al Hagan

James Copley

Jason Kyle

G. Scott Huggins

Michael Morton

Charles Hackney

Jon LaForce

Jason Weiser

Kal Spriggs

Brian Gifford

Charli Cox

Dan Kemp

Jonathan Shuerger

J.R. Wise

Steve Vickers

More Books from Cannon Publishing

Irregular Scout Team One

In July of 2016 a plague swept the world, and the civilization collapsed and fell. For a lone National Guard sergeant, a veteran of the wars overseas who had settled down to a new life, the nightmare began on a hot summer evening at the barricades. Orders and chaos, gunfire and being overrun, his unit dwindles away in the face of the infected. Months later, living in the ruins, the thud of helicopter rotors followed by a crash and the rescue of a downed pilot leads Sergeant First Class Nick Agostine back into the arms of the US military. From his experience comes the idea of teams, military and civilians experienced in dealing with the undead and barbarism of the wilds. The first Irregular Scout Team leads the way for Task Force Liberty to advance down the Mohawk Valley in Upstate NY, making contact with survivors and clearing out the infected with stealth and firepower.

Volume 1
Volume 2
Volume 3: Civil War
Volume 4: Bad Company
Volume 5: End of Days

The Line

When the world descends into chaos and anarchy with an unbelievably swift plague, turning victims into ravenous maniacs, the soldiers of America's storied 1st Infantry are asked to hold the line. From the brutal streets of urban combat to the bloodied, desperate defense on the plains of Kansas, they fight a war against an unrelenting enemy who used to be their fellow citizens. As civilization falls, can they hold the line?

The Thin Dead Line
Dead Storm Rising
The Big Dead One

Fallen Empire

What's a soldier to do when the war is over? When he's only known conflict his whole life? Since time immemorial the solution has been to find another war, this time for pay. Whoever has the credits and wins the high bid gets the experienced fighter. Sometimes, though, the credits aren't enough to cover the price. Empires rise, but Empires also fall. The Terran Union has spent five centuries under the control of the alien Grausians, like a barbarian tribe under the thumb of Rome. Now, after almost two decades of civil war and succession struggles, the formerly subject races have settled back in their ancient territories to lick their wounds and re-arm, leaving hundreds of settled planets to exist in a political vacuum. Into that space steps the free companies, mercenary units that fight for gold, honor, power and glory. Veterans who can't get the wars out of their souls, new recruits looking for adventure, corporations with their own agenda. Join us in a 27th Century that echoes history.

The Irish Brigade

Overrun

Silent Violence

Doom Company

Athenaeum, Inc

The Professor has problems, and not just what decades of soldiering did to his back and his knees. His boss just died, leaving him as CEO of the extremely discreet intelligence contractor Athenaeum, Incorporated. His old buddy the Operations Director is a highly skilled Army Ranger veteran but his finance chief is slightly unhinged and spends her money on highly inappropriate work outfits. The surviving old men on the Board of Directors are stuck in the 1970s. Running Athenaeum out of an old Cold War bunker and keeping their roster of experts together is expensive, but the government contracts are drying up or going to bigger, flashier corporate players.

Door Number Three
Doubling Down

When nuclear war erupts on Earth, the American colony in the Alpha Centauri system is left stranded. As the new day dawns, a furious attack by the native inhabitants threatens to overwhelm the colony's defenses. It's left to the thin red line of the US Army's 9th Regiment to stem the tide and ensure humanity's survival in this harsh new world. From two time Dragon Finalist and author of the best selling series "Irregular Scout Team One" and "Invasion" comes a new tale that tells of the struggle for survival on a brutal planet.

Offworld: Ragnarok
Offworld: Expeditions

Cannon Fodder: Tales From the Gun Crew

Fifteen stories from Cannon Publishing Authors, each taking from the universes of their novels to bring you perspectives and deepen their world. From 27th century mercenaries fighting on distant planets and young soldiers riding with Arthur to defeat Saxon hordes, to enchanted weapons dealing damage in hands of Fae, we bring you the best of Science Fiction and Fantasy!

Valkyrie

Humanity engages in a desperate struggle with an alien species for this side of the Orion Arm. Space ships die in instantaneous bursts of light and turn into vapor, but on the ground Marines scream and lie wounded in the mud and blood, praying for the Valkyries to come save them. They aren't wishing for death and a Nordic goddess to take them to Valhalla, the wounded are praying for the men and women of the '348th Field Hospital MEDEVAC to dive through fire and hell to come save them. Because they know that …Valkyries never die!

Valkyrie
Valkyrie: Rebellion
Valkyrie: Attrition

High Caliber Awards

The Cannon High Caliber Awards are an annual contest for new writers. In it we ask them to submit a novella length story of Science Fiction, Military or Fantasy genre to challenge their skills.

2024

2025

The Wishkiller Saga

While on patrol Captain Aethal Paaling discovers evidence that an ancient terror has reached the rich soil of his home: the Lotus, a prolific growth whose addictive leaves devour their victims from within turning their hosts into horrible, terrifyingly violent mockeries of humanity. Created at the dawn of history by the twisted power of a godly relic called the Well, the return of the Lotus may be a harbinger of even more horrors to come. Carrying the fatal news to the capital, Aethal discovers that even in the face of death itself, the Lords Paramount of Verlaen will fight to keep their secrets and their power. With only the guidance of his legendary Greater Rifle and the aid of the Pheonix Lancers, the soldier must find his way through the halls of a forgotten holy order and into deep dens of crime seeking answers. He must find the truth as quickly as he can, because the Lotus may have already taken root among those he loves... and fighting it may cost him everything, including his soul.

A Cold and Mortal Spring
War of the Shattered Moon

When nine out of ten people in the world have died in a brutal plague, what do those who remain do to pick up the pieces? Does the creed, "Duty, Honor, Country" have a place any more if there's no country left? On his way across the devastated remains of Texas, Marine Corps veteran and survivor Eric Marten rescues a young woman from a vicious attack by men who have turned into savages. As Dani slowly learns to trust him, they try to stay alive in the deathlands that America has become, using all their wits to survive a post-apocalyptic nightmare.

90% Death Rate: A Post Apocalyptic Thriller
Angel of Death: A Post Apocalyptic Thriller
The Bloody Princess: A Post Apocalyptic Thriller

A single train carries what might be the last vestige of civilization through a hellish nightmare. A few hundred alive out of millions, lights going out all across what was once America as the possessed arose from the dead and murdered the living. A few hundred survivors travel across the country in an armored train, seeking some place to shelter in a fallen world. All that remains is a dystopian nightmare marked by rains of blood, impossible horrors, and portals to Hell opening in the skies.US Army Captain Jack Zamora is responsible for their safety, a self-imposed burden that wears on him every day. Fighting off undead, protecting the survivors, keeping the train running and supplied as his team desperately plans their next moves. Starvation and disease threaten. but it gets worse, because the ancient gods have sent their emissaries, horrific beings of myth and legend that walk the Earth. Things that can drain a man's very life essence or even that of an entire city.

Hell Train: All Aboard

Sometimes a hero isn't what you expect, and the one you need comes from the castaways of society. Nearly broken and at the end of his rope, former decorated scout pilot and prisoner of war, Red has finally accepted the inevitable. He and his kin have no future in the Human Confederation of Worlds, being gene mods and barely human themselves. With the help of his friend he flees Terra for adventure and fortune out in the reaches of the galaxy. Along the way he's dragged back into conflict that calls on all his piloting skills and he learns the deeper meaning of Kin, as his crew becomes his family.

Path to Freedom: The Path, Book One

More than a decade after the Confederated Earth Forces were defeated, their commanding general, a boyhood protegee, lives in exile and disgrace. His life on an isolated farm is forever changed when two strangers show up at his homestead, and the war comes crashing back down on him. The problem though, remains the same. How do you fight an enemy that is technologically superior and holds the high ground?

Invasion: Resistance

Invasion: Day of Battle

Invasion: Total War

Military Sci-Fi/Fantasy Anthology

The military experience is timeless, and echoes down from our past and into our future. Along the way, not everything is as it seems. Thirteen stories from established and new writers in the field of Military Science Fiction and Military Fantasy bring you tales of the terrors of combat and the even greater fear of the unknown in Cannon Publishing's first Bi-Annual Military Anthology.

The Hundred Worlds

Fifteen classic Science Fiction stories from both masters of the craft and up and coming new writers! A tyrannical United Nations pulls the strings of its colony worlds, ruling with an iron fist. Corporate interests take precedence, and brushfire rebellions smolder on the edges. One system, home to the only alien species yet discovered, with human allies throws off the yoke and calls itself Independence.

Feedback from the slight pressure of a hand closing sends a powerful mechanical arm smashing into an opponent. A neural link hurls blustering plasma fire from your suit's shoulder mounted cannon. Your reactor levels scream with overload as return fire smashes into your armor, and damage alarms wail while you hurl your twenty ton body sideways for cover. You're a Mecha, a mechanical fighting machine with a human pilot. The guy that the infantry curse at in training and pray for in combat. The machine that the last hopes of your people ride on. The construct that strikes fear deep into alien hearts as they hear your turbines power up. The one able to pass through hell and come out the other side victorious, or die trying.

In the near future, massive empires rule the stars, and west of the Reach, they are battling for control of new systems. In the no-mans land between the front lines, Captain Nate Meric and the crew of the privateer Lexington fight for prize money, and loyalty to their ship and their friends. Beneath it all, though, runs a hidden dream. To see America restored, and take her rightful place among the stars.

Sea of Fire: Demonrise

Brian Corel, former slave, gladiator, ex-fiance to an Empress, exiled Captain of the Taland Royal Guard and now owner of the frigate *Widowmaker,* does the best he can to balance the lives of his crew with his own desire to live life as a free man. Skirting the border between being a privateer and an outright pirate, Corel stumbles into a war with a religious cult intent on corrupting the kingdom of an old friend and has to set things right while grieving over his lost love. Along the way he signs a dragon into his crew and has to risk everything to rescue his brother from the grasp of a demon that has destroyed an entire continent.

Chosen by the Sword

There are some things a PhD doesn't prepare you for, like running two feet of steel through the guts of a flesh-eating monster straight out of a nightmare, while ducking razor sharp claws. Or having the sword critique your fighting style while you do it. Dave Howard had a problem. Last week, he was out looking for a teaching job in the middle of a wrecked job market. This week he was neck deep in green blood and hellfire. Dragged into it by the very sword, his grandfathers' mysterious possessed blade, that was now walking him through hacking up a ghoul without getting his own head cut off. This wasn't exactly what he had gone to school for, and the University he had just taken a job with seemed to be anything BUT an academic institution. More like some kind of monster hunting bunch of weirdo nerds. Maybe his degree in Personality Psychology might be useful there, at least. The fighting though ... as he dodged another swipe of claws and awkwardly tried to follow the instructions the sword was screaming at him, he shot back at it, "Hell, I'm Canadian! Swordplay isn't in my cultural DNA!"

Beyond the Wall: A Novel of Post-Roman Britain

The legions are but a memory, the glory of Rome only a shadow of crumbling ruins and broken walls. A darkening tide of barbarism was washing across Britain's shores and the lights of civilization were slowly flickering out into darkness, only kept burning by the legendary Red Dragons cavalry unit. Led by their Tribune, Arthur, who serves no kingdom but goes where the fight is hardest and most crucial, they wage desperate battles to keep back the tide. The Red Dragons ride the length of Britannia to fight the invading Saxons, Scoti and Picts, wherever they show, from across the seas or down from the Highlands. At sixteen years old Peredur of Gwynedd has listened all his life to the stories of his father Pelinor fighting with Ambrosius Aurelianus. When word comes that his older brother has been slain in battle with the Saxons, his desire for revenge leads him to follow in his father's footsteps as a warrior, becoming a cavalryman with the Red Dragons. Along the way he may either find himself a warrior and leader worthy of Arthur or be left lying forgotten in the dust of history.

Two souls collide in the middle of a deadly war.

Sergeant Sylvie Lyons of Her Majesty's Royal Engineers wishes she'd listened to her grandda's advice and stayed away from the military.

USMC Sergeant Hondo Cassidy wants nothing more in life than being a Marine and fighting. Hondo and Sylvie find themselves thrown together when his artillerymen are assigned to provide security for her engineers deep in the desert of Afghanistan.. Amidst death, destruction, cultural misunderstanding and the inevitable that happens when you mix an all male unit of Marines with an engineer unit that is mostly female, Sylvie and Hondo find in each other a reason to live. That is, if they can survive.

The dead rose expecting a feast. What they got was a firefight.

Sergeant Alex Slaughter and the Marines of Alpha Squad were on a routine training exercise near Quantico when everything went silent. No comms. No command. No clue.

What they find when they return to base is worse than anything they trained for: a bioweapon has unleashed a zombie virus that has shattered civilization, and now they must survive the Collapse.

But as the squad pushes deeper into hostile territory—through the death-choked streets of Arlington and into the rot-stained corridors beneath D.C.—they discover that the undead aren't the only threat. Desperate survivors, rogue military units, and darker truths buried beneath the weight of secrecy will test their loyalty, their mission, and their very humanity.

Written by USMC veteran Jonathan Shuerger and set in J.F. Holmes's brutal and unrelenting Irregular Scout Team One universe, Semper Die delivers pulse-pounding action, authentic military detail, and a terrifying vision of what happens when duty and apocalypse collide.

Lock. Load. Semper Fi. Semper Die.

More From the Fae Wars

Get the full series!

Onslaught

What would you do if America and the world were invaded tomorrow by a relentless and brutal enemy? In an alternate 2015, a US Army Special Forces Team, part of the legendary black ops unit "Delta", is in midtown Manhattan to take out a Chinese spy and his handlers, sending a message short of outright conflict. All goes smoothly until they find themselves in a full blown shooting war through the canyons of the City. Portals from another world have opened in Central Park, making a way for figures out of historical nightmare to invade. The Fae, creatures banished from Earth thousands of years ago and now only part of our legends, have returned with Dragon fire, spell and sword to conquer and take revenge. The first volume of The Fae Wars covers Team Three, G squadron, Special Forces Detachment (Delta) as they fight their way off Manhattan and then join the defense of the refugees as the Fae assault the bridges. The fabled 69th Infantry puts up an epic fight against superior weaponry and then the war descends into the asymmetric hell that the Delta Operators know so well. Along the way they find new allies and old powers that come to their aid.

The Fall

For the first time in two hundred years an enemy has stepped foot on American soil and war has come to our cities. The US military is rocked back on its heels and driven into a fighting retreat as each defense line falls. The foe is unstoppable and ... Fae. Creatures from a legendary past who have come to reclaim the Earth in the name of magic and revenge. In the hills of Pennsylvania a ragtag, devastated army prepares to make a last stand against dragon fire capable of melting an Abrams tank and wizardry that stops fifth generation fighter jets in mid-air. Inevitably it comes down to shining steel verses human will, and Sergeant Oliva Acevedo transforms from a hospital clerk to a hardened fighter. Volume Two of the best selling "Fae Wars" follows the fighting retreat of the US Army as the Fae establish control of a shattered America.

Futures Past

Two thousand years ago the Fae were banished from Earth and they've spent that time plotting return and revenge. When their portals open around the world and start crushing the human's military with spell encased steel and dragon fire, it becomes a massive struggle between technology and magic. When the Fae Invasion hammers the West Coast, Captain James Powers and his California Army National Guard artillery battery is caught on its way home from Annual Training. In a running battle the unit is smashed by combat with orcs and elves, leaving their commander struggling to keep his people together and alive. Along the way a dying priest with a strange ability to see the future manipulates people and events to bring Captain Powers to his true calling as a Seer. As they run and fight, the humans gain new allies, Fea tinkerers who love all things mechanical and hate the elves. With their help they begin to take the war to the enemy in a brutal mayhem of ambush and assassination. Book Three of the Fae Wars series following the bestselling "Onslaught" (set in NY City) and "The Fall" (Pennsylvania)

Tales From the Occupation: A Fae Wars Anthology

Wars end, enemies are defeated and territories are conquered and the combatants have to return to a life changed. America and the rest of humanity have fallen to the Fae, ancient mortal enemies of mankind. After building their strength for two thousand years, the Elves have claimed their vengeance and now rule Earth with an iron fist and dragon fire. Down but not out, a human resistance is building, but first daily life needs to be lived. An anthology of stories exploring life during the Occupation in the best-selling Fae Wars universe.

Insurgent

Wars come and wars go. Eventually even the most belligerent of combatants will arrive at some kind of living arrangement, either through exhaustion or slaughter. Kill enough, down to the last child, and there will be no more war … until the next one, of course.

In August 2015, the war started, portals opening up between their world and ours, allowing the Fae to return to our (or their) home world in blood, fire and magic. Conventional forces fought back as well as they could, but the invasion had been planned to hit us in the middle of our civilization. America's military was scattered overseas or concentrated in large bases that were quickly overwhelmed by forces that were dropped right in the middle of their units. The fighting was brutal and horrific, magic overwhelming technology. It took six weeks, and the President surrendered to spare the civilian population. A puppet government was put in place and the Fae started to divide the conquered lands into principalities run by their Great Houses, slowly turning America into a land of feudal slavery. Thing is, though, the Fae had lived in their exile for thousands of years, fighting wars among themselves and against various races that populated their new home. Pitched battles where there was a clear-cut winner and loser. They had never fought an insurgency and had no idea how bloody it could get. Major David Kincaid. United States Army 1st Special Forces Operational Detachment–Delta, soldier of a defeated but unbroken nation, was going to show them. If, that is, he can keep the faith. The follow up novel to the bestselling "Fae Wars: Onslaught" by J.F. Holmes.

Ghost

There are wars, and then there's War. The all-encompassing thing that is fought on many levels, and with many kinds of weapons, many kinds of warriors. Even ghosts.

Alex was no one, a man just trying to get by at his paperwork job at the new Homeland Security. A man grieving for his wife, who had died in the Invasion. Someone just trying to keep his head down while the elves appointed him to do the paperwork of putting their boots on the necks of a conquered American people. Thing is, even a nobody paper shuffling clerk has a weapon, one that had lit the fires of revolution in America hundreds of years ago. His mind, and his words. The internet was still up and running, somehow and someway, and Alex takes to his keyboard. Inspired by his hero Patrick Henry, soon the words of the "Ghost" start inciting attacks on the Fae and the District of Columbia rings with explosions, gunshots and cries of Freedom. The Resistance notices, and Alex is soon assigned a bodyguard and a handler, an ex-police officer who is running from her own hidden past. Together they work to keep the flame of resistance alive and escape from the tightening net of the Fae. The consequences are, as always, Liberty or Death.

the tale of Tukor and Misty is a front seat view of the occupation in the Southwest that no one expected, least of all Tukor himself.

Relics of Empire

In a world shattered by elven conquest, where magic crackles and dragons soar, the Navajo Nation stands as a defiant refuge. Living there is Ben Yazzie, a battle scarred Marine veteran who wants no more war—until a brutal encounter with elven oppressors at a remote gas station ignites a spark of rebellion. Alongside Maria Hernandez, a grieving widow fueled by vengeance, and a band of unlikely allies, Ben is thrust into a fight against an empire wielding arcane power and ruthless ambition.

As ancient ley lines awaken, unleashing chaos across the American Southwest, Ben uncovers a legacy of resistance tied to his ancestors and a mysterious relic from a forgotten era. Magic surges and the earth itself stirs, forcing Ben to embrace his destiny as the Coyote, the elusive and mysterious warrior leading a desperate stand against an otherworldly tyranny.

From the dusty trails of Arizona to the neon-lit chaos of Las Vegas, *The Fae Wars: Relics of Empire* is a pulse-pounding tale of courage, sacrifice, and defiance against overwhelming odds. Will the old ways and a warrior's heart be enough to reclaim a shattered land?

The rebellion begins here.

John Holmes

J.F. Holmes is a retired Army Senior Noncommissioned Officer, having served for 22 years in both the Regular Army and Army National Guard. During that time, he served as everything from an artillery section leader to a member of a Division level planning staff, with tours in Cuba and Iraq, as well as responding to the terrorists attacks in NYC on 9-11.

From 2010 to 2014 he wrote the immensely popular military cartoon strip, "Power Point Ranger", poking fun at military life in the tradition of Beetle Bailey and Willy & Joe.

His books range from Military Sci-Fi to Space Opera to Detective to Fantasy, with a lot in between, and in 2017 two are finalists for the prestigious Dragon Awards.

In 2018, he launched Cannon Publishing, www.cannonpublishing.us specializing in military science fiction, fantasy and thrillers, with an emphasis on works from up and coming authors.

Lucas Marcum

Lucas Marcum is a critical care nurse practitioner and an officer in the US Army Reserve. When he's not working, or performing his reserve duties, he can be found hiking, reading, attempting to perfect his soft pretzel recipe and spending time with his family.

James Copley

James Copley is a former Non-Commissioned Officer of the U.S. Army, having served over twenty-one years in both Active and Reserve/Guard units, variously trained as Infantry, Communications, and Ordnance specialties before finally retiring from the Army National Guard in 2016. During his service, he deployed four separate times, twice to Iraq and twice to Afghanistan.

He is currently working as a software engineer in Central California with his wife, two children, and two dogs. Reading was his number one passion from a very young age, and more recently he decided to try writing his own. Feel free to join him on his writing journey!

Charli Cox

Charli Cox is a best-selling Military Sci-Fi and Horror Comedy author. She also writes Sci-Fi, Alternate History, and Military Fantasy stories.

If you enjoyed Fae Wars: Northwest Front and want to see more stories about Ash and "Gunny," Cannon Publishing has you covered. Burnt Mountain and Sasquatch will be coming to your Kindle later in 2025. Also, please be sure to leave a review!

Representing #teamandmore, Charli's first published short story is in The Phoenix Initiative: First Missions from Chris Kennedy Publishing. She has stories in Bureau 42 and Express Elevator to Hell, also from CKP.

Look for Whistles of the Wendigo, an Alternate History/Military Fantasy novel set in the Joint Task Force 13 universe from Three Ravens Publishing, due to release soon.

Charli's previous experience has been as a Realtor, HVAC Business Manager, IT Office Manager, and freelance bookkeeper. Professional skills such as drafting strongly worded emails transition surprisingly well into writing fiction.

An animal lover and #boymom, she lives in SW Oregon with her Leg husband, two sons, an Arabian mare, and two Husky mixes who think they are hooman.

Learn more about Charli and sign up for her newsletter on her website. Hang out with her on Facebook, Instagram, and/or TikTok.

Jason Weiser

Mr. Weiser has been a government contractor for the last eleven years, and before that, a writer working odd jobs trying to get by. He has a BA in History from CUNY Brooklyn. Mr. Weiser released his first novel in 2025, with Cannon Publishing, but before that, released a short story in their 2018 Spring Military Sci Fi Anthology.

Mr. Weiser is also an avid wargamer and has been published quite a bit in the hobby, having most recently run "Military Miniature" magazine as it's editor in chief from 2021-2023. Before that, he wrote for EpochXperience (a division of SJR Research) as a contributing writer for their blog on wargaming and military history topics from 2020 to 2021.

He also wrote two scenario books on Cold War wargaming topics, "Red Star, Burning Streets" and "Red Star, White Lights".

Mr. Weiser encourages all his fans to visit Cannon Publishing at their website

Brian Gifford

A military veteran with more than 25 years of service in the U.S. Air Force and Army (in an order that would surprise you!), Brian is a lifelong science fiction and fantasy nerd of the highest order. A student of the hard sciences and the arcane arts of cybersecurity and IT alike, Brian has spent a lifetime accumulating his unique view of the world, which he now insists on sharing with everyone else. He is a husband in awe of the magnificence that is his wife and the proud father of three awesome sons, and looks forward to retiring from the military in the near future to focus on his family and his writing.

More from Irregular Scout Team

Volume 1

In July of 2016 a plague swept the world, and the civilization collapsed and fell. For a lone National Guard sergeant, a veteran of the wars overseas who had settled down to a new life, the nightmare began on a hot summer evening at the barricades. Orders and chaos, gunfire and being overrun, his unit dwindles away in the face of the infected.

Months later, living in the ruins, the thud of helicopter rotors followed by a crash and the rescue of a downed pilot leads Nick Agostine back into the arms of the US military. From his experience comes the idea of teams, military and civilians experienced in dealing with the undead and barbarism of the wilds. The first Irregular Scout Team leads the way for Task Force Liberty to advance down the Mohawk Valley in Upstate NY, making contact with survivors and clearing out the infected with stealth and firepower.

This is a remastering of the best selling Zombie Killers series, combining the 2017 Dragon Awards finalist "Falling" with book 11, "Patient Zero", placing the story in proper chronological order and connecting the stories together.

Volume 2

A year has passed since the plague destroyed most of civilization around the world and the U.S. military is slowly starting to move out into a devastated country. From their bastion in the Pacific Northwest mechanized task forces take the fight for America onto the offensive.

In front of the military, deep into the wild ruins, go the Irregular Scout Teams. A mix of hardened military veterans and experienced civilians who can operate for long periods of time on their own. Checking the road, rail, and water transportation infrastructure, identifying groups of survivors for reinforcement or evacuation, running rather than fighting. The Teams have all the might of their task forces' firepower on call but it's better to be unheard by the infected and unseen by the lawless.

IST-1, the first team and the most experienced, is ordered to operate on their home ground of the ruined Upper Hudson Valley. Sergeant First Class Nick

Agostine, the Team Leader, driven to fulfill his oath to the Constitution and his county while haunted by the memory of his dead family. His fellow NCO and Team Medic, Doc Hamilton, trying to keep everyone alive. Ahmed Yassir, a man without a country or tribe, deadly at a thousand meters with is calm shooting. Isaiah Jones, a giant of a man with a machine gun and a booming laugh, who grew up surrounded by violence. Brit O'Neill, the fiery red head with the ice blue eyes, who is just as ready to take off an infected's head with her shotgun as she is to put at teammate into their place with her sarcasm. Former Serbian soldier Sasha Zivcovic, who is a born killer living in his preferred element, war.

As the eyes and ears of Task Force Empire, it's their job to save the lives of thousands of soldiers by providing accurate intelligence. That's the mission, in theory, but incompetence, the fog of war and politics get in their way, putting the entire teams' lives at risk.

This isn't a book about the Apocalypse. It's a book about the men and women of Irregular Scout Team One and how they lay their lives on the line for each other in the face of incredible danger. A book about how a bad decision or just plain bad luck can put yourself and the ones you love at risk. In the end, though, it's a book about ...

... Hope.

Volume 3: Civil War

Three years after the Undead virus / parasite infected the world, civilization struggles on. The United States is scraping by as a nation by the skin of its teeth, with forty million people crammed into the Pacific Northwest, living in squalid refugee camps. Army units have made inroads into the ruins of the rest of America, working on clearing the major cities.

Outside America, England survived, as did other island nations. The survivors are struggling back to their feet, fighting a long, exhaustive campaign to regain the Japanese Islands and Europe.

On an island in the Hudson River, thirty miles north of the nearest Army outpost, several families have homesteaded. Mixed military and civilian, planting crops and salvaging the land, they are survivors of the Army's elite scout teams. Children are born, old friends mourned, rivers run clean and trees grow in the ruins. The fight, though, still goes on ..

Irregular Scout Team One, call sign "Lost Boys", is working clearing operations in support of Task Force Liberty, designating targets for Close AIr Support. Their assignment is interrupted by the Task Force commander, who gives them an off the books mission that will plunge the nation into civil war.

This book contains the original books four and five of the Irregular Scout Team One series, "Civil War" and "Endgame". The entire series has been remastered and put in the proper order.

Volume 4: Bad Company

The world has fallen, swept away by plague and civil war. In a quiet corner of what remains of the United States, former Scout Team leader Nick Agostine struggles to adjust to peace, wanting to raise corn and kids with his wife. He has a good crop of both growing when the reality of violent war shatters his precious peace.

Called back to active duty, Colonel Agostine is tasked with planning reconnaissance missions for the Scout Teams to take out the leadership of the rebellions Mountain Republic. A final strike to end the last war, but when nuclear weapons become involved, Irregular Scout Team One travels to Florida in chase of a renegade traitor. Disaster overtakes the Team and Agostine sets out on desperate search to find his missing wife.

Through it all, the question runs, what price loyalty, and does the dream of America still live on in the hearts of men, or has it died in the ashes of barbarism?

Volume 5: End of Days

The plague has come and gone, followed by Civil War and the ruin of America. Still, the torch of hope is held aloft by those who haven't forgotten their oath...

As the Federal government battles the remnants of the Mountain Republic, Colonel Nick Agostine settles into a calm life of running a trading post and farm north of Albany. Feeling restless, after the harvest, he sets out with most of IST -1 to explore a long valley north of the remains of New York City, searching for survivors and looking for places where refugees can resettle.

Along the way old hatreds thought long buried resurface and the Team finds itself caught in a brutal ambush. As bullets fly and grenades crack, casualties mount and a shot sends the Scout Team leader spinning to the ground. He awakens to find himself facing torture and death in his most desperate situation yet. It could be ...

The End of Days.